Happy Hawkins

by

Robert Alexander Wason

Double 9
BOOKS

Happy Hawkins
by Robert Alexander Wason

Copyright © 2024

All Rights reserved.

ISBN: 978-93-62204-04-2

Published by

DOUBLE 9 BOOKS

2/13-B, Ansari Road
Daryaganj, New Delhi – 110002
info@double9books.com
www.double9books.com
Tel. 011-40042856

This book is under public domain

ABOUT THE AUTHOR

Robert Alexander Wason was an American writer. He was most known for authoring western-themed novels and short stories, some of which were serialized. Wason was born in Toledo, Ohio, to merchants Robert Alexander Wason and Gertrude Louise Paddock. He attended high school in Delphi, Indiana, and then clerked for his father for eight years, interrupted by periods of tramping and camping throughout the West. Wason served in the United States Army (artillery) for nine months during the Spanish-American War (1898-99) and worked in a number of vocations and locations before settling into a career penning westerns, which incorporate elements from his real experiences. In addition to clerking for his father, he worked as an office boy, a grip for the San Francisco cable car system, a miner in a Nevada mercury mine, and a farmer near Delphi, Indiana. Throughout his life, he lived in Ohio, Indiana, San Francisco, Detroit, Orr's Island, Maine, Temple, Arizona, Arden, Delaware, Norwalk, Connecticut, and Mountain Lakes, New Jersey. Wason married Emma Louise Brownell in Peru, Indiana, in 1911. They had two sons and one daughter. He died at Mountain Lakes, New Jersey.

CONTENTS

CHAPTER ONE
THE DIAMOND DOT

I wasn't really a Westerner an' that's why I'm so different from most of 'em. Take your regular bonie fide Westerner an' when he dies he don't turn to dust, he turns to alkali; but when it comes my turn to settle, I'll jest natchely become the good rich soil o' the Indiana cornbelt.

I was born in Indiana and I never left it till after I was ten years old. That's about the time boys generally start out to hunt Injuns; but I kept on goin' till I found mine—but I didn't kill him—nor him me neither, as far as that goes.

I allus did have the misfortune o' gettin' hungry at the most inconvenient times, an' after I'd been gone about two weeks I got quite powerful hungry, so I natchely got a job waitin' on a lunch counter back in Omaha. The third day I was there I was all alone in the front room when in walked an Injun. He was about eight feet high, I reckon; and the fiercest Injun I ever see. I took one look at him a' then I dropped behind the counter and wiggled back to the kitchen where the boss was. I gasped out that the Injuns was upon us an' then I flew for my firearms.

When the boss discovered that the Injun and fourteen doughnuts, almost new, had vanished, he was some put out, and after we had discussed the matter, I acted on his advice and came farther West. That business experience lasted me a good long while. I don't like business an' I don't blame any one who has to follow it for a livin' for wantin' to have a vacation so he can get out where the air is fit to breathe.

Just imagine bein' hived up day after day with nothin' to see but walls an' nothin' to do but customers. You first got to be friendly with your visitors to make 'em feel at home, an' then you got to get as much of their money as you can in order to keep on bein' friendly with 'em in order to keep on gettin' as much of their money as you can.

Now out in the open a feller don't have to be a hypocrite: once I worked a whole year for a man who hated me so he wouldn't speak to me; but I didn't care, I liked the work and I did it an' he raised my wages twice an' gave me a pony when I quit.

He was the sourest tempered man I ever see; but it was good trainin' to live with him a spell. Lots of men has streaks of bein' unbearable; but this man was the only one I ever met up with who was solid that way, and didn't have one single streak of bein' likeable. He was the only man I ever see who wouldn't talk to me. I was a noticing sort of a kid an' I saw mighty early that what wins the hearts o' ninety-nine men out of a hundred is listenin' to 'em talk. That's why I don't talk much myself. But you couldn't listen to old Spike Williams, 'cause the' wasn't no opportunity—he didn't even cuss.

We was snowed up for two weeks one time an' I took a vow 'at I'd make him talk. I tried every subject I'd ever heard of; but he didn't even grunt. Just when things was clearin' off, I sez to him, usin' my biggest trump: "Spike," sez I, "do you know what they say about you?"

"No," sez he, "but you know what I say about them," an' he went on with his packin'.

I thought for a while 'at the year I'd spent with Spike Williams was a total loss; but jest the contrary. It had kept me studyin' an' schemin' an' analysin' until, after that year had been stored away to season, I discovered it was the best year I'd ever put in, an' while I hadn't got overly well acquainted with Spike, I had become mighty friendly with myself and was surprised to find out how much the' was to me.

Did you ever think of that? You start out an' a feller comes along an' throws an opinion around your off fore foot an' you go down in a heap an' that opinion holds you fast for some time. When you start on again another feller ropes you with a new opinion, an' the first thing you know you are all cluttered up an' loaded down with other fellers' opinions, an' the' ain't enough o' your own self left to tell what you're like; but after that winter with Spike I was pretty well able to dodge an opinion until I had time to learn what it meant.

But the main good I got out of Spike was learnin' how to take old Cast Steel Judson. It was some years after this before I met up with him; but the good effect hadn't worn off and me an' Cast Steel just merged together like butter an' a hot penny. I wasn't much more 'an a kid even then, but law! I wish I knew just half as much now as I thought I did then. My self respect was certainly a bulky article those days an' I wasn't in the habit of undervaluin' my own judgment—not to any great extent; but that habit o' study I'd formed with Spike was my balance wheel, an' I generally managed to keep my conceit from shuttin' out the entire landscape. The' wasn't a great deal escaped my eye, 'cause I begun to notice purty tol'able young that experience is consid'able like a bank account: takes a heap o' sweat to get her started, but she's comfortable to draw on in a pinch.

Ol' man Judson was a curious affair, had his own way o' doin' every blessed thing, an' whenever he hired a man he always went through the same rigamarole. "Now what I'm contractin' for," he'd say, "is just only your time an' whatever part o' your thinkin' apparatus as is needed in doin' YOUR share o' my business. If I detail you to sit in the shade an' count clouds, I don't want no argument, I want the clouds counted. When I don't specially express a hungerin' for any of your advice, that's the very time when you don't need to give any. Whenever you think you have a kick comin'—why think again. Then if you still see the kick, make it to the foreman. If that don't work make it to me; but when you make it to me, you want to be mighty sure it will hold water. Above all things I hate a liar, a coward, an' a sneak. Now get busy 'cause life is short an' time is fleetin'.'"

That was the way he used to talk, an' some used to set him down as a tyrant, an' some had him guessed in as a rough old codger with a soft heart,—everybody took a guess at him,—but the blood in the turnip was that ol' Jabez Judson was purty tol'able sizey when you carne to fence him in. Everybody called him Cast Steel Judson, an' you might work through the langwidge five times without adding much to the description. Hard he was an' stern an' no bend to him; but at the same time you could count on him acting up to his nature. He wa'n't no hypocrite, an' th''s a heap o' comfort jest in that. A feller ain't got no kick comin' when a rattler lands on him; but if a wood dove was to poison him, he'd have a fair right to be put out. The only child 'at Cast Steel had was one daughter; but that don't indicate that paternity was one long vacation for Jabez. Barbie—her full name was Barbara—was the sweetest an' the gamest an' the most surpriseable creature a human being ever met up with, an' ol' Jabez could 'a' got along handier with seven sons than he did with that one girl. Oh, the eyes of her were like the two stars over old Savage, snappin' an' twinklin' an' sparklin' in the clear winter nights, or soft an' shy an' tender when the hazy spring moon cuddles up to them. She wasn't afraid of anything 'at walks the face o' the earth, an' Jabez had a hard time gettin' used to this—'cause he thought she ought to be afraid o' him.

Still, he fair worshipped her, an' if he'd been given full charge o' the earth for jest one day, an' anything would 'a' pestered the girl durin' that day, why the map-maker would sure have had a job on the day follerin'; 'cause from his standpoint, that girl was what the sun shone for an' the rain rained for an' the blossoms blossomed for.

We was allus havin' a lot o' Easterners string along during the summer, an' they generally was easy to entice into makin' a little visit with us. Some of 'em would spend their time crackin' stones an' makin' up tales about their bein' speciments o' the Zelooic age or the Palazoric age or some such a fool thing. They was mostly heathens, an' it didn't do no good to spring the Bible on 'em—in fact after we got able to read their signs we never contraried 'em at all, but just let 'em heave out any tale they could think up an' pretend 'at we believed it; an' hanged if I don't begin to suspicion that the' 's a heap o' truth in some o' their nonsense.

Purty near every one of 'em insisted that at one time all those mountains, even old Savage, had been under water, an' they'd take us out an' show us the signs; but we couldn't stomach that until we found out that this was one o' the Injun traditions too, an' then we give in.

Well, one o' these strays was what they call an astronomer. His speciality was the stars, nothing less; an' he knew 'em by name an' could tell you how far off they are an' what they weigh an' how many moons they had an'—oh, he knew 'em the same as I know the home herd, an' he didn't only know what they had done—he knew what they was a-goin' to do, an' when he called the turn on 'em, why they up an' done it. Comets an' eclipses an' sech like miracles were jest the same to this feller as winter an' summer was to me, an' we fed him until he like to founder himself, tryin' to hold him through the winter; but at last he had to go, an' after he'd gone Cast Steel was purty down-hearted for quite a spell.

"It ain't fair, Happy," sez he to me one day after the astronomer had gone.

"No," sez I, "I reckon it will rain before mornin'."

"I mean it ain't a fair shake," sez he. "Jupiter has eight of 'em an' we ain't but one an' the' ain't nobody lives there, while—"

"What do you happen to be talkin' of?" sez I.

"Why moons," sez he. "It seems too doggone bad for that confounded planet to have eight moons an' no one to enjoy 'em while my little girl jest dotes on 'em an' we only have one—an' IT don't work more'n half the time."

That was Cast Steel: he didn't look on life or death, or wealth or poverty, or anything else except in the way it applied to Barbie—but she was worth it, she was worth it, an' I never blamed him none.

But you needn't get the idea that Jabez was one o' these fond an' lovin' parents what sez: "My child, right if perfectly convenient, but right or wrong, my child." Not on your future prospects! Jabez, he sez: "My child, right from the shoes up, if the Rocky Mountains has to be ground to powder to make her so."

I remember the day she was six year old; he hardly ever laid out the details for her conduct, he jest sort o' schemed out a general plan and left her free to adjust herself to it, like a feller does with a dog or a pony he expects to keep a long time an' don't want to turn into a machine. He had told Barbie he didn't want her to ride nothin' 'at wasn't safe. Well, on the mornin' she became a six-year-old he came out o' the side door an' saw her disappearin' in the distance on top a big pinto 'at he had sent over for Buck Harmon to bust; it havin' already pitched Spider Kelley an' dislocated his shoulder.

"Who roped that pony for her?" yelled Cast Steel.

"I did," sez I. "She said 'at this was her birthday an' she was tired of actin' like a kid an' intended to ride a real ridin' hoss."

"If a hair of her head is injured, hell won't hide ya!" sez Cast Steel, an' his lip trembled an' his eyes fairly smoked.

"She's jest as safe as if she was in her bed," sez I, as gentle as I could. "I taught her how to ride, an' I ain't ashamed o' the job. She can give Spider Kelley cards an' spades an' beat him to it every time. But as far as that goes—"

I didn't get to finish because here she come, tearin' back on the pinto. Her hair was flyin', her eyes was dancin', an' she was laughin'—laughin' out loud. Light an' easy she pulled the pinto up beside us an' calls out: "Oh, daddy, this is lovely, this is mag-ni-fi-cent"—the little scamp used to pick up big words from the Easterners, an' when she had one to fit she never wasted time on a measly little ranch word—"oh, I'm never goin' to ride old Kate again."

"Git off that pony," sez Jabez, makin' a reach for the bit; but the pony shied, whirled, an' purty nigh kicked his head off. He stood still in a daze while Barbie was circling the pony an' gettin' him quiet again.

"How's she goin' to get off?" asked Jabez, turnin' to me.

"Simply climb down," sez I purty short. I had some temper those days, an' I hadn't got over his insinuations, an' I didn't intend to.

"She'll be killed!" sez Jabez. I never said a word.

"She'll be killed!" he repeated, an' his voice was filled with anguish.

"Get down off the pony, Barbie," sez I, an' she threw her little leg over the saddle an' hit the grass like an antelope. The pony never stirred. Ol'

Jabez stood watchin' her with his eyes poppin' out. "Turn the brute loose!" he shouts. "What for?" sez she. "'Cause I say so!" he fairly roars.

Well, she walks up, pats the pinto on the nose, an' slips the bridle off his head. He just stands still an' watches her as mild as a pint o' cream.

"Rope that pony," sez Cast Steel to me.

"Get one o' your own men to rope it," sez I.

He looked into my eyes a moment an' then he called to George Hendricks to rope the pinto; but when George hove in sight with his rope the pinto took to his heels an' made for the horizon. "There goes a ninety-dollar saddle," sez Jabez to me, "an' it's all your damned nonsense."

"It ain't either," sez Barbie, as fierce as a wounded bear, "it's all your damned nonsense. Happy has been trainin' that pony nights for my birthday an'—"

"Barbara!" yells Jabez, "what do you mean by usin' such langwidge? I'll line you out for this. You know mighty well—"

"Now you play accordin' to the rule," sez Barbie. "You was teachin' me to play seven up last week an' you said that everybody had to play by the same rule. I reckon that goes in cussin' too."

Well, they looked into each other's eyes for quite some while, an' then Jabez sez: "Go into the house, Barbara, an' we'll both think it over, an' as soon as we get time we'll settle it."

"All right," sez Barbie, an' she turns around an' marches to the house, her little head held like a colonel's. Just before she reached the house she turned an' calls: "You'll get the pinto for me, won't you, Happy?" I sort o' half nodded my head, an' she went on into the house.

"Did you ever see such grit?" sez Cast Steel, "an' her only six. Kids oughtn't to act so grown up at six, had they, Happy?"

"I reckon 'at kids are pretty much like colts an' puppies an' other young things: give 'em dolls to play with an' they'll play like children, but start 'em out on cards an' ponies, an' range 'em off with nothin' but grown folks, an' they're bound to have ways like grown folks'."

Jabez fidgeted around a while, an' then he sez, "Are you goin' to try to catch the pinto?

"I am goin' to catch it," sez I, rollin' a cigarette.

He kind o' nervoused around a few minutes longer an' then he sez, "What did you mean a while ago?"

"Jest whatever I said," sez I. "I don't know what you're a-referrin' to, but if I said it, that's what I meant."

"When I asked you to rope the pinto you told me to git one o' my own men to rope it; what does that mean?"

"It means that when a man tells me that hell can't hide me from his wrath, I'm free to consider myself foot loose. A man don't want to slaughter none of his own hands, an' if it should be that any one feels called upon to go after my hide, I don't want to feel that the time I'm wastin' in takin' care o' that hide rightfully belongs to another man who is payin' for it. Therefore I have quit. I'm goin' to rope the pinto for Barbie, but I wouldn't do it for you, an' when I get back I'll call around for what's comin' to me."

"Well, go an' be hanged! You always was the most obstinate, high-headed, bull-intellected thin-skin 'at ever drew down top wages for punchin' cows. You're nothin' more than a kid, an' yet you swell around an' expect a man—"

"Well, I don't expect nothin' from you, ceptin' my wages," sez I.

"You go to Jericho, will you!" snaps Jabez. "You don't need to think that I'd try to argue any man on earth into workin' for me. I can get an army o' riders as good or better than you—but the gel likes you, Happy, an'—"

"An' that's why I'm goin' after the pinto," sez I, an' I flopped onto a pony an' sailed out to a little glen in the foothills where I knew I'd find him, an' as soon as I had towed him back to the corral I put my saddle on the old beast I had rode there an' set off.

Just as I rode around the edge o' the corral, ol' man Judson stood there grittin' his teeth. "What are you ridin' that old skin for?" sez he.

"'Cause it's the only pony I got," sez I.

"You leave it here an' take your pick out o' the five-year-olds," sez he.

"All I want out o' this ranch is what I have earned," sez I.

"If you don't get something 'at your pride'll earn some day, I'm the biggest fool this side o' the big ditch. Here's your pay. You've been a fair hand, but don't forget that I never hire a man twice, an' I've hired you once already."

"Now look here, Jabez," sez I, "I ain't so old as I'll get if I live as long as I may, but I'm old enough to know that it's just as easy, to find a good boss as it is to find a good man. I've done my work without fussin', an' you've seen me in a pinch or two; an' yet this very mornin' you intimated than I'd risk Barbie on a pony she couldn't ride. The' ain't nothin' I wouldn't do for that child, but you don't understand her, an' if you go on in your high-handed way with her you 're in for the sorrow o' your life—mark my words."

"Here's your money. You ain't got sense enough to know your place an' I 'm glad to be shut of you." Jabez handed me my pay an' stamped over to the ranch house, while I kept on down the valley trail.

When I reached the turn I twisted about in my saddle an' looked at the cluster o' buildings. They looked soft an' gray with old Mount Savage standin' on guard back of 'em, an' the' was a bigger lump under my necktie than I generally wore. I didn't have mach call to go anywhere, an' I sat there on my old pony, wonderin' whether or not it paid to be game.

If my mother had been alive, jest at that point would have been where the West would have lost the benefit of my personal supervision—but then if my mother had lived I shouldn't never 'a' left home. I stood a stepmother six months out o' respect to my Dad, but I wouldn't 'a' stood that one a year—well, anyway, not unless I'd been chained an' muzzled.

It's a funny thing to me how a man can drink an' fight an' carry on for a year at a clip an' then all of a sudden feel a hurtin' somewhere inside that nothin' wouldn't help but a little pettin'. He knows doggone well 'at there ain't none comin' to him, so he hides it by cuttin' up a little worse than usual but it's there, an' Gee! but it does rest heavy when it comes. Why, take me even now when the' wouldn't nothin' but a grizzly bear have the nerve to coddle me, an' yet week before last I felt so blue an' solitary 'at I couldn't 'a' told to save me whether I was homesick or whether it was only 'cause the beans was a little sour.

I sat there on the old pony a good long time, an' then I heaved a sigh 'at made me swell out like an accordion, an' headed back to the valley trail. When I turned around, there, standin' in the trail before me with a streak down each cheek, stood Barbie.

"Ya ain't goin', are ya?" sez she.

"I got to go, honey," sez I.

"Ain't ya never comin' back?" asked she.

"Oh, I'll come back some day, ridin' a big black hoss with silver trimmed leather—an' what shall I bring little Barbie?" sez I, tryin' to be gay.

"Just bring me yourself, Happy, that's all the present I want. I love you because you're the handsomest man in the world"—yes, it was me she meant, only o' course that was some years ago an' the child was unthinkable young—"an' cause you tell me the nicest stories, an' train pintos, an'—an' I'm goin' to marry you when I grow up."

"Marry me, kitten?" sez I, laughin' free an' natural this time. "Why, bless your heart, where did you ever hear o' marriage?"

"My Daddy tells me of my mother, an' what a beautiful lady she was, an' how happy they were together—an' I'm goin' to marry you when you come back."

"Well, Barbie," sez I right soberly, "you be true to me an' I'll be true to you, an' now we'll kiss to bind the promise."

So I lifted her to my saddle an' kissed her. "How did you get here, child?" sez I.

She didn't answer for a minute. "I rode old Kate," said she at last, "but I didn't want you to know it. She's over behind that rock. And now, Happy, don't you dare to forget me. Good-bye."

I set her down in the road with her eyes misty an' her white teeth set in her lips, an' my own eyes were so hazy like that I couldn't see her when I looked back, an' then I rode away down the valley trail.

CHAPTER TWO
CONVINCING A COOK

I'm as wild as any comet when I first swing out o' my regular orbit, an' I rode on an' on, sometimes puttin' up for the night at a ranch house an' sometimes campin' out in the open, where I'd lay till dawn gazin' up at the stars an' wonderin' how things were goin', back at the Diamond Dot. I mooned on until at last I wound up in the Pan Handle without a red copper, an' my pony sore footed an' lookin' like what a crow gets when the coyotes invite him out to dinner.

I drew rein one night along side a most allurin' camp fire. I had noticed the herd when I came along in, an' they was dandies; big solid five-year-olds, hog fat, but they wasn't contented—kept fidgetin' around. When I struck the fire, a fair haired young feller was readin' a book, two Greasers an' a half blood Injun was playin' poker with an old bunch o' whiskers 'at wasn't a ridin' man at all while the cook had turned in without washin' the dishes.

"If anybody's at home," sez I, "I'd like to ask permission to set down an' rest."

"Why, certainly, make yourself at home," sez the fair hair. The balance o' the bunch only give me the side eye.

"Would you need any more help?" I asked, most respectful.

"No, thank you," sez the young feller, "I think we'll make it all right."

"You have a nice bunch here," sez I, "an' I thought perhaps you might want to get 'em to market in good shape. I am referrin' to the cows"—I continued, kind o' takin' the cover off my voice.

"We expect to get them to market in good shape," sez the fair-hair, uncoilin' his dignity. I rolled a cigarette.

"What makes you think we won't get them to market in good shape?" sez he.

"'Cause your cook's got a sour temper, an' the' ain't no one bossin' the job—'at knows how," sez I, mild an' open-faced, an' lookin' into the fire.

The fair-hair straightens up with a snort, while the pot-openers begin to cuss sort o' growly.

"Where are you from an' how long have you been making my business your own?" asked the fair-hair.

"Oh, I come from up no'th a ways; but I ain't ever made your business mine. I never saw your outfit until twenty minutes ago—but I've seen other outfits."

"Can you handle cattle?" sez he.

"Yes," sez I—"and men."

"Well, I think you can join us," sez he, kind o' slow. "The cattle don't seem to be as gentle as they did when we started. I think it is because we are short handed and have to be a little too rough with them." I didn't answer.

"Well, do you want the job?" sez he.

"Who's the foreman?" sez I.

"I am in charge," he answers stiff like.

"You're the owner, I know, but who's in charge o' the men?"

"I take full supervision," sez he.

"I don't want the job," sez I.

"All right," he snaps, "I don't recall havin' sent for you."

"No offense," sez I, "but up my way it's generally polite to inquire about the appetite. If any one was to ask me, I'd say I was hungry. If any one was to urge me, I'd be obliged to meet up with a little food." I looked him gently in the eyes. He dropped his an' looked put out.

"Tell you the truth, I'm havin' a dog's time of it with my cook. He's gone to bed an' I don't think there's a thing to eat."

"What'll the night riders do?" I asked.

"Oh, they'll raise Cain as usual, but that's all the good it'll do 'em."

"That ain't all they'll do," sez I. "Chances are they'll take it out on the cattle, an' they may—they may even go so far as to get the cattle to cut up until the day shift has to turn out an' help quiet 'em."

"Is that the reason?" he asked, his face lightin' up.

"I don't know for sure, but that's my first guess," sez I.

He looked down at his feet an' I looked him over. He was a nice lookin', well built boy, but he was up against it for about the first time, an' I saw his finish. "I would take the job o' foreman," I sez.

"I hire you—ten a month advance over regular wages, an' you to begin to-morrow."

"No," sez I, "me to begin to-night—with supper."

"All right," sez he, laughin', "help yourself."

I walked over to the cook wagon, as I hit the shadow I loosened my guns, an' the very minute they slipped in their holsters my lone-sickness rolled off like a cloud an' the hurtin' melted out o' my inwards. They was somethin' rolled up in a Navajo under the cook wagon an' I sized it up. It appeared to be seven feet long, but I kicked it in the ribs. Things began to happen at once. A huge creature of a man slid out on the opposite side of the cook wagon, an' when he came around the tail of it he was holdin' a bear gun so it would explode without much ceremony. He was usin' some language an' his speed was a thing to covet; but I just stood with my back to the fire, waitin' until I could get a chance to introduce myself. He was in the light, an' he was enough to make a man reform. Nigger, Greaser, Injun—oh, he was the hardest lookin' specimen I had ever seen, an' the think that occurred to me was that some time a woman had rocked him to sleep an'—kissed him. That's the queer thing about me. My face don't change, but I never got into a mess in my life without some outlandish, foreign idea poppin' into my head an' tryin' to hog my attention.

My attention wasn't much required just at that moment anyhow. He held the bear gun loose in his hand an' swore on like the roar of a mountain torrent. Once I glanced over my shoulder an' saw a pained look on the fair-hair's face, while the ante-up bunch was grinning wickedly an' waitin' for my finish. Me lookin' younger an' easier at that time than I really was, proved a big thing in my favor. Well, as soon as the mongrel cook had cussed himself clean an' dry, he yells at me, "Who in the hell are you an' what in the hell do you want?"

"I'm the new foreman," sez I in a school-girl voice, "an' I want my supper."

He wasn't prepared for it an' dropped his gun to his side while he began to narrate false an' profane eulogies about my breedin' an' past history. He took a few steps toward me so as I wouldn't lose none of his remarks, an' all of a sudden I swung half around an' kicked him in the jaw with my heel, which a trick I had learned from a French sailor. It took me forty-five minutes to come to, after I received my first an' only lesson, an' I wasted a full year huntin' for that sailor. Any time durin' the first six months I'd have ventilated him completely, but after that I wanted to thank him, 'cause I had learned an' tried the trick by that time, an' it was worth all it cost.

But this cook was no wax figger, an' he only lay quiet a moment before he began to roll around an' groan. I picked up a neck yoke what was handy, an' I went for him. I hit him in the butt o' the ear an' on the back o' the neck an' in the center o' the forehead—I tried him out in all the most stylish places, until finally he dozed off.

"Bring me a lantern—you man with the whiskers," I called out.

He riz to his feet like a machine. "It ain't filled," he said.

"I don't know much about fillin' LANTERNS," I remarked to him kindly, "but I have had some experience in fillin' other things. Bring me the lantern, filled an' lighted—and don't keep me waitin'."

I then noticed two fellers a hoss back. "Do you belong to this outfit?" sez I.

"Yes, we're the night riders," answered one o' 'em stickin' up his hands, which plan seemed good to the other one also.

"What are you doin' here this time o' the evenin'?" I asked 'em.

"We heard the racket an' we—we thought something was wrong, an' we—we came in to see—"

"That's all right," sez I, "I'm the new foreman. You don't need to put your hands up every time we meet, but I want you to understand right now that I don't want those cows pestered any more. This outfit is going to run smoother from this on, an' as soon as the cook feels better he is going to cook my supper. I'll see that there is plenty o' coffee for your midnight lunch, an' I want you to enjoy yourselves—but I don't stand for no nonsense."

I made a motion with my eye an' they rode back to the herd, an' by that time the lantern had arrived, an' I poked around in the cook's belongings an' confiscated two shootin' irons an' a wicked Mexican knife. Then I threw a bucket o' water in his face an' he came out of it.

"How do you feel?" I asked him.

"Oh, hell," he moaned, an' he meant every word of it, an' more.

"Now see here, cook," sez I, in a mild voice, "I hate trouble, an' I don't intend to be pestered with it. Do you know how to cook?"

"Yes," he muttered.

"Speak out free an' easy," I sez; "no blood at all is better than bad blood, an' if you don't feel able to forgive me an' go about your work in a friendly way, why I'll feel compelled to remove you from our midst. You're not injured none, only bruised a bit, and I'm famished for my supper. I'm always quick tempered when I'm hungry an' I'm gettin' hungrier every minute. Are you ready to begin?"

He slowly got up to his feet an' looked at me. "Come over to the fire an' have a good look," I said, as though we were old friends.

He followed me over to the fire an' he sure gave me a lookover. "You're bigger'n I thought you was, an' you've been purty well seasoned. I ain't never yet been licked without a gun an' I didn't think it could be did. Will you fight me again—without weapons?" "I'll never fight you again but once," sez I, an' my lips were smiling, but all of a sudden a hatred of his cruel, evil eyes came over me, an' my lips curled back over my teeth. "If you had known I was your foreman an' had mixed with me I'd 'a' killed you a few moments ago. The very next time you cross me I'll kill you. I sleep light—when I do sleep. Are you goin' to cook my supper?"

"Yes, you blasted rattler," sez he, with a grin, "you're the killin' kind an' you're the killin' age, but I know when the jig's up. I know your name all right, but hanged if I can see through your game. I ain't goin' to try, either. As long as you choose to play at bein' foreman, I'll play at bein' cook, an' when you start on again, I'm willin' to join ya. I'll get your supper in a jiffey, Kid."

I sauntered over to the fair-hair, tryin' to act as if this was an every day occurrence. He had never changed his position all through it, although his hands were tremblin'.

I sat down beside him an' he chuckled softly—I liked that chuckle. It was boyish an' friendly, but most of all it showed a good foundation. He was new to the game, but he was the kind that learned.

"I suppose I'm purt nigh as old as you," he blurted out.

"In some things, mebbe—not in the cattle business," sez I.

"No," he grinned, "nor in the man-handlin' business, but I want to tell you right now that I have enjoyed this evenin's performance, no matter what happens from it. I ain't carryin' much cash with me," he added after a moment's thought.

"I ain't carryin' any," sez I.

He looked into my face again an' gave his chuckle. A feller couldn't help but echo when that fair-hair chuckled. "I heard the cook say he knew you an' he called you Kid—I suppose you are the Pan Handle Kid?" he asked.

"I didn't know the' was a Pan Handle Kid, but they're pretty common an' they're all a good bit alike. Forced to begin killin' before they're able to put the right value on life, an' once they begin, no way to stop. Now I'll tell you confidential that I'm not the Pan Handle, nor any other kind of a kid, although I once was the makin' of one. Still, it will make matters easier if this bunch thinks I am, so we'll just let it go at that. My name is Happy Hawkins; what might I call you?"

"Happy?"—he opens his eyes like saucers an' then he laughs like a boy. "Well, I watched you goin' after the cook with the neck yoke an' I never in the world would have called you Happy."

"Well, you'll see me trail in this bunch o' beef cattle, smooth an' contented an' with every man jack rollin' fat an' dimpled to the knuckles. They've had their last fuss. I'll feed 'em an' I'll work 'em from now on, an' you won't know 'em when we hit the market. Where you headin' for, K.C.?"

"Yes. My name is Mister Jamison—James Jamison."

"This is a warm climate," sez I.

"Yes," he sez sort o' surprised, "it is."

"It has an awful meltin' effect on names," I continued.

He chuckled again. "I'm mighty glad you arrived, Happy," sez he. "What do you suppose'll happen to my name?"

"Well" I sez, "if you get yours before they learn to like you, it'll probably be James Jamison on the headboard, but if you make good, it'll be Jim Jimison on Sundays an' jest plain Jim for every day." "That suits me," sez he. "I'm entered for the whole race, an' I'm glad to get off as soon as possible."

"Supper's ready," called the cooks, an' when I gave a whoop an' bolted for it he giggled like a big fat mammy. I had turned up the side of his nature 'at would be most useful to our business. I took a sip o' the coffee while he kept his eyes glued on me. "Come over here, Jim," I called.

Jim came over lookin' a little anxious. "Taste that stuff," sez I.

He tasted it an' his face changed as though he had caught a vision of the better world, but I kept my face like the face of an angry bear. "What do you call this stuff?" I asked the cook, an' his face grew dark as a thunder cloud.

"That's coffee!" he roared.

"When was the pot cleaned?" I asked, with my brows drawn down to the bridge of my nose.

"Not more'n ten minutes ago," he yelled; and I got up an' holding my cup in my hand I danced about twenty different dances, while that cook like to split his sides laughin'. He was a cook, the' was no gettin' around it, an' Jim, he turned in an' fed his face while first his cheeks would dimple with the gladness o' the moment, an' then his eyes would sadden as he thought of all the good eatin' he had missed by not knowin' the proper kind o' diplomacy to use in handlin' a cook. An' me!—say, I mowed away until my skin begun to creak under the strain an' I couldn't roll my eyes more'n two degrees. Then I got up an' I shook hands with the cook.

"Cook," I sez, "no matter how devilish wicked you've been in the past, an' no matter how faithful you live up to your inner nature in the future, you're sure of a number nine crown an' a spotless robe jest fer this one meal"; an' the cook, he fairly glistened in the firelight.

Well, this was about all they was to that expedition. We all got to be so friendly with one another that by the time we had trailed that bunch into the stock yards, we was like one big family of elder brothers, an' Jim, he teased me into goin' back to the Pan Handle with him.

Jim was an Englishman—a younger brother. Up to that time I had allus supposed 'at bein' a younger brother was somewhat in the nature of an accident, an' not a thing to be hurled in a feller's teeth; but over in England it's looked upon as a heinius crime, an' the only thing a younger brother can do to square himself is to get out o' sight. That's how Tim happened to be in the Texas Pan Handle with a tidy little fortune his aunt had left him, tucked away in a good-sized, well-stocked ranch.

I took a good deal o' pains with him, 'cause he didn't have nothin' but a book education, an' it wasn't altogether easy to get him to see the true value o' things. He used to talk about Eton an' Oxford purty solemn, until one night he helped me mill the herd durin' a Norther', an' after that he took more kindly to the vital things o' life, but he was a man, Jim was, an' he kept raisin' my wages right along until I got that opulent feelin'. I never could stand prosperity those days; just as soon as I had a weight o' money 'at I could notice, I begun to grow restless, an' nothin' 'at Jim could do or say had much effect.

If things hadn't run in oil, I'd a-stayed right along, I reckon; but it got so 'at the' wasn't a hitch from week to week, an' I couldn't stand it. I never had a better friend in the world'n that cook was after he'd saved my life.

Jim had a kid sort o' chorin' around the place an' keepin' us from gettin' old an' stupid. One nice bright winter's day the kid went out for a ride; his pony came lopin' in just at sun down in the face of a blizzard, an' I went out to look for the kid. I found him trudgin' toward home an' cussin' his luck somethin' terrible. I put him up behind me an' by that time the wind was shootin' needles o' sleet into my face 'till I couldn't see a yard ahead. The kid snuggled up to me an' went to sleep, an' I gave the pony his head an' trusted to luck—no, come to think about it, that night I trusted to somethin' higher than luck, 'cause it was a perfect demon of a night.

The pony dropped from a lope to a walk an' then he put his nose to the ground an' fairly shuffled along. I was wearin' sheepskin with the wool on, but after a time the needles began to creep in an' I grew numb as a stone, while my flesh seemed shook loose from my bones, an' it hurt me to breathe. Oh, Lord, but it was cold! If it hadn't 'a' been for the kid I'd have gotten down an' walked alongside the pony, but as it was, he was out o' the wind an' sleepin' peaceful, so I just sat an' took it.

At last I sort o' drowsed off myself. I didn't sleep, but I wasn't awake; I seemed to be back at the Diamond Dot an' playin' in a little sheltered dell with Barbie. She had made up a game called Fairy Princess; sometimes she was the Fairy Princess an' sometimes I was, an' it was a mighty amusin' sort of a game, but different from most o' the games I was familiar with.

Well, that night out in the Texas blizzard I was playin' that game with little Barbie, an' all of a sudden—smash! Before I knowed what had happened we had been run into an' knocked down a ravine an' both the kid an' the pony was lyin' on top o' me. The kid got up an' begun to cuss as usual, but the pony never moved. I'd a heap sight rather had the conditions reversed, 'cause the pony was on my right leg an' my right leg was on a sharp stone.

"Shut up, kid," sez I, "this ain't no time for such talk. Here, you curl up alongside the pony an' I'll spread part o' my coat over you."

That kid was a home-maker all right; nothin' ever surprised him, an' wherever he lit he made himself comfortable. In two minutes he was asleep, while I began to puzzle it out. We were in a sheltered spot an' the wind swept above us; but it was so dark that you couldn't see ten inches. The wind was from the no'th, an' I went over every bit o' landscape in the country until at last I figgered out the' was only one place in Texas that filled the bill. A path swung around a crag an' the' was a shelf of stone ten feet below it an' eight feet wide, then it cut off sheer, fifty feet to the rocky bank of a creek. I reached out with my hand an' felt the edge of it, an' it give me an awful chill. I don't like to come quite so close.

After a time the wind veered around a little more to the east an' then it sucked up through the cut an' I began to freeze. I didn't care a great deal 'cause it stopped the horrid hurtin' in my leg; but the dead pony began to cool, an' I knew it was only a question o' minutes. Finally I awoke the kid. "Where is your gun, kid?" I sez.

"I shot all my catridges tryin' to bring some one out on a pony," sez the kid, drowsily, an' then he dozes off again.

We were only a mile from the ranch house; it was again the wind an' it wasn't much use to waste ammunition, but I finally got out my gun an' begun to shoot at intervals.

"What the deuce you makin' that racket for?" grunted the kid at the third shot. I boxed his ears and went on shootin' until at last the cold went through sheepskin an' woolens an' hide an' flesh, an' I grew warm an' contented; an' the next I knew, the cook was rubbin' my wrists an' pourin' hot coffee into me. I was purty mad at bein' dragged back to earth an' grumbled about it free an' hearty, but the cook kept croonin' to me the same as if I'd been a baby: "Neveh mind, honey, neveh mind; ol' Monody'll bring ya around all right. Take another sip o' coffee, chile, that's right, that's right."

It took me quite a spell before I could tell whether I was alive or not, 'cause while the cook had changed a heap since I'd first met up with him, I'd never heard any such talk as this; but after a time I came out of it an' the anguish I underwent gettin' back to life wasn't nowise worth the experiment.

It had stopped blowin', but it was colder than ever, an' at last I began to take enough interest in things to want 'em to get settled one way or another. As soon as I was able to think along a straight line, the cook would give a heave to the pony an' I would give myself a jerk. The lantern shed a splash o' light on the shelf, but the jump-off looked like the mouth o' the pit, an' I jerked purty tol'able careful. At last I was out, an' if you'll believe it, my leg was only broke in two places. I thought it was broken clear off. I couldn't get back up the cliff to the trail any way we could figger, so the cook said I should roll up in the Navajos he'd brought an' he'd take the kid an' go back an' bring a couple o' the boys an' pack me in.

The kid had found the blankets all right an' had rolled himself up, an' we had to shake the stuffin' out of him to rouse him again. He complained most bitter when he found he had to go back to the ranch house; but at last they got started an' it wasn't long before they had me there too, an' next day Phil McLaughlin rode over an' brought out a doctor who lined up my bones as good as new, while Jim told me about the cook.

Old Monody was like a salamander for heat, an' you couldn't drag him away from the fire in the winter time; but when I didn't return he began to worry: "If the' was a man left in this outfit I reckon he'd go out an' get him," he'd say scornful. "Riders! you call yourselves riders? You're loafers an' eaters, that's what you are! I'm a cook, but if nobody else has the nerve to go an' git him, I'll go myself."

Jim started to go at last, but he wouldn't let him. "You got the grit, Jim, but you ain't got the night sense yet. You stay where you are or you'd be on our hands too." Well, he steamed up an' down makin' new hot coffee an' drinkin' it by the bowl. All of a sudden he give a scream: "Oh, oh! there he goes over the cliff! Get me a pony—get me a pony, while I wrap up some coffee an' pick out some blankets!" Well, the cook was so blame wild by this time 'at they was glad to get shut of him; so they rigged him out an' he rode a bee line right to me, an' what led him you can figger out for yourselves. He was a queer cook, but after that night he was different: he acted as though he had adopted me; he petted me an' spoiled me an' you can talk all you want to about the flesh-pots of Egypt—why, that cook could fix beans eleven different ways, an' each one better'n the other.

But while I was lyin' there waitin' for my leg to knit up, I kept thinkin' o' the little lass back at the Diamond Dot, an' when I got about again, I knew I was signed for a trip No'th.

The cook was mighty good to me while I was backin' it; he used to deal out fussy little fixin's 'at kept the appetite an' the fever both down, an' when they wasn't no one around he used to pat out my pillers an' oncet he smoothed back my hair. He cut out his cussin' too, an' he used to line up the kid for it.

"You're from the South, ain't ya, Happy?" sez he to me one day.

"Not so you could notice," sez I. "I reckon this is the southest I ever got before."

"Hu," sez the cook, "Texas ain't south. Texas is just the rubbish heap o' this whole country. Where did you hook up to that word 'reckon'?"

"I dunno," sez I, thinkin' back. "A feller just catches words like the mumps, I suppose; but my pap, he used to use it right often."

"Where did your folks come from?" sez the cook.

"Oh, they come from Kentucky, an' before that from Virginia an' No'th Carolina, an' before that they came from Scotch Irish an' English, an' go clear back to Adam an' you'll find us Hawkinses was a ramblin' crew, I reckon; but what on earth you drivin' at, Monody, an' where on earth did your line hail from?"

He sat there a moment with lights an' shades dartin' over his ugly face, which somehow wasn't ugly to me any more, an' at last he said: "I have the blood of an Injun chief an' an African king an' a Spanish nobleman in my veins, an'—"

"Lord, man, you ought to let some of it out," I interrupted. "You'll have an eruption in your in'ards some day 'at'll blow you into a million pieces."

"No, I got 'em all whipped out now, Happy, an' I reckon 'at you did it. You're the only man I ever met 'at I ain't once felt like killin'."

"It's pleasant to think o' what a good neighbor you've been all your life, cook; but I'm glad you've turned over since I met up with you. Anyhow, you've been a heap o' comfort to me, an' anything I got is on your list too, don't you never forget it."

But just the same, as soon as I got up an' around again, I had a terrible tuggin' from the no'th an' I couldn't resist it. I'd be makin' plans for the summer an' then all of a sudden I'd find myself sayin', "What in the world do you reckon 'at that child is doin' now. She'll be eight years old shortly, an' I simply have to see her on her next birthday, even if she don't see me." At last I couldn't stand it no longer, so I told the boys I had to cut, an' it fell like a stone on a lamp chimney; but the cook, he took it harder'n any one else. I liked the boys an' I liked Jim an' I liked the job; but there was that tuggin' allus at my heart, an' in the end I set a day. Jim, he made me all kinds of offers, 'cause things were gettin' easy with him; but when I made it clear to him, he saw how it was an' he sez: "I know 'at you'll come back to me some day, Happy, an' if you'll settle down, you can be a rich man. I've kept back five hundred dollars for you 'at I haven't mentioned in your wages, an' you can take your pick o' the colts an' just as soon as you've had your little flier I want you back; we all want you back."

It's a comfortin' feelin' to know 'at you're goin' to be missed; but I couldn't savvy that cook. He had one big tearin' time of it an' sluiced himself out with gin an' dug up his old profanity, an' then he simmered down an' just cooked himself into a new record. Gee! it was hard to separate from that mess table; but I had set my day an' the' was no goin' back.

Jim had a black Arabian stallion an' a couple o' high grade mares an' he was showin' up something fancy in the hoss line. He raised the colts just like range ponies, an' while they wasn't quite so tough when it came to livin' on sage brush an' pleasant memories, they could eat up the ground like a prairie fire, an' they was gentle. I bought a silver trimmed bridle an' some Mexican didoes, an' then I said good-bye to all of 'em except the cook—he wasn't there.

I hunted for him an hour; but he had so many peculiar ways 'at I just let it go at that an' finally gave him up; so I left him a nifty present an' pulled out with about a thousand yellow ones in my belt an' the best mount in the West.

I hadn't gone more than two miles before I turned a corner an' came face to face with ol' Monody. He was settin' on a big bald-faced roan, an' he had a serious look on his face. "Well, I wondered if you was goin' to let me go away without sayin' good-bye," sez I, tryin' to talk light an' easy.

"I'd be apt to," sez he. "Why, I've been peacefuller since you been here'n ever I was in my life before, an' it ain't likely I'd let you scoot out an' leave me. I'm goin' along."

Well, what do you think of that! Me startin' up to where I wasn't sure of a welcome an' takin' such a tow as ol' Monody along with me. I argued with him for an hour, an' then I got hot an' told him that merely savin' my life didn't give him no mortgage on me an' that he couldn't nowise keep up with me, an' by the time he reached the Diamond Dot, the chances were 'at I'd be on my way back to the Lion Head. He didn't waste no time in words, just sat sour an' moody, an' every tine I'd stop he'd growl out, "I don't care where you go or how fast you go or nothin' at all about it. I'm goin' along, an' I'll catch up with you sometime."

I sure gave him a chase; I wanted the black hoss to show up well when I landed, but I sent him along pretty steady an' took extra care of him. Ol' Monody had picked out the toughest pony at the Lion Head, an' he had good hands, but he never sighted me till the night I reached the ranch and was busy wipin' Starlight's legs. "I got some news for ya," sez ol' Monody, gettin' down slow from his leg-weary roan. "I'll tell it to ya while you 're eatin supper,"—an' I was sure glad to see him—an' glad to eat food again.

CHAPTER THREE
UNDER FIRE

As soon as I finished takin' care o' Starlight, I give Monody's mount a look-over. The old bald-face was whipcord an' steel; but he looked purty near ready to own up.

"Monody, confound you," I sez. "What the deuce did you hammer this old skin over the road like this for?"

"That's my pony," he growled.

"Since when?"

"Since I bought him, that's since when."

"When did you buy him?"

"It ain't none o' your business when I bought him. I bought him the mo'nin' you pulled out."

"What did you pay for him?"

"Are you goin' to talk about that ol' cayuse all night?" he snorts, gettin' wrought up.

"I'm goin' to talk about him until I find out about him," sez I, "an' you might as well come out of it an' tell what the' is to tell."

"I don't have to tell nothin' about him. He neveh belonged to you. Jim, he owed me some money on my wages so I just took the pony for the money. An' now I hope you're through pesterin' me."

"How much did he owe ya?" sez I.

"Now you gone about far enough with this!" yells Monody. "I don't know how much he owed me, an' I don't care. I reckon he owed me more'n the pony's worth, 'n if he didn't he can just pertend he raised my wages last month."

"Why didn't you let him raise your wages a little more, an' bring along a bunch o' five-year-olds too?" sez I, grinning. I was mighty glad to see the old scamp, an' I knew he had drawed the worst end o' the bargain; but I wanted him to understand that it was embarrassin' to go again my wishes without my consent. He had the pot o' coffee just ready to set on the rock where we was goin' to eat, an' all of a sudden he straightened up an' shot a scowl into me. "Look here, Happy." sez he, "I don't care a sky blue flap doodle for the whole Jim Jimison outfit! I told you I was comin' along, an' I come. I tells you again that I'm goin' wherever you go; but if you don't shet up about that royally sequestered ol' ball faced camel, I'll dash this scaldin' hot coffee—right on the ground!"

Well, I fell on my knees an' begged him to spare me, an' I kept it up until he was gigglin' with laughter—he had a funny way o' laughin'—an' then we sat on the stone an'—well, the' never was a human mortal 'at was qualified to carry water for ol' Monody's cookin'.

"What's your news, Monody?" I sez, after I 'd satisfied myself that I couldn't swaller another crumb.

"You're headin' for the Diamond Dot, ain't ya?" sez he.

"This is a corner o' the Diamond Dot range," sez I, lollin' back an' puffin' slow an' comfortable at my pipe.

"The pony corral stands at the mouth of a little canon, don't it?"

"Yes," sez I.

"An' the cook house is to the right of it?"

"Yes," sez I.

"An' the ranch house is kind o' sprawly with—"

"Look here, Monody," sez I, interruptin', "this ain't no news. What are you gettin' at?"

"You got friends there, ain't ya?" sez he.

"I got one friend anyhow," sez I, "but as long as you've insisted on taggin' along after me, you'll see the place an' you'll see my friend; though I somehow doubt if you'll be invited in for a meal."

"Is your friend a lady?" sez Monody.

"Oh, no," sez I, sarcastic, "she 's a two-year-old heifer. I wouldn't think o' goin' this distance just to call on a lady."

"How old is she?" asked Monody.

"Now you look here, you old pest," sez I, "if you're just tryin' to get even with me about the bald-faced roan, why cut it; but if you've got anything to tell, why tell it, 'cause I'm gettin' sleepy. She'll be eight years old to-morrow."

Old Monody shook with silent laughter for a moment. "A lady!" sez he. Then he sobered an' sez, "Is it your child?"

I heaved a rock at him which he dodged, an' then I sez, "You wicked of beast you, do I look old enough to have an eight-year-old daughter?"

"Sometimes you do an' sometimes you don't. You're one o' these fellers 'at ain't got no age o' their own, but just age up accordin' to what's goin' on," —an' ol' Monody stumbled on a bit o' truth when he said this, an' it's still true.

"Well, what are you gettin' at?" sez I.

"The Diamond Dot is goin' to be raided to-night," sez he.

I jumped to my feet. "Who by?" I sez.

"You're fifteen years older right now than you was two minutes ago," sez Monody. "I stumbled onto Bill Brophy's gang last night. Bill has seven o' the lowest grade wolves 'at ever wore man-hide—I—I used to know Bill down in the Territory, an' Bill he thought I was still on the grab. He put me on. I'm supposed to be at the pony corral at midnight to turn the ponies loose an' bottle up the house gang in their shack. Brophy's bad medicine; you'd better pass up your eight-year-old lady friend an' come on back to the Lion Head with ol' Monody."

I walked up an' down a time or two, thinkin' it over. "We can ride right into the ravine 'at leads to the pony corral from here," sez I. "It's a good average four hours' ride. Now I can do it in three on Starlight; the old bald-face couldn't do it at all to-night—"

"Look at him now," sez Monody. There he was eatin' grass as lively as a cricket. "Well, you follow as you can, only you'd better lay low unless I whistle the Lion Head signal. If I get time to break you gentle to the home gang, it'll be all right; but you ain't apt to be due for a cordial welcome, not when strangers to you are lookin' for hold-ups."

He had tossed the saddles an' bridles on the hosses by this time, an' we left our outfit lyin' on the rocks. We hit the saddles in the same tick an' settled into a swing. Big an' heavy as ol' Monody was, he was a light rider, an' the bald-face hung at my cinch for the best part of an hour an' then we slowly oozed away from him. The stars were all full power that night, an' a feller could see most as plain as if the'd been a moon.

It smelt good to be back at the old place again, an' my blood was racin' through my veins till I fair tingled. Finally I reached the canon an' began to ride careful. It was only about eleven; but I didn't want any o' Brophy's gang to take a pot shot at me. All of a sudden something moved on a little grassy shelf on the side of the cliff. Starlight shied off to the left an' my gun flew up over my head, ready to drop on whatever it happened to be. My eyes were drillin' into the gloom when a mite of a creature with her hands clasped rose up an' said, "Oh, Happy, Happy! is it really you? an' ridin' on the black hoss with the silver trimmed leather!"

"Barbie, child!" I cried, "what on earth you doin' out here this time o' night an' all by your lone?"

"I just couldn't sleep, Happy," she said, comin' to the edge o' the shelf an' sittin' down with her little bare feet swingin' over; "I got to wonderin' how it would feel just when the birthday was a-comin' on; so I sneaked out here, an' I was just beginnin' to feel it when you hove into sight. I been thinkin' o' you lots lately, Happy."

"You little minx, you," sez I, "I doubt if you've thought of me twice since I been away, while I've been thinkin' of you every minute. But come, jump down behind me an' we'll hurry on. I want you to go in an' wake Daddy up an' tell him I've got something mighty important to say to him, while I scurry over an' wake up the home gang."

"The home gang ain't here," sez Barbie. "The ponies vamoosed this afternoon—they nearly always do the days I turn Mr. H. Hawkins with them,—that's what I call the pinto. He's an awful scamp; but the best pony on the place."

"Then I reckon they'll bring 'em around the twist an' down this canon. Now you get down here an' sneak into the house while I stake out Starlight in the big cathedral—see how well I remember everything."

I set the child down, rode Starlight into a big open nook with a narrow mouth, an' then hustled into the house. Old Cast Steel was standin' in the dining room in his stockin'-feet with a gun in each hand an' a question in his eyes. "Get ready for a raid, Jabez," sez I. "Who from?" sez he.

"From the Brophy gang," sez I.

"How do you know?" sez he. "They are due to arrive here at midnight, Jabez," sez I. "I don't know why; but I think we'd better get ready for 'em now an' argue about it to-morrow."

"I know why," sez lie. "One of 'em stole one o' my ponies an' started to run off a bunch o' my own cows with it. I strung him up an' he said 'at Bill Brophy'd get even with me for it. That was two months ago, an' the' hasn't been a minute since 'at I was so bad prepared for 'em. How many's in the gang?"

"Bill an' seven others. I found out through the meanest lookin' mortal you ever set eyes on. He's a giant, nearly black, an' the ugliest critter you ever set eyes on; but he's white inside. He'll be along as soon as he can get here—don't shoot him."

"I ain't apt to shoot any help this night," grins Jabez.

"If it wasn't for the little girl, Happy, I'd be right satisfied to have it out with Bill; but I hate to think of what may happen to her. How'll we fix for 'em?"

"Get in the dug-out cellar," sez I, for I'd been plannin' it all along.

"I reckon they'll burn the house down," sez Jabez; "but I'd rather they destroyed the whole blame outfit than to have anything happen to the little lass."

"Where's Melisse?" sez I. "She left," sez Jabez; an' I hadn't time to learn particulars.

By this time we had everything barricaded, an' gettin' Barbie we made a run for the dug-out. It was only two hundred yards; but we hadn't left the shadow of the house before a rifle sings out followed by two revolver shots. The' was a big pile o' winter wood in the L of the ranch house, an' without sayin' a word I swung Jabez with little Barbie in his arms back of the wood pile.

We didn't shoot much, although the gang kept pepperin' at the wood pile purty frequent from behind the cook house. "They'll fire the house purty soon," mutters Jabez, after we'd beat'em off on their second rush. "We'll have to try for the dug-out sooner or later."

Just at this minute the six notes o' the Lion Head signal floated in. "There's ol' Monody," sez I. "I wish Barbie was safe an' we'd show'em a merry time of it." I answered the call an' the' was silence for a long time. Presently we heard a rattlin' volley, an' the cook rolled around the corner o' the house an' joined us.

"The next time they rush," sez Jabez, "we'll charge out after 'em an' try for the dug-out. They won't monkey much longer."

They didn't monkey at all. Two of 'em had broke into the house from in front, an' the next we knew a window had been flung open at our back an' we would a-got it right then, but Monody heard 'em, an' as soon as the window shutter flew back he emptied his gun inside. At the same time the remainin' six charged in a body, an' for the next few minutes we was some busy. But we beat'em off, an' as they scurried for shelter to load, we made for the dug-out; me in front, ol' Jabez in the center, an' Monody closin' up the rear.

Just before we reached it, a revolver cracked in the doorway o' the dug-out, I felt a sting in the left shoulder, spun around and fell, but jumped up just as Jabez changed directions for the cook shack. It was only a step from the dug-out an' we rushed in, slammed the door, dropped in the bar, an' turned to face a man with two guns on us. Monody dropped on him, an' I was about to shoot from the hip when of Jabez sez, "By George, Jim, I'd forgot all about you—we can sure fix'em now. These is friends, Jim." Jim was a savage lookin' brute an' I eyed him purty close. "This feller is cookin' while Flapjack is on his bender, Happy," sez Jabez.

The cook shack was built out o' pine logs at the bottom, an' fixed so the upper sides'd swing out like awnings in hot weather. We felt purty comfortable. The' was a square window at each end an' one on the side facin' the house; the stove was on the other side. We made little Barbie sit in the corner behind the stove. Jabez took the window facin' the house, me the one facin' the dug-out, an' the sub-cook facin' the corral. I could shoot cleaner'n Monody, so he stood by to do my loadin', an' we proceeded to waste ammunition. It's enough to make the oldest man the' is reckless, when you think of the weight o' lead good aimers can throw without spillin' any blood.

After a bit things grew quiet, an' then we saw a small freight-wagon backin' down to the door with a lot o' wood across the back of it. Jabez came over to my window an' we shot into an' under the wagon; but it still backed up. The' was a little grade down to the cook shack, an' after they got it started the' wasn't much to do but guide. They had fixed a stick o' wood pointin' straight back from the rear axle, an' when it hit the door the bar broke an' the door flew off its hinges an' clear across the room.

But gettin' the wagon away for their rush was a different matter, an' we all shot at one another purty regardless. Once I reached back my hand for a fresh gun an' failed to get any. I turned around, an' there was Monody holdin' the sub-cook's right wrist with his left hand an' grippin' at his throat with his right. The' was a horrid look on the sub-cook's face, an' just as I turned to interfere, Monody gave a wrench which tore out the cook's wind-pipe, gave him a sling which landed him under the table, an' handed me a fresh gun. I was some bothered about this; but that wa'n't no time to hold an investigation, so I begun shootin' at flashes again.

"How's your catridges holdin' out?" sez Jabez.

"Ain't many left," sez Monody.

"I'm about cleaned myself," sez Jabez. "Where's Jim?"

"I think he's about once through," sez I, an' we proceeded to shoot more economical.

Purty soon they quit firin' again an' then the freight wagon started up the hill. They had put their ropes on the tongue an' were draggin' it out with ponies. We knew what that meant an' took a brace.

The lull what followed was the hardest part o' the whole business. Ther' wasn't a blasted thing we could do, an' it seemed hours before the neat volley came from the corner o' the dug-out. We didn't reply to it, which was most uncommon lucky for us; 'cause first thing we knew, they came rompin' around each corner an' poured in on top of us. They was used to fightin' against odds, an' it irritated 'em consid'able to take so long at a job with the odds in their favor. Outside, the starlight give us a purty fair aim, while they couldn't do more than guess at us—so we beat 'em off once more.

"The's only three shots in this gun," sez Monody, cheerfully, as he handed my iron back to me.

"What's that?" sez Jabez.

"We're about out o' fuel, Jabez," sez I.

I heard him grit his teeth in the darkness. "Where is she, Happy?" sez he.

"She's still in her corner back of the stove with the shack door in front of her. They won't hurt her, Jabez—no matter what happens, an' the' 's a good fight in us yet. Ol' Monody here don't begin to fight till the ammunition has give out; so keep your mind easy for the next rush," sez I.

Next moment they surged down on us, shootin' as fast as they could fan. We didn't explode a catridge until they was bunched in the door an' then we emptied out. They cussed an' groaned consid'able; but they surged on into the cabin, just the same. The smoke was like a cloud inside, an' a newcomer couldn't see an inch; so I backed into my corner with my left arm danglin' at my side an' holdin' my gun by the barrel.

The shootin' stopped in a flash an' the silence hurt a feller's ears. The' was a sloppy, floppin' sound over under the table an' now an' again a low groan. "Fetch the lantern out o' the freight wagon, an' let's chalk up." said a deep, heavy voice. In about a minute a light ripped its way into darkness an' I never saw a worse sight. Jabez was lyin' face down with a hairy viper on top of him face up. The feller'd been pinked in the bridge o' the nose an' it was most horrid ghastly. Two others lay still with their bodies inside the shack an' their legs outside; while another was lyin' just at my feet. Some one had swatted him in the temple with a revolver butt; but the sight that just about made me homesick was Jim, the deputy cook.

Monody hadn't broken the windpipe, an' he wasn't dead yet. It was him 'at made the floppin' sound. Oh, it was sickening! Brophy was a fine lookin' man—I recognized him from his description right at once—an' he hadn't been even grazed. He looked around cool but quick, an' just about took it all in, in the snap of a finger. Then he loaded both his guns before us an' made the feller with the lantern do the same. After which he looked into Monody's eyes—looked into 'em until Monody's ugly black face turned ashy; but Brophy hadn't even a scowl, an' when he spoke, his deep voice was steady an' calm. "How did that happen, Monody?" sez he, pointin' to the sub-cook.

"I—I reckon one o' the boys mistook him in the dark," sez Monody.

"I reckon you lie," sez Brophy. "The' ain't no white man would be beast enough. It's one o' your own heathen tricks."

I was surprised at the way Brophy talked. I'd allus heard 'at he was a rip-snortin' screamer, an' here he was talkin' low an' level like, as if he was conversin' about the weather; but when I looked into Monody's face an' saw it gray an' quivery, I knew 'at Brophy wasn't no bluffer, whether he yelled or whether he whispered.

I moved about an inch 'cause my leg was strainin', an' three guns dropped on me. "Don't try nothin'," sez Brophy. I didn't—I stood mighty still.

The man under the table give a gaspy squawk, Brophy dropped on one knee to look at him, an' I could see him shudder as he looked at the torn throat. "My God!" he muttered, an' then he started to git up, his voice fairly snarlin' with rage. "Monody, you beast!" he yelled, snap-pin' back the hammer of his gun, "I'll—"

He never finished it. With a queer, guttural cry Monody took a step forward with his left foot an' kicked him under the chin, lifted him clear from the ground, an' rolled him over, a crumpled an' broken thing, on top o' the sub-cook The man with the lantern began to fan-shoot into Monody, an' I jumped for him an' hit him in the temple with the butt, o' my gun. He went down with a crash an' the lantern went out.

"Monody!" I called. "Monody, are you hurt?" The' wasn't no answer; the' wasn't a sound. I felt like the last man on earth. Then I thought of the girl. I waited a moment to quiet my voice, an' then I sez, "Are you all right, little Barbie?" Still the' wasn't no answer, an' I fairly yelled to her.

"Yes, I'm all right, Happy, but I want to get out. Are you all right?" Her voice was steady, but it sounded a long ways off.

"Yes, Honey Bird, I'm all right," I sez.

"And is my Daddy all right?" she asked.

My! but it was a world o' comfort to hear the child's voice again, an' some way I felt unreasonable tickled to think 'at she had asked about me first. "Your Daddy ain't here just now, Barbie," I sez. "You'd better just stay where you are until we make sure 'at they're all gone."

"Well, all right," she said in the same muffled voice; "but I'd like to get out."

I hunted through my pockets for a match, but I couldn't find one, an' what I wanted just then was light—Lord, how I did want a light!

And then I heard a tramplin' an' a poundin' as the herd swept down the ravine an' into the corral, an' next minute I heard George Hendricks give the yell he allus give when a job was done, an' I yelled back—yelled till my voice cracked; an' it was the biggest relief I ever had.

CHAPTER FOUR
PROFESSIONAL DUTY

I kept on yellin' until they got to the cook shack. "What the bloomin' blue blasted blazes is the matter?" sez Spider Kelley. "An' who the fiber fingered flub-dub are ya?"

"Get a light, get a light an' see!" I yells, hatin' to move.

"It's Happy Hawkins!" yells the whole bunch, an' the tone they used was all-fired welcome.

Purty soon they come in with a lantern, an' then they stopped askin' questions. For a moment we all just looked at that floor, an' it was sure a hideous sight. I put my finger on my lips an' pointed to the corner back of the stove where I'd put the shack door in front o' little Barbie, an' then I motioned for 'em to drag the bodies out. Monody was alive an' he had a satisfied grin on his face when I helped to carry him out in the air. Jabez never moved, an' the boys lifted him mighty tender—he'd been a good man to work for, spite of his queer ways. The two men in the doorway were still gaspin', but the rest of Brophy's gang had passed on as they had a right to expect, wearin' their boots an' their guns hot in their hands. Brophy himself had his neck broken, but his face didn't look bad. It was peaceful under the lantern light.

As soon as they was all lined up on the side porch I took the shack door down, but Barbie wasn't there. "Barbie!" I called. "Barbie, child! where are you?"

"Here I am, Happy," answered a muted voice. "I'm in the oven. Can't I come out now?" I opened the door to the big oven an' there she was, wrapped in a coat an' all rumpled up as if she'd been sleepin'. "Who put you in there, child?" I asked.

"A woman," she answered. "A woman with a soft, kind voice. She put me in here an' she told me to go to sleep, an' I did sleep most o' the time. When you'd all shoot together it would wake me up; but then after a minute I'd doze off again, an' now it's gettin' daylight an' I'm eight years old, an' I didn't get to see how it felt comin' on. Where's my Daddy, an' are all the robbers gone?"

"A woman!" sez I.

"Yes, an' she had the kindest voice," sez Barbie. "Ain't she here now? I want to talk to her. I've missed ol' Melisse something fierce—but I never let on to Daddy. Where is Daddy, Happy?"

"You ask more questions'n an almanac, Barbie," sez I, tryin' to speak easy. "I'm goin' to carry you in an' put you to bed, an' you can go on dreamin' about your beautiful lady, an' then in the mornin' I'll tell you all about what's happened."

My heart weighed about a ton in my breast as I carried the child into the house with the gray dawn light drippin' over her an' the still form of her father lyin' around on the side porch. I thought o' the mother she hadn't never seen, an' I hoped that things was fixed so 'at that mother could keep on comin' back now an' again to put a dream into her lonely little heart like she'd already done that night; but I carried her into her little white bedroom hummin' a dance-tune, took off her shoes an' stockin's, covered her up warm, an' told her she could sleep late, as we wasn't goin' to have an early breakfast. The big lids closed down over her bright little eyes, an' purty soon she was breathin' soft an' quiet, an' then I left her. I stopped in the doorway an' looked back, an' my heart ached when I thought of her havin' to wake up an' face it all. It ain't just killin' a man that's so bad, it's the awful hole most of 'em makes in some innocent woman's heart.

When I got back to the side porch my breath liked to 'a' stopped, for there was Jabez sittin' up an' complainin' most bitter because he had an achin' in the back of his neck. I stopped in my tracks gappin' at him, an' purty soon he noticed me an' sez, "Well, what are YOU starin' at? Remember 'at I ain't no chicken heart, an' remember 'at what I hate worse'n anything else is a liar. Now where is my child?"

"She's in bed and asleep, an' if you're sure you 're alive you've lifted a ton off my heart. I thought you was dead," sez I.

"This whole pack of idiots thinks so yet," he yells, "an' they won't let me get up. I got to see her, Happy, I got to touch her an' make sure for myself that she's all right."

"Where was you hit, Jabez?" I sez.

"I was creased—I was creased the same as they crease a mustang" he sez. "I was just touched in the back o' the neck an' it paralyzed me. These blame pin-heads are crazy to strip me an' see if I ain't shot all to pieces, but I won't stand for it." He tried to get up, but his legs wouldn't work, an' he sank back again.

"You just set an' rest a bit, Jabez," I sez. "I want to see how old Monody is."

The boys hadn't paid much attention to him, thinkin' him one o' Brophy's gang, an' not carin' much whether or not he was comfortable, 'cause he was the most bloodthirsty lookin' of the whole bunch. "Are you hurt bad, Monody" I said. His face lit up with a smile. "I don't hurt at all, Happy, but I reckon I 'm done for—the' ain't no feelin' in me from the waist down."

I got three o' the boys to help me, an' we put him on the shack door an' packed him into the house an' put him into one o' the spare beds. He was shot three times in the left shoulder, an' it wasn't till I noticed it that I recalled my own fix. Monody's shoulder was all shattered to smash, but still, it wasn't no reason for him to die, so I begun to kid him about it. He grinned an' said he didn't intend to die on purpose, but he reckoned it was his turn, an' he didn't intend to side step. He was most unreasonable an' wouldn't let us bandage him nor nothin', said he had a salve 'at beat anything a doctor had, an' we got it for him out of his coat which was the one wrapped around Barbie. He examined my shoulder with his right hand, an' his fingers worked around inside my bones clear and true, but some way without hurtin' me much. "It ain't broke," sez he, "just grooved a bit. You got bones like a grizzly."

When his salve came he rubbed it on me an' then he rubbed it on himself, an' then he told us to clear out so he could sleep. We all left him after a little, an' I sent Spider Kelley after the doctor. The' was only one member of Brophy's gang alive when I got back to the side porch, an' he was sinkin' fast. He had told Jabez 'at then intended to clean him out completely, an' that Jim, the sub-cook, was one o' the gang an' had let the ridin' ponies loose so 'at the' was no choice but to walk after the herd when they stampeded. He said that if he hadn't 'a' had that chance he would 'a' put knock-out drops in the coffee that night, which made all the men madder'n ever. Knock-out drops ain't no fair way o' fightin'.

Well, this feller had been with Brophy a long time, an' he gave us a purty complete list of his doin's an' his ways. As a rule a man only lasted about a year with the gang, an' when it was possible Brophy tried to get boys to fill up the vacancies,—boys likin' the game an' not carin' much for the consequences. He tried to tell us where Brophy had a lot o' gold salted down in Nevada, but it was hard to understand him, an' before he made it clear he tuckered out.

We sent out word to the neighbors, an' that evening about forty of 'em rode over to the buryin', and they made a good bit of a fuss over us, 'cause the gang had been worse'n a plague an' a famine. You can judge o' their nerve when they made war on the Diamond Dot, we havin' one o' the biggest outfits in the territory, an' all patriotic toward the old man. Jabez give me more credit'n was due me, but he sure tried to do the fair thing by of Monody too. Monody had saved us all, an' that was the simple truth. It seemed odd to think of how that kick I had in the jaw won me a friend in Monody, an' then, when it was passed on, saved the Diamond Dot. I'd like to know what it did for the French sailor an' the feller what handed it to him. Funny thing, life.

We tried to get Monody to take his clothes off an' be comfortable; the boys fairly pestered the life out of him tryin' to do somethin' for him, but he was obstinate, said 'at his clothes was clean, an' he didn't intend to take 'em off till they got dirty. They bothered him so that finally he made me bring him one of his guns, an' he swore he'd use it before they got his clothes off. "I want to be buried in 'em, Happy," he said to me, most earnest. "If I die with 'em on you won't let 'em take 'em off, will ya?" He had a lot o' fever, so I humored him; but I wished, myself, he wasn't so set in his ways. His salve was the bulliest stuff I ever used on a bullet hole, an' my arm begun to mend right from the start. His shoulder was splintered purty bad, but still, it didn't seem as if it ought to have bothered his legs none. The next day he was a little wobbly in his head, an' it seemed to rest him to hold my hand. He didn't want no one else in the room, so I just sat an' talked nonsense to him, an' twice Barbie came in to see him.

In spite of his ugly face the child wasn't a mite afraid of him, an' she would smooth back his black, coarse hair; but she didn't talk to him much — just looked into his eyes an' smiled.

"I wish Melisse was here," she said to me once when Monody was dozin', "she'd cook somethin' nice an' tasty, an' she's such a good nurse."

"Melisse?" sez Monody comein' to, "who's Melisse?"

"She's my old nurse," sez Barbie. "I told her a story—just a little one— an' she wouldn't whip me for it, so Daddy told her to clear out until she was willin' to do her duty. He thinks she's gone for good, but I know where she is."

"Melisse, Melisse," muttered Monody. "Well, after all, it might be. The' ain't nothin' too strange to happen."

I see 'at he was a bit out of his head, so I didn't question him none. "Where is she, Barbie?" I asked in a low tone.

"I don't know just exactly where she is or I'd go bring her back, of course," she sez; "but I know 'at she's somewhere hereabouts, 'cause the day before my birthday—why, it was only day before yesterday, wasn't it? It seems years ago. Well, day before yesterday I found a big pan o' cakes in my playhouse, an' no one can't bake 'em but Melisse."

Monody didn't say anything more until after Barbie'd gone from the room, and then he made me tell him all I knew of Jabez, which was mighty little. He lay there a long time without speakin', an' then he sez: "O' course the' may not be anything in it, but if ever you an' this Jabez lock horns, you just ask him about the Creole Belle, an' if he's the man I mean—an' he sure favors him—it'll most likely unnerve him. Now I want to sleep."

Spider Kelley an' the doctor got back about ten that night, an' ol' Monody was in a ragin' fever an' some out of his head, but he kept his gun handy an' wouldn't stand for any one startin' to undress him.

"The''s somethin' worse'n that shoulder," sez the doctor, "though that's bad enough, goodness knows. He's hurt somewhere in the spine, an' I'll have to examine him. Take that fool gun away from him."

I put my hand on Monody's an' he loosened his hold on the gun an' took hold of my hand, his face lightin' up contented. Then I handed the gun to one o' the boys an' took tight hold of his right arm while the doctor started to unbutton his shirt. Ol' Monody's eyes opened with a jerk, an' the fever had left 'em. "Happy, Happy!" he pleaded. "You know 'at I'd give my life for ya! You won't let 'em bother me, will ya? I'm done for, I know it; an' the' ain't nothin' to do. Happy, Happy, let me go in peace, won't ya? Let me die like a man!"

The' wa'n't no fever in his eyes, an' he was sure earnest about it. I knew 'at if things was changed an' I was in his place he'd give me my way, so I sez to the doctor, "Dock, ol' Monody here is a cure-all himself; he give me the best salve ever I see for my own shoulder, an' when he sez it's all up with him, he ain't bluffin'. I reckon you'd better just let him alone." I hadn't never seen this doctor before; he was a youngish buck with sharp features an' an obstinate chin. "No," sez he, "it wouldn't be professional. I got to make an examination. Now some o' you boys hold his feet an' some o' you hold his good hands an'—"

"Some o' you go to hell!" sez I. "If ol' Monody here wants to die with his clothes on he's sure goin' to do it or else the' 's goin' to be consid'able more funerals on this place than we've already had. Now you git!"

The Dock, he was the first to go, an' then the rest o' the boys filed out.

"You're square, Happy," sez Monody, after they'd gone. "You're square, an' I knew it the first time I looked into your eyes. If I'd fell in with square ones at the start it would 'a' been a heap easier—a heap easier."

Cast Steel hadn't hardly taken his eyes off Barbie since lie 'd got up an' around again, but right after the Dock had left, in he popped. "What's this I hear, Happy?" he sez, excited.

"I don't know, Jabez," I replied.

"Dock Wilson sez 'at you chased hire out o' the room with a gun an' wouldn't let him examine this man."

"Well," sez I, "as far as that goes, this man has a right to judge for himself. He saved your life an' your outfit an' your daughter, an' I don't reckon you're goin' to tie him into a knot so as a doctor can go pokin' around in him when he don't want it."

"You're as obstinate as ever!" shouts Jabez. "He 's probably out of his head."

"No, he ain't out of his head," sez Monody, in a low, soft voice, but without openin' his eyes more'n a crack.

"He ain't out of his head an' he ain't forgot nothin' he ever knew, an' it'll be better all around if he's allowed to go in peace."

Jabez looked at him in surprise, and Monody scowled up his face till he looked like a wounded Silver Tip, but the' came a queer hunted look into Jabez' eyes for a moment, an' then he muttered, "Well, this is a free country an' I reckon lie has the right to decide. He has sure saved us, an' if the' 's anything on earth I can give him, all lie has to do is to ask for it, an' I hope he pulls through in his own way."

Jabez fidgeted around a minute or two longer an' then he oozed out o' the room. When he'd gone of Monody chuckled a wicked, contented chuckle, an' after a bit he sez, "It's him all right, it's him, but he never did me any harm, an' I wouldn't worry the child, not for worlds. She ought to have a woman around her though. You get old Melisse back, Happy, an' remember—if it ever comes to a question of you or him—just call him George Jordan an' say 'at Jack Whitman wasn't killed "—Monody chuckled again, an' then sobered—"but don't spring it except as a last resort, 'cause the little girl couldn't help nothin' about the Creole Belle, an' she ain't no call to be worried by it. Jim Jimison, he's white, Happy, but he 'd 'a' been killed that trip if you hadn't taken bolt when you did. He's learned the game purty well now, though, an' I reckon he'll make good."

Poor old Monody kept on talkin' disconnected until about midnight, first tellin' some devilish deed he'd seen or took part in, an' then tellin' o' some joke or some act o' kindness. Just at midnight he took my hand, an' the' came a look into his eyes like as if he was about overcome by some beautiful vision; but in a moment he cohered down an' he gripped my hand till it hurt. "Happy," he gasped, "I allus loved ya, Happy. You won't let— you won't let 'em—" an' it was all over with ol' Monody.

I sat by the bed a long time thinkin' it over, an' then I went out into the settin' room. Jabez an' a couple o' the boys was there an' I told 'em it was over. I went out into the night to have a look at the stars. Whenever somethin' has happened in my little wobbly life down here I like to get out an' see the same old stars in their same old places, calm an' steady an' true. That was one thing which allus drew me to the child Barbie,—she was a star-worshiper too, same as me.

When I got back I see the little doctor explainin' somethin' to Jabez. I thought he had gone long ago, but the hooked-nosed buzzard couldn't leave without satisfyin' his curiosity. "What do you reckon was the reason your friend wouldn't let himself be examined?" sez he, with a leer.

"It wasn't nowise my business," sez I, "so I didn't think about it at all."

"Well, it was because he wasn't a man at all—he was a woman."

For a moment I stood an' looked at him, while a lot o' things became clear as day to me. A woman—ol' Monody was a woman! When I thought of what a girl is, an' what it must have took to make one want to really be a man, I felt plumb ashamed o' my sex; but here was another creature in man's clothes standin' an' grinnin' into my face as though he had done somethin' smart.

"How do you know?" I sez soft an' steady.

"I went in an' examined—it was my professional duty. She had been shot in the abdomen and the bullet had lodged in the spine. She had stuffed a rag into the hole an' all the bleedin' was internal. I found that—"

"Who was with you?" I asked him.

"Nobody," he said with pride; "I went in alone an' I found—"

"I'm obliged to ya, Boys," sez I, "an' I'll be obliged to you still more if you'll just stand to one side an' watch me make an examination. I only got one arm, so it's perfectly fair. It seems to be the fashion now days to examine human beings who wear men's clothes—but who ain't men—so I feel it my PROFESSIONAL DUTY to examine this here speciment before us."

The grin kind o' left his face when I started for him. He wasn't near my size, but me only havin' one workin' arm made it fair. He looked to the boys to help him, but they was unusual placid. I reached out an' grabbed him by the collar an' put my knee in his stomach as a brace; he struck me in the face an' in my wounded shoulder, but in about one minute I had his clothes off him, an' there he stood the shamedest thing I ever see. "Now you get out o' here an' ride home," sez I, "an' I believe if I was you I'd pick myself out a new home—one 'at would take about six weeks to ride to. You won't be popular around here from this on."

"Can't I put my clothes on," he sez.

"Not these," sez I. "If you have any more where you've been livin' you can put them on; but I hope in my heart the sun peels your back before you arrive, an' I hope when you do arrive the' 'll be enough women awake to give you a raw-hidin' for bein' indecent. Now git."

He looked into the boys' faces again, but they wasn't friendly—they wasn't even smilin', an' then he went outside, got his pony, an' rode away. He rode clear out o' the West I reckon, 'cause while I heard of the story purty much everywhere I went after that, I ain't never heard o' the buzzard himself since that day long, long ago.

It was dawn by the time he'd rode out o' sight with his white skin shinin' on his hunched up form, an' then I went in to set with ol' Monody a while.

CHAPTER FIVE
JUST MONODY—A MAN

He looked mighty peaceful, did ol' Monody. Curious thing about death, is the way it seems to beautify a person. In life Monody was the homeliest human I ever see, an' yet the' was something so kindly, an' gentle, an'—an' satisfied in his face there under the lamplight, that I reached out an' patted his hand, almost envious—even though my fool eyes was a-winkin' mighty fast.

We all of us would give the first ten years of our life to know what it's like out yonder; when he was here, ol' Monody would 'a' done anything he could for me,—well, he lay down his life an' I reckon that's about skinnin' the deck,—but here I was achin' to know how it was with him, an' there he was with all his guesses answered, an' him not able to pass back a single tip to me.

It wasn't him that I was lookin' down at, it was just the shell of him, scarred and battered and bruised, but all his life—or at least most of it—he had twisted up his face to make it as ugly as possible, so 'at no one wouldn't take him for a woman. Now it could relax an' give a sort of a hint as to what it might have been if he'd had a chance to live. Oh, it's sure a crime the way we torture some o' the white souls 'at drift to this Sorrowful Star, as I once heard a feller call it.

Injun, Nigger, an' Greaser—why, such a combination as that ain't entitled to trial in a civilized nation—it's guilty on sight. Any one would know 'at such a bein' would be cruel an' treacherous an' thievin' an' everything else 'at was bad—but yet the' come a good streak into Monody some way or other. All in the world I had ever done for him was to beat him over the head when he acted like a beast, an' then to treat hint like a human when he acted like one. The' wasn't nothin' especially kind nor thoughtful in it, just simple justice as you might say, an' yet in spite of his treacherous mixture he wasn't askin' no favors; all he wanted was a square deal, an' when he got it he was square clear to the finish. It's a funny thing, life.

In spite of all he'd done to kill it the' was a mother streak in him which made him fair hungry for somethin' to pet an' fondle. He was allus good to any kind of an animal, an' though I didn't notice it at the time, he was allus motherin' me; an' look at the way he had soothed little Barbie with a touch that night in the cook shack! O' course I ain't questioning the judgment o' the Almighty, but for the life o' me the I can't see why it was necessary to make a woman as big an' as tall as ol' Monody was, an' yet perhaps if I just knew the story from the beginnin', I 'd see it was a mercy, after all.

Anyhow, it made it easy enough for him to work out his scheme.

The' ain't no rules for women anyhow, 'cause their hearts won't never surrender to their heads; when they do, they ain't all woman. Well, yes, there is one rule 'at 's safe for a man to foller In dealin with woman, an' that is that when a woman's in love, she 's in love all over. Sometimes a man's in love up to his pocket-book, sometimes up to his appetite, an' sometimes up to his heart, but he's mighty seldom in love all over. If nothin' else stays dry he's generally able to take care of his head, but with a woman everything goes; so I'm purty tol'able sure that away back at the beginnin' it was love 'at drove ol' Monody out of her own sex down into ours.

When the news spread abroad 'at the man who had killed Bill Brophy without a weapon had cashed in, the neighbors gathered from ninety miles around, and we sure gave Monody the rip-snortin'est funeral ever seen in those parts. We didn't say nothin' about him not really bein' a man, an' though I reckon 'at every feller there knew of it, the' wasn't a single one of 'em spoke of it—so we didn't have no trouble at all.

He lies on a little knoll about a mile to the north of the ranch house. Up back of him ol' Mount Savage stands guard an' fights off the roughest of the storms; while the soft winds from the south steal gently up a little cut in the rocks an' seem to circle about him, whisperin' secrets of countries far away. If the' 's a single bird in Wyoming, you can find it hoppin' about his narrow bed or singin' in the oak tree 'at stands above him, spreadin' out its branches like a priest givin' the blessin'. Winter or summer, Monody's grave is the quietest, peacefullest, purtiest spot 'at lies outdoors, as if the old Earth had repented of the way it had treated him, and was tryin' to make it up to him now.

Take it in winter when the' 's a clean sheet o' soft, white snow over everything, an' I like to go out an' stand on another little knoll about a half mile this side. The last speck of light in the valley comes through a narrow cleft an' falls on Monody's grave. As the sun sinks lower an' lower the crimson glory on the soft fleecy snow seems to come up out of the grave an' climb the black shadow of the mountain, like—but pshaw, I reckon it'd be a mighty tame sight to ol' Monody himself.

I never speak of him, an' I never think of him, as anything but a man. He lived like a man, God knows he died like a man; and on the little stone at his head the' ain't nothin' carved except just—Monody, a Man.

CHAPTER SIX
THE RACE

It was mighty pleasant back at the Diamond Dot after things got settled again. Barbie had become a curious little trick with a way of doin' strange things in a sober old-fashioned manner like as if she was a hundred years of age, but was tryin' to hide it.

She was more like Jabez too, which give me a heap of amusement, seein' which one was goin' to win when they straddled a question. Barbie wasn't sassy, not at all; she just didn't seem able to savvy that a few small matters, like age an' parentage an' ownin' the ranch, gave Jabez a sort of a majority vote, as you might say, on all questions. No, Barbie couldn't seem to get callous to this, an' she fought out all differences of opinion from the mere facts o' the case, an' I got to do Jabez the justice of admittin' that he never retreated behind his authority until after he'd been well licked in the open; an' unless it was a mighty important question he took his lickin' like a man. Barbie was game about it too, an' when she got the worst of a fair fight she never put up a howl; but when she had won in the open it used to grind her something fierce to be told point blank that she had to do such an' so, "'Cause she was a girl."

"If tobacco stunts your growth, how's it come 'at old Tank Williams an' George Hendricks an' Happy an' a lot more o' the boys is all over six feet tall," she sez one day durin' a try-out, "while Flap Jack is the smallest man on the place an' he don't never use it at all—'cept when he cuts his finger."

"Things don't allus work alike," sez Jabez, slow an' cautious. "The tall ones would all 'av' been taller if they hadn't used it, an' Flappy, he wouldn't 'a' been able to see out of his boots if he had."

"Well, I don't see as it makes much difference, anyhow," sez she. "I don't want to be so everlastin' tall, so I reckon I'll just smoke four a day an' that'll—"

"I reckon you won't smoke any a day," sez Jabez, gettin' riled. "Smokin' cigarettes is a nasty, filthy habit, an'—"

"Then I'll smoke a pipe," sez Barbie.

"No you won't smoke a pipe! I don't intend to have a gal child of mine smokin' anything. It's disgustin', an—"

"It ain't as disgustin' as chewin', an' you chew," sez Barbie.

"Now you look here!" yells Jabez, hot as a hornet, "I'm a man an' you ain't, an' that makes a heap o' difference. I had to give up cussin' on your account, but I don't intend to go to wearin' dresses complete, just to keep you halfway respectable."

"Yes, an' I got three cusses comin' to me too," sez Barbie. "I heard you over at the hay-barn yesterday."

"That don't count—the agreement was, 'about the house'; an' besides, you didn't have no call to be there."

"Yes I did. I couldn't light my cigarette out in the wind so I got behind the barn. You are the one 'at didn't have no call to cuss. The' wasn't anything wrong at the hay-barn an' you was all alone. I just know 'at you went there to cuss 'cause I made you own up at breakfast that it wasn't no worse for me to fling the oatmeal out the window when it didn't suit me than it was for you to fling the coffee."

The old man just stood an' stared at her so I knew 'at the little witch had rooted out his devisement. "When you are older, Barbara," ol' Cast Steel sez in his coldest tone, "you will understand these things an' be glad of the care I took of you; but now I am compelled to lay down a law. You are never to smoke again until you're of legal age."

"What's legal age?" sez she.

"Twenty-one years," sez Jabez.

"That'll be thirteen years," sez Barbie. "All right; but I'm goin' to roll three cigarettes a day for thirteen years an' the very day I'm twenty-one I'm goin' to smoke 'em all."

"You go to your room an' stay there," sez Jabez, white-hot.

"I will," she answers as cool as an icicle, "an' I'm goin' to figure up how many it will be, so I'll have some sort of fun to look forward to—when I get of legal age."

After she'd gone Jabez set down on a stone an' wiped his forehead. "She ain't a child, Happy. She ain't nothin' like a child," sez Jabez to me. "Here she is only eight year old an' she's got me out beyond my depth already. I don't know what I ought to do with her. She went to the spring round-up this year an' slept in a Navajo right outdoors. She wants to go bear huntin' or anything else 'at's wild an' dis-accordin' to her nature. What on earth am I goin' to do with her?"

"You ought to have children to play with her. She wants to play all right, she tries to play; but the only kind of play she knows is grown-up play. Get some children an' dolls an' pet kittens an' such things for her; that'll give her a chance," sez I.

"I tried it," sez Jabez. "I tried it last summer, but she about killed 'em. The only children I could get was two little Injuns, but she about ruined 'em. The only game she would play was war, an' when they wouldn't stand for her way o' playin' it she got on her pinto—the one you broke for her—an' roped 'em both an' like to dragged the hide off 'em. I don't know what to do."

"You ought to send her to school," sez I. "They'll be white children there an' they won't be slow an' gentle like the little Injuns; they'll be just as full o' devil as what she is, an' she'll get the sharp corners wore off her."

"Hang it I tried that too. I sent her when she was six year old—I'd been lookin' forward to it a good long time too, but it didn't do no good.

"She put in the first day all right, but things went too slow for her after that, an' she brought home her books an' made me pester over 'em with her, an' she went into it like a game, an' now she's gone through about four years' work in two. It's a blame shame, 'cause the school is only ten miles away an' she could go as well as not, but she's so terrible impatient. She reads all kinds o' books already, an' sez she's goin' to read 'em all before she quits. She ain't a bit like a child an' I don't think it's natural. I wish she'd pester me for dolls an' pink dresses an' things like that instead of wantin' all kinds of firearms, an' playin' poker with the boys."

Ol' Cast Steel was all worked up over it, an' I thought a long time before I answered him, then I sez, "Jabez, you're hard enough on the child an' you're strict enough with her, but you ain't strict enough with yourself. When it comes to a show down,—when you actually say yes and now,— why, she gives in; but when you argue with her she's just as sharp as you are, an' the' 's a heap o' things all children has to do 'at I reckon the' ain't no real sense in, so when you try to dig up a reason for 'em you give 'em the whip hand. Just like religion: lots of it is better just stated an' not mussed up tryin' to be explained. When a parson tries to tell me why God created this universe, it don't sound reasonable; but when I go out an' look at the stars an' the mountains an' the big sweep o' the plains an' then try to round up all that astronomer feller said about things, why, I just know 'at nobody but God could 'a' done it—an' I reckon it's that way with a child. She trusts you until you get down to her level an' then she sees that the' ain't much difference between you, an' she naturally expects you to play the same game by the same rules. You send her to school an' tell her it's for her own good, an' let her'n the teacher fight it out. That's a teacher's business an' they know how."

Well, they was a heap o' sense in what I said, an' I'd been thinkin' over it a long spell; so when school opened up again in the fall Barbie had her orders an' the' wasn't much in the way of trouble.

I didn't have any regular duties at the Diamond Dot—the worst trouble about the Diamond Dot was that nobody had any regular duties. Jabez was notionable to a degree, an' we all just floated along, doin' what we did do right, but not havin' much of a plan for it. I could have handled the place with ten less men an' got through on a tighter schedule, but it was a fine place to work at an' we all got what was comin' to us. Through the winter I used to ride over with Barbie when the days was anyways rough, an' it took her a long time to find out that Starlight really could beat her pinto. I reckon that child was the best rider 'at ever backed a pony. As you might say she grew up with a pony between her knees, an' the way she could play a bit in a hoss's mouth was the finest sight I ever see. I ain't much of a fool when it comes to pickin' out a ridin' critter, an' the pinto was able—most uncommon able.

One Saturday morning she told me that she was tired o' seein' Starlight beat Hawkins on ten-mile dashes, an' she was goin' to have a real race that day. She allus called the pinto "Hawkins" after I got back; she had said it wouldn't be polite to call us both "Happy" an' as long as I had owned both names the longest, she was willin' to give me my choice—an' then she said 'at that wouldn't be quite fair to the pinto—she was mighty rigid on bein' square—so she said 'at we'd have to draw for 'em. She wrote "Happy" on one piece of paper an' "Hawkins" on the other, put her hat in the pony's mouth,—she had taught him a lot o' tricks,—an' I had to turn my back while she dropped in the names. My luck was good, so I drawed "Happy," an' the pony was called "Hawkins." I was feared I might have to go back to John, an' John's a sort of a heavy baggage for a careless cuss to be luggin' around.

It was spring, an' the range was smooth an' tough. All through the snow Starlight's long legs had given him a big advantage, but now her weight made it a purty good bet either way. "Let 'em go grassin', Barbie," sez I. "This fine young grass—"

"I knew you were afraid to make a fair test of it," she sez scornful.

"I ain't neither afraid," I sez, "but what's the use of a race just to satisfy our curiosity?"

"What's the use of curiosity except to satisfy it?" sez Barbie, an' she had me sure enough. A feller was a fool to argue with that little witch. She allus had a come-back, an' the only way to get ahead of her was either to boss or beg. I hadn't no authority to boss, an' I was too blame young to beg, so she just about had me roped an' tied. "How far are you goin' to race?" sez I.

"A hundred miles," sez she.

"Pshaw," sez I, "the country's wider'n that. Why don't you give'em a decent work out."

"That'll be enough for this time," sez she, "an' if you hustle you can have'em ready by five o'clock."

"Does the boss know?" sez I.

"He will sometime," sez she. "Now hustle."

It was a glorious day, an' I own up I was amused at the prospect. Both hosses was hard as flint an' nervy. If I'd 'a' stayed at the ranch I'd have collected up brandin' irons an' other truck for the round-up, an' a hundred miles through spring sweetness was a heap sight more temptin' to me; so I give in an' soon we was under way. "Where is the course laid out, Barbie?" I sez. "You know I won't see much of you back there in the ruck an' I want to know the path."

"All you need to do is to foller Hawkins's trail," sez she, "but in case you can't find it just circle Mount Savage an' that'll be the distance, so the boys say."

We started out at a comfortable gait, an' I watched her pretty close. Once I tried her out by sendin' Starlight along for a mile, but she just kept the pinto pluggin' away, an' I sensed I was up against some head ridin'. Oh, it was gratifyin' to watch the little rascal ridin' with her brain, like I'd taught her. She didn't throw the reins down on her pony's neck, an' she didn't pull in on the bit; she just played it in his mouth to keep remindin' him that this was his busy day, an' that he'd better tend to his knittin'. Old Starlight knew every move I made, an' he was resigned to a good long pump of it.

I nonsensed a while, tryin' to get her to laugh an' cut up, but not her. "Now don't talk unless you have somethin' to say, Happy," sez she. "I don't want Hawkins to imagine 'at we're out ridin' for an appetite. I want him to believe 'at we're on mighty important business."

"Oh, he'll sure enough think it," sez I, "when we swing around Mount Savage an' he gets to see home through Starlight's dust."

"When it comes to that, I'll bet he won't be complainin' o' the dullness of the business he's been on. Now just practice thinkin' a while."

We watered about noon at a little snow stream on the opposite side of old Savage; but we et our vittles on hoss back an' we didn't waste any time on the waterin'. I figured we'd scaled up about fifty miles, an' the pinto was still tonguin' his bit an' waitin' for somethin' interestin' to turn up. Starlight was gettin' some disgusted with the monotony.

We rode on for another hour an' then Barbie began to ride a little. The pinto let out a couple of links as cheerful as a rainbow, an' I rode at his cinch. I knew I could beat her in the brush, an' she was easin' the pinto too much to make it a question of grit unless she began to herd him mighty shortly. Well she did begin ridin' purty soon, an' brother Hawkins responded like an echo. He was a hog for distance, was that pinto. He was short on top with plenty of depth to him, and his belly cut up quick, showin' he had lots o' room for his heart an' his lungs an' his forage. Starlight's nostrils worked a shade more than his did, but we were gettin' purty close to the pinto's speed, an' Starlight had a load of it left, and he'd pay out the last ounce of it when I said the word. I knew I could beat her this time, but I was feared she might call for a repeat the next day—an' I intended to remind Jabez it was the Sabbath.

Starlight was pretty wet with sweat, while the pinto was bone dry when we struck Trouble Creek which was boilin' full. In we went, an' the water hissed and sucked around our waists; but we crossed at about the same time, an' then it was only ten miles to the ranch house an' Barbie shook her quirt. Away shot the pinto, but Starlight had his fussy streak warm by this time, an' I let him edge ahead as fast as he wanted to. He knew the distance now, an' he knew I wanted to cover it in the least possible time, an' he knew just how much the' was left in him, so I drew a tight rein, eased it off again, an' we dropped a gap between us an' the shorter legs of Barbie's mount. We only gained an inch at a time an' I wasn't sure I'd be the one to do the braggin' even yet, when all of a sudden we swept around a point of rock an' there was Melisse hot-footin' it to the ranch house. She heard us the minute we saw her, an' when we drew up to her she gasped: "Pluto has about killed ol' Cast Steel, an' Spider Kelley has gone for the doctor."

Barbie caught the words, but she never made a reply or asked a single question; she just laid the quirt without a sting over Hawkins's foreshoulder an' raced on. I stopped long enough to tell Melisse that I would send the buckboard after her, an' then I took after Barbie. It looked like a race, sure enough. I was worried. Pluto was a high grade stallion Jabez had got after I lined up Starlight alongside the range ponies, an' he had the meanest temper I ever see put into a hoss. I had been tendin' him 'cause I'd got wise to the ways o' these thin-skinned fellers down at the Lion Head, but I never quite trusted him, an' I feared 'at maybe Barbie's goin' off without notice had riled the old man an' he had tried to take it out on Pluto.

We only had five miles to go, an' we sure went it. I beat her to the ranch house, but Starlight hadn't got his breath back when she rode in, an' the pinto only took one long breath an' shook his head. I turned the hosses over to one o' the boys 'at were hangin' around the door lookin' troubled, an' hustled inside. Jabez lay on the lounge with a face like soured vinegar. He had a bandage round his head an' another around his arm, while his leg was propped up on pillows.

"What's the damage, Jabez?" I asked.

"Where's Barbie?" he demanded, not payin' any heed to my question. She had flung herself from the pinto an' came running into the room. "Oh, Daddy," she said, throwin' her arms around him.

"Where have you been?" sez he.

"I been racin' with Happy," she said. "Are you bad hurt, Daddy?"

"Who beat?" sez he.

"Happy did, about a hundred yards."

"It wasn't more'n fifty," sez I.

"How far did you race?" asked Jabez, grittin' his teeth.

"A hundred miles," sez Barbie.

"A hundred miles?" sez Jabez, grinnin' painful. "A hundred miles, an' the black hoss beat your pinto carryin' a hundred'n fifty pounds more weight. Hendricks—tell those blame fools not to kill Pluto. Happy, you go an' see that they don't even hurt him. It was my fault. Now, Barbie, tell me about the race."

I went out to the big open stall where Pluto was kept all by himself, but first I sent one o' the boys with the buckboard after Melisse. I found Pluto in the middle of his stall with three ropes around his neck an' the boys snubbin' him to posts. They wasn't minded to let him go, even on Hendricks's say-so, but I went into the stall an' told 'em to ease off. "He's whipped one man in a fair fight," sez I, "an' if another man don't whip him in a fair fight the' won't be any handlin' of him from this on. Ease off these ropes."

Well, I whipped that hoss in a fair fight, an' then I went in to see how Jabez was gettin' along. I said a fair fight an' I meant a fair fight. Yes, the' is a way to fight a hoss fair—that is, as fair as any fight is. If you look at it one way, the' can't never be a fair fight, 'cause one is bound to have an advantage—skill, luck, experience, or courage; but what I mean is, that I fought that hoss with nothing but just my own hands an' I whipped him.

Why the way I did it was this: as soon as they slacked off the ropes I slipped up beside him an' jerked 'em over his head, an' we two stood alone in the big box stall with size in his favor an' brains in mine. I had some consid'able size in those days, an' he was almost too brainy for a hoss; but I own up 'at I 'd had the most experience.

First I stood off an' insulted him: I cussed him an' I called him all manner of names an' then I laughed at him—you think a hoss, a hoss like Pluto, can't be insulted? Why, pshaw! they're as high feelin' as children. He was out o' humor to begin with, an' purty soon his ears went back an' his eyes got red. I've heard tell about an animal not bein' able to look a man in the eyes, an' I never saw the wild animal 'at could; but I've seen three man-eatin' stallions in my time 'at could look clear to your liver, an' a bulldog can do it too.

First off he tried to bite, but I got him a shoulder-blow right on the nose. It made him wink, an' he reared an' struck at me with his front hoofs. I ducked to the left an' the minute his hoofs came down I slipped thumb an' forefinger into his nostrils, an' tried to jerk his head around to the right; but I'd thrown him once before that way an' he was too quick. He threw up his head before I could grip his mane with my left, an' a reachin' kick with his right hind foot tore my vest away.

He floundered me around consid'able for a spell, but at last in tryin' to jam me against the wall I got hold of his mane. I braced my feet against the wall an' liftin' myself, I got his ear in my mouth an' I bit it. It was a trick I'd learned from ol' Monody, an' I sure bit hard an' close to the head. For mighty nigh a minute he stood it fightin', an' then he give a groan. He hadn't had a sniff of air through his nose since I'd grabbed it, an' he wasn't no bulldog, he was a satin-skinned thoroughbred, an' he couldn't stand the anguish in his ear.

He groaned an' then he shivered an' then of a sudden I let go his ear, jerked his head around to the right, pulled up his left front foot with my left hand an' heaved with my shoulder. Down he went an' as he fell I leaped across him, an' put my weight on his head. Then I took my fingers out of his nose an' patted him.

I hate to whip a hoss, I hate to break the pride of any livin' creature; but when I start in to do it I don't just pester him. I wait until I have good reason an' then I convince him—whether he's able to live through it or not. I stroked old Pluto's ears an' nose, all the time murmurin' to him, an' durin' the murmurin' I told the boys to file out. I never shame nobody in front of anybody if the' 's any other way round.

Well, Pluto was drippin' with sweat an' havin' his bit ear rubbed was mighty soothin' to him. We all like a lot of babyin' after we've been hurt, whether we own up to it or not, an' Pluto wasn't any exception to the rule. After a while I explained everything to him an' told him that if he'd just act like a human bein', he'd be treated like a king; but if he wanted to carry on like some savage varmint we'd have to remove his hide an inch at a time; an' when I finally let him up he was mortal shamed of himself.

It was plumb dark by the time I let him up, an' I watered him an' fed him an' rubbed him until he began to eat, an' that was the last bother any man ever had with Pluto; but I was the only one he'd mind without bein' chainbitted. He counted me his best friend, an' after a while he got so he'd play with me—nip my ear with his lips an' such things, which I count as bein' a game way of takin' punishment. Still, it ain't just gettin' beat, it's havin' it rubbed in that makes a feller bitter.

I walked around to where Starlight an' Hawkins was enjoyin' their evenin' meal, an' I was mortal proud of the condition they was in. I reckon the' wasn't another pair in the territory 'at could 'a' covered their ante that day, an' it was a feather in Uncle Happy's cap all right.

But all the time I was thinkin' o' these things I was dreadin' havin' it out with Jabez. He was contrairy enough at the best; but all bunged up, I could see my self-control gettin' strained twice a minute. I knew enough about us both to know 'at whenever it came to a show down, it meant a breakin' of home ties, an' I hated to cut loose from Barbie. After a while, I washed up, fed up, an' went in to have it over with.

CHAPTER SEVEN
MENTAL TREATMENT FOR A BROKEN LEG

Barbie an' three of the boys were in the room when I went in. Barbie was tellin' the old man of our ride, an' the three punchers sat with the rims of their lids between thumb an' finger, lookin' at the floor as solemn as if they was on trial for their life. Barbie had just finished about our meetin' up with Melisse when I stepped in.

"Who's boss o' this place?" sez Jabez to me.

"If the' is any boss," sez I, "I reckon you're it."

"Who told you you could be gone all day?" sez he.

"Nobody told me. Nobody told me what was to be done if I stayed. Nobody hasn't told me what to do on a ranch for some several years. Why?"

"Looks to me as if you 'd have sense enough not to risk this child's life with your fool nonsense," sez he. I looked at him calm an' steady, an' I didn't grin—much.

He knew all 'at I was thinkin' of,—about my leavin' the last time an' also about my comin' back,—but he also knew 'at I knew he was thinkin' of the same thing, an' that we'd neither of us mention it, an' that it wouldn't ever weigh an ounce in whatever happened to come between us. I didn't say anything.

"What makes you humor her in everything for?" sez he.

"As far as I know, she ain't my child," sez I.

He give a start an' it made him groan. "What's the matter with your leg?" sez I. "It's broke!" he yells. "Do you think I got it stuck up on pillers 'cause my foot's asleep?"

"Is it easy that way?" sez I.

"No it ain't," he snaps.

"Perhaps if you'd get it fixed easy you might be able to talk easy," I sez. "Do you want me to fix it easy?"

"For heaven's sake, yes, if you know how," he sez; so I examined it. It was a nasty break. It seems 'at Jabez had hunted over the place to find something to fuss about as soon as he discovered 'at Barbie an' me had flown the coop. Luck was in his favor when Slinky Bill left Pluto's door open an' he got out. It took 'em some time to get him back, an' they finally roped him. None o' the boys seemed anxious to go into his stall an' take the rope off unless he'd let them ride him a while to get the ginger out of him. Jabez took a short club an' went in an' took off the rope, an' if the boys hadn't been handy he'd 'a' been took off himself. As it was the hoss had smashed his leg something fierce.

"Get a board," sez I. The three boys left in a body to get the board. I lined up the bones as well as I could, 'cause the leg was some swelled. Then I bandaged it purty tight, next took an old boot-leg an' bandaged that in, an' finally split a joint of stovepipe an' packed cotton to fit the leg, tyin' the whole business to the board when it arrived, an' proppin' the board up on pillers with one at each side of the foot. Then I wet the bandage on his head an' arm, puttin' in plenty of turpentine on the arm to prevent poisonin'. The turpentine made him twist an' grunt, but when it stopped burnin' his face cleared up.

"My leg's a heap easier," he sez. I only nodded. I knew he had a lot more steam on his mind. Presently he said, "But we might as well settle things now as any time. Who are you workin' for?"

"I settled that a long time ago," sez I. "I'm workin' for myself."

"Then what the deuce do you mean takin' my wages?" sez he.

"I ain't takin' your wages, I'm takin' my own," sez I; "but if I was you I'd keep calm. You'll raise your fever."

"It's my fever!" he yells, an' even the three punchers had to grin.

"Look here, Jabez," sez I, "the' ain't any sense in your gettin' riled. You ain't dangerous when you rant around, an' I know it; but you're most uncommon irritatin'. We didn't run any risk in our ride to-day, an' it proved 'at my way o' feedin' is the right way. You don't own a pair o' hosses 'at can go out to-morrow an' keep in sight o' Starlight an' the pinto. An' my way o' handlin' Pluto is the right way too, but if you don't like my way o' workin' for myself on your ranch—why, the' 's plenty of other ranches. The' ain't no use o' your makin' us both miserable, quarrellin' like a pair o' children."

"That's what I say," sez Barbie.

"You wait till you're spoke to," sez Jabez; but at that moment the buckboard came in with old Melisse, an' the very first thing she did was to chase the three punchers out o' the house, fix up a mess of her own to put on Jabez's head an' arm, an' then she picks up Barbie in her arms an' I saw the little chap's lip begin to quiver; I saw Jabez wink his eyes too fast for comfort; I saw the tears rollin' down the cheeks of old Melisse, an' I went out into the starlight to look up toward Mount Savage where Monody was sleepin'. It's a funny thing, life. After a while I went back inside an' they were purty cozy again. "You been away purt nigh a year," sez Jabez, "where you been?"

Melisse grinned; she was a Mexican an' had been good lookin' a century or so before. She was the silent sort, but she could do a heap sight keener thinkin' 'an lots of 'em 'at kicks up more dust at it.

"Part o' the time I been right here at the ranch," she sez, "but when the snow was heavy I stayed in a little cave right up the ravine from the pony corral. You don't reckon 'at I'd leave this child just on your account, do ya?"

It was some comical to see Jabez's face. "Lord, no!" sez he. "I'm in the habit o' payin' wages to people 'at work for themselves, an' I don't reckon I got the authority to make anybody get off my ranch. If you've been foolin' around here, how come the dogs never barked at ya?"

"Dogs ain't apt to forget the hand that feeds 'em. After a dog has thought well of ya for a while, he don't turn on ya just because you've become out o' favor for a spell; the friendship of a dog works both ways—dogs ain't like human beings, Jabez Judson."

Melisse had a low, musical voice; but I kind o' felt my hair raisin' in pity for the man on the sofey. It seemed like she had stuck a knife into him, an' was twistin' it around slow without losin' her temper. He squirmed, he bit his lip, his thumbs kept runnin' over the inside of his fingers. It was some time before he spoke, an' then he said, "How much longer you goin' to keep that child awake?"

"She's been asleep in my arms for some time," sez Melisse, lookin' down at Barbie's face, which was nestled up close to hers. "I reckon I'll put her to bed now." She got up an' carried Barbie to the door an' then she turned an' sez in a low tone: "You're mighty proud o' being called Cast Steel, you love to trample over people; but I want to tell you somethin' to remember; I sha'n't never be separated from this child again except by her own will. Next time I can't live around you I'll take her with me. You've known me a long time"—an' she shut the door without slammin' it.

"Oh, I don't reckon it's allus some one else's fault," I sez, after he had got through cussin' about his luck.

"Am I a hard man to work for?" sez he.

"You ain't," sez I.

"When am I ever unjust?" sez he.

"When you go off halfcock," sez I.

"What is it allus about?" sez he.

I thought over everything before I answered. "Why, it's allus about the child Barbie."

"I ain't Cast Steel about her; I'm spring steel where she's concerned, an' you fellers ought to know the way spring steel works if any one does."

"That's all right," sez I,—I was still smartin' a little,—"but the deuce of the thing is that you go off at halfcock, an' then you allus expect the other feller to pay the damage. It's goin' hard with you some day, Jabez, if you don't watch closer."

"Oh, you can't understand it. If you only knew what lyin' an' disobedience sometimes does, you wouldn't talk so calm about it, neither. The' ain't nothin' I wouldn't do for Barbara—except see her get started wrong. You're different from the rest, some way, an' she thinks more of you than the others. That's one reason why I give you a wider circle to range in, an' why I give you foreman's pay for odd-job work—"

"Now if you think 'at I don't earn all you're payin' me," sez I—but he broke in: "If I didn't think I wouldn't pay it," sez he.

"I can go down to the Lion Head any time I want an' get more'n you're payin' me," sez I.

"I can pay you as much as any man in the West," sez he.

"You couldn't hire me at all if it wasn't for Barbie," sez I.

"An' I wouldn't hire you at all if it wasn't for her," he snaps. "You can do the right thing at the right time better'n any other man I ever had; but you're the contrariest man to work with on the job. You're allus flyin' up, an' you'd talk back if your throat was cut."

"I'm free," sez I, "an' what's more, I know it. The' ain't no law ever been framed up yet 'at can herd me in with the cows, an' I don't never intend to act like a cow. I'm man to man wherever I am, an' a lot o' you fellers with big outfits are beginnin' to forget that proposition; but I don't forget it, an'—"

"Well, for heaven's sake," he yells, "I ain't tryin' to put a bit in your mouth; though I must confess if I had my way about it, I'd like to put a quart o' bran there sometimes. What I'm tryin' to do is to come to an understandin' about the child."

"Hasn't she gone to school every day this term?" sez I.

"There's another thing," sez he. "When I told you to give that schoolmaster a rawhidin', you wouldn't do it."

"Course I wouldn't do it," sez I. "He may have been in the right as far as I know, an' anyway, she gave him the worst of it."

"I don't want her to give 'em the worst of it. I want her to act like a gal child. Ridin' her pony into the schoolroom an' ropin' the master ain't no way for a gal child to act. What I want is for the teachers to play fair. It ain't reasonable to suppose 'at these mountains was ever under water."

"You stood for it when the astronomer said so," sez I; "an' the Bible sez so, an' — "

"Well, that's all right when it comes to grown-ups; but the' ain't no use makin' a child say somethin' it don't nowise believe. The truth is more important than a lot of water 'at dried up millions of years ago—if it ever was here."

"Well, the truth is a heap o' bother to Barbie's teachers at the best," sez I. "Look at her spellin'—she comes upon a cross-bred word in a book an' the teacher sez it's pronounced one way, an' you another, an' me another, until she thinks we're all liars; and she knows it the next day when she comes across another word spelled almost alike an' pronounced just the opposite. How you goin' to teach a child to spell an' be honest both?"

"It's a damned outrage!" sez Jabez, his eyes flashin'. "Take 'thought' an' through,' an' 'though'—why, it's enough to ruin the morals of the best child the' is. Hang it, I — "

"Well, you had your own way about it," sez I. "You've had three different teachers here this term."

"Who built the school?" sez Jabez. "Didn't I build it with my own money, just so I'd have it handy, an' didn't I offer to pay the teacher if they'd put it right here at the ranch?"

"You ain't got money enough to bring the world here to her feet, Jabez," sez I, "an' it wouldn't be the best thing for her if you could."

Well, I sat there the whole blessed night, cheerin' him up. Every time he'd get to thinkin' about his arm or his leg, I'd say somethin' to rile him an' take his mind off his afflictions, an' along about dawn he fell asleep. Spider Kelley had found the doctor almost in our neighborhood, an' he arrived with him by ten in the mornin'. He paid me a high compliment on the leg, an' after he'd rounded up a few splinters it wasn't no trouble at all to set it; but Jabez was in for a good long spell of it, an' the Spring round-up in sight.

You might think that this would rile him up too; but he took it like a hero, an' I kept him in touch with everything.

We didn't have a regular foreman at the Diamond Dot. George Hendricks took charge around the house, an' Omaha was a sort of ridin' over-see-er; but Jabez himself tended to even little details when he felt like it. When he didn't feel that way, any one else who thought of it did. After the round-up Flap Jack decided to go on a bender. I tried to talk him out of it, but he insisted, an' finally I sent him into Jabez.

Flappy came away just tearin' mad. "He's the hardest-hearted old tyrant ever breathed," sez Flappy to me.

"What now?" sez I.

"Last time I came back I was a day late," sez Flappy. "He fair frothed at the mouth at it, an' made me promise to give him a month's notice next time. How's a man to know a month ahead when he's goin' to be in the notion for a bender. I'm fair ravin' for it now; but like's not I'll be all out o' the notion in a month."

"Then you'll be a sight o' money ahead," sez I.

"Money? What's money for? Can you buy a thirst like mine with money? Why, I could take this thirst o' mine to a city an' get independent rich, just rentin' it out by the night. I've watched fellers drinkin' when they didn't crave it, an' it hurt 'em somethin' dreadful. If you don't want it, you can't enjoy it until you're under the influence of it, an' after you're under the influence of it half the fun o' drinkin' it is gone."

Flappy had studied this question more'n airy other man I ever see, an' it was edicatin' to hear him lecture on it.

"The's only one way to get around ol' Cast Steel," sez I, winkin'; so he got Barbie to beg for him when she went in that evenin', an' she got Jabez to let him go next day; but after Jabez'd had time to think it over, he sez to me, "Now see what I've done—I've let that child wheedle me into changin' my mind an' lettin' a man break his word."

"Well, he needed it mighty bad," sez I.

"An' another thing; it ain't no fit thing for a gal child to be beggin' for a man to go get drunk," sez Jabez. "Maybe not," sez I, "but he sure needed it."

CHAPTER EIGHT
THE LETTER

It all came about through me bein' edicated. Most any one can read print words, if they're of a reasonable size,—the words I mean,—but I could read handwritin' too. I never was no great mathematician when you got above fractions, an' I was some particular in what I read; but if I 'd been minded that way, I reckon I could have waded through purty much any kind of a book ever was written. At that time, however, I was still middlin' young in some things, an' I sure was suspicious of any kind of book 'at looked like a school book.

If you'd have school books did up in paper with the right kind of pictures on the covers you could easy get children to peruse 'em. Did you ever notice bear cubs gettin' an edication? They ain't beat into it, they has to be helt back. Same with the Injun kids; they was up on edge to learn until they got to schoolin' 'em, then they fought again it just like the white kids. The reason is that we make children learn things they ain't curious about. I bet if you was to try an' keep it a secret about George Washington bein' made President because he wouldn't lie about choppin' down that cherry tree, the kids would stay awake nights to pry into it. Kids is only human, any way you take 'em.

But this business was sure a fetcher to me, an' Barbie, she just stumbled on it too. One afternoon me an' her went for a little ride up into the foothills, an' after we'd built our fire, like we allus did, no matter how hot it was, she lay there rollin' cigarettes for me to smoke, like she allus did—the little scamp used to get on the lee side o' me so the smoke would blow in her face; but we never mentioned it.

Well, after a while she begun to talk of romances, an' to ask me questions about 'em. I told her as many as I could remember, an' the one what suited her best was "Claud, the Boy Hero of Gore Gulch." It allus used to fret her to think 'at the' wasn't nothing she could do to make her a boy, an' she tried to even up by plannin' to herself what she'd have done if so be she had been a boy. We talked along about as usual; but I see the' was somethin' on her mind. She wasn't the one to flare up an' shout for information. She allus talked in a circle like an Injun when she really needed news.

After a while she fished out a funny old letter. It wasn't put into an envelope, it was just wrapped inside itself an' stuck fast with a gob o' some kind o' wax which had been broke before it was opened. The' had been a name on the outside, but it had been rubbed out. Inside at the beginning was the name "Rose Cottage, San Francisco," and a date; but I've forgotten the date. The letter began, "Dearest George." I read that much an' then I looked at Barbie. "Where'd you get this?" sez I.

She reddened a little, an' then she looked me straight in the face, and sez "I found it in the attic. I wanted a new box to put my cigarettes in, an' one day Daddy left the attic door open an' I went in. The' was just a dandy chest there an' he had left the key in it. I opened it an' this letter was on top. He goes to the attic alone every now an' again,—mostly at night,—an' he won't never let me go with him."

"I suppose that was the reason you thought he wanted you to go alone to the attic, too," sez I. She flushed again. "If a person don't trust me he ain't got no call to be surprised when I don't suit him."

I shook my head. Now in talkin' to her you forgot she was a child, 'cause she didn't talk broken like most of 'em do—nor she didn't think broken neither; but when you looked at her, little and slim an' purty as a picture, you couldn't help but wonder if she hadn't got her soul changed off with some one else, like what they say the Chinese believe. She had the same rules that I did for so many things that it floored me to understand how she got 'em that young, me havin' had to figger 'em out with a heap o' sweat.

"Was the letter to you?" I sez, gettin' around to facts.

"No, it wasn't; but I read it, an' I wisht I knew what it means."

"I ain't a-goin' to read it," sez I.

"You're a coward," sez she.

"That's nothing," sez I; "if it wasn't for the cowards the' would be a heap o' vacant land in this country," sez I.

"I thought you was my friend," sez she, takin' back the letter an' holdin' it open in her hand. "If Spider Kelley could read he would read it for me."

"So would Hawkins, your pinto," sez I, grinnin'. "What you ought to do is to tell your Dad that you have the letter. If you don't tell him, I reckon I'll have to."

At first she was mad as hops, an' then she looked into my eyes an' laughed. "I'll dare you to," sez she. The' was some woman in her even then.

The' wasn't no way to bluff her, so I said serious, "Well, what do you intend to do about it?"

"I don't know," said she. "Dad has lost so many other things beside his temper, stumpin' around with that cane, that he thinks he has lost the key to the chest. He goes around grumblin' an' lookin' for it; but he don't ask if any one has found it. Why do you suppose that is?"

"It ain't any of my supposin'," sez I. "What are you goin' to do about it?"

"As soon as I get through with this letter—an' make up my mind not to hunt through the chest—I'm goin' to slip the key into his pocket—an' then watch his face when he finds it."

"You oughtn't to treat your own father so, Barbara," sez I.

She laughed. "Barbara! that's a good soundin' name on your tongue, Happy," sez she. Then she sobered. "I don't care nothing for what you say or what he says; the' 's things I'm goin' to find out; an' I have a right to. I never told him why it was that I whopped those two girls over at school last winter, an' I never told even you. I whopped 'em 'cause they said I never had a mother. Everything has to have a mother, even a snake, an' I had one too. Why don't he tell me about her? Why does he allus turn me off when I ask about her? I don't intend to just let him tell me that she was the most beautiful woman in the world an' too good to stay here, an' such things. I am going to find out who she was, an' if you wasn't a coward you'd help me. Now."

It was true what she said, an' I might have known she was studyin' about it. I might, if I'd had the sense of a hoss, have known that this was what made her old-like—studyin' about things she never ought to have been forced to study about.

"Does that letter tell about her, Barbie?" I asked.

"That's what I want to know; but you ain't got the sand to read it, an' I can't make it out. Here, read it."

I took it an' read it. The writin' was fine an' like what was in Barbie's writin' book along the top. It sounded like as if a young girl had written it partly against her will, although it was purty lovesome too. It told about how lonely she was, an' that she hadn't never been able to tell whether it was Jack or him she was most in love with until Jack had asked her, an' then after Jack had deceived her an' he had been so kind, she found out 'at he was the one she had loved the most all the time. She reminded him 'at she had written to him before acceptin' Jack, an' that now if he was still sure he wanted her, she would accept him; but she could never live near the Creole Belle. She closed with love, an' signed herself Barbara.

I kept on lookin' at the page a long time after I had read it. I remembered what Monody had said when I thought he was out of his head—about George Jordan an' Jack Whitman, an' the Creole Belle. I knew 'at Barbie was studyin' my face, an' I pertended to spell out the words a letter at a time until I could get full control o' myself.

"What kind of a bell is a Creole Bell?" sez I. "She ain't got it spelled right neither."

"A Creole Belle is a beautiful woman of French an' Spanish blood who lives in New Orleans," sez Barbie. "What do you make out about it?"

I was thinkin' fast as I could, but I still pertended to read the letter. So Jabez had been in a scrape with some cross-breed woman, an' he an' this Jack Whitman had loved the same girl, an' the' was a bad mix-up somewhere.

"Little girl," I sez, "the' 's a lot o' wickedness in this world you don't know about—"

"An' the' a lot o' wickedness I do know about 'at I ain't supposed to," she snaps in. "Do you reckon I could knock around this ranch the way I have an' not know nothin' except about flowers an' moonlight? You cut out the little girl part an' play square."

"Well, you look here," I sez. "I don't know what you do know an' I don't know what you don't know; but I do know 'at lots of the things you think you know ain't so, if you picked it up from the fool stories some o' these damn cow punchers tell; an' you ought to be ashamed to listen to 'em."

"Oh, yes, of course!" she fires up. "I am the one what ought to be ashamed of the stories the cow punchers tell! That's the way from one end to the other; somebody else says somethin' an' I ought to be ashamed 'cause I ain't too deaf to hear it. Now the' 's a lot of questions I'm goin' to ask you as soon as I get time. I want to know why—"

"No, you don't!" I yells, jumpin' to my feet an' blushin' clear to my ears. "I ain't neither one o' your parents an' I ain't your teacher. If you want to know things you ask Melisse. If you don't put a curb on yourself I'm goin' to flop myself on Starlight an' streak for the Lion Head this very minute, an' I won't stop before reachin' the Pan Handle."

She knew enough to stop bettin' up a pair o' tens when she see the other feller wasn't to be bluffed; so she sez, "Well, I'm goin' to find it out some way or other—I'm going to find out everything I want to know before I'm done. I love my Daddy, but he don't always play fair; an' I'm goin' to find out what I want to find out—whether he wants me to or not."

I was in a sweat. "Barbie," I sez at last, "supposin' he is playin' fair? Supposin' he has sacrificed his own happiness to keep sorrow out of your life, an' supposin' you nose around an' discover it—who'd be the one 'at played un-fair then? You're powerful young yet; you're a heap younger'n you realize, an' you can't know it all in a day. He'll tell you when he can, an' you ought to trust him. He loves you more'n anything else in this wide world. You ought to trust him, Barbie."

She trembled tryin' to steady herself, an' I looked off into the valley for a moment. "I know he loves me, an' I wouldn't hurt him for the world; but I think I'm old enough to know, an' I'm goin' to ask him. If he won't tell me now he has to set a date to tell me. I ain't goin' to have no dirty-faced school kids askin' me questions I can't answer."

"I reckon all you want to know is in that chest in the garret," sez I; "an' I reckon it's kept for you to read after—well some day; but if I was you, I'd put back the letter an' I'd not think about it any more'n I could help. Supposin' your Dad had had to kill a man to save your mother, an' didn't want you to know 'at he had ever killed a man—"

"Humph!" she snaps in. "Didn't Claud kill fourteen men in Gore Gulch, an' didn't I think it was fine? If he's killed a man I'd be proud of it."

"It's different in real life," sez I. "I like to read about Claud myself, but I wouldn't want to slaughter men in the quantities he does."

"You killed a man oncet yourself," sez she.

"When?" sez I.

"You killed at least one o' the Brophy gang with the butt of your gun," sez she.

"It couldn't be proved," sez I.

"It couldn't be denied," sez she. "If that's all you think it is I'm goin' to ask him."

"Supposin' your mother had made him promise not to tell you until you came of age,—you know what store he sets on keepin' his word,—would you be glad to know 'at you had made him break it? This Barbara might have been his sister, an' some one else might have been your mother."

"Oh, I see it now—my mother was the Creole Belle, the beautiful lady. He allus said she was beautiful, the most beautiful woman in the world—" She sat there with her eyes flashin', but I didn't want to let her make up things 'at wasn't so an' then be disappointed. "Who do you suppose George was, an' Jack?" sez I quiet.

She drew her brows together an' sat diggin' her spur into the dirt. "That's so, too," she said, thinkin' aloud. "But Barbara certainly did have something to do with me, an' I wisht I knew! Oh, I wish I could grow as big as I feel—I hate this bein' a child. I hate it!"

"Will you put the letter back an' try to forget it?" I said at last.

"I'll put it back at once, I'll give him the key at once; that is, I'll slip it into his pocket, an' I won't pester him about it—now; but you got to promise to tell me if you ever find it out. Will ya?"

"Yes," sez I. "If I ever find it all out I'll tell you, honest across my heart."

"An' you won't say nothin' about this letter to Daddy, until I let you?" she said, fixin' her eyes on me.

"No, I won't say a word about that until you tell me to," sez I.

"Now, then, let's play tag goin' back to the house," she said, with her lip stiff again. Oh, she had a heart in her, that child had.

"You know the pinto has Starlight beat on turns an' twists," sez I.

"Yes," she sez, "an' on a two-hundred mile race, too." She played away through the summer an' never spoke a word on the subject again; but she hid it most too careful, and Jabez saw the' was somethin' on her mind. "Have you any idea what the child's thinkin' about?" he asked me one day when we was figurin' some on the beef round-up.

I didn't answer straight off, an' he noticed it. "What is she studyin' about?" sez he, mighty shrewd.

"How can a body tell what that child is studyin' about?" sez I.

"You're with her most of the time—fact is, about all you do is to play with her these days."

"Any time my work here don't suit you," I began; but he snaps in, "It ain't a question o' work. If you amuse her you're worth more to me'n any other ten men; but I have some rights. I want to know what you think."

"Have you asked her?" sez I.

"I'm askin' you," sez he.

"Well, I want you to understand 'at I ain't no spy," sez I, glad of a way out. "I don't know all 'at 's on her mind, an' I don't propose to guess; and if I did know, I wouldn't tell unless she told me to. If you know any way to make me tell, why go ahead and I'll stand by and watch the proceedin's."

Well, he ranted up an' down a while, an' finally he pulls himself down an' sez, "Now look here, Happy, the' 's a difference between a parent an' anybody else."

"I own too to that," sez I; "but what have I got to do with it?"

"Well, you can sort of hint around until you find out what's on her mind, an' if it ain't somethin' fit, you can tell her so; because if it comes to a show down, she thinks I ought to tell her anything she wants to know."

"Well, hadn't you?" sez I.

"Yes, sometime, I suppose—but hang it, it's mighty hard to answer some of her questions, or to give reasons why I can't answer 'em."

"Have you asked her what's on her mind this time?" sez I.

He fidgeted around a while, an' then he sez, "Yes, I asked her."

"What did she say?" sez I.

"She looked me plumb in the eyes, an' said, 'Do you want me to ask you what I want to find out?'"

"What did you say?" sez I.

"Why, I said, 'Yes, Barbara, if it is something you ought to know.'"

"Well?" I sez, after waitin' a bit.

"Why, she flared up," sez Jabez, "an' went on sarcastic about it bein' strange to her why girls was so much different from other folks, an' there bein' so many things 'at they wasn't fit to know; an' finally she said to me point blank, 'Do you want me to ask you what I want to know, an' if I do ask you will you answer?'"

"What did you say?" I sez.

"I didn't know what to say," sez Jabez. "She looked different from any way she had ever looked before, and after a minute I sez, 'No, Barbara, I don't think you had better ask me, an' I don't think you had better think of it any more.' Don't you think I did right?"

"No," sez I, "you did not. You simply side-stepped; you wilted under fire, an' she hates a coward as much as you do. Why didn't you face it right then?"

"Happy," he sez, an' his voice wrung my heart, "the' 's things she'll have to know sometime, but she ain't old enough to know 'em yet." He stopped, an' his face grew hard as stone when he went on. "But the' 's some things that she never can know, an' I don't want her to even learn that there are such things. That's why you have to find out what's on her mind."

"Now you know, Jabez, that I have my own ideas on what I have to do; but you tell me what kind o' things there are that she mustn't ever learn, an' maybe I'll see your way of it."

Jabez looked down at the ground, an' the sweat broke out on his forehead before he answered me. When he did the' wasn't a trace of friendliness in his tone. "You have done a heap for me, Happy, and if there's anything in the money line that you think I owe you, why, name it an' it's yours; but you can see for yourself that we can't go on this way. I haven't asked you to do anything unreasonable and you have refused point blank. I don't intend to explain myself to one of my own men, and I don't intend to have an argument with him every time I want anything done my way. This is my ranch and as long 's my own way suits me, that's the only man it has to suit."

"Yes, you own this ranch," sez I; "but you don't own the earth, so I'll move on."

"I haven't fired you," sez Jabez. "You're welcome to work here as long as you want to; but you'll have to be like the other men from this on. You've been like one of the family so long 'at we don't pull together any more, and so if you stay I'll have to send you out with the riding gangs."

I looked into his face and laughed, though even then I was sorry for him. He led a lonely life, an' I knew 'at he'd miss me; but we was both as we was, so I rolled up my stuff, loaded up Starlight, an' said good-bye to little Barbie. That was the hard part of it. She didn't cry when I told her I was goin'—that would 'a' been too girlish-like for her; she just breathed hard an' jerky for a couple o' minutes while we looked in opposite directions, an' then she said, "How'll you come back next time, Happy? It's over three years ago since you left that other time, an' you came back just as you said, ridin' on a black hoss with silver trimmed leather. How'll you come back next time?"

"I don't know, Barbie," I said, "but I'll sure come back, true to you."

"Yes," she said, "an' I'll sure be true to you, all the time you're away and when you come back."

"Barbie," I said, "you haven't treated your father right. You've let him see that you're worryin' about somethin', an' it bothers him."

"I ain't made out o' wood," she snaps out fierce. "I try to be contented, but I get tired o' bein' a girl. I've half a mind to go with you, Happy."

"Yes, but the other half of your mind is the best half, Barbie," I said. "Now I'm goin' to tell you a secret; your daddy is twice as lonesome as you are, and he's been through a heap of trouble sometime. You miss the mother that you never did see, but he misses the mother that he knew and loved; and I want you to promise to do all you can to cheer him up and make him happy."

"I never thought o' that before," said she, "I'll do the best I can—but you'll come back to me sometime, won't you, Happy?"

"I sure will," I said, an' we shook hands on it. Then I decided that I'd leave Starlight with her. He wasn't as good for knockin' around as a range pony, and I didn't know what I'd be doin', so I took my stuff off him, picked out a tough little mustang from the home herd, shook hands with her again, an' started. I glanced up toward old Savage, and she read my thoughts. "I'll take flowers to him now and again," sez she, "and I'll go up there and talk to him about you; and Happy, Happy, we'll both be lonesome until you come back!" And so I kissed her on the lips, and rode away the second time.

CHAPTER NINE
ADRIFT AGAIN

Well, I rode purty tol'able slow. Some way I didn't want to go back to the Lion Head Ranch. I knew 'at Jim would be glad to see me, but I knew I'd be lonesomer there than among total strangers; so I just floated, punchin' cows most o' the time, but not runnin' very long over the same range.

It was just about this period that I begun to lose my serious view o' life and get more man-like. The usual idea is that a boy is a careless, happy, easy-goin' sort of a creature, and a man is a steady, serious minded, thoughtful kind of an outfit; but just the reverse. A boy starts out believin' most o' what's told him an' thinkin' that it's his duty to reform the world; an' about the only thing he is careless of is human life—his own or any one else's. Fact o' the matter is that if you watch him close enough you'll find out that even in his games a boy is about the solemnest thing on earth, an' you have to know the game purty thorough to tell when it drifts into a real fight. That's why all wars have been fought by boys. They believe in any cause 'at looks big enough to lay down their lives for, an' that's their chief ambition. A man, though; gets to see after a time that the' 's most generally somebody up behind who's working the wires, an' he gets so 'at he don't want to lay down ANYBODY's life, except as a last resort. He looks favorable upon amusement, an' after a while he kind o' sort o' gets hardened to the fact that the whole thing's a joke and he'd rather laugh than shoot. Why, I'd be more afraid of a boy with a popgun than I 'd be of a man with a standin' army.

So as I said, it was just about this time in my life that I begun to hunt up pleasant places to eat and sleep; an' if I heard of trouble in the next county I turned out an' went around. I did a little of everything; even lugged a chain in a surveyor outfit, but the' wasn't enough chance in that. I got to have a trace of gamblin' in anything I do; so the first thing I knew I was down in Nevada lookin' for the treasure 'at Bill Brophy had buried there. The last of his gang had tried to describe the place, but his description would have done for 'most any place in Nevada—she not bein' what you might call free-handed in the way of variety.

Well, I ragged around in the mountains between Nevada and California, lookin' for a flat-shaped rock with a mountain-peak on each side of it, an' a cold wind sweepin' up the canon—I don't know just how the cold wind got included, but the dyin' outlaw dwelt upon that cold wind something particular. I stayed out puny late in the season, an' if cold winds was identifyin', Brophy had his treasure buried purty unpartially all over the West.

I reckon I'd have died if I had it fallen in with Slocum. Slocum was a queer lookin' speciment when you first came upon him. His skin didn't fit him very well, bein' a trifle too big, an' wrankled an' baggy in consequence; his eyes was kind of a washy blue, an' they stuck out from his face, givin' him the most sorrowful expression I ever see. You just couldn't be suspicious of a man with such eyes as that; he seemed to have throwed himself wide open an' invited the whole world to come an' look inside. Why, a perfect stranger would have trusted Slocum with his last plug of tobacoo, and like as not he'd have gotten part of it back. Well, as I said, I was headin' for warmer weather, but I got overtook an' had about given up all hope when I noticed the smell of smoke in the air. I was walkin' on foot an' pullin' a burro with a pack behind me, an' after a time I located that smoke comin' right up through the snow.

I yelled and shouted around for a while without gettin' any response. Night and the snow was both fallin' fast, an' that smoke was exceeding temptin'. Finally I took a piece of burlap off the pack, put it over the hole where the smoke was comin' up through, an' piled snow on top of it. I was curious to see what would happen. I waited—perhaps it was only five minutes, but it seemed that many hours—an' then a low, calm voice, down somewhere beneath me, sez, "Get off that chimney!"

"I will," sez I, "when you tell me how to get to the fire."

I waited again, an' then a man with a lantern emerged into the cut about forty feet below me, an' told me how I could wind around and come down to him. Well, me an' the burro finally worked it out, an' there was a man with long whiskers standin' in his shirt-sleeves in front of a hole in the snow.

"You like to 'a' smothered me," he grumbled. "Don't you know better'n to stop up a chimney that's workin'?"

"I wanted the chimney to work double," sez I, "an' that was the only way I could think up to attract your attention."

"Do you live around here?" sez he. "Not very much," sez I, "but I 'm minded to try it a while, if there 's room in your burrow for two."

"Got any tobacco?" sez he.

"Plenty," sez I.

"You're welcome," sez he.

We took the burro over to a clump of pine woods an' turned him loose, an' then I crawled in through the tunnel to Slocum's fire. It was in a cave which had a natural chimney runnin' up the hill, an' it looked considerable much like Paradise to me. We ate an' smoked together for a week, an' then one day our fire went out an' a flood of water poured down through the chimney. We worked like beavers for a while, gettin' our stuff outdoors, an' it was as hot as summer outside.

"That's the only drawback to this cave," said Slocum. "It will be all to the good when the winter settles in earnest, but it will be some bother while it's still snowin' an' thawin'."

I told him that I agreed with him to such an extent that if I could locate the burro I'd rather risk gettin' back to humanity than to dyin' there of rheumatiz. I was wringin' wet through.

"Nobody can't die of rheumatiz around me," sez Slocum, an' he went to one of his packs an' got out a piece of root.

"Chew this," sez he, "an' it will drive the rheumatiz out of your system."

Anybody would have trusted those eyes, so I chewed the root for about a minute, an' then I chewed snow an' mud an' tobacco an' red pepper for an hour, tryin' to get rid of the taste. Drive the rheumatiz out of your system? Why, the blame stuff would drive out your system too if you chewed it long enough. It was the tarnationest stuff 'at ever a human man met up with.

"It's most too strong to take pure," sez Slocum, "but if you grind it an' put a shall pinch in a quart of alcohol it makes a fine remedy. Don't throw the rest o' that root away. There is enough there to do you a lifetime."

"Yes," sez I, "there is, an' more."

A feller once told me that man was a slave to his envirament—envirament is anything around you, scenery, books, evil companions, an' sech; well, a burro ain't no slave to his envirament 'cause he generally eats it. My burro was fat, an' the clump of pine trees had mostly disappeared. I loaded up my stuff, shook hands with Slocum, and started down the mountain. Just as I got fully started Slocum sez to me, "I 'm sure sorry to see you go. I don't generally get much friendly with folks any more, but I took to you from the first, an' any time I can do you a favor, all you got to do is to wink."

"What's your general plan of occupation, Slocum?" sez I.

"All that I ever expect to do for the remainder of my days," sez he, "is to search for my Rheumatiz Remedy."

"Well," sez I, "any time you get to do me a favor in that line, it'll be when I'm too weak to wink." So we parted the best o' friends, an' I went on to a lumber camp where I put in the winter bossin' a gang. I didn't know much about lumber, but the men there was just the same as anywhere else, an' we got along fine.

I was bossin' a little ranch up in Idaho next June when I heard tell of a big strike in the Esmeralda range—not such a great distance from where I had spent the week with Slocum. The report had it that a feller named Slocum had located the big ace of gold mines, an' I was some et up with curiosity to see if it was the same Slocum; but I was needed at the ranch that winter, an' as I took a likin' for the young feller who was tryin' to make it go, I stuck to him, an' it wasn't until the followin' July that I pulled out an' floated down that way.

Well, it was the same old Slocum sure enough. He was the most onlucky cuss 'at ever breathed, I reckon. Every time he had made up his mind to do something, Fate had stepped up an' voted again it. He had wasted the best part of his life locatin' gold mines 'at wouldn't hang out, until at last even he got disgusted an' went to huntin' for his Injun root to cure rheumatiz with. First thing he knew, he had stumbled on a bonanza lode in the Esmeralda range. This here lode was a peach. Ten-foot face on top, just soggy with gold an' silver, an' copper an' tin enough to pay expenses. It just looked as if they's said, "Now then, there's Slocum; he been hammered so long he's got callous to it. Let's jus' see how he'd act if we switched his luck on him." An' they sure done it.

Slocum, he scratched around until he see that it wasn't no joke, an' then he set bait for a couple o' capitalists. He trapped two beauties, an' they put up the assets an' went in, equal partners. They sunk shafts an' built stamp mills an' smelters an' retorts; oh, they sure made plans to get the metal wholesale. As soon as it began to flow in they built stores an' shacks an' a big hotel—they wasn't timorous about puttin' their coin into circulation, you bet your life, an' it looked as if they was going to flood the market.

Well, Slocum, he owned a third of everything, mind, an' his expression flopped square over like a dry moon, an' stayed points up. He forgot all those years 'at he'd been havin' the muddy end of it, an' after a time he got 'em to call the mine "Slocum's Luck." The' wasn't no call to hurl such an insult as that into the mouth of an honest, hard-workin' mine, an' naturally, as soon as it was done, the mine laid down in its tracts an' refused to give up another ounce.

They came to a break in the lode an' couldn't find the beginnin' again. The same twist that had hove one edge out of the ground had unjointed the other. But they had got out a tidy sum already, an' they knew the' must be a loose end somewhere, so they was anxious to keep their outfit in good order.

Slocum hadn't swelled clear out of shape with his new fortune, an' when I made myself known to him he had give me a purty tol'able decent sort of a job, where there was more bossin' an' responsibility than brute labor; an' I felt kindly toward him. Winter lasted full four months out there. It was a good ninety miles to the railroad, an' so when the mornin's begun to get frosty every one else scooted for humanity, an' I, bein' more or less weak-minded, took the job o' watchman, at forty a month an' my needin's. I always was a hog for litachure, so I got a bushel o' libraries an' started in to play it alone.

The' wasn't a blessed thing to do, so I read 'em through by New Years, an' got out of tobacco by the first of February. From that on I begun to think in a circle, an' my intellect creaked like a dry axle before the bluebirds began to sing. Quiet? I could hear the shadows crawlin' along the side of the house. The snow was seventy-five feet deep in the canyons, so you might say I was duty bound to stay there. As a general rule, I don't shirk breakin' a path, but when the snow is more than fifty feet higher than my head, I'd rather walk fourth or fifth.

When the outfit came back in the spring I was the entire reception committee; but I bet the' never was one more able to do its part.

CHAPTER TEN
A WINTER AT SLOCUM'S LUCK

They only brought out about half a gang that summer, an' they kept them probin' around all over the neighborhood; but though they found enough stuff to about pay expenses, they couldn't get back on the main track. Both the Eastern capitalists showed up along toward fall to see what was doin', an' when it came time to knock off work, they tried to get me to repeat my little performance as watchman.

I thanked 'em for their trustfulness, but I politely declined the honor. I told 'em 'at I was purty tol'able quick-witted, an' it didn't take me four months to study out what I was goin' to say next. But I compromised by sayin' that if they would give me two other fellers for company I'd stay; otherwise they'd have to rustle up some poor devil 'at needed the money. They knew 'at I was reliable, so they agreed; an' I selected out my two companions in affliction. What I mostly wanted was a heap of variety, an' when the number is limited to two, a feller has to be some choicy; but I reckon I got the best the' was.

There'd been a little light-haired feller there all season, kind o' gettin' familiar with labor, like. He was no account to work, he couldn't even learn to tie a knot; but he talked kin' o' blotchy, an' it was divertin' to listen to him. One day we was kiddin' him about bein' so thumby, an' he sez, "That's right, boys, laugh while you can; but I'll have you all between the covers of a book some day, an' then it will be my grin. I ain't swore no everlastin' felicity to the holy cause o' labor; I'm just gettin' local color now."

Next day he fell into a barrel of red paint he was swobbin' on the hotel to keep her from warpin', an' every blessed man in camp passed out about six jokes apiece relatin' to local color. He never saddened up none, though, just smiled sorrowful, as though he pitied us, an' went on tanglin' up everything he touched.

An' then there was another curious speciment there; a tall thin feller, with one o' them lean, chinny faces. He claimed 'at he had been a show actor, but his lungs had given out—claimed he was a tragudian, but Great Scott! he couldn't even turn a handspring.

He said he was recuperatin', an' he sure did hit his liquor purty hard; but I never could make out what he expected to get out of a minin' camp, 'cause he was full as useless as Local Color. About half the fellers you meet strayin' around out here are a bit one-sided, but we don't care so long as they're peaceable. When you'd guy this one a little stout, he'd fold his arms, throw back his head, an' say, "Laugh, varlets, laugh! Like the cracklin' o' thorns under a pot, is the laughter of fools." This was the brand of langwidge 'at flowed from this one, an' he wasn't no ways stingy with it.

Well, they had kept these two at boys' jobs an' boys' wages, an' when I offered 'em the position of deputy watchmen, they fair jumped at it. Said Local Color, "It will be a golden opportunity to perpetuate the seething thoughts which crowd upon my brain." Said Hamlet, "I thank thee, sir, for this, thy proposition fair. In sooth I'll try the cold-air cure, and in the majesty of prime-evil silence, I shall make the snow-capped mountains echo to the wonderful rhapsodies of Shakespeare." Well, the' was a super-abundance of cold air an' prime-evil silence an' snow-capped mountains, an' I didn't care a hang what he did to 'em, so long as it kept me from gettin' everlastin' sick o' my own company.

I never see any company yet 'at wasn't a shade better'n just my own. I knew I could stand these two innocents for four months, an' if they got violent I could rope an' tie 'em. When everybody begun to get ready to pull out, I took the twenty-mule team down to town to get our needin's. I took the children along with me, an' I sez to 'em, "Now, boys, no drinkin' goes up above through the winter. We simply have to go out an' get disgusted with it before we start back."

Well, we sure had a work-out. On the sixth day Hamlet, he throws his arm around my neck an' busts out cryin' an' sez, "Happy, it is the inflexible destiny o' the human race to weary of all things mortal, an' I'm dog-tired o' bein' drunk—an' 'sides, I'm busted."

It turned out that he didn't have any advantage over me an' Locals in this respect, so we went to the company store an' got three bushels o' nickle libraries, enough grub to do six men six months, enough tobacco to do twelve men a car, an' a little yeller pup 'at we give six bits for. I didn't 'low to run any risks this deal.

When we got back 'most everybody had pulled out, an' the roads was beginnin' to choke up. Slocum an' the two capitalists was there waitin' for us, but when all their stuff was loaded on the wagon the' wasn't room for the men; so Miller, the youngest capitalist, who was a bit of a highroller, an' had been shakin' up the coast off an' on, he took off four trunks, an' sez to me, "Happy, if you run out of clothes, here's four trunks-full." Then they hopped on the wagon an' left us alone in our glory.

I reckon, take it all in all, that was about the most florid winter I ever put in, an' it purt' nigh spoilt me for hard work. I did the cookin', the innocents did the chores, an' we got along as bully as a fat bear for a while, livin' in the hotel. The' was a hundred rooms, but we didn't use 'em all. Locals, he wrote most of the time, when he wasn't lookin' at the ceiling an' tryin' to think. Hammy, he walked barefoot in the snow, on' hollered at the snow-capped mountains. I read nickle libraries, an' we didn't care a dang for the Czar of Russia, until along toward Christmas a spark lit in my pile of litachure, an' doggone near burned the hotel down. Then we began to feel snowed-in. Locals had writ himself dry, Hammy was tired of listenin' to himself, besides havin' chilblains up to his knees, an' I was half crazy, 'count of havin' nothing to read. We didn't have a nickle between us, so we couldn't gamble, an' I resigned my mind that when spring climbed up the trail the 'd be two corpses an' one maniac in that cussed hotel.

One day Hammy came stalkin' in to where me an' Locals was playin' guess. Guess ain't never apt to be a popular pastime 'cause it has to be played without any kind o' cheatin' whatever. The one who is it, guesses what the other one is thinkin' of, an' if he guesses before he falls asleep, he wins. Well, Hammy, he breaks in on our game just the same as if we hadn't been doin' anything at all, an' I knew by his action that the' was somethin' afoot. Whenever Hammy was ready to speak something, he always walked like a hoss 'at was string-haltered in all four legs. Well, he paraded up to us that day, hip action, knee action, and instep action all workin', stopped in front of us, folded his arms, an' sez, "Good sirs, I have conceived a fitting fete."

"The only fate I expect is to go mad an' cut my own throat," sez Locals; but Hammy frowned an' went on in a scoldy, indignant voice. "When Wisdom speaks, Folly replies with jest; yet, having little choice of company, I needs must make the best of what I have."

Well, those two had what they called a war of wits until finally Locals hit Hammy with a chair, which was the way most o' their discussions ended; but it turned out that what Hammy was tryin' to say was that we should open the trunks, dress ourselves in the clothes, an' give a show. He said he knew parts to fit any make-ups we'd find; an' after Locals found out what it was 'at Hammy had schemed out, he joined in enthusiastic, an' said that if the' had never been a part writ to fit 'em yet, he could do it on the spot, an' he wasn't swamped with business right then anyway. "Yes," I sez, "it's a great idee, an' we'll sure draw a mammoth crowd. We'll charge 'em a library apiece an' get enough litachure to last us a hundred years."

"At best, sarcasm is out of season; at worst, the season 's out of it," sez Hammy to me: "and furthermore, good friend, in life, as on the stage, your part must be a role of actions, not of words." I used to say over the things 'at this pair made up, until I had 'em by heart, an' since then I've had a lot o' fun springin' 'em on strangers. They used to speak to me as though I was a horse, and of me as though I was part of the furniture. Hammy sez to me one day, "Me good man, you do very well with your hands, but kindly Nature designed your head merely for a hatrack."

They could say these little things right off the roll, an' it allus made me feel like a fish out o' water, somehow, but I stored 'em up in my memory, an' I've got my worth out of 'em all right.

We did open the trunks a week or so after this—and clothes! Well, say, Miller sure was the dresser. The' was fifteen hats in a little trunk built a-purpose for 'em, an' the' was all kinds of vests an' pants an' neckties 'at a feller could imagine. But best of all was a book 'at we found at the bottom of one o' the trunks. It was a hard-shelled book, an' I never took much stock in that kind. When it's my turn to read a book, a little old paper-back fits me out all right. I've been fooled on them hard-shells too often; but this here one was a hummer.

I ain't no tenderfoot when it comes to a book, but this one was sure the corkin'est I ever met up with. I had allus thought 'at "Seventeen Buckets o' Blood; or the Mormon Widder's Revenge" was about the extreme limit in books, but this here one lays over even that. It was called "Monte Cristo," an' had the darndest set o' Dago names in it ever a mortal human bein' laid eyes on. I tried to mine it out by myself at first, but pshaw, every cuss in the book had a name like an Injun town, an' the' was about as many characters in the book as the' is on the earth; so I delegated Hammy to read her out loud. This suited Hammy to the limit, an' he didn't only read her—he acted her. He'd roar an' screech an' whisper an' glare into your eyes so blame natural that a feller never used the back of his chair from start to finish, an' twice I was on the point of shootin' him, thinkin' it was real.

If you ain't never read the book it'll pay you to fling up your job an' wrastle through it. It starts out with a nice, decent young feller sailin' home to marry his steady, but all his friends turn in an' stack the cards on him, an' get him chucked into the rottenest dungeon in France. He knowed how they soak it to a feller citizen in that country, an' at first he was all for killin' himself; but after he'd studied it over ten or twelve years, he suddenly heard a queer scratchin' noise.

In that same prison was another prisoner, an Abbey. An Abbey is a kind of foreman priest. Well, this Abbey wasn't one to throw out a prayer an' then set down to wait for results, not him. He was one o' these nervous, fretty fellers what like to do their own drivin', an' he makes him a set o' minin' tools out of a tin saucepan an' a bed-castor, an' runs a level from his own cell into Eddie's—an' that was the queer, scratchin' sound that made Eddie decide not to kill himself.

By George, if I could find a prison what had an Abbey shut up in it, the' wouldn't be any way in the world to keep me out. This Abbey, he cottoned to Eddie right from the start, an' durin' the next few years they mine around in the prison till she's as holey as a Switzer cheeze; an' durin' their leisure he edicates Eddie till he knows more'n a college professor.

Then the Abbey begins to have fits, an' when all the medicine 'at he could make out of old soot an' sulphur matches an' such stuff is gone, he gives up an' tells Eddie where he has a little holler island, chuck full o' diamonds an' money an' such like plunder. Then he dies, an' Eddie gets in the sack. They chain a round shot to Eddie's feet an' hurl him off a cliff into the angry sea, an' when it comes to that part you can't hardly breathe; but Eddie kicks off the chain, rips open the sack, an' when he strikes the water he's a free man.

He swims along for a couple of days until he overtakes a smuggler, an' he climbs on board an' shows 'em how to run their business accordin' to Hoyle. He only stays with 'em long enough to learn all their secrets, an' then he gives 'em the slip an' goes to his little holler island. He pulls off the top, an' it's all so, what the Abbey told him. Then he lifts up his hand an' he sez, sez he, "I'll be avenged!" And he sure done it.

He didn't believe in none o' your cheap little killin's. He gives 'em all the range they wanted while he was fixin' up the cards; but when he was ready to call their hands, the' was somethin' doin' every minute, an' don't you never forget it. Oh, he was a deep one. It is creepy to think of any one like him bein' turned loose on the earth, 'cause a feller might do somethin' 'at didn't suit him, an' the' wasn't no place you could hide in afterward. He kept watchin' all the while, an' nobody couldn't commit a crime nowheres on earth but what he knew of it, an' he'd go an' call the feller over to one side an' say, "Young man, you are doomed to die; but if you'll promise to do anything I want you to, I'll give the Pope, or the Emp'rer of Chinee, or whoever the main stem happened to be, a scuttle o' diamonds an' get you free—what's the word?"

Well, in a few years the' wasn't half a dozen criminals in the whole world who wasn't bound to carry out his orders, an' you can see what an outfit he had to back him up. Some of 'em he'd make his body-servants; but that wasn't no snap, you can bet, 'cause he was notionable to a degree. He'd make plans for a little party, an' he'd send one man to Siberia for a fish, an' another to Asia for a fowl, an' another to Chinee for a bird's nest—to make soup of—an' so on. He never give his guests nothin' to eat 'at growed in the same country the feast was to be give in. Then he'd say to his steward, who had the hardest job of all, "Bill"—Bill wasn't his name, but it'll do—"Bill, where did I see that six-foot vase, made out of a single ruby?"

An' Bill would turn pale an' say, "It was in the secret vault of the Em'prer of Chince, your Excellency." Then Monte Cristo, he'd say, "Ah, yes, so it was. 'Tell, go an' get it an' have it here by the twenty-fifth day of next month."

Well, Bill, he'd just about flicker out, an' begin to tell how it couldn't be did; but Xlonte, he'd only look at him cold, an' say, "Never mind the details, Bill—get the vase. If you think you need the British Navy, why, buy it, but don't bother me. It seems to me, Bill, 'at you ought to begin gittin' on to my curves purty soon. Good-bye."

This was the way he carried on. He'd go to a prison an' he'd say, "Young man, you was buried to death when you was a baby, but I figgered I could use you later on, so I had you transplanted. You come out o' this prison, get an edication, an' on the ninth o' next June you show up at number forty-nine, Rue de Champaign, Paris, at two fifteen P. M.—sharp. Here's a million francs to pay expenses. Don't be a tight-wad—the's plenty more." A franc is worth five dollars, but he didn't give a durn for 'em. That was HIS style.

He'd come to town an' buy a tenement house 'at wouldn't rent, because it was haunted; an' he'd tear it all down except the rooms 'at had been most popular to commit murder in. Then next day he'd run up a swell mansion around these rooms—big an' gorgeous, like the Capitol at Cheyenne, with full-grown trees from all over the world, standin' in the front yard. Then he 'd give a party to all the substantial citizens who had once used those rooms to commit murders in, an' he'd bring 'em face to face with the ones they thought they had murdered—an' it was comical to see 'em fallin' around in faints; but Monte, he'd pretend 'at he hadn't noticed anything unusual, an' he'd get 'em a glass of wine an' make 'em face the torture, till it gives a feller a cold sweat, just to read about it.

You might think that a man runnin' for congress in this country has a hard time sinkin' his reputation; but the way 'at Monte Cristo mined around in a feller's past was enough to scare a cat out of a cellar. They don't run things over in France like they do here; they make Counts an' Markusses an' Bankers out of the bad men, an' slap the innocent ones into dungeons to keep 'em from gettin' spoilt. But this didn't suit Monte for a minute; so when he gets the gang all settin' up in front of him like a herd o' tenpins he sez, "Let her go!" an' you ought to have seen 'em drop.

He don't do none o' the dirty work himself—no more prisons for him. He just goes around like a Sunday-school director at Christmas time, while his enemies turn to an' poison an' stab an' mutilate each other in a way to turn a butcher pale; but his favorite plan is to make 'em go insane an' have their hair turn white in a single night. That got to be his private brand.

Well, Hammy read the book to us so natural that we all slept in one bed for company; but it cheered us a heap, an' we begun to feel rich, ourselves, an' talked about millions as easy an' natural as though we each had little holler islands of our own. Miller was about my size, so 'at all his clothes fit me like the skin on a potato. Hammy was a leetle too tall an' thin, and Locals, a foot or so short; but they fished out a couple of swell outfits too.

We found a lot of empty check-books, an' used to play draw, settlin' at night by check. It was purty good fun for a while—until we woke up. Hammy owed me ten million francs an' Locals was into me for fifteen. I offered to give 'em a receipt in full if they'd give me their interest in the yeller pup. As long as the pup had three bosses he wouldn't mind no one, an' I wanted to teach him somethin' besides eatin' an' sleepin; but them two cusses wouldn't sell out at the price. When I saw that a hundred an' twenty-five million dollars wouldn't buy two-thirds of a seventy-five cent pup, I understood what the spell-binders mean by a debased currency, an' I felt hurt an' lonesome again.

One day Hammy stacked himself in front of a window an' began to talk about the gloomy ghastliness of solitude, until me an' Locals couldn't stand it no longer, an' we heaved him out into a drift. Under ordinary circumstances he would have rolled his eyes, pulled his hair, an' ranted around about the base ungratitude of man; but this time he looked up to the sky an' hollered, "Come out here quick! Hurry up! COME ON!"

We went out, an' the' was somethin' a-floatin' away up yonder, lookin' like a flyspeck on a new tablecloth. "What is it?" asked Hammy. "Is it a bird?" asked Locals. Under such conditions I never say nothin' until I have somethin' to say, so we stood an' gazed. In about ten minutes we all shouted together, "It's a balloon!"

An' by jinks, that's what it was. We hollered an' fired off guns, an' after a while it settled down an' lodged in a tree. The' was only one man in it, but he was dyked out in Sunday clothes, an' purt' nigh froze to death. We fed an' warmed him, an' he was about as much surprised at us as we was at him. I was wearin' a Prince Albert coat an' a high plug hat, Locals had on a white flannel yachtin' rig, an' Hammy was sportin' a velvet suit with yeller leggin's an' a belt around the waist. After we had fitted him out with a pipe he sez, "Gentlemen, I may possibly be able to repay you at some future time. I am Lord Arthur Cleighton, second son of the Earl o' Clarenden."

When he registered himself thus, I see Locals an' Hammy open their eyes, an' I knew 'at we had landed somethin' purty stately.

"I am pleased to meet you, me lord," sez Hammy, in his most gorgeous manner. "I am Gene De Arcy. You may have heard of my father, the multimillionaire."

Locals, he looked at Lord Arthur, an' see that Hammy's bluff had stuck, so he girded up his loins an' sez, "Sir, it gives me great pleasure to make your acquaintance. My uncle, Silas Martin, the late copper king, has just died, leavin' me as his sole heir; an' I have been seein' a bit of my own country, preparatory to a prolonged trip around the world."

Lord Arthur, he jumps to his feet an' shakes hands with 'em, tellin' 'em to just cut out his title, as he was a simple Democrat while in the United States.

I hardly knew what to do. I didn't hold openers, an' yet if I didn't draw some cards an' see it out I stood to lose entirely. I had been corralin' a heap o' city langwidge since I had been cooped up with Locals an' Hammy, but my heart failed me. I knew I was still some shy on society manners; but I also knew 'at the' was a heap o' bluffin' goin' on, so I stuck up my bet an' called.

"Artie," I sez, holdin' out my hand, "you're the first lord my eyes has ever feasted on; but I like you—you're game. It ain't many 'at will own up to bein' a Democrat these days, not even in the secrecy of the ballot box, but here in Nevada you're safe. Pa has just retired from business, leavin' me this little mine; but it only pays about ten million a year now, so I've made up my mind not to bother with it, but to shut it down an' go on a tour of the world with my two friends here. I never cared much for school, so this will be a good way to finish my edication. We was up here last fall seein' that things was closed in proper order, an' waited for the watchman to come up from below, when we expected to drive down to our special train an' start for Paris. But the snow came unexpected, and the expected watchman failed to come; and here we are, with no food fit for a human, an' all our servants in the special train, ninety miles away."

When I begun my oration Locals and Hammy leaned forward, holdin' their breath; but when they see 'at I wasn't turnin' out no schoolboy article of a lie, they settled back with a long sigh, an' I could tell by their faces 'at they were takin' pride in my work. They was about the best qualified judges o' that kind o' work I ever met up with, an' I'll own 'at I never felt prouder in my life 'an I did when Hammy slapped me on the back as soon as I finished an' sez to Artie, "Me Lord, this is a typical American. He plans his life on larger things than rules; but you can depend on him—yea, though the heavens fall, you can depend on Jack here."

I was glad we didn't have any liquor there, or like as not we'd 'a' burned the hotel down just for a lark. We was so full of that doggone Monte Cristo book that we believed our own lies as easy as Artie did, an' begun to talk to each other like we was society folks at a banquet.

But Artie was a good, decent sort of a chap, as common as we were, when we got to know him. He never kicked none on the grub, an' his appetite was a thing to make preparations for; but, as Locals said, his high descent came out the minute he was brought face to face with work—he didn't recognize it. Now he didn't try to dodge it, nor he didn't apologize for not doing it; he just didn't seem to know the' was such a thing. It never occurred to him that the only way to have clean dishes was to wash dirty ones. Hammy and Locals, those freeborn sons of Independence, was glad an' proud to have the chance to wait on him; but I must confess that the day he sat by the fire with a pile of wood within reachin' distance, an' let the fire go out, I grew a trifle loquacious about it.

Hammy overheard me mutterin' to myself in a voice 'at could be heard anywhere in the hotel, an' he drew me to one side an' sez, "Hush, presumptuous peasant; for all you know the blood of Alfred flows within his veins."

"That ain't my fault," sez I; "but some of it will flow down this mountain side if he don't begin stayin' awake daytimes."

Still, all in all, he was a likeable young feller an' the' ain't no doubt but what he saved us from bein' lonesome any more. He said 'at this balloon had been exhibited in Los Angeles, an' he had got into it just for fun; but the rope had parted an' he had been fifteen hours on the way. It was only by luck 'at he had happened to have his overcoat along.

He had four or five newspapers, which he had tied around his feet to keep 'em warm, but nare a library; so after we had lied our imaginations sore for a week or so, we fell back on draw, settlin' by checks at night. By a dazzling piece of luck Artie had his money in the same New York bank 'at Miller had, so he could use our checks, an' things began to brighten. Three of us were playin' for real money, an' the other feller thought he was—it was genuine poker, an' the stiffest game I ever sat in.

Time didn't drag none now. Artie knew the game, an' it kept me in a sweat to beat him. White chips was a hundred dollars apiece; but we bet colored ones mostly, to keep from litterin' up the table. Spring began to loosen up about the first of March, an' by that time Artie owed me two million real dollars. Locals an' Hammy was into me for close to a billion, but I didn't treasure their humble offerings much, 'ceptin' as pipe-lighters. We was keyed up to a high pitch by this time, an' was beginnin' to get thin and ringey about the eyes. Artie from losin', me from longin' for the time to come when I should start out to be a little Monte Cristo on my own hook, an' Locals an' Hammy, from pityin' Artie an' envyin' me.

On the twenty-fifth of March a wagon-load of grub an' four men came out to get things started. I see 'em comin' up the grade, an' I piked down an' told 'em 'at I had landed a good thing, an' to just treat me as the boss for a few days an' I'd make it all right with 'em.

When Artie saw the new men he turned pale about the gills. He owed me close to three millions, an' blame if I didn't feel a little sorry for him. Still, I'd played fair all the while, an' I 'lowed 'at the Earl o' Clarenden could stand it, and I needed the money a heap more'n some who might 'a' won it.

When old Bill Sykes came in to report to me I was wearin' a plug hat on the back o' my head an' sportin' a white vest an' a red necktie, so I looked enough like the real thing to make it easy for him to act his part. He came in an' blurted out, right while we was boostin' up a jack-pot. "That'll do, me good man," sez I, "wait until this hand is played." Bill, he took off his hat an' stood humble until Artie had scooped in a hundred thousand dollars, an' then I told Bill he might talk.

"The watchman was found froze to death, Mr. Hawkins," sez Bill to me mighty respectful, "an' your train waited until two relief parties had been drove back by storms, an' then it pulled out for 'Frisco. We are all ready to take charge here, an' as soon as you wish you can drive down in the wagon an' telegraph for the train."

Bill backed out bowin', an' we made plans to emigrate a little. I promised Locals an' Hammy a generous rake-off, an' we fixed to have a tol'able fair time as soon as I cashed in.

Next mornin' I found a letter addressed to Mr. John Hawkins, Esq. Artie wasn't around, but Locals an' Hammy was, so I opened the letter an' read it. This here is the letter. It's one o' my greatest treasures.

"GENTLEMEN,—You have all treated me fine an' I hate to skin out without saying good-bye but I have not the nerve. I have lied to you all the time. I am not a real lord at all. My father was gardener at Clarenden Castle an' I was under groom at St. James Court. When the younger son came to this country, I came with him but left him an' became a waiter in New York City. I went to an excursion to Long Branch an' got to flirting with a widow just for pastime. She dogged my life after that and my wife is something terrible so I took her and came to Los Angeles. We was as happy as any one could be with a wife like mine until the widow showed up. Then I stood between two fires and either one of them was hell so I got into the balloon and cut the rope expecting to drift over into Mexico. You are all rich and will not need the money but I always play fair and I hate to skin out this way;

"yours truly "
L. A. C.

"P.S. It was all I could do to keep from helping with the work 'cause some of your cooking was rotten and you did not wash the dishes clean but I knew if I worked you would not think me a real lord. I hope some day I may be able to repay you for all your kindness."

I didn't say a word after I finished readin' the letter. I had fallen too far to have any breath left for talkin'; but Hammy an' Locals unbosomed their hearts something terrible.

"A murrian on the filthy swine!" sez Hammy, after he began to quiet down a little. "I would I had his treacherous throat within my grasp, that I might squeeze his inky soul back to the lower depths from whence he sprung."

"Hush, you punkin headed peasant," sez I. "The' 's just as much of Alfred's blood flowin' through his veins now as the' ever was."

"'T is not the money I have lost that makes me mad," sez Locals. "It's finding out that a man can become so degenerate that he will impose upon the very ones who save his life—deceive them, lie to them!"

"Oh, he ain't the only liar 'at was ever in this hotel," sez I; "an' when it comes to the money YOU'VE lost, that'd be a small matter to get mad over. He risked just as much money as we did, an' if he'd 'a' won, he wouldn't 'a' won a cent more."

After a while they grew more resigned in their langwidge; but after we had driven down to town without finding him, Hammy sez, "In sooth 't is bitter truth that all the world's a stage; yet Fate, however cruel, never decreed that I should play the second season, as servile server to a worn out mine—my health is all right again, an' I'm goin' back where a feller gets paid decent wages for makin' a fool of himself."

Suddenly Locals gave a yell of joy and shouted, "My fortune's made! I can take this thing and have a runaway boy and a lost orphan and a rich uncle and a villanous cousin, and write the novel of the age about it."

"No, no!" sez Hammy, catchin' the excitement, "tragedy—make it a tragedy. It is for the stage! Think of them lost without food and the balloon coming into sight! Think of the scenic effects, the low music as the orphan kneels in the middle of the stage and prays that the balloon may bring them food; and then have the villanous cousin in the balloon—"

Well, they purt' nigh fought about it, and they were still at it when I left them. The tingle of spring in the air made me wild to get back to the range again. I thought of little Barbie and what a great girl she must be by this time. I thought of the big-eyed winter calves huggin' up to their mothers and wonderin' what it all meant. I thought of old Mount Savage, and all of a sudden somethin' seemed pullin' at my breast like a rope, an' I drew down my winter wages, an' set out for the no'th, eager as a hound pup on his first hunt.

CHAPTER ELEVEN
DRESS REFORM AT THE DIAMOND DOT

I've heard it called Christian fortitude, an' I've heard it called Injun stoickcism, an' I've heard it called bulldog grit; but it's a handy thing to have, no matter what it is. I mean the thing that keeps a feller good company when the' 's a hurtin' in his heart that he never quite forgets. A little child away from home an' just sick to go back, a man who has to grit his teeth an'—but no, the first expresses the feelin' better—a child, homesick, but keepin' a stiff upper lip; and it don't make much difference what the age, that's a condition 'at nobody ever outgrows.

Well, all the years I'd been away the' was a little empty sore spot in my heart that I couldn't quite forget; but I never aired it none, an' I don't believe I knew myself how big it was, until I left Slocum's Luck behind me an' headed for the Diamond Dot. Then I spread a grin on my face that nothin' wouldn't wipe off, an' I stepped so high an' light that I was like a nervous man goin' barefoot through a thistle patch. I was headed for home; an' even a mule that gets dressed down regular with the neck-yoke gives a little simmer of joy when he's headed toward home, while a dog,—well, a dog will just naturally joyful himself all over when the trail doubles back on itself, an' a dog ain't no parlor loafer, neither, if I'm any judge.

Why, for two years I hadn't polished a saddle, an' I whistled like a boy when I pictured to myself the feel of a hoss under me. The' 's somethin' about feelin' a hoss's strength slide into your legs an' up through your body that must be a good deal like the sensation a saint enjoys the first fly he takes with his new wings. A little pop-eyed drug merchant was out here on a tour oncet, an' he asked me the usual list of blame-fool questions, about what we et an' where we washed an' if it didn't make us ache to sleep on the hard ground, an so on. When I had made answers to his queries accordin' to the amount of information I thought it wise to load him with, he shakes his head solemn like an' sez, "I do not see where you get any compensation for such a life as this."

"We don't get any compensation," sez I, "but look at all the hoss-back ridin' we get to make up for it."

An' there I was with the spring drippin' all about me, the plains standin' beckonin' to me on every side, just coaxin' to be rode over, an' me walkin' on foot with flat-heeled boots on!

I had rode out on Sam Cutler's freighter to within' twenty miles o' the ranch house, an' I built a little fire an' unrolled my blankets; but I couldn't sleep. I just lay lookin' up at the stars an' tryin' to imagine what Barbie looked like an' whether Starlight was still at the ranch, an' every now an' again I tried to decide as to whether I'd grin or be haughty when I first spied Jabez. I was some anxious to come upon Barbie first. I knew she'd be glad to see me, but I was rather leery about Jabez. He would 'a' welcomed a projical son of his own as often as occasion offered, but he wasn't just the sort of a man to be a public welcomer. I couldn't picture him puttin' up a sign sayin', "Projical sons turn to the left. If chicken is preferred to veal, shoot in the air twice when you get within a mile of the house."

But I was too much elated to worry much, an' along about one o'clock I rolled up my blankets, kicked out my fire, an' started to drill. When the sun rose I was in sight of the ranch house, an' the sun seemed to throw an arm around my shoulder an' go skippin' along by my side—an' I did skip now an' again.

When I got about a mile from the house I came upon Jabez, walkin' slow an' lookin' down-hearted. He hadn't changed a mite in the five years—in fact from what I could see he hadn't even changed his clothes; so for a moment I thought his sour look was the same ill humor I'd left him in; an' then I saw it was more serious, an' my heart stopped with a thump.

He looked up just then an' we stared at each other without speakin'. "Ain't you dead?" sez he.

"No I ain't," sez I.

"We heard you was," sez he; "killed in a muss over at Danders."

"I don't believe it," sez I, "an' besides, I ain't been in Danders for over seven years."

"Well, then, what made you stay away so long for?" sez he, sort o' snappy.

"I don't remember you sheddin' any tears when I left, an' I don't recall you beggin' me to hurry back," sez I. I was pleased at the way I was bein' received an' I meant to make him show his hand.

"You know as well as I do that things allus go better on this ranch when you're here."

"Yes," sez I.

"An' you know 'at I don't like to beg no man to do anything; but you ought to see that I know that you're the usefullest man I ever had, an' you oughtn't to be so fly-uppity," sez he.

"Now see here, Jabez," sez I, "you're one o' the kind o' men who never own up 'at a man was fit to live until after he's dead. You're like some o' these Easterners—they get so everlastin' entranced with the beautiful scenery that they forget to water their ridin' hosses. I don't ask no special favors, but I ain't so mortal thick-skinned myself, an' you ought to learn sometime that there is hosses 'at work better when they're not beat up an' yelled at."

"Are you goin' to stay this time?" sez he.

"As long as it's agreeable—all around," sez I. "Is everything goin' smooth?"

The down-hearted look came into his eyes again. "She won't speak to me," sez he.

"You don't mean to say 'at you've gone an' got married," sez I, "or that you are tryin' to?"

"I ain't such a fool," he snaps. "It's Barbie, I mean."

"How long has this been goin' on?" sez I.

"This is the fourth meal," sez he; an' he was so solemn about it that I was some inclined to snicker, but then it flashed upon me that when I left, the child was all het up over the letter she'd found in the attic, and I sobered an' sez, "Is it something 'at's goin' to be hard to smooth over?"

"I don't see how the deuce it's ever goin' to be smoothed over," sez Jabez, desperately.

"Would you feel like sort o' hintin' what it was about?" sez I.

"Well, it's about the way she acts," sez Jabez. "Confound it, Happy, she's the best gal child ever was on this earth, I reckon, but she don't want to be one, an' she won't act like it, an' she—she won't dress like it. Every time I argue with her she beats me to it, an' I'm plumb stumped. Yesterday I told her she had to take 'em off an' wear dresses, an' she did; but now she won't speak to me."

"You mean that you said that she was never to argue with you again?" sez I, indignant.

"No, I mean that I sez she must take those confounded buckskin pants off! She's big enough now to begin to train to become a woman—not a man."

I had to grin a little, but even though it didn't seem as skeptical to me as it did to him, I saw he might be right about it. Still, I wasn't goin' to take sides without hearin' all the evidence, so I sez, "Is she healthy, Jabez?"

"Healthy?" he sez. "Why, that child could winter through without shelter an' come out in the spring kickin' up her heels an' snortin'."

"Well, that much is in her favor," sez I. "Is she good at her studies?"

"Where you been that you haven't heard about it?" sez he. "Last winter she out-ciphered an' out-spelt the schoolmarm, an' she fuddled up one o' these missionary preachers till he didn't know where he was at. She has been studyin' about all kinds o' things, an' she cornered him up on the first chapter o' Genesis. She lined out the school-marm first, an' the schoolmarm came an' told me that she was an infidel—the' ain't no sense in havin' women teach school, Happy. You can't reason with 'em an' you can't fight with 'em an' they just about pester a body to death. I don't see how Barbie stands it."

"Well, what did you do about her bein' an infidel?" sez I.

"I couldn't do anything to the teacher except tell her what I thought of her; but next Sunday I had Barbie read to me the first chapter o' Genesis. Did you ever read it, Happy?"

"Yes," sez I, "I read all of that book an' most of the next one. Me an' another feller had a dispute about the Bible one time, an' he said it was the best readin' the' was, an' I said it was too dry. He read me about a feller in it named Samson, who was full o' jokes an' the strongest man ever was, I reckon, before he let that Philistine woman loco him, an' he read about another feller, just a mite of a boy, who killed a giant with a slingshot in front of an army which had made fun of him an' was all ready to give in to the giant, an' he read me some poems about mountains; an' I had to give in that the Bible was the greatest book ever was. That was up at a little ranch in Idaho, an' he was goin' to read it all to me an' explain what it meant,—he was full edicated, this feller was, an' had a voice as soft as a far-off bell, an' an eye that seemed to reach right out an' shake hands with ya,—but one day when I was away a posse surprised him, an' though he potted two of 'em they finally put him out. He left me his Bible with a note in it which said that he had killed the man all right an' that he would do it again under the circumstances; but he couldn't tell a word in his own defense 'count of mixin' in a woman. We never found out a word about it, not even where the posse came from. Well, afterward I tried to read it alone; but I couldn't make any headway. For one thing, the' 's too many pedigrees to keep track of, an' the names are simply awful. I don't want to be profane nor nothin', but hanged if I think the Children of Israel was square enough to deserve all the heavenly favors they got; so I finally gave up tryin' to read it. But what about you an' Barbie?"

"Well," sez he, "I'd read the Bible clean through from cover to cover an' I never saw anything unreasonable in it, so I thought I could set Barbie right without any trouble. She read the first chapter, an' by that time I was runnin' for cover an' yellin' for help. The' ought to be something done about that book, it ain't right to try an' raise a child to be honest, an' tell 'em that they must believe the Bible, an' then have 'em find out what the Bible really sez."

"Well, what about it?" sez I.

"Well, it sez that the' was light an' darkness an' evenin' an' mornin' on the first day; on the third day the' was all kinds o' grass an' herbs yieldin' seeds, an' fruit trees yieldin' fruit; but the' wasn't no sun or stars until the fourth day. Now how could you have evenings an' mornings an' grass an' fruit trees without sunshine? You know that wouldn't work, an' when she put it up to me I simply threw up my hands, an' sent Spider Kelley with the buckboard to hunt up this missionary preacher. He was long-haired an' pius, an' when I saw him I felt purty sure he could straighten it out; but he wasn't game. Barbie argued fair an' square, an' he lost his temper an' called her an infidel an' a heretic an' a nagnostic; but she pulled a lot o' books on him, an' he couldn't understand 'em an' blasphemed 'em something terrible; but he see he was whipped, an' just simply ran away. I felt mighty bad about Barbie bein' an infidel until Friar Tuck came around. You remember Friar Tuck—the one they call an Episcolopian?" Course I remembered Friar Tuck. Everybody knew him an' he was about as easy to forget as a stiff neck—though for different reasons. Preachers are about as different as other humans to begin with, but the women seem more unanimously bent on spoilin' 'em; so as a general rule I wade in purty careful when I 'm startin' an acquaintance with a strange one, but I did know that this here one was all to the right, an' his time belonged to any one who demanded it. This made him purty wearin' on hosses, an' when one would give out on him he'd just turn it loose an' rope another 'thout makin' any preliminary about it; all the explanation a body got was just seein' a tired, stray pony eatin' grass. The first time he tried that game they gathered up a posse an' ran him down; but he pulled a Bible on 'em showin' where he got his commission from, threw a sermon into 'em 'at converted two an' made one other sign the pledge, an' that put an end to any unsolicited interference in his line o' work. He was a big man with two right hands, an' some one gave him the name of Friar Tuck out of a book, an' he was known by it the whole country over.

I nodded my head: "Did the Friar get fainty about Barbie bein' a heretic?" sez I.

"No, he didn't," sez Jabez, "he just laughed when I told him about it, an' he an' Barbie, they wrangled over it for a long time; but he played fair. When he didn't know the answer he owned up to it, an' then he told her that the Bible was written by a lot of different men, an' that the spirit of it was inspired; but that the' wasn't any words ever invented that could describe creation; because the origin of life was a thing 'at man wasn't wise enough to comprehend, an' that all the scientific books ever written couldn't come any nearer to it than that first chapter of Genesis, which had been written ages ago when the old Earth was still in its childhood."

"How did Barbie get around this?" sez I.

"Well, she didn't have much to say; he didn't climb up on a perch an' call her names, he just sat there by her side like they was both children together; an' then he took some of her books an' explained things she didn't understand an' pointed out things 'at other scientists didn't believe in, an' he actually said 'at he believed that after they had examined the earth all over, inside an' out with a magnifyin' glass, every last scientist the' was would be willin' to admit that it must have been created some way or another; and that we'd all be the better for the work these scientists was doin', but that she mustn't confuse the word with the spirit, for it was the spirit which giveth life. He's an A I man, Friar Tuck is; but when I offered him twice as much a year as he's gettin' to stay an' teach her, he just laughed again, an' said that I wasn't in no position to double the kind o' wages he was workin' for. I was a little put out at this, but Barbie said he was talkin' in parables."

"Was she wearin' the buckskin pants when he was here?" sez I.

"Yes, she was, an' I didn't much like the way he acted about that. At first he thought she was a boy, an' it made me hot; but he sez to me, 'Didn't God create man first?' I owned up that he did. 'Well, then,' said he, 'let this child develop the man side of her first, so that she may have strength an' courage for all her journey.' Everything that man sez has the ring o' truth in it, an' I didn't have much of a come-back, except to say that she was overdoing it. He called Barbie over to him an' looked into her eyes an' put his big hand on her head an' afterward he sez to me, 'You needn't worry; soon enough a soul which is all woman will stand before you and ask questions which will make you long for these days back again. Give her all the time she will take.'"

"What else did he say?" sez I.

"Well, he asked me if I had ever noticed a litter of pups. I said I had, and he wanted to know if the' was much difference in the way they played. I owned up that the' wasn't. Then he looked sort o' worried an' asked me if I had ever found any of 'em to get their sex mixed up bad enough to have the tangle last through life. I had to admit that I never had, an' he laughed at me good an' proper—but his laughs never hurt. I didn't mind about her wearin' the buckskins after that so much."

"Well, then, what made you rear up about 'em yesterday?" sez I.

"I hired a new man when she was out ridin',—day before yesterday it was,—an' when she came in he thought she was a boy an' kind o' got gay, an' she panned him out; an' he cussed her an' she drew a gun on him an' made him take it back, an' he might o' taken some spite out on her before he found out she was a girl. She is too sizey now, an' confound it, leggin's an' a short skirt ought to satisfy any female—but now she won't speak to me, an' I can't go back on my order, so I don't see how we're goin' to straighten it out."

I pertended to be mad. "Jabez," I sez, "I do wish I could come back to this ranch just once an' find it runnin' smooth. Here I come all the way from Nevada just to see it once again, an' I find the boss an' his daughter ain't on speakin' terms, an' I have to stand palaverin' for a solid hour without anything bein' asked about my appetite, an' me just finishin' a twenty-mile walk."

"By George, I'm sorry!" sez Jabez. "But hang it, Happy, you ought to savvy this place well enough by this time to know 'at no human ever has to set up an' beg for food. I'm glad to see you 'cause the little girl does set a heap by you, an' you seem to have a way o' straightenin' out the kinks. While you're eatin' breakfast see if you can't think up some way to get her to talkin' again." We started to walk to the house, an' I sez, "just what was your orders about these buckskins?"

"I told her to take 'em off at once an' throw 'em out the window, sez he.

"Did she do it?" sez I.

"She allus obeys orders when she drives me to issue 'em—but I allus get a sting out of it, some way or other. This time I issued the order at the supper table, an' she went upstairs to her room, stuffed the suit full o' pillows, stood in the window, an' screamed until me an' the boys ran out to see what was the matter. Then she threw the figger out an' we thought she had jumped, an' I made a fool o' myself. It's playin' with fire every time you cross her, but she allus obeys orders. Still, it's tarnation hard to be her father—not that I'd trade the job for any other in the country, at that."

Happy Hawkins | 95

I had to chuckle inward all the way to the house, an' just before we arrived to it I purt' nigh exploded. Here come a figger, heavily veiled an' wearin' a shapeless sort of a dress affair made out of a bedquilt an' draggin' behind on the ground. It walked along slow an' dignified, like some sort of a heathen ghost, an' when it came to a pebble in the path it would walk around it an' not step over, all the time holdin' a hand lookin' glass to see that her toe didn't show. I just took one side-eye at Jabez an' his face looked like a storm cloud at a picnic; but when Barbie see who I was she tore off the veil, gathered up her skirts, an' yelled, "Happy! Happy Hawkins, is it really you?"

"I'm ready to take my oath on it, madame," sez I, not crackin' a smile; "but if I might make so bold, who are you?"

"Oh, Happy, we thought you was dead," said she, with a little catch in her voice that made me wink a time or two. "Where have you been all these years, an' why didn't you come back to us?"

She stood lookin' into my eyes, half tender an' half cross, an' I couldn't help but try her out to see which would win. "I didn't know for sure that I'd be welcome," sez I.

"Oh. Happy!" she sez; an' she threw her arms around my neck an' kissed me, an' then we went in to breakfast. I answered her questions between bites, an' as soon as we'd finished I proposed we'd go for a ride. "I haven't crossed a saddle for two years," sez I. "Is Starlight here yet?"

"Well I should say he is, and fat an' bossy," sez she. "The' hasn't airy another body but me rode him neither. I divide my ridin' between him an' Hawkins, just ridin' a colt now an' again to keep from gettin' careless." Then she stopped an' looked down at the thing she was wearin' an' said, sadly, "But I reckon my ridin' days are over."

"Alas, yes," sez I, usin' Hammy's most solemn voice, "Old Age has set his seal upon your brow, an' I can see you sitting knitting by the fire for your few remainin' days."

"Where did you learn to talk that way?" sez she, quick as a wink. So I told her of my winter at Slocum's Luck, an' she asked me a million questions about Hammy an' Locals. When I was through she sat silent for a while an' then she sez, "Happy, I'm goin' to see more o' the world than just this ranch some day."

"Well, the' ain't much of it that's a whole lot better—an' I've seen it about all," sez I.

"You seen it about all?" sez she, scornful; "why, you haven't seen the inside of one real house."

I glanced around, but she snaps in, "This ain't a house, this is just shelter from the elements. I'm goin' to see mansions an' palaces, an' I'm goin' to see 'em from the inside too."

"Have you ever read Monte Cristo?" sez I.

"No," sez she.

"Then don't you do it," sez I. "Your head's about as far turned now as your neck'll stand, an' what you ought to do is to learn how to cook an' sew."

She looked at me with her eyes snappin', but in a second her face broke into a grin. "The' ain't a mite o' use in your tryin' that," sez she. "You like me just as I am, an' you don't need to feel it's your duty to work in any that teacher stuff. Gee, but I'm glad you came back It looks as if me an' Dad is in for a long siege of it this time, an' you'll keep me from gettin' lonesome."

"Not the right answer," sez I. "I'm goin' to leave tomorrow."

Her face grew long in a minute, when she see I meant it. "Happy—you don't really mean that, do you?"

"Barbie," I sez, "I had to leave before, or take sides. Well, you an' the boss are warrin' again; I can't fight you, an' I won't side again him. You don't leave me any choice—I just have to go away again."

"Oh, I don't want you to go away again," she sez. "You allus find more in things than the rest of 'em ever do, an' I want you to tell me all about those two queer men you spent the winter with, an' to teach me just the way the one you call Hammy used his voice. Happy, you just can't go away again."

"I don't want to go away again," sez I, an' I was down-right in earnest by this time, "but you make me. Barbie, you are hard-hearted. You know that your father thinks the world of you—"

"He don't think one speck more of me than I do of him," she snaps in.

"Yes, but he's different," I sez. "He's your father, an' he has to guide and correct you."

"Well, he don't have to throw in my teeth that I'm a girl every tine I want to do anything."

"I'm disappointed in you," I sez to her in a hard voice. "I thought that you would be game, but you're not."

"What ain't I game about?" sez she.

"You're ashamed of bein' a girl," sez I.

"I ain't," sez she. "I'm glad I'm a girl, an' I want to tell you that the' 's been just about as many heroines as heros too. I don't mean just these patient women who put up with things; I mean heroines in history. Look at Joan of Arc!"

"I never heard of her before," sez I, "but I reckon she must have been Noah's wife." She breaks in an' tells me the story of the French farm girl who got to be the leader of an army and whipped the king of England an' was finally burned; an' then, naturally, became a heroine an' a saint.

"She didn't wear boys clothes, did she?" I sez, thinkin' I had her.

"Yes, she did!" sez Barbie.

"Well, she ought to be ashamed of herself," I said; but I knew I was gettin' the worst of it, so I changes the subject. "But speakin' about the Ark," sez I, "there's another example of your obstinacy. When I went away from here you was fussin' with the school-teachers because they said this whole earth was once under water, an' now I find you cuttin' around an' linin' out missionary-preachers because you ain't suited with the way the Bible was wrote. It looks to me as if you ought to get old enough sometime to realize 'at you ain't nothin' but a child. Your father is willin' to give you a fair show; he don't ask you to act like a girl, all he wants is for you to look like one."

"If I have to wear a skirt, you know mighty well I can't ride," sez she.

"You don't have to wear a thing like what you have on now," I sez. "Why don't you get over your pout an' be sensible. He never asks you to humble yourself. All you need is to do what he wants, an' he'll drop it at once."

"Yes," sez she, "all I need to do is to give up my independence an' he'll think I'm a nice little girl."

"Why don't you figger out some kind of a dress that would look like a girl's and—and work like a boy's?" sez I.

She sat thinkin' for a minute an' then sez, "That wouldn't be a complete surrender, that would only be a compromise; an' I'd be mighty glad to do it if the' was only some way."

"Where's that picture of the girl who whipped the king?" sez I.

She ran an' got it, an' it was a dandy lookin' girl all right,—it looked a little mite like Barbie herself,—but she was wearin' clothes 'at most folks would think undesirable; they was made out of iron an' covered with cloth.

"You don't want to wear any such thing as that, Barbie," sez I, "it would be too blame hot, an' that bedquilt thing's bad enough."

"That's what they used to fight in," sez she.

"They must 'a' been blame poor shots," sez I. "Why, I could shoot 'em through those eye-holes as fast as they came up, an' she don't even wear any head part with hers." Then an idea struck me: "But why don't you make a suit like her outside one?" sez I. "It comes below her knees an' yet she can ride in it all right."

Well, we got old Melisse to help us, an' by four o'clock the thing was done. We had used up some dark-green flannel that Jabez had bought to have a dress made of, an' which she had kicked on. She took it up to her room an' I went out to find Jabez. I told him that she was always willin' to give in when any honorable way was pointed out, an' he was the tickledest man in the West. He went in to supper four times before it was ready, but when it finally was ready Barbie wouldn't come down.

Melisse went after her an' come back sayin' that Barbie didn't feel hungry an' was goin' to wait until after dark an' then wear it outdoors.

"What nonsense!" sez Jabez. "Here she's been wearin' regular buckskin pants, an' now she fusses up about what you say is a half dress. You go an' get her."

I went to the head of the stairs an' called her, an' she finally stuck her head out of her room an' sez, "Happy, I just can't wear this thing. It flaps!"

"Let it flap!" sez I. "You're just like a colt gettin' used to a single-tree; you won't mind it after the first hour. Let me see how it looks."

She opens the door an' stands with a queer new look on her face, an' her cheeks pink as wild roses. I hadn't never seen those cheeks pink up for anything but fun or anger before, an' it flashed upon me what Friar Tuck had told Jabez; an' I was willin' to bet that the time would come when he'd have full as much girl on his hands as any one man could wish.

The waist part of it was loose an' low in the neck an' came to a little below the knees where the leggin's began. The upper part of the leggin's which you couldn't see were loose an' easy. Her little legs looked cute an' shapely, an' her smooth, round throat came up from the open neck mighty winnin'—the whole thing was just right an' I sez to her, "Why, Barbie, this is the finest rig you ever had on, an' you're as purty as a picture."

Well, her face went the color of a sunset an' she slammed the door. "If I was your Dad," sez I to myself, "you'd go back to those buckskins to-morrow." I waited a moment an' then I began to make fun of her, and after a while she came out with her teeth set tight together an' we went down to the dinin' room; but it was the first time I had ever seen her take an awkward step.

"Now that's what I call a sensible garment," sez Jabez, heartily, an' then he begun talkin' to me. Jabez had a lot o' wisdom when he kept his head, an' by the time supper was over Barbie was purty well used to the feel, an' we all three went for a ride; me ridin' Starlight, Barbie, Hawkins, an' Jabez a strappin' bay, one of Pluto's colts, an' a beauty. Well, I'll never forget that ride: you know how tobacco tastes after a man owns up that he was only jokin' when he swore off; you know how liquor seems to ooz all through you after you've been out in the alkali for three months—well, that first ride, after bein' out o' commission for two years, makes these two sensations something like the affection a man has for sour-dough bread. Oh, it was glorious! we all felt like a flock o' birds—hosses an' all. In the first place it was spring, an' that was excuse enough if the' hadn't been any other; but two of us had gone into that day not on speakin' terms, an' now they were closer than ever, an' the third one had brought 'em together. The old sayin' is that three's a crowd, but it took a crowd to hold all the joyfulness that we was luggin' that night, an' it was ten o'clock before we turned around on the velvet carpet an' came swingin' back to the house.

We had to finish with a little race, an' I was rejoiced to see that old Starlight hadn't become a back number, even though the bay colt did make it a mighty close finish.

As soon as we unsaddled, Barbie sort o' whispered to me, "I 'm awful glad you came back, Happy"; an' then she ran into the house.

Jabez shook hands an' sez, "It seems to me, Happy, that I've been waitin' for you for months. I hope to goodness you don't fly up any more."

"I ain't goin' to look for trouble, Jabez," sez I. "This spot is the most homelike to me of any on earth; but I don't believe I'll turn in yet. I want to stroll around a little."

I walked off in the quiet to the little mound where Monody lay, an' I sat there a long while, thinkin' o' the last time I'd come back. The night was unusual warm, an' I hunted up all the stars that I knew, an' watched 'em as they dropped down one by one behind the mountains. I thought of all that Friar Tuck had said about the origin of life, an' what a nerve a child like Barbie had to even study on such a subject. Then I dropped back to all the happiness I'd had that day, an' the last thing I knew I was lookin' into Barbie's eyes an' wonderin' what made her face so pink. It was the cold, gray dawn-wind that woke me up.

CHAPTER TWELVE
THE LASSOO DUEL

That was a summer I love to think over; but the' wasn't nothin' happened to tell about. I was a little soft at first, but it didn't take me long to get my hand in, an' I roped my half o' the winter calves. It had been a mild winter an' the' was a big run of 'em, an' Jabez was in a good humor most o' the time.

The men mostly liked Jabez; but they used to talk a lot about him, as he was some different from the usual run. He had first come into that locality when Barbie was two years old, buyin' the big Sembrick ranch an' stockin' it up to the limit. Ye never said a word about his wife, nor his past; an' Jabez wasn't just the sort of character a man felt like pryin' private history out of.

The men laughed a good bit about the time Jabez had had with the Spike Crick school. He had a fool notion that money was entitled to do all the talkin', an' that's a hard position to make good in a new country. After his money had built the schoolhouse, they refused to elect him one o' the trustees; said it might lead to one-man control. Still, Jabez wasn't no blind worshiper of the law, an' when he found that they'd put a rope on him, he just sidles in an' asserts himself. It was easy enough to convince a teacher that the trustees was boss; but when Jabez began to get impatient, the school-teacher generally emigrated a little. Then they put a cinch on him for true. They hired a woman teacher. When it came to bluffin' a woman teacher, Jabez got tongue-handled so bad that once did him for all time to come.

But the' wasn't any difference of opinion when it came to Barbie. The' wasn't a man on the place who wasn't willin' to stretch a neck for her. She knew 'em all by name an' used to tease 'em an' contrary 'em; but she never hid behind bein' the boss's daughter. Any time they scored, she paid, an' that was the thing that made 'em worship her. She had changed a lot in the five years I'd been away; not only in size, in fact, that was the least noticed in her; but she had more thinkin' spells.

It used to be that she made up to every one right from the start; but now she was a little shy at first, especially with Easterners. Easterners generally are about as tantalizin' as it's possible for a human to get, but she had never minded 'em much until this summer. Now she'd answer the first twenty-five or thirty fool questions polite enough, but after that she got purty frosty an' would ask 'em some questions herself that would straighten 'em up right short in their tracks. About every time an Easterner would pull out I noticed that she'd put a little wider heal on the bottom of her skirt.

But she was purty much the same with me, an' after the spring round-up she used to keep me ridin' with her most o' the time when the' wasn't anything actually demandin' my attention. It was just about this time that Jabez hired a new man by the name of Bill Andrews. He was about as near speak-less as a man ever gets, an' he wasn't much liked by the rest of us; but he was a hard worker an' a good, all-around hand, so he got along all right.

When the fall round-up came, Barbie surprised every one by sayin' she wasn't goin' to do any of the ridin', but would wait until after we'd got all the sortin' out an' brandin' done, an' would then come out an' see the whole herd in a bunch. The' wasn't a thing the matter with her health an' we all wondered what was her reason; but I had my own private opinion—she was beginnin' to find out she was a girl, an' she wasn't quite used to it.

We finally rounded up in the big bend of Spike Crick, an' the stuff was in the suet, every one of 'em. Omaha was supposed to be straw boss; but he was too easy-goin' an' generally let the men do about as they pleased. Bill Andrews, the new man, had a sneer on his face about half the time, an' one mornin' when I came in from night ridin', he sez to a bunch o' the boys: "I didn't suppose the parlor boarder ever risked any night dampness."

They all grinned, 'cause the' wasn't any jokes barred with us; but I didn't grin. I walked over to the group an' I sez: "Is the' anybody else in this outfit that has any o' that brand o' supposin' about 'im?"

"Aw sit down, Happy," they sez; an' "What's the matter, Happy; you gettin' tender?" an' such like things; but Bill Andrews continued to sit an' grin, so I sez to him: "As a rule, the last comer in an outfit has sense enough to either use his eyes or ask questions. I admit that this is a purty easy-goin' place,—they don't even ask where a man comes from when they take him on,—but I've been here off an' on for some time, an' I reckon that the boss is able to figger out whether or not I've been worth what I cost."

"Yes," sez Andrews, slow an' drawly, "the boss—or his daughter."

Three o' the boys grabbed me, but Andrews never moved; so I let go of my gun an' sez, "It seems 'at you're the kind of a hound 'at picks out a safe time to snarl—but the' 'll be other times."

"Any time you wish," sez he, "but I didn't mean what you seem to think. I know well enough 'at the' 'll never be nothin' between you an' her—

the old man knows it too, an' you ain't kept here for nothin' except to be her play-mate."

I was so blame mad I couldn't see. I couldn't speak. I was so infernal het up that I choked an' spluttered; but when I got my hands on his throat I put my finger-prints on his neck-bone. The boys had a hard time tearin' us apart, an' a heap harder time startin' Andrews goin' again; but as soon as he was able to talk, I sez to him, "Now we ain't through with this yet. I'm willin' to give you your choice of settlements, but you sure have to settle some way. How do you want to settle?"

He had black blood—an' he was a coward. It's the hardest mix-up a man ever has to deal with. He jumped to his feet, his face all twisted up in a wolf-snarl, but he couldn't look me in the eyes, an' he finally tries to smile. Its a weak, sickly affair, but it is a smile all right, an' he sez, "We'll just compete to see which is the best man at a round-up, an' we'll settle it that way. The' ain't no use of us makin' fools of ourselves over nothin' at all. I was just jokin' an' I didn't think you'd be so blame pernicious about boldin' down an easy snap; so as the' ain't really nothin' between us, we'll settle it that way."

I had been doin' some quick thinkin' while he was talkin', an' when he finished, I broke out laughin', "Why, you blame rookie," sez I, "you don't really think I was mad, do you? I see 'at you was only jokin' right from the start, but I wanted to do a little play-actin' for the boys here. That'll be the best way of all to settle it—see who's the best man at a round-up."

He looked some relieved when he laughed—an' then he rubbed his neck. I indulged in some hoss-play with Omaha, an' began to eat my breakfast; but all the time I was thinkin'. I was thinkin' several different ways too: first, was the' some truth in what Bill Andrews had said—was I gettin' to be nothin' but the playmate of a girl? Then I wondered if Jabez had studied over it any—I never had myself before. I knew that he never cared nothin' about my wages, knowin' that I had saved him more the night I brought Monody back than he'd ever pay me—but I didn't want to be pensioned, an' I didn't care to be looked on as the ranch watchdog. But the thing that finally came an' refused to leave was a question—what right did I have to waste the best part of my life loafin' around with a child? The' was a lot more o' these pesterin' questions; but they all finally perched on Bill Andrews an' made me want to blow him up with dynamite.

That was the swiftest round-up ever the Diamond Dot had. Bill Andrews was a roper for true, an' I don't believe the' was a man in the West 'at could touch me those days. When me an' Barbie would be out ridin' I was always practicin' with a rope or a gun, an' I had a dozen foller-up throws 'at I've never seen beat. I did my work cleaner an' more showy'n he did, but it couldn't be done much quicker. We finished three days ahead of the schedule an' the boys said it was a tie. I had roped twenty-six more calves'n he had, but they wanted to see us contest a little more, an' they figgered out excuses for him. The' ain't nothin' ever satisfies a civilized human except a finish fight. He don't care a hang for points.

Well, we did all kinds o' fancy ropin', an' I was a shade the better at all of it; but those confounded cusses kept on claimin' it was a tic until I got het up a little, an' sez 'at we'll have a lassoo duel an' that'll settle it, even among blind men. This ain't all amusement, this lassoo-duel on hoss-back, an' I see Andrews look wickedly content. "Nothing barred," sez he; "we rope hoss or rider, either one."

"Sure thing," sez I. I don't know to this day whether or not he really thought I was green, but anyhow, he thought he had me at this game, an' I saw in a moment 'at he had trained his pony; but he didn't have any advantage over me. I was ridin' Hawkins, an' he had been dodgin' ropes all his life an' liked the sport. We fenced for an hour without bein' able to land, an' then he gets his noose over Hawkins' neck. Before he can draw it tight I rides straight at him; his pony has settled back for a jerk; I gets my noose over the pony's neck, a loop over Andrew's right wrist, when he tries to ward it off his own neck, an' then another loop over his shoulders, pinnin' the left arm an' the right wrist to his body. My rope was the shorter now so I sets Hawkins back an' takes a strain. I knew what was goin' to happen when that rope tightened—he would be twisted out of the saddle an' his right arm dislocated—an' he knew it too; an' he knew that I was goin' to do it. The boys was as silent as the ace o'clubs.

His face went pale an' he looked at me with beggin' eyes, but mine was hard as stone. I hated him for all the devil-thoughts he had put into my head, an' I wanted to see him twisted an' torn. Then I just happened to see two riders comin' in from toward the ranch house. I knew by instinct it was Jabez an' Barbie, an' just as Andrews started to twist in the saddle I touched Hawkins with the spurs, rode up to him, threw off the loops, put a smile on my face—an' shook hands with Bill Andrews, while all the boys give a cheer. I was pantin' an' tremblin', but I don't think it was noticed, as I kept that smile as easy-goin' an' good-natured as a floatin' cork.

Well, I kidded with the boys until Jabez got through decidin' on what he wanted done with the different bunches, an' then when he an' Barbie rode back to the house I went along. I made sure to brazen it out as much as possible, an' not to give the impression that I was as het up as I had been; but I knew that Bill Andrews was well aware of what had saved him. I also knew that he'd hate me to the day of his death—but he'd fear me to the last minute, an' he'd never start but one more contest.

The Diamond Dot didn't seem so homelike after that; it was a heap easier to get the best of Bill Andrews than it was to get rid of those questions; but I tried to act just as much the same as possible, only I did as much range ridin' as I could make seem natural. I supposed that Bill Andrews would leave, but he didn't; he stayed right along an' he worked hard an' he never kicked. He was allus friendly with me, but he didn't overdo it, an' things went along smooth as joint oil.

Barbie had gone through all the stuff they taught at the Spike Crick School, an' was studyin' some advance stuff with the teacher who was ambitious to finish her own edication. This was a big surprise to me; I had allus supposed that a teacher knew everything, but it seems not. The' 's lots they don't know, an' the front they put up before a pupil is two thirds bluff. A naked body's a disappointin' sight, but I bet a naked soul would make a crow laugh.

All through that winter I was tryin' to find an excuse to quarrel with Jabez, but the' wasn't none. The' wasn't one hitch in the whole outfit except that I'd lost my taste for it. I couldn't get it out of my head that one man had already taken me for a child's playmate, an' while I knew that this particular man had other views by this time, I didn't know how long it would be before some one else would find that same idea gettin' too big to keep under his breath; so the very second that spring opened I hunted up Jabez one mornin' after I had given old Pluto a special good rubbin', an' after talkin' a while about nothin' at all, I sez to him, "Jabez, I'm goin' to pull out purty soon."

"What for?" sez he.

"The' ain't no chance on this place for a man to get on," I sez.

"What do you want to get on for?" Sez he. Well, that was a fetcher. The great trouble in debatin' with a man is, that he never flushes up the kind of an idea 'at your gun is loaded to shoot. "What does any one want to get on for?" sez I.

"I don't know," sez Jabez, kind o' sad like. "It's been so long since I wanted to get on that I can't remember what fool notion it was that sicked me at it; but it looks to me as though you was doing purty well, considerin' the way you work."

There it was again. It was just for all the world as if the watchdog had gone on a strike for higher wages. "Well, you're right about that," sez I. "If I owned a place like this, I wouldn't board a man who didn't do more than I do. That's one reason why I'm goin' to travel on a little—I 'm gettin' so rusty that the creakin' o' my joints sets my teeth on edge."

"Poor old man," sez Jabez, sarcastic. "I saw you vaultin' over Pluto this mornin'. You'd better be careful, you're liable to snap some o' your brittle bones. I'll have to put you on a pension."

"Pension bell!" I snaps. "I've been pensioned too long already. The' ain't any chance for a man with get-up, over a low grade coffee-cooler on this place, an' I 'm sick of it. I'm goin' to hunt up a job where it will pay me to do my best."

"How much pay do you want, for heaven's sake?" sez he.

"I don't want any more pay for what I 'm doin'," sez I, "but I do want more opportunity. You don't keep any out an' out foreman here an'—"

"An' it wouldn't make any difference if I did," he snaps in. "It's allus best to get an imported foreman, an' not have any jealousy; but confound you, I pay six men on this place foremen's wages—an' you're one of 'em."

"Six?" sez I.

"Yes, I raised Bill Andrews' pay last week. He does more work than any of you, an' he ain't all the time growlin'. He won't never have any friends either, so if I was to choose a foreman he'd be my pick."

"I was foreman of the Lion Head a good many years ago," sez I, "an' I built it up, an' my work was appreciated: but I was a fool kid then. Now I 'm gettin' along in years an' I don't intend to waste any more o' my life."

"How old are ya, Happy?" sez he, laughin'.

"Well, I'll be thirty years old—before so many more years," sez I, lookin' full as indignant as I felt, I reckon.

"You're nothin' but a kid in most things," sez Jabez, an' his voice was so friendly that I began to cool. Then he said, "Why, I never think of you like I do the rest o' the boys, though I rely on you a heap more. You've allus been like one o' the family, like; an' you an' Barbie have played around together until most o' the time I think of ya as about the same age; but if it's anything in the money line, why speak out. I was a young feller myself once, an' if you've happened to run up any debts on some o' your town trips, why I'll pass you over a little extra an' take it out in laughin' at you."

By George, he made it hard for me. One moment he'd tramp on my corn an' the next he'd scratch me between the shoulders; but the more he said the more I see that I did not have any regular place in the team; I was just a colt playin; beside, an' it gritten on me something fierce.

"Jabez," I sez, "it's hard for me to explain myself. I like this place an' you know it; but if you had a son o' your own, you wouldn't like to see him settlin' down before he'd struggled up a little. I'm old enough now to take a practical view o' life, an' I intend to become a business man."

He tried not to grin, I'll say that for him, but he couldn't cut it. "Why, bless your heart, boy, you never will be practical, an' as for business, you have about the same talent for it as a grizzly bear. You enjoy life as you go along, an' you enjoy it full an' free; a business man don't enjoy anything but makin' money. You may be rich some day, but it won't be from attendin' to business. Now take a lay-off if you want to, an' get this nonsense out of your system, then come back here. You know 'at Barbie misses you every minute you're away."

"All right," I sez, "I'll try it. I want to leave this place once, the same as if we was both grownup, not as if we had had a child's quarrel. I'll go an' I'll take my lay-off by bucklin' tight down to business; but if it don't seem to agree with me, why, I'll come back here an' make a report."

"Now, don't stay away long, cause the little girl is lonesome for company, an' as she sez to me the other night, you're better company than any book, an' you've got more intelligence than a school-teacher."

"Yes," I went on, "an' I don't require beatin' as often as a fur rug, an' my hair don't shed off as bad as a dog's, an' if I could just forget that I'm a human bein' I wouldn't be any more bother than the rest o' the furnishings; but that is the one thing that's on my mind just now—I'm a man, an' it's time I began to practice at it."

Barbie wasn't quite so easy to get away from as Jabez was. She couldn't believe but what we'd been quarrelin'. When you came right down to givin' the actual reason for my departure without mentionin' any o' the true cause, it was a rather delicate project for a man who hadn't no experience in makin' political speeches: an' Barbie gave me a purty complete goin' over.

We talked it out for a week, but my mind was made up to go an' the' wasn't anything that could stop me, unless it was mighty important; an' at last she stopped arguin' an' just began to look sorry. That was hardest of all.

"Happy," she sez to me one night when we was ridin' back from Look Out, "don't you think I'm old enough now to ask Dad about what that letter meant?"

I turned an' looked at her; the sun was just about to duck behind the ridge, an' her face was in all its brightness. It was a lot different face from that of the child who had asked the question so long ago. It was serious with its question, an' it looked like the face of a woman. This was the first time she had mentioned the subject since I'd been back, an' I hadn't thought she dwelt on it any more; but I saw now that it lay close up to her heart, an' was the one thing she never could ride away from. "I'm purt' nigh fifteen," she went on. "Fifteen is a goodly age," I sez, but not sarcastic. I was thinkin' of Jabez an' myself that mornin', an' wonderin' if age cut so much figger after all. "Do you an' your dad ever talk about your mother any more?" I asked her.

"Not much," she said. "When one wants to know all, and one don't want to tell any, the' ain't much satisfaction in talkin' about—about even your own mother. Don't you still miss your mother?"

"Well, I wouldn't like to tell everybody," sez I, "but I sure do. Why, if the' was any way on earth that I could go back to her, I'd sure go—this very minute."

"At least you know about her. If I just knew about my mother it might be all right. You can't seem to get close to even a mother when you don't know a single thing about her. If you know people well, you can tell what they'd do under any kind of conditions, an' if you know what they have done, an' what they've been through, you know purty well what they are; but when you don't know anything at all, it makes it hard, awful hard."

I didn't have anything to say to her that would help, so I didn't say anything; an' after we had ridden on a while she said, "Happy, I don't want you to be a business man. The Easterners that rile me up worse than any other kind are the business men. They allus calculate how a thing could be turned into money. Why, if one of 'em lived out here he'd put a cash value on of Mount Savage. They allus make me think o' Dombey."

"What was th' about that buckskin mustang to make you think of a business man?" sez I, thinkin' she meant a little ridin' pony she used to have.

"I don't mean Dobbins," sez she, "I mean a character out of a book. He was such a good business man that he let most of life slip by him. I don't want you to do that." "Well, I'll try not to," sez I, "an' it may be that beginnin' late in life like I am, I won't become enough of a business man to get that way; but the' is one thing sure—I'm through with my nonsense. I'm not goin' around playin' like a boy any more, I'm goin' to start in an' stick to business all this summer, an' see what comes of it."

"Where you goin' to start in?" sez she.

"How do I know?" sez I. "I'm just goin' to knock around till I meet up with a business openin', an' then I 'm goin' to put my full might into it till I know the whole game."

"I don't believe that's the way they do it," sez she. "These ones that I've heard braggin' about bein' business men don't look to me as if they ever did much knockin' around. They generally have everything all planned out when they begin, and then follow out the plans. Are you goin' to start in some town or go into a big city?"

"Well, I can tell you more about it when I get back," sez I. "I stayed three days in San Francisco oncet, but I didn't like it—it was too cramped up. I'm thinkin' o' headin' that way though."

"Well, as soon as you've give business a good fair try-out, you'll come back here an' tell us about it, won't you?" sez she. The sun had dropped by this time; but I could still make out her face in the twilight. The eyes were big an' soft an' glisteny, the lips were parted an' were tremblin' a little; it was a brave little face, but it looked lonesome. Something began to tighten around my heart, an' I didn't want to go; but I had put my hands to the plow, an' I didn't intend to back-track till I'd turned one full furrow. "Yes," I sez. "Honor bright, just as soon as I've give it a fair trial I'll come back an' let you know."

"You'll come before it snows if you can, won't you?" she sez, an' I nodded.

Well, for my part, I'd rather quarrel when I'm goin' to break any ties. I stayed for five meals after that, but they was uncommon dismal. We all tried to act as if everything was runnin' to suit us, an' we all made a successful failure of it. When at last I was ready to leave, Jabez shook my hand and said, "Now this is just a vacation, Happy. Have your outing an' then come back an' settle down here. Do you want to take your money with you, or leave it in the bank until you decide to invest it?"

"What money?" sez I.

He grinned. "Oh, you'll make a business man all right. Don't you remember givin' me six hundred dollars after you came back from the Pan Handle? Well, it's been in the bank ever since, an' it's grew some, I reckon."

"Well, let her keep on growin'," sez I. "I'm goin' to learn the business before I invest in it."

"That's sense," sez he. "Did you ever have any experience?"

"I was clerk in a restaurant once," sez I; "but I didn't like it, an' I don't reckon I'll go into the restaurant business."

Barbie rode a long way with me, but we didn't talk much.

I don't suppose the' ever was a time when we both had so much to say; but we couldn't seem to say it, an' when we came to part all she said was, "Oh, Happy, I hate to see you go, but I'm sure you'll come back in the fall."

"I'll come back as soon as I feel I can," sez I; "an' now don't worry none yourself, an' don't fret your Dad—an' don't forget old Happy." We shook hands long an' firm, an' her eyes seemed tryin' to hold me until I couldn't look into 'em—but I didn't kiss her this time. We both noticed it, an' we both knew 'at while I was partin' from her she was partin' from her childhood. Partin' from anything 'at you've been fond of is mighty sad business; and so I rode away again.

CHAPTER THIRTEEN
BUSINESS IS BUSINESS

I felt entirely different this time. I wasn't smartin' under anger an' unjust treatment; I was goin' out of my own accord an' because I had left behind me the carelessness of boyhood, hood, an' was ready to plow an' plant an' wait for a crop. No more gaiety, no more frivolity, no more heedlessness. I was to scheme an' plan for the future an' not be led astray by every enticin' amusement that beckoned to me.

When I came in sight of Danders the second day, I didn't inquire how my thirst was feelin'—no more thirst emersions for mine. The' ain't any profit in that, sez I to myself; what I want to do is to ease this old skin of a pony along until I can get a piece of money for him; that's business.

I wasn't much acquainted over in Danders, an' I thought it would be easy slidin'; but the first feller I met was a useless sort of a cuss what had been punchin' cows at the Diamond Dot the time the Prophy Gang tried to clean it out, an' he has to tell 'em who I am, an' they had all heard about me an' Bill Andrews; so 'at it was purt' nigh impossible for me to hold out. I apologized for not drinkin', an' they let me off; but the old Diamond Dot hand said he was broke, an' wanted me to shove him a little stake.

Well, that was sure a bad opening: "Business," sez I, "don't let go one cent unless it's goin' to grab another an' fetch it back home;" an' I knew that all I gave this feller would keep in circulation for the balance of eternity. Then a brilliant thought struck me, an' I told him I'd give him one fourth of all he got for the pony over ten dollars. He looked at the pony an' sez, "Who gets the ten dollars?"

"I gets the ten dollars," sez I. "This is business: I own the pony, I pay you wages to sell him, the more you sell him for the more you get."

He looks at me a moment an' then he calls a gang around him an' sez to 'em: "Here's a rich one, fellers. You see this pony—well, he was too blame old to herd geese with when I was punchin' cows over at the Diamond Dot, ten year ago, an' now Happy wants me to sell him, me gettin' one fourth of all I rake in over ten dollars—an' HIM gettin' the ten dollars. What do ya think o' that for nerve?"

Course they all laughed like a lot o' guinea-hens, but I knew that a business man has to overlook the inborn ignorance of his customers, or else it's twice as hard to land 'em; so I just smiled polite.

"What is your first offer, men?" sez my salesman. "Who'll give me a hundred dollars for this grand old relic; this veteran of a hundred wars; this venerable and honorable souvynier of bygone ages?" Well, that blame fool went on pilin' it up while the crowd egged him on by offerin' two bits, an' four bits, an' six bits an' a drink; an' so on until I was disgusted and turned it off as a joke, tellin' the blasted rascal to take the pony an' try to trade him for a night's lodgin'.

He takes my saddle an' bridle off an' puts 'em careful in the hotel, an' then he takes the pony across the street an' begins to rub him down. He rubs him a while an' combs out his stringy mane an' tail with his fingers. Every now an' again he backs off an' examines that pony as though he was actually worth stealin'. I couldn't make out what he was up to, so I stood in front of the hotel watchin' him. Purty soon up comes a tourist what has been lurkin' around in the distance.

"What is the' about that pony that everybody takes such an interest in him for?" sez he, glancin' over to where us fellers was gawkin'.

"Don't you know?" sez the feller, in surprise. I can't quite recall his name now, but I think it was Bill. Anyhow, most fellers' names is Bill, so we'll call him Bill. "Don't you know who this pony is?" sez Bill.

"Why no," sez the tourist. "I just arrived this mornin', an' I'm waitin' for my uncle to send in after me."

"Is that so?" sez Bill. "Well, I'll bet your uncle knows who this pony is. This pony is Captain. Who is your Uncle?"

"Why, my uncle is Charles W. Hampton," sez the tourist.

"You don't say!" sez Bill. "Well, Cholly knows who Captain is all right."

"Oh, do you know him?" sez the tourist.

"Why, everybody knows him around here," sez Bill.

"That's funny; they told me he lived over a hundred and forty miles from here," sez the tourist. "But what is the' about Captain that makes him so wonderful? He don't look like much of a pony to me."

Bill looks at the pony and then he looks at the tourist, then he looks at the pony again an' sez in a low voice: "It ain't on his looks, it's for what he's done that makes Captain famous."

"What's he done?" sez the tourist.

"Did you ever hear of Custer's massacre?" sez Bill.

"Of course I have," sez the tourist, gettin' interested.

Bill, he walks up an' puts his hand on the pony's neck, an' then he turns an' sez proudly, "This here pony is the last survivin' remnant of that historical event."

"You don't say!" sez the tourist. "What are you goin' to do with him?"

"I don't want to say a word again the flag of my country," sez Bill, holdin' tip his hand, "but my country ain't got the gratitude it ort to have when it comes to hosses. I don't blame 'em for condemnin' the common run o' hosses an' sellin' 'em to wear out their pore lives in—in toilsome labor, but when it comes to a hoss with a record like Captain—well, I kept him as long as I could afford it. Now I'm goin' to give him a good groomin', spend my last penny in givin' him one more feed, an' then take him out on the broad free prairie of his native soil—an' shoot him. Of course I could sell him, but I won't do it. I'd rather give him a soldier's death than to have him hammered around in his old age, after all he's done for his country."

Well, the tourist, he gets all het up over it, an' then he comes over to where us fellers gathered. We're standin' in solemn awe, an' he sees the' ain't any of it put on; but he can't tell that it ain't respect for what the pony has done that makes us so solemn; he can't see 'at we 're off erin' up our tribute to Bill.

"Do any of you gentlemen know anything about that pony?" sez the tourist.

"Who, Captain!" sez a tall, lanky, sad-lookin' puncher. "Well, it ain't likely that you can find a man in the West who wouldn't recognize that pony by the description. That there pony was in the Custer Massacre."

"The gentleman what owns him is goin' to shoot him," sez the tourist.

"Well, perhaps it's all for the best," sez the sad one. "I ain't no millionaire, but I offered him thirty-seven dollars for that pony. He doubted that I'd take good care of him, so he wouldn't sell him to me. He said he didn't think I'd abuse the pony when I was sober, but I'll have to own up that when a friend—when a friend invites me to have a drink, I can't say no—an' I got a darn sight o' friends in this country."

The' ain't no use in draggin' this out. After that tourist had agreed to treat that pony like the saints of glory, Bill, he finally sold him to him for an even fifty dollars—an' it was me that bought the liquor for the crowd.

I'm good-natured enough to suit any one reasonable, but I own up I was sore. Here I'd started out with the best intentions in the world, with my mind all made up not to be led into temptation or turned from a set purpose, an' what was the first result? I had simply given my entire stock in trade away to a worthless loafer, an' had seen him sell it for fifty dollars after he had made all manner of fun of me for offerin' one fourth of all he made over ten. Why, the pony was worth seven dollars, an' I could have sold him for that money myself if I hadn't let them laugh me into showin' of. Then to top off with, I'd blown in about a month's wages just to show the gang I was able to take a joke when it was measured out to me.

I was ready right at that minute to own tip that business didn't come natural to me; but I enjoyed myself plenty enough until along toward mornin', an' then the penjalum begun to swing back. I sat over in the corner kickin' myself purty freely, when a funny, twisted little man came over an' sat across from me. He had pink-like cheeks an' shiny little eyes, an' he was middlin' well crowded with part of the wet goods I had been payin' for. "It was one o' the smoothest business deals I ever saw put through—on a small scale," sez he.

"Oh, hang business," sez I.

"Well, it's a hangin' matter often enough," sez he. "Do you know the reason why the' 's so much devilment in this world?"

"It's 'cause the' 's so many people here," sez I; "that's easy enough."

"It's 'cause the preachers ain't got the nerve to explain what the commandments mean," sez he.

It was an awful curious little man, an' I kind o' straightened up an' give him a searchin' look: "I've met a heap like you," sez I. "Some folks think that preachers is paid to make the world better, but they ain't. They're paid so that when a feller's conscience hurts him he can just lay all the sins of the whole world on the preachers."

"They deserve 'em," sez the little man. "What does it mean to steal?"

"Why, any fool knows what stealin' is," sez I. "It's takin' something that don't belong to you."

"How can you tell what does belong to you," he sez, leanin' forward as if he was makin' a point.

I looked at him an' saw that he really thought he was talkin' sense, so I sez: "You go talk to some one else. I'm too sleepy an' I'm too blame sore to bother with such nonsense."

"It ain't nonsense," sez he. "I'm an edicated man, an' I been studyin' life ever since I been born. My father was a preacher across the water, an' I got arrested for stealin' a bottle of whiskey when I wasn't nothin' but a boy. The whole family was disgraced on account of me, an' my father told 'em to go ahead an' give it to me hard. Now I stole that whiskey on a dare, an' I stole it from a good church member; but all the rest of my life I been stretchin' that there commandment until I tell you the whole human race is one set o' thieves."

Well, I was purty sleepy, but the little old man had an eye in him like a headlight, an' he just made you listen to him. "The' ain't no sense in your slingin' mud that way," sez I. "The' 's lots of men 'at wouldn't steal, if they had a chance."

"If I ruin my constitution through depravity, is it stealin'?" sez he.

"No," sez I, "it's darn foolishness."

"It is stealin'," sez he, "just as much as if I help to waste natural products what can't be replaced—stealin' from the children of the next generation, an' all the followin' generations."

"What rights have they got?" I sez, losin' my patience. "They ain't even born yet."

"Did you ever see a baby?" sez he.

"Yes," I sez, "I bet I've seen a dozen of 'em."

"Well," sez he, "was they polite? Did they beg for what they wanted? Did they have any doubt but that they'd be plenty of everything to go around?"

"Not them what I saw," sez I. "They'd give one little coo, to see if any one was handy, an' then they'd holler an' yell an' scold an' fuss until they got what they wanted."

"Do you suppose if they didn't have any rights they'd have the nerve to carry on that way?" sez he.

"Rights!" sez I. "They didn't have to have rights—they had mothers."

Well, that set him back a good ways, an' by the time he had thought up some new stuff I was asleep; but he shook me awake an' sez, "Of course the child's mother will do all she can; but supposin' she ain't got what the child wants—how'll she explain it to him?"

"She won't bother explainin' nothin' to a baby," sez I. "She'll just send the old man out to get it."

He looked sort o' disgusted like, as if he wasn't used to arguin' with a man what could handle logic an' make points. "You're just like the rest," sez he. "What I mean is, that every man who has ever been on earth is just sort of an overseer for them what is yet to come. We have the right to use everything we want in the right way, but we haven't any right to waste it or destroy it, or hog it up so that all can't enjoy it. Why, when you start to savin' an' draw in what ought to be circulatin', you steal from them what haven't had the chance 'at you've had. It's wicked to be thrifty."

"Well, you're the craziest one I've seen yet," sez I, laughin'. "Why, if you had your way you'd utterly ruin business."

"Business!" he yells, gettin' excited. "Do you know what business is?"

I thought a moment. "I don't know all the' is to know about it," sez I, "but I expect to give it a fair good work-out before I'm through with it."

"Business," he sez, leanin' across the table an' hittin' it with his fingernail, "business is simply havin' the laws fixed so you can steal without havin' to pay any fine. What is business? Ain't it figgerin' an' schemin' to get away from a man whatever he happens to have? That's nothin' but stealin'."

"Confound you," sez I, "do you mean to say that just because I'm goin' to engage in business I'm a thief?"

He looked at me a moment an' then he shook his head. "No," he sez, "you won't never be that kind, you'll be some other kind; but that's about all business is—just thievery. Why, I once knew two men 'at was the best friends 'at ever lived; an' they just ruined their lives 'cause they couldn't resist the temptation of each tryin' to grab all. It was over the Creole Belle—"

"Yes, but she was a woman!" I yells, jumpin' to my feet, an' leanin' over the table.

"No, it was a mine," sez he, sittin' still.

"A Creole is a cross-breed woman 'at came from New Orleans," sez I; "an' when they're good lookin' enough, they call 'em belles."

"Well this here mine 'at I'm goin' to tell you about was called the Creole Belle," he sez. "For a longtime it didn't pay to amount to anything, an' then it began to pay; an' the two friends got covetous, an' first George had Jack killed an' then he gets killed himself by Jack's—"

"No, he wasn't killed," I snaps in like a blame fool.

The old man looked at me with his little shiny eyes all scrouged up. "Who wasn't killed?" he sez, slow an' cautious. "Why, George Jordan wasn't killed," I sez.

"What would a kid like you know about it" sez he.

"Well, I do know 'at he wasn't killed," I sez. "I been workin' for him; he don't live but a short way from here. Tell the the whole story. I'll make it worth your while. Come on, what'll you have to drink?"

He leaned forward with his hand clutchin' at his side, an' his pink checks gray an' twisted. He coughed a dry, short cough, an' groans out between his set teeth. "It 's my heart; I got a bum pump. You tell George Jordan that I never breathed a word of it, but that Jack Whitman—Oh, my God! Get me a drink of whiskey! Get me a drink of hell-fire!"

He doubled up, grabbin' an' clawin' at his breast while I jumped to the bar yellin' for whiskey. I grabbed the bottle an' hustled back to him, but he was all crumpled up on the floor. We straightened him out an' rubbed his wrists an' poured whiskey down his throat, an' after a while he opened his eyes. The minute his senses got back to him he clutched at his heart again, rollin' an' writhin', an' makin' noises like a wounded beast. "I knew it would end this way," he gasped. "I'm goin' out now, but listen to what I say"—he helt his breath to keep from coughin'—"the' ain't no sin but stealin'. Don't never take nothin' that don't belong to ya."

All his muscles grew rigid an' twisted, an' then a smile came on his face an' he sank back. They had the doctor there by that time, but the' wasn't anything to be done, except to give a big heathen name to what had been the matter with him. There he lay on the bar-room floor; the' was filth an' refuse all around him, but the smile on his face was just plumb satisfied, an' yet it was a knowledgeable smile too. I could 'a' cried when I thought that this man, who could have told little Barbie what she wanted to know, had wasted all that time tryin' to convince me that business an' stealin' was all one. What he knew wouldn't do him a mite o' good, wherever he was; an' yet the' wasn't any way on earth to bring him back long enough to have him tell it.

They told me his name was Sandy Fergoson, an' that he was harmless crazy. He used to float around doin' odd jobs an' talkin' nonsense about stealin'; but nobody knew where he had come from, so I chipped in a little something to help bury him, an' gave up the rest of my money for a ticket to Frisco.

I didn't enjoy that trip to Frisco; business didn't seem so attractive when you once set out to find her, an' then again, I was broke. I don't mind bein' broke when I 'm on the range 'cause a feller can pick up a job anywhere; but I wasn't city-wise, an' I didn't know how long it would take me to track down the kind o' business I wanted to engage in.

I suppose cities must suit some folks, or they wouldn't keep on livin' in 'em; but cities sure don't suit me. I allus had a kind of an idea from what Slocum had told me that I'd enjoy the bankin' business, so I applied to the banks first. They're a blame offish set, bankers. They didn't laugh at me,—leastwise not until after I'd gone out,—but they didn't offer much encouragement. I tramped around that city for four days, an' by the time I finally got located in business my appetite was tearin' around inside my empty body till I couldn't sleep nights. Oh, it was not joyful! I had taken the position of porter in a mammoth big drygoods store, an' I was some glad when noon arrived; but no one called me to partake of dinner, so I went up to a young lad, an' sez, "Where do they spread it?"

"Spread what?" sez he.

"Dinner," sez I.

"I bring mine with me," sez he.

"Is the grub that rotten?" sez I.

"What grub?" sez he. "You surely don't think they serve meals here, do you?"

"Do you mean to tell me that I got to find myself, out of forty a month?" sez I.

He started to make up a joke, but I looked too famished to trifle with; so he explained to me that all we got was wages, an' we couldn't even sleep in the store. I was gettin' purty disgusted with business, but he told me that the man what owned the whole store had started in as a porter; so I went back an' portered harder than ever that afternoon, wonderin' what in thunder kind of a man it was who could save enough out of a porter's wages to buy a store like that. I was dressed some different from the rest o' the folks around there, so I attracted a lot of attention, an' the' wasn't much I did that wasn't enjoyed by more or less of a crowd. When quittin' time came I hustled up to the feller what had hired me an' told him I'd like to have my day's pay. "We don't pay until Saturday night," sez he, hustlin' out o' the store. I stood on the sidewalk thinkin'; an' what I was thinkin' of, was the nonsense 'at Sandy Fergoson had been talkin'. It didn't sound so foolish now.

The' was a little restaurant across the street, an' the owner of it had noticed me washin' the windows—he had seemed to enjoy it too. I went over an' told him that I would like to board with him if he would make me rates. He sized me up an' sez he would board me for six dollars a week. I didn't see how I could save enough to buy a store out of four dollars a week, an' after I got tired o' seein' the sights I'd have to rent a bed somewheres too; but what I needed then was food, so I agreed.

I sat down an' begun to eat slow, 'cause it's always best to warm up careful on a long job. I et away peaceful an' contented until I got good an' used to it again, an' then I kept the waiters hoppin' purty lively. The proprietor took a deep interest in me, an' dodged around so he could have an unobstructed view; while the rest of the guests got to noticin' too, an' when they'd finish they'd just stick around an' keep cases, until after a while things began to jam, an' every time I'd order in some new food they'd make bets on whether I'd be able to finish it or not. When I finally quit, the proprietor came up to me on a run an' sez, "Are you sure you have had all you wish?"

"Yes," I sez, "an' I ain't no fault to find with the cookin' either."

He eyed me all over, an' then he drew me to one side. "I don't want to go back on my word," sez he, "an' I don't intend to charge you a cent for this meal; but Great Scott, man, I wouldn't board you for six dollars a day, let alone six dollars a week."

I didn't intend to let him know that I was stone broke, 'cause it didn't seem the thing in a business man; but I did tell him that I hardly ever et quite so much as I had that night. Still, he wouldn't take any chances, so I took my blankets an' went on. I was purty sleepy after my meal, an' it was just all I could do to stagger up an' down the hills, before I found a place to flop in. It was under a little tree in a big yard, an' I got out at sun-up 'cause I didn't want any one to see a business man occupyin' such quarters as that. I didn't miss breakfast much that day, an' I went about my work singin' an' whistlin'. Just before noon I found a hundred dollars on the floor close to the door.

I asked every one around if they had lost any money, an' most of 'em said no, an' them what bad lost any—an' the' was a purty high average that mornin'—had all lost the wrong amount, or else it was in a different kind of a sack; so I knocked off at noon, went to a new restaurant, an' et a fair meal, which they charged me one dollar for. I thought that was goin' a little stout for a porter, but I knew I'd find a place where I could live on my income as soon as I got better acquainted, an' I was purty light-hearted when I got back that noon.

"You're nineteen minutes late," sez the floor boss.

"Is that so; what's happened?" sez I, pleasantly.

"You are not supposed to take more than an hour for lunch," sez he.

"Well, you can just take the nineteen minutes out of the time I saved up yesterday," sez I.

"You must understand right at the start that business depends on method," sez he, sour like. "Mr. Hailsworth wishes to see you at once."

Hailsworth was the capital letter o' that outfit, an' I was glad o' the chance to see him, 'cause the' was some several changes I wanted to make in the porterin' department. I follered the floor boss upstairs an' back to a private room, where a little wizen-faced old man sat up an' looked at me over his spectacles. "I understand you found some money?" sez he.

"I did," sez I. "Do you know who lost it?"

"Well, no, not yet," sez he; "but of course you understand that any money that is found in this building belongs to the firm, unless its rightful owner claims it."

"Well that's a new wrinkle" sez I. "Why don't it belong to me?"

"'Cause you have hired your time to me, an' whatever you find here you find in my time, so it's mine. This is the law, an' I am very busy. Just hand it over at once."

"That ain't right," sez I, "an' I don't intend to hand over a nickle of it."

"Then we'll have to arrest you," sez he. I put my hand down to my leg, but both my guns was rolled up in my blankets. "I'm goin' out to see a lawyer," sez I, thinkin' that would be more business-like than to tell him I 'd blow the top of his head off. The' was lots more things I wanted to tell him, but it took most o' my strength to manage my self-control; an' I allus like to have good footin' when I make my spring. I didn't feel at home, either, an' that's a heap. It kind o' got on my nerves to see that little shrimp squattin' there behind his spectacles an' tellin' me what I had to do, the same as if I was a hoss. I turned on my heel and strode out o' that store head up an' I was some glad that Hammy had taught me what strodin' was, 'cause the rest o' the gang opened up a path you could 'a' drove a street-sprinkler through.

I didn't like the looks o' that lawyer, he reminded me of a rat. I don't care much for the law anyhow. All the law is fit for is to take care o' the weak an' the ignorant—an' they can't afford it. I've noticed that much, the little time I've been penned up in cities. This lawyer o' mine had full command o' the kind o' talk that bottles up a man an' keeps him from expressin' himself. He said I had a good case an' that he would save me my findin's, but that I had to give him half of it for his services—in advance. If you don't tell a lawyer the truth he can't fight your case; an' if you do you put yourself in his power. Course I don't claim to be authority, but I just actually don't like the law.

When I came away from the law office, a nice friendly feller got into conversation with me, an' after I'd bought him a couple o' drinks, he grew confidential an' told me his troubles. He was owner of a whole block of buildin's an' a lot o' residence houses, but he was stone broke. He had had a quarrel with the banks, an' couldn't raise a penny, an' he had lost ten thousand dollars the night before, gamblin'. He said it would take forty dollars for him to go to Los Angeles, where he had friends who would lend him any amount. Otherwise they would foreclose the little mortgage he had on the business block.

He talked along until I couldn't stand it any longer, so I give him the forty on the condition that I was to be his collecting agent at wages of two hundred a month, as soon as he got back from Los Angeles.

I went down to the station with him and then I hunted up a place where I took board and lodging for a week at six dollars in advance. This left me purt' nigh two dollars to go on until the real estate owner got back. I called around at my lawyer's every day, an' he told me just to lay low an' he'd keep me out o' trouble. Then the sixth day passed without the real estate owner I told the lawyer about it an' asked him if he thought anything might have happened. He got awful mad an' said he'd ought to be kicked for not chargin' me ninety-five dollars for his services in the first place; an' by Jinks that was the truth: that rascally real-estate owner wasn't nothing but a flim-flammer.

At first I couldn't believe that the block he had showed me over didn't belong to him; but when I did I was ready to wreak vengeance. The lawyer said that wreakin' vengeance wasn't a thing that paid in city life, but that if I ever met up with that flim-flammer I could scare a lot of money out of him. My lawyer was a purty good sort of a feller, after all, an' he gave me a lot of high-class advice. He told me that it might be years before my case came up, an' that the' wasn't any use of me waitin' around for it. Then he talked about business, an' he an' Sandy Fergoson had about the same ideas of it, though they used different words. He told me that it was all right for a boy to start in in some old business an' learn the trade, but that the thing for a man to do was to get a start in a smaller town, an' then after he'd learned the ropes to come to the big town an' cut things wide open.

The more I thought over this the better it looked to me; but I hardly knew where to start in. Then the thought struck me that about the best business move I could make was to go to Los Angeles an' scare enough money out of the flim-flammer to give me a good start in some little business of my own. My board bein' out an' my cash bein' likewise, I had to travel on foot; but as my back was pointed toward Frisco, I didn't mind that much.

I trudged along for several days, an' the' was enough people along the line to welcome me to my meals, so I begun to get more resigned to bein' a human again. The farther I got from Frisco the nearer I got to Los Angeles, an' though I was some anxious to meet up with the flim-flammer, I finally began to doubt if he was worth the bother, an' besides, he might not be there anyway.

I was beginnin' to get good an' sick of business; an' I was more than convinced that gettin' a feller's own consent to engage in it wasn't the hardest step he'd ever have to take. Wayside friends was beginnin' to get mighty scarce, an' I was feelin' lonesome above the average one mornin', when I came to a pause in front of one o' these little six-acre ranches where they raise lawn grass an' fresh air. It was a purty, restful sort of a place, with a double row of trees leadin' up to the house, an' somethin' seemed to be drawin' me in at the front gate, although I couldn't smell any food cookin', either. I only waited about a minute, an' then I followed the draw.

I'm a firm believer in Fate. Fate is a funny word: leave the first letter off, an' it's the cause; leave the last letter off, an' it's the result. Barbie found this out one night when we was discussin' Fate. But I mean the sober side o' Fate, when I say I believe in it. A train starts out o' New York city just the same time that a fool cow puncher ropes a pony so he can ride to town for a big time. The puncher reaches the washed-out railroad bridge five minutes before the train—what do you call that?

I was thinkin' o' these things while I was walkin' up the drive-way; an' when I raised up my hand to knock, I felt just as if I'd been sent for.

CHAPTER FOURTEEN
THE CHINESE QUESTION

It happened just like I thought it would. I hadn't more than struck the fourth or fifth tap before the door was opened by the finest little woman you ever saw. She had a worried lock on her face, but when she saw me the clouds rolled away an' she smiled clear into my heart. She was a real lady— it stuck out all over her, like a keep-off-the-grass sign.

"Are you the man?" sez she.

"Well, I'm one of 'em," sez I.

"You know I sent clear to San Francisco for a man," sez she, "an' I suppose you're the man."

"To tell you the honest truth," sez I, "I was so preoccupied in Frisco that I clean forgot to stop around for my mail, but as long as we're conversin' on this subject, I'll just be bold enough to say 'at I'll take the job, without askin' what it is."

"Have you had a wide experience?" sez she.

"Wide?" sez I. "Wide, only just begins to give you a hint at it. I ain't filled with the lust of vanity, nor I ain't overly much given to tootin' my own horn; but in my humble an' modest way I guarantee to be able to do anything on this good, green earth 'at don't require a book edication."

"Can I trust you?" sez she, lookin' into my face mighty searchin'.

"If you sell me anything," sez I, smilin' as near like a baby as I could, "you'll have to trust me, 'cause I'm dead broke." She just stood an' looked in through my face; an' I tell ya, boys, I was mighty glad that in all this rip-snortin' world the' wasn't one single woman who could rise up an' say that I hadn't played fair. She kept on lookin' into me, until I knew she was readin' everything I had ever done or said or thought, an' the sweat was tricklin' down my back like meltin' snow.

"Yes," she sez finally, "I can trust you."

"Don't you never doubt it," sez I. "All you need to do is to issue the orders, an' if I don't carry 'em out, why, just tell the folks not to send flowers. I ain't long on talk, but I'll agree to carry out any plan you've got, from ditchin' a limited to shootin' up a Methodist Church. That's me," sez I, "an' now let's have the news."

Talk about bein' surprised! I thought she had a fence war on her hands at the least; but what she wanted me to do was to take care of a gentle old pair o' hosses, milk a cow, tend a garden, cut the grass, an' help around the house. By the time she finished the program, I felt like a fightin' bulldog when a week-old kitten spits at him. Here I was, willin' to leave my hide tacked up on her barn, an' all she wanted was a kind of lady-gardener. I just sort o' wilted down on the steps, an' I must 'a' turned pale, 'cause she said to me, "Why, you must be hungry. Haven't you had your breakfast?"

"Oh, yes," sez I, "day before yesterday."

Then she begun to rustle about an' fix me up a snack, an' I was glad I had followed the finger o' Fate. The bill o' fare seemed altogether adapted to my disposition.

While I was fillin' up the chinks an' crevices, she dealt out a varigated assortment of facts. It seemed they lived there on account o' the health o' the baby. Her husband had had to go East, an' would be there some six weeks longer. When he had left, she had an Irish cook, an' a Chinaman as polite as an insurance agent; but as soon as he was gone, the Chink began to take liberties, the cook packed up her brogue an' headed for an inhabited community, an' then the Chink concluded that all he saw was his'n. She finally took a brace a' told him to hit the trail, an' he had gone off, vowin' to come back an' burn down the whole place. This was her first year there, an' the closest neighbor was seven miles across country, an' not well acquainted.

She expected her cousin in a week or so, but as it was, she was beginnin' to have trouble with her nerves. Then I was glad that I had made her my little openin' address, 'cause she had joyfulled up like a desert poney when he smells water.

Well, I put in a rich an' useful day, as the preacher sez. First, I rode one o' the veterans over to the station about ten miles away, an telegraphed the other man not to bother; then I came back an' wed the onions, washed the dishes, ran the washin' machine—say, I was bein' entertained all right, but every minute I felt like reachin' to see if my back hair wasn't comin' down.

Me an' the cow had the time of our life that night. She had missed a couple o' milkin's, an' didn't seem to care much about resumin' payment; so I finally had to rope an' tie her, an' milk up hill into a fruit-jar. Talk about bein' handy? I didn't know but what next day I'd be doin' some plain sewin', or tuckin' the crust around a vinegar pie.

That night after supper she put the kid to bed an' then came down, an' we went around nailin' the house up. Finally she showed me where to flop. It was in her husband's cave, I believe she called it—a little room full o' books an' pipes an' resty-lookin' furniture. The' was a big leather bunk, an' that was where I was to get mine. Her room was at the head of the stairs, an' she had a rope goin' over the transom with a bell hangin' to it, close in front of my door. The bell was to be my signal if she heard the Chink attack before I did. Just before she went upstairs she reached into the bosom of her dress an' fished out a real revolver, about the size of a watch-charm. She held it in her hand and looked into my eyes with her lips tight set.

"Are the mosquitoes as bad as that?" sez I.

"I carry this all the time, to defend myself an' child," sez she, rufflin' up like a hen when you pick up her chicken, an' she was so earnest about it that I nearly choked, swallerin' a grin; 'cause honest, I could 'a' snuffed the thing up my nose.

I pulled a long face an' sez to her as solemn as a judge, "Is there enough food and water in the house to stand a siege, in case the Chinaman'd pen us up?" Her face grew drawn an' worried until she caught the twinkle in my eye, an' then she broke into a simile an' tripped upstairs like a girl. I stood out in the hall a moment lookin' after her an' I was mighty glad I had come. We was both in need of company; her mind was a heap easier than it had been that mornin', an' I felt better than I had for some several days. I couldn't see where Sandy Fergoson had told me anything that would get me any nearer what Barbie wanted to know; an' yet I couldn't keep my mind off studyin' over it, except when I was busy. It was the same with Bill Andrews, an' I was glad to have some one new to worry over until I got tuned up again.

As soon as she shut an' locked her door, I backed into my stall an' looked about. The' was some invitin' lookin' books on the wall, an' I read over the titles, finally selectin' one called, "The Ten Years' Conflict." Now, if ever the' was a name framed up to deceive the innocent, this here was the name. I opened the book with my mouth waterin', thinkin' I was about to wade through two volumes of gore; but it started out to tell about the Church of Scotland, an' I wasn't able to keep awake to even the beginnin' of the scrap; so I started to prepare myself for the morrow's duties, as the preacher sez.

After I had opened my roll an' took out my guns, so I could show 'em to her in the mornin' an' sort o' cheer her up, I shed my boots an' proceeded to occupy my bunk. Say, it was like floppin' down on a tubful o' suds. Springs! Well, you should have seen Uncle Happy bouncin' up an' down. I reckon I went to sleep in mid-air, 'cause I was too tired to remember whether I was a husky maid or a tender man.

When I came to, I thought it must sure be the last day, an' that I had waited for the very last call. The dinner-bell was a-knockin' all the echoes in the house loose an' they was fallin' on my ear-drums in bunches. I rushed out into the hall an' grabbed that bell by the tongue, an' give a yell to let her know that I was ready for orders. She opened the door an' came to the head of the stairs, an' sez, "Hush-shh! Don't make any noise."

"Noise!" sez I. "The' ain't any left. You used up all the raw material. What seems to be wrong?"

"Fido has just been growlin'," sez she, in a low whisper, "an' I heard a noise out in the bushes."

"What shall I do?" sez I. "Come up there an' toss Fido out into the bushes, so as to kill two birds with one stone?"

"No," sez she. "If you are willin' to take the risk, I wish that you would go out the front door an' lock it after you. Then look around careful and see if he is settin' fire to the house. Take my revolver an' Fido, an' do be careful not to get hurt—an' don't kill him unless you have to."

"I won't kill him unless I see him, an' he won't hurt me unless he sees me first," sez I. "You better keep Fido an' the gun. I don't want to be bothered with a couple o' noncombatants."

Fido was a little black woolly-faced dog, an' he didn't impress me as bein' no old Injun-fighter. I went out an' chased a cat out o' the bushes; but didn't flush up a single thing wantin' to disturb the peace, except the goat. He was the most frolicsome goat I ever see, an' he about got my tag before I heard him comin'. I rummaged the place purty thorough, an' after tellin' her that all was well, I folded my wings an' went to roost on the leather bunk again.

Twice more that night the clanging bell summoned me to go forth an' chase imaginary Chinamen, an' then my patience begun to get baggy at the knees. I wanted to be up in time to gather the milk before the heat of the day, an' I was a couple o' nights shy on my sleep already. The last time I took Fido along an' dropped him into the feed-bin, where he could hunt Chinamen to his heart's content 'thout disturbin' my beauty sleep.

Our days flowed along smooth an' peaceful; but most o' the nights I put in huntin' Chinamen. No, I wouldn't have killed one if I could have found him—well, not all at once. I got so I could churn an' dust an' do fancy cookin', until if they'd been any men in that locality, I reckon one would have chose me to be his wife—an' then came the cousin.

She'd been tellin' me all about him—it's miraculous the way a woman's talk'll flow after it's been dammed up a spell. He was from Virginie an' was goin' to college to study chemistry, whatever that is; an' he was an athlete an' a quarter-back an' a coxswain—oh, he was the whole herd, the cousin was. I begun to feel shy whenever I thought of him. I feared he might arrive when I was peelin' spuds with my apron on, an' he might choose to kiss me.

I drove to the station after him; but nobody got off the train except a nice lookin' boy with outlandish clothes, an' a couple o' trunks. After the train had pulled out, he sez to me, "Can you tell me the way to Mrs. B. A. Cameron's?"

"I can sight you purty close," sez I. "That's my present headquarters. You—you ain't Ralph Chester Stuart, are ya?"

"You win," sez he, as though we had made mud-pies together. "Come on, let's load the trunks an' trip toward where ther's a noise like food. I'm troubled with what they call a famine."

We drove along, an' he was as merry as a bug an' talked a langwidge the like of nothin' that I had ever met up with before; but I was tryin' to fit his real size with my idea of it. I had been lookin' for a six-footer with bulgy muscles an' a grippy jaw. This pink-cheeked boy didn't look like no athlete to me. He was so cute an' sweet that I felt like hangin' a string o' coral beads around his neck an' savin' him for my adopted daughter. I had just concluded to hand over the dish-washin' right at the start, when he fished up a pipe out of a case, filled it, an' begun to puff like a grown-up, an' then I savvied that dish-washin' wasn't one of his hobbies. "Any sport here?" sez he.

"If you're good at dreamin'," sez I, "you can have the time of your life huntin' Chinamen. I never see a place yet where the huntin' was so plentiful an' the game so scarce."

He got interested in a minute an' told me he had a shotgun, a rifle, an' three revolvers.

"I wish I could write Chinese," sez I.

"What for?" sez he.

"So I could put up a sign warnin' him away," sez I. "Why, if we'd all three get a chance at that Chinaman, it'd take me a solid week to clean him off the lawn."

Ches an' me got along fine. He was a game little rooster, an' his college stories used to tickle me half to death. I never would have believed that a little feller could 'a' been a college athlete; but Ches had got his pictures in the papers, time an' again. At college they race in a boat about the size an' shape of a telegraph pole, eight of 'em rowin' an' the coxswain perched tip behind, pickin' out the path an' tellin' the rowers not to think of their future, but to kill theirselves right then if it will win the race. Ches sez that the coxswain is the most important man in the boat. He had a good deal the same views about the quarter-back, in fact he took what they call a purely personal estimate of life.

He showed me how to play football. It's pleasant pastime, but too excitin' for a frail thing like me. He gave me his cap to carry, an' told me to back off about twenty feet, an' try to run over him, or stick my stiff-arm in his face or dodge him—any way at all to get by. I backed off an' then I looked at him. He looked about as hard to get by as a toadstool.

"Now, Ches, I don't want to have your blood on my head," I sez, "an if you've just been jokin', why say so." But no, nothin' would do but I must run him down. I never won much of a reputation for bein' slow, an' I weigh one ninety when I'm ganted down to workin' trim. I took a full breath an' sailed into him. I intended to give a jump just before I reached him an' go clear over his head, but I lacked the time. Just as I took my jump he gave a lunge, wrapped himself about my lower extremities, an' we sailed up among the tree-tops. All the way up I was tryin' to figure out how it happened; but when we struck the earth again, I didn't care. I knew it would never happen again. I'd shoot first.

We lit on top of my face an' whirled around a few times an' then sort o' crumbled up in a heap, with him still shuttin' off the circulation in my legs. "Down!" sez he, "an' now the ball is dead."

"I can't answer for the ball," sez I, "but I'm about as near bein' in the coffin mood myself as I ever get at this season of the year. What game did you say we was indulgin' in?"

"This is football," sez he.

"I'm glad to know it," sez I, "so that in the future when any one issues an invitation for me to play football I can make arrangements for provin' an alibi. If I HAD to play a game like this I should choose to be the ball."

He was full o' little ways like this an' entertained me fine; but it was mighty hard to wring any useful work out of him. He used to prune the rose vines, and now and again he'd do a little dustin'; but once when I had to bake sourdough bread, I pointed out that the garden needed weedin', an' explained to him just what effect weedin' had on garden truck. He sez to me, "My motto is, 'Competition results in the survival of the fittest.' I ain't no Socialist." When I asked him what this bunch of words meant, he told me that he didn't know of any exercise 'at would do me so much good as learnin' to think for myself; an' that's all the satisfaction I could get out of him. He was some like other edicated persons I've met up with: when you tried to get him to do something useful, he'd fall back on his book knowledge, roll out a string of high steppin' words, an' then look prepossessed.

He was good about one thing, though: he just about took the night trick off my hands, so that I begun catchin' up with my sleep again. He used to load himself down with firearms an' he and Fido would hunt Chinamen two or three hours every night, but he never had no luck. Several times the neighbors rode by an' they told us that the' was a gang breakin' into houses an' stealin', but they couldn't seem to get any track of 'em.

One mornin' I was tryin' to find out what made the sewin' machine drop stitches, when he came runnin' in with his eyes stickin' out like a toad's.

"He's been sleepin' in the barn," sez he.

"Who—the horse?" sez I, thinkin' it was one of his jokes.

"No," sez he, "the Chinaman."

Well, I looked at him, an' he explained how his suspicions had been aroused, an' that he had made a practice of stirrin' up the straw each evenin', an' then each mornin' would find the print of a man's body but that he had put tar on the ladder without gettin' any evidence.

I pricked up my ears at this, an' turned the machine out on pasture for a while. We went to the barn, an' there, sure enough, was the print of a man's body. Then we adjourned to the shade to hatch up a sub-tile plot. We smoked an' hatched until it was time for me to go in an' help with dinner. We was both thinkin' hard, an' finally I sez, "Now, Ches, the craftiest thing for us to do, is for me to cover up in the straw, an' when he lays down, explode my gun against his ribs." He had pestered me a mighty sight, an' I never was partial to 'em nohow. Ches never made any reply; he was what you call engrossed. All of a sudden he leaps to his feet an' slaps me on the shoulder.

"Happy," sez he, "are ya game?"

I looked at him a while, an' then I sez gently, "Now look here, Mister, I ain't no hero, an' if you happen to have any more college festivities to introduce, why I'll own up to a yellow streak a foot wide; but I don't recollect just what day it was that any livin' man accused me of bein' down-right pale-blooded. If you got any hair-raisin' projec' in your head, don't bother to break it gentle. Just tell it right out, an' I'll lean up against this tree, so as not to hurt myself should I faint."

"Well," sez he, chucklin' like a prairie-dog. "I propose we paint up the goat with phosphorus, put him in the barn, an' me an' you get up in the trees to watch."

"What's the goat done?" sez I.

"The goat ain't done nothin'," sez he, "but he'll scare the Chink to death, an' when he comes out we can shoot him in the leg or something."

"No," sez I, "it won't work. The Chink knows the goat better'n we do; an' it'll be the goat that'll come out an' get shot in the leg, while the Chink'll get away."

"Oh, rats!" sez Ches. "He won't even know it's a goat. Can't you see that?"

"Why won't he know it's a goat?" I sez, gettin' impatient. "A Chinaman's got just as much sense as a human being, an' you'll find it out sometime too."

"Yes, but didn't I tell you I was goin' to paint him with phosphorus?" sez Ches, all het up.

"I don't know what phosphorus is," sez I, "but you'll have to do a master job of painting to make that William goat look like a pinchin'-bug. Still, this is your projec' an' if you want to play the wheel one whirl, why I'll help stick up the stake."

I was busy about the house all afternoon, an' Ches kept himself penned up in his labatory. He had brought out a lot of stuff in cans an' bottles, had turned the woodshed into what he called a labatory, an' spent a good part of his time there, mixin' up peculiar stenches. They used to smell something frightful; but they only exploded about half the time. No matter what they did do, he always claimed that it was just exactly what he intended; but his hands was colored up constant like a fried egg, an' I never took much joy in loafin' about the woodshed.

That night as soon as I had my dishes washed an' the kitchen red up, we caught the goat an' took him to the barn. He was considerable of a goat, this one was, with horns on him a foot long an' a fright of a temper. He was one o' these fellers what is always out o' humor, only sometimes farther out than common. Still, me with my rope, an' Ches with his football habits, was one too many for Mr. Goat; an' we soon had him up in the haymow. Then

I passed up the can o' paint, an' took a stroll around to see that no one had been givin' us the look-over.

The can o' paint did have a pretty fierce smell, but I didn't put much faith in it. I'd been in opium joints, an' I knew that a Chinaman would FATTEN on a smell 'at would suffocate a goat; an' when it comes to vigorous an' able-bodied odors, a billy-goat ain't no tenderfoot himself.

After a time Ches came down with a heavenly smile on his face, so I knew the goat hadn't smothered yet; an' then we went into the house an' handled the lights in just the regular way; but when the time came, instead of goin' to bed, we went out an' cooned up a big tree, about on a level with the mow-window. Ches had nailed up a kind of platform, which was rickety enough to keep a sensible man on the watch; but first I knew he was wakin' me up. He had his hand over my mouth, an' whispered, "He's in the yard now."

I ain't one o' them what yawns an' grunts an' stretches; I wake up like an antelope—all in a bunch.

The' was a little rustlin' back in some bushes over by the fence. Then, after a pause, we heard a queer scratchin' noise. He was climbin' up a tree at the back o' the barn so as to get in through a scuttle in the roof. 'T was gettin' interestin', an' I got out my guns an' held 'em ready. Ches had a whole arsenal spread out around him, an' I could easy see a week's work ahead of me, a-policin' up the premises.

The sky was just literally soggy with stars, an' you could see the outline of things purty plain. It was one o' those nights when everything is so still that you hear with the inside of your head, an' any little real noise fair puts a crimp in ya.

We was leanin' on the rail of Ches's platform, when all of a sudden we hear the greatest jabberin' ever a human man heard. A goat an' a Chinaman speaks the same langwidge, an' goodness only knows what Billy Buck was a-tellin' him but the tone was insistent an' the effect was most exhilaratin'. I had my ears stretched out to catch every sound—an' sounds wasn't nowise scarce just then. Squeals an' groans, an' wrastlin' an' blows, kept a feller all keyed up, an' we was bitin' our lips to keep from laughin'—an' then it happened!

The door o' that mow flew open as though it was struck by eleven engines, a dark form shot out, followed by two more—an' then the devil, himself, poked his head out through that haymow window. Talk about faces—Lord! I attended a ghost dance over in the Sioux country onct; but it was a Sunday-school picnic alongside the face that poked its way out of that door.

The' was rings of fire around the eyes, nose, an' mouth, the whiskers was one long waverin', ghastly flame, an' the horns was two others. The' was a blue gritchety sort o' smoke curlin' up around the face, an' my heart laid right down in its tracks an' rolled over on its back. I only saw that face a second, but I can shut my eyes an' see it right now. Gosh!

I ain't much superstiticus, 'cept when I'm gamblin', but of course I know the' 's such things as ghosts an' devils an' sich, an' I don't take no liberties with 'em. I screeched out, a "Great Scott! what's that?" My hands shut up voluntary, both my guns went off in the air, the rail broke, an' me an' Ches sort o' chuck-lucked to the ground. We didn't miss any limbs on the way down, nor the guns didn't neither. Every time they bumped a limb, they went off, an' it sounded like Custer's last stand.

We weren't hurt none, an' scrambled to our feet in a second. The' was an awful squawkin' goin' on under the haymow window, an' that horrible, fire-faced devil seemed to be eatin' the heads off the Chinamen. I got a better view of it this time, an' I see it was one o' the dragons they worship. It made me feel a little better, 'cause I didn't see why he'd have any grudge against a Christian. Still, I wasn't takin' no chances, so I grabbed Ches by the arm an' headed for the kitchen—him stickin' his heels in the ground an' callin' me coward. I thought he had lost his mind, so I didn't pay any heed to him.

We threw ourselves against the kitchen door, an' I hammered on it with my knuckles, while Ches kicked me on the shins an' tried to get away. Finally Mrs. Cameron raised an upstairs window an' began shootin' with her bean-blower. I've no idy what she was shootin' at; but she hit me twice in the boot-leg, an' blame if it didn't sting like a whip.

Ches jerked loose while I was rubbin' the sore spot, an' as I glanced up I saw the three dark forms comin' after us followed closer by the devil-dragon, his face fairly drippin' with liquid fire. The whole bunch of 'em looked outrageous big, an' I felt about as massive an' forceful as an angle-worm; but at that, I managed to open the celler door, an' tried to get Ches to come in too. "Ches," I whispered, for I hadn't strength enough to yell, "Ches, come on in an' save yourself;" but he never gave no heed. He just stood crouching over in the shadow while they headed for him, devil-dragon an' all.

I wanted to crawl into the cellar alone, but I lacked just one grain of havin' moral courage enough, so I stood still with my knees beatin' together, watchin' 'em come. My heart ached to think that he was out of his head an' fairly throwin' himself away, an' then all of a sudden, it flashed upon me that the blame fool was playin' football. On they charged like a stampeded herd, a-screechin' like a run-away freight wagon with dry axles, while that pink-checked tenderfoot stood in his tracks, as calm an' cool as the North Star, until they arrived at the proper distance, an' then he sorted out the big one in the center an' dove for his legs.

They went up in the air, like a long-horn foolin' with the leg-throw for the first time, the other two bumped into them, the fire-faced devil-dragon slipped through, caught me full in the pantry, an' we all avalanched into the celler in one mixed up tangle. I can't describe it to you. I saw a photograph oncet of the bottomless pit at a revival meeting, and this lay-out was a card out of the same deck. I ain't stuck-up nor exclusive; but hang me if I ever want to get into such a mixed crowd again. We bit an' kicked an' hammered each other till I felt like quartz at a stamp-mill. The only light we had, came from the Chinese devil'-an' I 'd a heap sooner had none.

Finally I got hold of two cues, an' it give me a logical purpose. I simply took a short hold on those cues an' bumped the heads they belonged to, together, until that dragon caught sight of me an' hit me a thump in the back that loosened all my teeth. Something began to make an awful bawling sound, an' it scared the life out of me until I see the Chinese devil go up the stairs leaving a trail of flame behind him; an' then I knew that one of our own Medicines had arrived.

This was some the worst roar I ever heard. It would start in with a lot of foreign words an' end up with Rah! Rah Rah! The voice sounded something like Chess; but when I called him he didn't answer, an' I feared it was his spirit.

The' didn't seem to be any use in bumpin' my two heads together any more, so purty soon I dropped 'em, an' straightened up. The' wasn't a sound, an' it was enough sight scarier than the noise had been. I looked around in the dark, an' the' was ghastly waverin' flames all over an' I could see hideous faces grinnin' at me.

I scuttled out o' that cellar like a homin' rabbit, an' ran around to the side door. Mrs. Cameron put her head out after a bit, an' when she found out who I was, she let her lantern down to me on a string, an' I screwed up my courage an' went back to the cellar. I listened a moment, an' it was quiet as a grave—it was too much like a grave to suit me. I needed the touch of an old friend, so I went back an' hunted up one of my guns, loaded it, an' went down into that cellar—an' I never want my nerves stretched no tighter than the' were right at that minute. I see three Chinamen an' Ches stretched out in a heap, Ches still huggin' the big one he had picked out first.

I carried the two of 'em upstairs still locked together, an' laid 'em on the porch. As I did so, Ches opened his eyes an' smiled weakly, ail sez to me most beseechful, "Gi' me the ball, gi' me the ball, an' let Hodge an' Roger throw me over the line. It's no use tryin' to buck through." The doggone loon still thought the was playin' football, I don't reckon a railroad wreck would give one o' them football players a single new sensation.

He jumps up after a minute, shakes himself, an' seems as good as new. I was for lettin' the Chinks go, an' gettin' indoors; but not for him, so we ties 'em; but I ain't a mite easy in my mind. I was still lookin' for old Mister Devil-Dragon to come chargin' back with his Fourth o' July face, an' put an' everlastin' crimp in us. His man had a cut in the back of the head, while my two was merely softened up a little; an' as soon as we got 'em in the kitchen an' threw some water in their faces, they revived out of it an' began to jabber enough to give a steam whistle the headache.

"I'd better go an' let my cousin know we're all right," sez Ches.

"Yes, we'll both go," sez I, quickly.

"You'd better stay an' keep guard," sez Ches.

"The door's locked an' they're tied," sez I.

We went together, an' Mrs. Cameron laughed an' wept an' made a great fuss. When we came back, the Chinks were gone.

"I told you to stay on guard," yells Ches.

"Well, I'm mighty glad I didn't," sez I.

"What do you mean?" sez he.

"Can't you see what happened?" sez I. "Their blamed fire-faced dragon came back an' took 'em off, an' if I'd been here, like as not, he'd have taken me too. He'd 'a' taken 'em down cellar; but your Good Medicine came an' gave a shriek an' scared him away."

Ches stood an' looked at me. "If you are really crazy, I don't mind your talkin' this way;" he sez finally, "but if you have a grain of sense left, tell me what you mean."

"Do you mean to tell me that you didn't see him?" I sez. "He had horns an' a long beard, an' was about six feet high an' spouted fire, an' —"

"Do you mean the goat?" he snaps in.

"Goat!" I sez, gettin' mad. "Now don't get gay. The goat has tried to butt me fifty times since I been here, an' I guess I know him by sight; but this thing—"

He see I was in earnest, took a match, wet it, an' held it in a dark corner. "The goat was painted with that," sez he, an' I saw it all, an' I—well, I just natchly shriveled. I thought it all over. "Well, then," sez I, "what was the thing that gave the spirit call in the cellar?"

"That was my college yell," sez Ches, an' he gave it again, an' gee, but it would 'a' made an Injun's mouth water.

I was beginnin' to see that the' was a heap more in a college edication than I'd ever supposed.

CHAPTER FIFTEEN
THE DIAMOND DOT AGAIN

Next day we searched the barn an' found her just soggy with stolen stuff. We started out the news an' most of it was claimed up by the neighbors for a hundred miles around. They heroed me an' Ches right consid'able; but we didn't tell 'em about the goat. It might put the Chinamen wise, you see. They took up a purse of eighteen hundred dollars for us which had been offered in rewards one place an' another, an' we felt purty tol'able contented.

But I was beginnin' to get lonesome, the same as I allus do when I've been in one o' these quiet, stagnant places for a spell. I was fond o' Mrs. Cameron an' the baby an' the place an' the cookin', an' I thought the world o' Ches; but the' was a constant tuggin' at my heart to get back to the Diamond Dot, back to the big, free sweep o' plains, back to little Barbie.

I'd been soakin' away all Ches's stories an' ways, an' I knew she'd be full as interested in 'em as I was. I had had enough o' business too. I could easy see 'at I wasn't cut out for a business man, but I generally managed to round up a little wealth one way or another. I knew all along that I didn't really have a taste for business; it was just that fool talk o' Bill Andrews that made me want to cut loose from the Diamond Dot. I'd made up my mind now on that question, an' it was surprisin' how simple the answer was after I'd finally worked it out. The answer was this: I had as good a right anywhere on earth as any one else did. I was some company for Barbie at the Diamond Dot, an' it suited us both first rate. If it got on Bill Andrews' nerves till he couldn't keep it under his breath, why I'd have to furnish him with an excuse for movin'; but as for myself, I'd just stick around until things began to creak a little.

When Mr. Cameron came back, he made a big fuss over me an' Ches—he was an' A1 sort of a man, Cameron was—an' he wanted me to stay right along offerin' me big wages, which was a thing that Mrs. Cameron had forgot all about, an' me too; but I didn't feel like stayin'; so I set a date an' then it was settled. Besides, Ches would be goin' back to college again soon.

Cameron was a real estate broker in the East, but was beginnin' to study up on minin' propositions. He knew all about Slocum's Luck, that is, he knew the' was such a mine, an' that they was still lawin' over it; but when I asked him about ever havin' heard of a mine called the Creole Belle, he shook his head an' said he never had. He hadn't heard of Jack Whitman, nor George Jordan, nor even Sandy Fergoson; so I see the' wasn't any use in stayin' around there, an' while I hated to part with 'em, I was glad when the time came for me to say good-bye.

They wanted to give some kind of a present when I left; but the only thing I'd accept of, was a pair of chickens. I had got used to eatin' eggs whilst I was there, an' I knew 'at Barbie would like 'em; so they put me up a rooster an' a hen in a basket, an' I rolled up my roll, an' drove off to the depot with Ches. He was mighty sober when we got out of sight of the house, an' after he did get to talkin' it was mostly of all the good times we had had, an' how he wished I was goin' back with him, or else he was goin' on with me. I told him all about the Diamond Dot, an' how to get to it, an' invited him out for a visit any time he could get away. I didn't tell him much about Barbie; but I made him promise that if ever his Cousin found out the facts about the Creole Belle mine, he'd let me know at once. I couldn't bring myself to believe that Sandy Fergoson had been crazy, an' I was beginnin' to come to the conclusion that the' must have been both a woman an' a mine mixed up—an' that's a combination to bowl over the best of us.

Ches said he was so stuck on the West that he half believed he'd learn to be a minin' engineer an' come out here an' live. He tried to get me to promise to come an' visit him, but I told him that I ranged over the same territory mostly, an' wouldn't know how to act in the East; but that if I ever did head in that direction, I'd sure look him 'up. He bought my ticket while I was gettin' my roll out of the wagon, an' I couldn't make him take the money for it.

"This ain't on me," he sez, "the Camerons's payin' for this; but even if I was, I reckon I could afford it. You've brought me my luck."

"How about it bein' your bringin' me mine?" sez I, but he wouldn't stand for it, so I got on the train with purty close to a thousand dollars in my clothes an' a pair of chickens in my basket. He stood on the platform until we were out o' sight, an' then I settled back to think things over.

People are more different than the other kinds of animals, an' yet they're a heap alike, too. Now, me an' Ches was about as different as they ever get, most ways, an' yet we pulled a level double-tree out in the open. I could see the difference between my kind o' talk an' his; but neither one of 'em was the booky kind that Mr. Cameron talked, an' yet we had all three sat out one night watchin' the stars, an' the' wasn't much difference in what we thought about a lot o' things; but by the time we reached Oakland, I wasn't takin' such friendly views of humanity.

Now, I don't mind what a feller does as long as it don't interfere with me, an' even then, I can put up with a sight o' bother; but all the passengers on that train, an' the train crew too, seemed to think that it just about capped the climax to see a man o' my build totin' along a pair o' chickens. The' wasn't anybody on that train who behaved any better'n those chickens did, except the first time I tried to water'em out o' the cup; but they nearly pestered me to death tryin' to find out what was mysterious about 'em I told 'em the full reasons for my takin' 'em up to the Diamond Dot; but that didn't suit 'em, they had to have some outlandish excuse. I stuck to the truth until my good nature began to blister an' then I fixed up a past history for those chickens that wasn't nowise common.

When you just glance at it, a chicken ain't a creature that's apt to have a adventurous life; but long before we reached Oakland, folks was gettin' on the train every place we stopped, just to have a look at chickens what had been taught to tell counterfeit money. It was easy enough when I got started. Every one knows that a chicken's eye is mighty detectin'. They stroll along pickin' up bugs 'at you or I can't see with a magnascope, an' all 'at would be necessary to make 'em experts at money, would be to get 'em interested.

The' 's allus somebody in a crowd who don't swaller bait as easy as the rest, an' bye an' bye a feller holds up a silver dollar to the rooster. The rooster was a pretty beast, all red an' blue, an' a good feeler; but he didn't care a hang for money. He turned his head away, an' I sez, "The dollar's good."

But the feller had to keep on makin' tests, which didn't interest the rooster any until finally the rooster begun to get some exasperated. The feller held out a five-dollar bill to the rooster, an' he was tired o' such nonsense an' took a sudden peck at it an' tore it in two. "It's bad," sez I.

"I knew it was bad," sez he. "I said when I took it that I bet it wasn't any good; but one o' these smooth Easterners give it to me. If I'd had a bird like that I wouldn't 'a' got stuck. What'll you take for him?"

I smiled and sez, "I don't reckon you'd believe what these birds is worth, but I wouldn't want to sell 'em even if I got my price. I wish you'd give me that counterfeit bill though. The hen ain't fully taught an' bills like that are scarce."

He give me the bill, an' offered me all kinds o' prices for the poultry; but I wanted to take 'em to Barbie, an' I finally stuck 'em under the seat an' refused to let any one see 'em. That blame fool offered me seventy-five dollars for that pair o' chickens when he got off the train at Oakland, an' I was blame glad I had give up business, 'cause it was sure good business to take a price like that. The five-dollar bill was all right an' I spent part of it at the restaurants along the way.

When I got off the train at Webb Station, who did I see but Spider Kelley an' the home freight-wagon. Well, we was both glad to see each other, an' he stayed sober just so we could chat together on the home ride.

"How did you like business?" sez he. "Oh, it pays—in a money way," sez I, "but it's too monotonous. I don't like it."

"You ain't been gone long enough to make much money," sez he.

"Oh, no, not what you would call money in business," sez I, "but I've handled several pieces o' coin since I been away, an' I'll have nine hundred for ol' Cast Steel to put out on pasture for me."

"Nine hundred! Well, by gee!" sez Spider. "What kind o' business have you been in, Happy?"

"Oh, I tried hosses first, but they wasn't enough change in it, then I went to Frisco an' give the dry-goods business a work-out. I tried the real estate business next; but, Spider, you'll be surprised to learn that I made more money out o' goats an' chickens than any other business I got into."

"Well, that sure is wonderful," sez Spider. "Are you goin' to stay here a spell, or are you just goin' to try to get Old Cast Steel interested in poultry? I doubt if he goes into chickens deep, he allus likes to herd on a big scale."

"I'm goin' to give this here pair to Barbie," sez I. "If the old man wants me to take on for the fall round-up, why it's likely I'll do it, an' I may even stay through the winter. Money ain't the whole o' life, an' I like this range better'n any I ever rode over."

"Well, he'll be glad enough to take you on for the round-up," sez Spider. "Omaha has quit."

"The deuce he has," sez I. "What did he quit for?"

"Him an' Bill Andrews had some words, an' I got to own up that Bill was in the right of it. Cast Steel didn't take any sides, an' Omaha, he finally pulled out week before last. Bill Andrews is the nearest thing we got to a foreman now."

"How's everything goin'?" sez I.

"Smoother'n oil," sez he. "I've been around the ranch house ever since you been away, tendin' to Pluto an' breakin' colts."

"I'm goin' to get out an' walk back," sez I.

"What the 'ell for?" sez he.

"I never struck this place before when it wasn't in a tangle," sez I, "an' I feel in my bones, it betokens bad luck."

"Oh, hoofs," sez he, "you ain't that superstitious are you? Did you leave last time in the same humor as usual?"

Then I felt a shade easier. "No," sez I, "every other time me an' Cast Steel had had a little difference; but this time, I was simply tired o' the place. Well, I'll go on an' chance it; but I'm leery that somethin' will happen."

We arrived next day in time for supper, an' Barbie an' Jabez was mighty glad to see me. Barbie went wild over the chickens, just as I knew she would, an' Jabez said that he used to like eggs himself when he was a boy, an' would have got some poultry long ago if he'd only thought of it. They both of 'em laughed to think that I had at last come back to the Diamond Dot without findin' any kind of warfare; an' when I told 'em that it sort o' worried me, they only laughed the more.

"How did you like business, Happy?" sez Jabez.

"I got nine hundred dollars I wish you'd range out with the rest o' my herd," sez I, "but to tell you the simple truth, I don't like business, not one mite."

I thought I could stall 'em off without tellin' 'em what kind o' business I'd made my stake in, but they wormed it out o' me before that first meal was over. It was a merry meal, an' lasted about three hours. I enjoyed it, but I made up my mind that if I took on again, I was goin' to eat with the rest of the boys. I had allus et with Barbie an' Jabez; but I didn't want to have any o' the outfit get to thinkin' that I wasn't nothin' but a visitor. When bedtime hove around, Jabez sez, "Well, you'll find your old room ready, Happy."

"Why, I reckon I'll sleep in the bunk shack from this on," sez I.

"I reckon you won't," sez he. "You're worth more to me as a sort o' reserve than you 'd be as a straight puncher, an' the' ain't no use o' your gettin' so blame finicky all of a sudden. What's got into you lately?"

"Now, you knob' how it is, Jabez," sez I, "if I cut loose from the rest o' the bunch, they're bound to talk about it an' —"

"Let 'em talk," he snaps in. "Talk ain't expensive; but I don't think they're a jealous lot. They all like you, Happy, an' I got a sort of a suspicion that those who don't won't pester you overly much. I ain't heard the straight of it, but I have heard some talk about him overestimatin' his ability in the ridin' line. Now cut out this nonsense an' just begin where you left off. Barbie here'll be mighty glad of some company again."

It didn't take 'em long to talk me into it—it generally is easy to break down a man's will when it ain't braced up by his natural desires; so after I'd balked as long as seemed polite, I settled into the collar again an' trotted along just in the same old gait.

It was just as I thought. Barbie was plumb wild to hear all those college stories, an' the queer words that Ches used to talk with. She asked me about a thousand questions that I wasn't sure on the answers; but I made out to interest her, an' Jabez' face used to beam when he'd hear her laugh ring out.

We were sure a happy household; but I noticed mighty soon that Barbie was more restless than ever; but also had more control over herself. She wasn't so quick about either askin' questions nor givin' answers as she used to be, an' she noticed things closer—an' this was goin' some too; 'cause she allus did inspect everything that came on her range.

We had a gang o' tourists swoop down on us for a couple o' days, an' it tickled me to see her watch 'em an' draw back in her shell any time she thought they was watchin' her. I knew every line in her face, an' mighty few of her thoughts came as a surprise when she framed 'em into words. She never said it all now, unless she was het up about something, an' I like to listen to any one 'at talks like that. Her best thoughts were never accented, they just came in as packin' like, an' it added to the interest. When a feller hands out a little commonplace idy an' then sends along a couple o' verses to tell what it means, I get weary; but when I'm able to see into somethin' that lays too close to his heart to say out, an' too close to forget, why I feel as if I had found a real jewel, an' that was the way with Barbie. I knew that somethin' was tuggin' at her; but when I found out exactly what it was, it came with almost as much of a shock as if I hadn't known it was there all the time.

CHAPTER SIXTEEN
THE HIGHER EDUCATION OF WOMAN

Barbie had grown some more, even durin' the little time 'at I'd been away. She had got used to the new rig she wore an' wasn't a mite awkward, an' her face was firmer an' more self-composed. She was purtier too, though it don't seem possible. It even seems more impossible when I tell ya that she looked more like of Cast Steel than ever. He an' the girl was a heap alike, 'cept that he was big an' raw-boned an' spare-featured; while she was as dainty as an antelope, an' as far as looks went, she was the Queen Bee of Creation, I reckon.

When it came to ridin' a bucker or shootin' off an eye-winker or expressin' herself free an' frank, she didn't have to import no testimony to prove 'at she was his daughter either. She had him skinned on ridin' though; 'cause while he was able to set anything on four feet, he allus showed 'at he had begun late in life, an' he sometimes jerked the bit unintentional; while she—well, I reckon she must 'a' been born on hoss-back, an' besides, I had give her all the pointers the' was.

One mornin' about ten days after I'd come back, I heard 'em discussin' purty heatedly out back of the corral; an' I just sauntered over to harken to it. It wasn't a case of eavesdroppin', 'cause when them two had any comments to make they didn't care a blue bean what the prevailin' style in opinions happened to be, they nailed their own personal jedgments on the wall an' then stuck around handy to back 'em up. I was particular anxious to know what they was crossin' words over, 'cause I couldn't get it out o' my head but what my comin' back an' findin' 'em peaceable betokened something.

Jabez was standin' with his feet wide apart, his hands on his hips, his hat tilted over one ear, his chin stickin' out with the lips pursed up, an' his eyes had a dogged look in 'em. Line by line an' feature by feature, she shadowed him to the last item; an' neither one of 'em saw a twinkle o' comicalness in it, neither.

"Do you know who you're talkin' to?" he yells just as I arrived. "I'm your father!"

"What of it?" she snaps back. "It's too late to remedy that—I just got to make the best of it. But do you know who you're talkin' to? I'm the future owner of the Diamond Dot, an' I ain't a-layin' no plans to have the lalakadinks from the civilized parts o' this country come out an' round up my langwidge, same as they gather Injun speciments. You may be my father, but you can just bet your saddle that before I reach the end o' my trail, a stranger won't be able to guess it from our talk."

Now the old man was mighty savin' with his cuss-words, a' he put out a purty tol'able fair grade o' grammar; but the girl had an eye in her head and an ear to listen with, an' she had been for a long time takin' notice o' the side winks o' the Easterners. Some Easterners put on their manners the same as their complexions, an' the open air is apt to put cracks in 'em.

The of man looked at her a good long while, but she never blinked a winker; an' he finally turned away an' said in a soft-like voice, "I know, child, I ain't been able to fill the part full measure—but it ain't 'cause I haven't tried. I reckon you'll have to go, honey; but it'll sure be lonesome while you're away; an' when you do come back you'll never be my little kid any more." His voice kept gettin' sadder an' sadder until I about snuffled myself when he continued "I'll rub up my talk all I can while you're away, an' then if you bring out any friends next summer you can tell 'em that I'm the foreman an' that you let me eat in the house while your father is takin' a trip to Europe."

The ol' man would have played that part about as natural as a bull buffalo, but he fooled himself into believin' it, an' his voice was purty shaky at the end. Barbie's eyes filled up with tears, an' when he stopped an' began to totter feebly toward the house, she ran up an' threw her arms about his neck, an' said. "Dad. I just hate you—you don't play fair. You start the game under one set o' rules an' then when you get the worst of it you just simply crawfish. When we were sayin' mean things out in the open, I just natchly put it all over you; an' now you flop over on your back an' work that 'coals o' fire' stunt, an' I just hate you. You know in your heart I'd be proud of you in any company on earth, but the' is a heap o' difference between you an' me. You have been successful, an' strangers will respect you for it; but it's got to be a show-down with me every time. If I don't learn the new gaits, so a stranger will think I'm city-broke, some fresh tourist is apt to get the idee that I'm as uncivilized as my manners, an' it won't do to tramp on my toes— not overly often. But I don't have to leave you. I'll just turn in an' do the job right here on the ranch, an' accordin' to the very latest models. You get me a lot o' books an' all the magazines an' fashion papers, an' hanged if I don't turn out a job 'at'll fool the best of 'em. You're a mean old Daddy, you are, for a fact; but we snake too dandy a duet for me to go away an' leave you to grind out a solo all alone. But—but I sure wanted to go."

Well, Jabez grinned all over; but I saw that he wasn't through with it so easy. Barbie wasn't the one to throw her rope before she was all braced for the jerk, an' the' wouldn't be any kinks in her logic, neither. She had thrown a purty stout string of arguments, an' I was full prepared when they told me that he was to have his way about it, an' she was to go to college that very fall.

She did go in less'n a month to a prep-school clear down East. A prep-school is a sort of a calf college, you know; an' she had to train there a solid year before they had the nerve to turn her loose on a full-grown university. But she had a head on her, Barbie had; an' when she got squared away, she made 'em all get down an' scratch. They do say that she put more life an' vim in that institution than anybody what had ever give it a work-out before.

Ol' Cast Steel went down twice the first winter, an' never let her know 'at he was in the neighborhood, for fear it would make her think 'at he was pinin' for her. He just went down there an' bought some store clothes an' prowled around waitin' for the chance to see her at a distance—never even lined out the professors to see if they were doin' their duty, nor mixed in the game the slightest bit. Talk about bein' game? I reckon that puts a shadow on anything ever that man had to face.

She used to come back every summer, bringin' a lot of chums an' all kinds o' pets with her. She was just daffy over any kind of a wild animal from an Injun papoose to a white mouse; an' when she'd go back in the fall, Jabez had his hands full with parrots an' alligators an' butterfly coons an' sech—to say nothin' of a lot of potted flowers what was mighty notionable in their tastes.

I was so busy tendin' to this branch o' the outfit that about all the ridin' I did was for exercise—yes, an' for company, 'cause it allus seemed as if she was along when I'd be out on the range. Then, again, I allus felt a kind of drawin', myself, to the silent people, who think an' wish an' feel, just the same as we do, but aren't able to handle our langwidge. I got so I could purt' nigh tell what an animal had on his mind, just from tendin' to her speciments.

She had one speciment which was a possom, an' the blame thing bit me eight times one winter, me tryin' to give it baths—an' then she wrote back home that the doggone critter didn't need'em nohow. She purt'nigh got expended for takin' a rattlesnake back to the university an' keepin' it hid in her room; an' after I'd had a deuce of a time catchin' 'em, they made her send a bob-cat an' a mountain lion to some kind of a garden—wouldn't let her keep 'em at all. The professors allus was a sore trial to her, but once she began a thing she allus fought it through, so she put up with 'em the best way she could.

She used to tell us that bein' housed up like to 'a' drove her crazy at first, an' they was so tarnation fussy that she felt like a hobbled pony in a stampede. They wouldn't even let her picket her ponies out in what they call the campus, which she said was just drippin' fat with rich grass, an' nary a hoof to graze it. Why, they even had fool notions about havin' certain hours about goin' to bed, an' even when you had to put your lights out.

One night she got fidgety an' nervous with the lonesomeness of it, an' she got up about one o'clock an' fired her revolvers out the window,—just for sport, you know, like a feller sometimes will when he's—well, when his soul gets kind o' itchy like,—an' it purt' nigh started a riot. She said 'at we wouldn't never believe how different the people was down there. I reckon a university must be run a good bit like a penitentiary. But as I said, she wasn't no quitter, an' I reckon, takin' it all in all, she give 'em back about as good as they sent.

Course we could see a lot o' change in her when she'd first come back, but it seemed to slide off as the tan came on, an' by the time she left in the fall again she'd be purty much the same old Barbie. She went full five years, countin' the prep-school, an' I don't suppose they was much in the way o' learnin' they didn't filter through her; but it didn't spoil her, an' the very moment her knees clamped on a pony again you could see that her blood was as red as ever, even if her face was roses an' cream. My heart allus beat out of time when I knew she was headin' back; but the very minute she gave my hand the old-time grip I knew she was still the old-time girl, an' when she'd turn to the chums an' say, "Girls, this is Happy," why, I was big brother to the lot, an' before they went back I'd teach 'em ridin' till they could giggle on hoss-back without fallin' off. They all owned up that she was the takin'est girl at the university, and while her pals was a mighty attractive lot, they didn't have to use any arguments to convince me it was the truth.

She allus left me so much to do when she was away that I never felt like leavin' through the winter; while durin' vacation time I wouldn't have gone without bein' drove; but toward the middle of her fourth year, me an' Bill Andrews had another little run in.

We was havin' a terrible streak of weather, an' Bill wanted to move a herd over to the southwest corner of the ranch where the' was some extra good bunch grass. It was a wise move all right, an' I said so; but when he wanted me to help trail 'em, I vetoed it. I was watchin' up some experiments with silkworms an' I didn't want to leave 'em. We were short-handed an' Jabez 'lowed 'at I'd better go. Well, we argued back an' forth until he finally said that he could take full care o' the silkworms, an' intimated that my work with 'em wasn't much but pastime, anyway.

That settled it with me. I helped drive the herd, an' it was the bitterest weather we'd ever had. The sleet blew in the cow's faces an' it was simply one long fight. Three o' the boys gave up an' pulled back to the ranch house, but not me. I don't believe I slept on that drive, night or day, an' when, the boys finally told Bill Andrews that it couldn't be done, I told 'em that it could, an' that if any more of 'ern dropped out I'd count it a personal insult. We got 'em there all right, an' then I rode back to the ranch house.

Jabez had let the silkworms die—an' I told him what I thought of him, an' pulled out. It was cold weather an' I was travelin' on foot, but it wasn't cold I was suffer in' from, it was heat.

CHAPTER SEVENTEEN
IN RETIREMENT

I plugged along through the cold, gettin' hotter an' hotter all the time, 'cause I didn't want to go away at all. Barbie'd be home in a few months and I wanted to be there when she came—but I couldn't get over those silkworms. She was goin' to write somethin' about 'em for some kind of a paper, an' it meant a good deal to her, an' I had kept a record of all the projec's she'd written me to do with 'em—only to have Cast Steel an' flint fool Bill Andrews flounder in with that herd o' cows.

I piked on over to Danders thinkin' I'd get on a train an' go somewhere; but on my way there I met the foreman o' the E. Z. outfit ridin' into town to see if he couldn't pick up a fence-rider. Then I see old Mrs. Fate nudgin' me in the ribs with her finger again. We was all down on fences at the Diamond Dot. Jabez said that as far as he was concerned, he preferred to have his fences mounted on hoss-back, 'cause they was easiest moved, an' we didn't have a foot o' wire on the place. I knew that no one would ever think o' me ridin' fence, so I just up an' spoke for the job. The foreman, Hank Midders was his name, didn't know me an' he was suspicious of me bein' on foot. "Can you ride?" sez he.

"I used to could," sez I. "How many days' ridin' does it take to go around?"

"We don't ride that way," sez he, "we put two men in a camp an' they ride out fifteen miles an' then double back."

"They waste the return trip," sez I.

"We think different," sez he. "We keep a big run o' cows, an' we want the whole fence rode twice a day. We allus have plenty o' good ridin' ponies."

"Well, they ain't ridin' on my time," sez I, "so it ain't nothing to me. Do I get the job?"

"Where you been ridin' at?" sez he.

"At the Lion Head, for Jim Jimison," sez I.

"I've seen some o' their stuff," sez he. "It's a good outfit; but it's a rather lengthy walk from here."

"Yes, I stopped off a while in Californie an' Idaho to rest," sez I. "Do I get the job?"

"We don't find a man's saddle an' bridle for him," sez he.

"I got mine cached over at Danders," sez I, recallin' the ones I had left there before I went into business.

"What's your name?" sez he.

"I ain't nowise choicy," sez I, "call me anything you want."

"I guess you won't do," sez he, ridin' on into Danders.

I reached it myself about two hours later, an' went to the hotel. Hank was settin' by the stove when I came into the bar-room. The' was eight or ten other fellers still restin' from last summer's work, but I didn't see the old landlord. "Where's Peabody?" sez I.

"He's dead," sez a tall, snarley lookin' feller; "what do ya want with him?"

"I don't want nothin' with him—if he's dead," sez I. "Who's runnin' this place now?"

"I am," sez the snarley one. I didn't take to him at all.

"Would you be so kind enough as to tell me where my saddle an' bridle is?" sez I in my softest voice. "What the 'ell do I know about your saddle an' bridle?" sez he.

"I left 'em here with Peabody," sez I.

"How would I know it was yours?" sez he, sneerin'.

"I'd recognize it," sez I. "It had H. H. burned into it."

"What does H. H. stand for?" sez he.

"It stands for Henry Higinson—sometimes," sez I. Then I turned to the bar mop an' said, "Where's that saddle an' bridle?"

"Why, it's back in—" he began; but Snarley snaps in "You shut up, will ya? Even if this puncher did leave an old saddle here years ago, I bought everything on the place from Peabody, an' the storage on the rubbish would amount to more than it's worth."

"That 's kind o' new doctrine out this way," sez I; "an' I'm 'bliged to request you to produce the articles so I can claim 'em up."

"You go ahead an' make me do it," sez he, grinnin'.

"Wouldn't you sooner do it of your own free will?" sez I, like a missionary tryin' to get up enthusiasm over a donation.

"I'm good an' sick o' your fool nonsense," sez he, comin' down toward me. I was wearin' a gun on each leg, an' I pulled 'em out an' punctuated both his ears at one time; but I never stopped smilin'. He grabbed an ear in each hand an' begun to swear in a foreign langwidge, dancin' around most comical. "Won't you please get my leather for me," sez I, "or would you sooner have me guess off the center o' those two shots?"

"Yes," he roared, usin' a lot o' high-power words 'at ain't needful in repetin', "take your blame junk an' get out o' here." I nodded to the bar mop. "Shall I get 'em, Frenchy?" sez he.

"Yes, for heaven's sake, get 'em," sez the snarley one, while some o' the boys snickered, but not too noticeable.

Well, they was my saddle an' bridle all right, an' I thanked the bar mop an' flung 'em in a corner. Then I went over an' sat down by Hank Midders. "Did you get your fence-rider yet?" sez I.

"No, I ain't got him yet, but I got two days to look for him in," he sez.

Just then who should come in but the same old Diamond Dot hand who had beat me out of the pony. "Well, sign my name! If there ain't Happy Hawkins!" sez he, rushin' over an' shakin' my hand, "Still in business, Happy?" sez he.

"Nope, I've retired," sez I.

"You'd ought to have stuck around here until that tourist went home from his vacation," sez Bill,—I reckon his name was still Bill, though for the life o' me I can't remember it plain,—"he got the whole town hilarious on account o' the joke we'd played on him. He was game all right, an' he got me a job out to his uncle's, which I've held ever since—off an' on."

"Happy?" sez Hank Midders, "Happy what?"

"Happy Hawkins," sez Bill. "Haven't you never heard o' Happy Hawkins?"

"Happy Hawkins is down in the Texas-Pan Handle," sez I, in a matter-o'-fact voice. "Don't forget that, Bill."

"Surest thing there is," sez Bill, winkin'. "I seen him get on the train myself."

"When will supper be ready, Frenchy?" I sez to the snarley one, who had been puttin' some grease on his ears an' wishin' he'd had better manners.

"In about an hour," sez he, an' I knew the' wouldn't be any more trouble from him. He was one o' these fellers what can take a lickin' without gettin' all broke up over it, an' he'd be just as gay about bluffin' the next stranger as ever, an' he'd be just as dominatin' over them what he had already bluffed.

"Well, I'm goin' out for a little stroll," sez I, "but I'll be back in time for supper, an' I'll likely be hungry."

I knew they'd all want to ask a few questions, so I went outside an' walked down the street. I couldn't make up my mind what to do, an' I wanted that fence-ridin' job more than ever. When T turned around to come back, I see Hank Midders walkin' toward me. "So you're Happy Hawkins?" sez he.

"Well, that's what some folks call me," sez I.

"I thought 'at you had finally settled down at the Diamond Dot?" sez he.

"The' ain't nothin' that I know of that changes any oftener than the style in thoughts," sez I. "Do you think it's goin' to snow?"

He laughed. "You're Happy Hawkins all right," sez he. "Do you want that fence-ridin' job?"

"That's what I went to the trouble o' rootin' out that saddle an' bridle for," sez I, "but I don't care to have it advertised that I'm ridin' fence at my time o' life, an' I don't promise to continue at it more'n a few months."

"I see," sez he, "an' it'll be all right. Kid Porter'll be down with the buckboard day after to-morrow, an' you can go out with him."

When I went back I see that Bill hadn't spared no details to make me interestin', an' all the boys was friendly to me—an' called me Higinson. Me an' Frenchy got along all right, an' when I threw my saddle an' bridle into the back o' the buckboard, an' sez, "Well, good-bye, fellers! I'm on my way to the Pan Handle," they all calls out, "Goodbye, Happy! If any o' your friends inquire for you we'll tell 'em we saw you start; but the next time you come this way, Higinson, don't forget to drop in for a little sport."

Things generally even up pretty well in this life, an' before we had driven very far I was able to see where I had got full value out o' that seven-dollar pony 'at Bill had beat me out of. Kid Porter explained things to me an' I saw it was goin' to be a purty fair sort of a layout. Our shack was closer to Danders than it was to headquarters, so we got our needin's there. He said that Colonel Scott was an allright man to work for, but that he'd only seen him once since he'd been on the job.

Ridin' fence is about as excitin' as waitin' for sun-up, an' after a couple of months at it I was feelin' the need of a little change, so I drove down to Danders the first day of April, an' while I was standin' on the platform watchin' the train pull in an' take water, a cute little feller dismounted an' after givin' me a complete look-over, he sez: "Me good man, are you a type of this community?"

I put my hand to my ear as though I had heard a noise close to the ground. After a bit I let my gaze rest on him sort o' surprised like, an' then I sez in a soft, oozy voice, like a cow conversin' to her first calf, "Be you speakin' to me, little one?" sez I.

It allus riles me some, to be called "me good man." It seems to give me a curious, itchy feelin' in the right hand, an' I have had to make several extra peculiar speciments dance a few steps for no other reason; but this little cuss never batted an eye. He looks me square in the face, an' sez, "It is perfectly obvious that I could be addressin' nobody else. I am out in the West hunting for a place to study the most pronounced types of American citizens, an' I am very favorable impressed with your appearance."

Did you ever have a stranger brace you like that? I suppose the fat lady an' the livin' skeleton gets used to it, but I allus feel a trifle too big for my background. I stand six foot two an' dress easy an' comfortable, an' some o' the guys on the trains allus seem to think 'at I'm part of the show, out for an airin'.

"Well, to tell you the truth, honey," I sez to the little feller, "I ain't fully maychured yet. We get hair on our faces pretty young out here, but we don't get our growth till we're twenty-five. I'm water-boy to the E. Z. outfit. If you want to see somethin' worth lookin' at, you ought to come out where the men are. You'll find American citizens out there, a darn sight harder type to pronounce than what I am. They sent me to town on an errant."

He examined me, but I never blinked a winker, an' then his face lit up, like as if he'd found a whole plug of tobacco, when he thought his last chew was gone. Finally he gave a wink an' a chuckle, an' sez, "Here, smoke a cigar on me, an' tell me if I can get board out your way. I think you'll make copy."

He was just what I needed as a time-killer, so I spun him a yarn about the lovely life me an' Kid Porter was livin'. We jerked out his trunk just before the train left, bought a month's grub, an' came along out to our shack. His name was William Sinclair Hammersly, an' the' never was a squarer boy on the face o' the earth, after he'd shed off those spectator ways. He won my affections, as the storybooks say, before we was out o' sight o' Danders.

He said he had relations scattered all over the British Empire, an' owned up that he had just come back from a long visit to England, where he had picked up the "good man" habit. I told him that it might suit that climate all right, but that out our way I couldn't recommend it to a peace-lovin' man for every-day use. He thanked me an' said he was ashamed to know so little about his own country, this bein' the first time he had ever been west of Philadelphia. He said that he was minded to become an author, an' had come out to study the aboriginal types an' get the true local color. Whenever I hear this little bunch o' sounds, I know I got a nibble. Any time a man goes nosin' around after local color, you can bet your saddle he's got several zigzags in his think-organ.

These fellers is a breed to themselves. I wouldn't exactly call 'em wise—wordy'd come a sight nearer fittin' these local-color fellers without wrinklin'. The''s a ringin' in my ears yet from the time that I was penned up with Hammy an' Locals, an' this one had a good many o' the same outward an' visible signs, but more o' the inward an' spiritual grace, as Friar Tuck sez.

Bill slid right into our mode of livin' like a younger brother, but it took us some consid'able time to savvy his little private oddities. The' was one wide bunk in the shack an' one narrow one. Me an' Bill took the wide one, but it wasn't so eternal wide that a feller could flop around altogether accordin' to the dictates of his own conscience. When she was carryin' double we had to hold a little consultation of war, to see whether we'd turn over or not.

We used to start out early in the mornin', an' if the' wasn't much fixin' to be done we got back long before dark. About seven-thirty was our perchin' time before Bill took a hand, but after that we got so convivual that sometimes we'd sit up till purt' nigh half-past nine, playin' cut-throat an' swappin' tales. Sleep allus was a kind of a nuisance to Bill. Purt' nigh every night when me an' the Kid would stretch ourselves out, Bill would speak a piece about "God bless the man what first invented sleep"; but he was only joshin', an' all the time he was sayin' it he'd be buildin' up the fire an' changin' his clothes. He had one suit which he never wore for nothin' except just to sleep in. Pajamers, he called 'em, an' they sure was purty.

Well, he'd put on this suit an' a pair o' red-pointed slippers, light his pipe, pick his guitar, an' saw his fiddle till along toward mornin', all the while singin' little batches o' song an' speakin' pieces. Then he'd heave a sigh an' lay down alongside o' me; but in about fifteen minutes he'd jump out o' bed, sayin', "That's good! That's great! I mustn't lose that!" an' he'd get out a book an' write something into it. Sometimes he'd laugh over it an' sometimes he'd cry.

The Kid'd never had no experiences with geniuses before, an' at first he feared that he might get violent durin' the night, so he took his gun to bed with him, but I knowed the' wasn't a mite o' danger in him. When breakfast was ready we purt' nigh had to get a hoss to pull him out o' bed.

I was interested in his tales of foreign countries, an' he used to tell me all about the castles he had been to. One day I happened to think of the letter what the drug clerk at Slocum's Luck had wrote us, an' I asked Bill what kind of a lookin' place Clarenden Castle was. "Clarenden Castle?" sez Bill. "Where the deuce did you ever hear of Clarenden Castle?"

"Well, I might have heard of it from the younger son," sez I. "He came over to this country, you know."

"Where is he now?" sez Bill, mighty interested.

"Minin' law is, that the first feller what stakes out a claim gets it," sez I. "Now my question staked out the first claim. You answer my questions an' then we'll be ready for yours."

"Humph," sez Bill.

"Where is St. James Court, Bill?" sez I.

"Well, I never expected you to know anything about such things!" sez Bill.

"'Tis wonderful how intelligent some trained animals are, ain't it?" sez I, sarcastic. "But you must remember, little one, that I've been livin' right in the house with folks a good part of my life. Now if you'll just answer my questions the same as if I was human, I'll sit up an' beg, jump over a stick, an' do all my other tricks for you."

Bill would allus tumble if you hit him hard enough, so after a bit he grinned an' said, "Well, Clarenden Castle is one o' the seats of the Cleighton family—"

"Seat?" sez I. "I allus thought it was a house."

"You see, over in England they call—" Bill began to explain it to me an' then he saw me grinnin' an' he broke off short. "I know what a seat is, Bill," sez I. "They have country seats an' town seats; but some o' you fellers pout when you're obliged to live up to the rules, an' I wanted to see if you was square enough to own up after you'd been shown—the's lots o' fellers, not as well edicated as you, who can't do it without groanin'."

Bill studied out this last remark before he answered, an' I was glad to notice it. Most fellers look for a marked passage, but I like to train 'em out to pan everything I say, an' then do their own testin'. Bill was all right. "Now, dear teacher," sez he, "if we are through with that lesson, we shall return to the original subject." We both laughed, lookin' into each other's eyes, an' it did us good.

"Now this Cleighton family is a great family in England and Scotland," sez Bill, "The Earl of Clarenden is the head of one branch an' the Duke of Avondale is the head of another. The sons are called lords, an' they have lots of land, but are running shy on money, an' the main stem of the family is getting purty well thinned out."

"About this younger son that came to America, now?" sez I.

"Well, the present Earl married beneath him—I visited close to Clarenden Castle, an' I know all about it," sez Bill. "He married an American girl with lots of money, Florence Jamison of Philadelphia."

"Jamison?" sez I.

"Yes, Jamison," sez Bill. "I suppose you are well acquainted with the Philadelphia Jamisons?"

"Well, that name does awaken a purty tol'able fairsized echo," sez I, "but still, to be perfectly frank with you, me an' the Jamisons ain't on what you could call intimate terms any more."

"I'm glad to learn it," sez Bill. "I'd hate to think that I had irritated you by implicatin' that it was a come-down for an English Earl to marry into your circle." Bill most generally squoze all the dampness out of his jokes. "This was his second marriage," Bill went on, "an' he had one son by it, named James Arthur Fitzhugh Patrick—"

"That's plenty for me," sez I, breakin' in. "The first two names is interestin' to me, but the' ain't no use loadin' down a feller with names till he has to pay excess baggage on 'em. Now, how did this one get to be a younger son?"

"Why, the first marriage of the Earl also resulted in a son," sez Bill. "His first wife was a lady of quality, but she had a weak constitution an' the son has epolepsy. The younger son was fitted for the army, but he got into a scrape, was given a lump sum by his father, an' came to this country, where he disappeared. He also had an inheritance from an aunt, a maiden sister of his mother, who didn't like the first son for a minute."

"What kind of a scrape did the youngster get into, Bill?" sez I.

"He was engaged to the daughter of the curat at Avondale Chapel," sez Bill, "an' he bein' the heir presumptive to the title—"

"What is that, Bill?" sez I.

"The one what gets the title as soon as the one who is holding it, dies, is the heir apparent, an' the one who gets the next chance is the heir presumptive. It's a legal term an'—"

"Never mind explainin' it then," sez I, "If I was to live as long as Methusleh, all I'd know about law would be that ignorance wasn't no excuse for it; but what is a curat?"

"A curate is a sort of preacher," sez Bill.

"I thought it was some kind of a doctor. But what in thunder did you mean when you said that gettin' engaged to the daughter of one was a scrape?" sez I.

"Why, it wouldn't do for the heir presumptive to Clarenden, and a possible claimant to Avondale, to get engaged to a person in that station of life; he had to make up either to a heap of money or else a big title; he simply had to marry a lady of quality," sez Bill.

"So he could contribute his share of epolepsy to the family collection, I suppose," sez I.

"Well, James gets an awful callin' down," sez Bill, "an' he cuts loose from the family an' goes to live in London, where he's a leftenant. Richard Cleighton, his cousin, who is the heir presumptive, once removed, sneaks down there an' comes back with the report that James is married to Alice LeMoyne, a music-hall dancer."

"Jim swung purty wide in his taste for women, didn't he?" sez I.

"The upshot of it was," sez Bill, never heedin' me, "that they settled with James, an' he lit out—his mother had died several years before. About four years after, this Alice LeMoyne dies, an' on her deathbed she confesses that she is the wife of Richard Cleighton an' helped to put up the job on James to get him out of the way, as the heir apparent didn't look like a long-liver, an' she thought she would like to be an Erless, with a chance of being a Duchess even."

"An' you mean to tell me that this low-grade Dick Cleighton puts up that job on Jim, just so he can beat him to the title?" sez I.

"Yes," sez Bill, "you see he was the heir presumptive, only once removed."

"Well, if I'd had the job o' removin'," sez I, "once, would 'a' been plenty."

"That put Richard out o' the runnin'," sez Bill, "Lord Wilfred, the apparent, was livin' along all right, an' the old Earl had come to the conclusion that when it came to a presumptive, he'd sooner have Jim; so he turned the hose on Dick, an' started out to find Jim. Jim wrote 'em from New York that he was goin' to South Africa, an' then he wrote 'em from Australia that he was goin' to India, an' then he wrote 'em from—"

"Oh, those was only jokes," sez I. "Jim's all right; but what become of Dick?"

"Nobody knows," sez Bill, "an' nobody cares. He's got lots better health than Lord Wilfred, but he's got some epolepsy, too, an' he's a mean sneak. His mother was insane, but she left him a little bunch of money."

"She must have had more quality than the average of 'em;" sez I, "but hanged if I wouldn't sooner do without the quality than to have all that epolepsy thrown in with it. Jim's all right though, I'll say that for the breed."

"Yes, Jim was a fine feller from all accounts," sez Bill, "but where the Jink did you meet up with him?"

"It's a state secret," sez I, "or I'd let you in. Jim's doin' fine an' I wouldn't for the world have him dragged down where he'd have to marry up with a lot o' quality. Now while you're givin' your concert, I'm goin' out an' check up the stars."

I was purty yell pleased with Bill. I had bothered him all I could in the tellin' an' yet he had kept his temper an' handed out the facts; an' I wanted to go over 'em forward an' hack till I could get the full hang of 'em. It was wonderful queer how a ridin' man like me had brushed shoulders, as you might say, with the Earl of Clarenden, an' I was beginnin' to think that old Mrs. Fate was stirrin' things up a shade extra. As a usual thing I don't go into scandal an' gossip so prodigious; but I was hungry to have another look at Jim, now that I knew he was the son of an Earl, an' I decided to pull out an' give the Pan Handle a look-over as soon as it was handy. I spent about two hours that night lookin' at the stars an' wishin' they could tell me all they'd ever seen. They knew all that Barbie wanted to know, an' I didn't seem able to git on the track, in spite of me readin' detective stories every chance I had.

CHAPTER EIGHTEEN
CUPID

Well, I didn't go down to the Pan Handle after all. I just fatten on a new variety of entertainment an' the sample that Bill was puttin' out amused me to the limit. Me an' Bill drove down to Danders on the first o' May to get some grub. Most o' this breed has a purty tol'able active thirst, but Bill was unusual harmless when it came to storin' away liquor. About the only excitement Danders held out to a temperance crank was goin' down to the depot to watch the train come in. This time the west-bound had to take a sidin' and wait twenty minutes for the east bound; an' a feller got his dog out o' the baggage car an' started to climb the mountains.

You fellers all know how this air is, but a stranger thinks he can spit on a mountain that's ten miles off. When the whistle blew, he made a good run an' got on all right; but the pup was havin' the time of his life an' missed his chance of gettin' on the same car that the feller did. He was game all right an' give a purty jump onto the front platform of the last car, where a big buck nigger was standin' with a white coat on. He give the pup a kick under the chin an' sent him rollin' over backward.

"Why, the vile wretch!" yells Bill, at the same time snatchin' my gun out of the holster. I had barely time to bump up his arm, an' even as it was he knocked the paint off right above the coon's head. Bill turned on me with his eyes snappin' sparks, an' in a voice as cold as the click of a Winchester, he sez, "Next time, John Hawkins, I'll thank you to mind your own business." An' he held the gun kind o' friendly like, with the muzzle pointin' at my watch pocket.

I own up I was jarred; he'd been as gentle as a butterfly up to that minute, an' here he was lookin' into me with the chilly eyes of a killin' man; but I put a little edge on my own voice an' sez, "Heretofore, I allus counted it my business to look after what my own gun was engaged in doin'. When you're sure that you're all through with it, I'll thank you to return it to where you found it."

Then I turned on my heel an' strode up toward town; but he grabbed me by the shoulder an' whirled me around. "Here's your gun, Happy." sez he. "You know I didn't aim to offend you. It was that confounded Zulu 'at riled me up."

The pup had give up his chase after the train an' was comin' back the track to town, lookin' mighty down in the mouth—he had a purty prominent mouth, too, the pup had. He was a brindle bull; not one o' these that look like an Injun idol, but a nice, clean-built, upstandin' feller with a quiet, business-like air.

"Purty tough on the pup to be turned out to starve this way," sez I.

"Who's goin' to let him starve?" sez Bill. "Come here, old feller." "Better look out," sez I, "bulldogs is fierce."

"So is men," sez Bill; "an' besides, this ain't no bulldog, this is a London brindle bull-terrier, an' a crackerjack. Look at the brass collar he's wearin'. This is ain't no stray. I'll telegraph ahead an' see if they want him expressed."

Bill caught the feller at the next station, an' he telegraphed back that he'd been havin' trouble with the pup all along the line; an' if we'd keep him a month, he'd stop an' get him on his way back. He sent us ten dollars to pay expenses. I never believed that they could send money by telegraph before; but I saw the agent give it to Bill, with my own eyes.

We all went to the hotel for dinner, the pup lookin' miserable sorrowful. Frenchy was goin' to kick the pup out—he was a low-grade heathen, but he was big an' he didn't mind a little trouble now and again.

"If this dog can't eat here, neither can I," sez Bill, "but as for your kickin' him out, you 'd better pray for guidance before you tackle that job."

"Do you think I'm afraid o' that cur?" sneers Frenchy.

"Cur!" yells Bill. "Cur? Why you maul-headed, misshapen blotch on the face o' nature, what do you mean by callin' this dog a cur! I never saw this dog before to-day; but I'll bet ten to one that I can find out who his great-great-grandfather's great-great-grandfather was; an' I doubt if you know who your own father happened to be."

Bill was firin' at random o' course, but it looked as if he had hit somethin'. Frenchy was fair crazy. He pulled out his gun an' came chargin' down on us. Bill tried to get mine again, but I thought I'd better run it myself just then. I covered Frenchy, Frenchy covered Bill, an' the bull pup turned his back on us and looked down toward the depot, to see if his train was comin' back.

"Better put up your gun, Frenchy," I sez, soft as a wood dove, "or you'll get this office all mussed up."

Well, he knew me; so we arbitrated a little an' then we all went in an' the pup et his dinner like any other Christian, payin' for it himself out of his own money. First thing after dinner, Bill went out an' bought a gun of his own, an' I scented trouble. He wasn't old enough to shoot only from principle, not merely for practice.

The' was another young feller at Frenchy's with a lot o' hot money in his clothes. He seemed to have a deep-felt prejudice against fire, too, the way he was blowin' it in. When Bill came back, the young feller tried to buy the dog from him. Bill was polite an' refused to sell, givin' as the main reason that the dog didn't fully belong to him yet, but the feller pestered around until finally he offered Bill two hundred dollars for the dog.

"You ain't no fool when it comes to a dog," sez Bill, "but I'm givin' you the honest truth. This here pup don't belong to me—though if I can buy him I sure intend to do it."

"How far would you go when it came to payin' for him?" sez the man.

"Well, I'd give two fifty for him just on speculation," sez Bill. "He's put together, this pup is; but I didn't suppose 'at you people out here in the cattle country would know enough about the points of a dog, to offer two hundred for just a fancy one."

"I don't know nothin' about the points o' that dog," sez the feller. "I never even saw a dog like that one before; but when I see a man willin' to go the pace you went for this dog, I'd kind o' sort o' like to own the dog."

Bill got interested in the feller an' began pumpin' him for what he called copy. The young feller had punched cattle most of his life, blowin' in his wages at variegated intervals. About a month before he had slipped over to Laramie an' had gone against Silver Dick's game, winnin' over eleven hundred dollars. He said that Silver Dick was plumb on the square an' that he never intended to work again, just spend down to his last hundred an' then go an' play at Silver Dick's. Bill got a paper an' figured out what he called percents, showin' how an outsider was bound to lose to the game in the end; but most o' the fellers there had been up against Dick's game an' they took sides against Bill, tryin' to prove that they stood a show to win, until finally Bill give it up an' we started back home.

When we started home, Bill was still discoursin' about us Westerners. He said that we wasn't nothin' but a lot o' children playin' games an' believin' in fairy tales, that we never provided for the future, that we was allus willin' to risk anything we had on some fool thing that wouldn't benefit us none, an' so on until I got weary of it, an' after I'd took a shuffle I dealt him out this hand.

"An' the"s another breed," sez I, "that ain't nothin' but children an' that's the writers. An idea comes along an' stings 'em like a bee, an' they immejetly begin to swell. They swell an' swell until the whole earth ain't nothin' but the background for that bee-sting. They howl about it as if it was the most important thing in creation; but if you call around next week, you find that swellin' gone down an' they're howlin' just as fierce over a new swellin' where a different idea has stung 'em; ain't it so?"

"Not exactly," sez Bill; "for we set down our thoughts an' emotions while we're smartin' from the sting an' the other fellers can get the sense of 'em an' pass judgment on 'em in cold blood without gettin' stung at all."

"Well, you landed there," sez I, "but the' wasn't one o' those fellers there to-day, who was a quarter whit more childish'n what you was. Talk about providin' For their future! Why, the way you went on over this stray pup, purt' nigh put you in the position of a man who didn't have no future to provide for, an' what in thunder good can this here pup ever do you, no matter what happens?"

The pup was sittin' with his head between Bill's knees, an' Bill pulled his ear a time or two, an' then sez, "I reckon you're right; the whole earth ain't nothin' but a kindergarten. We all play different games an' when you stop an' look at it they all cost about the same in the end an' they all bring in about the same profit; but I'm glad I'm livin' anyhow; an' I'm glad I've got this dog. I'm special fond o' dogs."

You couldn't help likin' Bill; he allus played in the open an' when he kept score, he give you all the points you made without fussin' over 'em; but I didn't like the look o' that new outfit on his hip. He was too impulsive to carry a gun, an' he was too young. Take it when a man has had some experience in gun-fightin', he gets purty sober over the effect of it; but a young feller—well, who on earth knows what way a young feller is goin' to jump when he gets touched up a little?

"That's a purty likely lookin' gun you got there, Bill," sez I. "Do you savvy how to run one?"

He took it out of his pocket an' looked around, but the' wasn't nothin' in sight that needed killin', so he began to pop at an old single-tree lyin' about thirty yards away. The ponies were trottin' along purty jerky, but hanged if he didn't hit it four times out of six.

"It don't just hang to suit me," sez Bill, "but I'll learn it after a bit."

I looked at him a moment, but he was merely speakin' his mind, an' I sez: "Bill, where in Goshen did you get to be a killin' man?"

"Me?" sez Bill. "I never shot a man in my life, but I used to knock down glass balls purty accurate, an' I've hunted big game in Africa an' India. I don't want no trouble, but I'm set in my ways about dogs. It's a heap o' responsibility to raise a pup; but I'm goin' to give this one a fair show, an' I'm goin' to own him some way or another—I feel it in my bones that this here dog was sent to me. I had a dog, the livin' picture o' this feller once, an' he traded his life for mine, out there in the Indian Jungle. Now don't ask me any questions about it."

That night after we'd got the supper things red up, Bill sez; "Now I don't want no one to punish this dog but me, till he gets his edication. I don't care a bean for a trick dog; all I expect him to learn is jest English an' a part o' the sign langwidge, so as he'll be pleasant company an' useful in an emergency. I'll pay for any property he destroys, but please don't punish him."

The pup was about fifteen months old when he came, an' at first he sorrowed a heap for his old boss; but purty soon he see that Bill knew more about dogs'n he did himself, so he just transferred his affections over to Bill. Bill never raised his voice, he never whipped him nor even threatened him; he just reasoned with him an' explained why it was necessary to learn the conventionalities o' polite society. It took him a solid week to learn that pup how to shake hands, an' yet Bill told us confidential that he was certain that the pup knew it all the while; but at the end of the week the pup gave in, an' from that on he was as eager for knowledge as a new-born baby.

Cupid was the name of the pup, engraved right on to his brass collar, an' when he set his mind on acquirin' an edication, he made me an' the Kid leery 'at he'd beat us at the finish in spite of our start. He could walk on his hind legs an' speak an' open an' shut doors an' wipe his feet on the door-mat an' roll over an' pray an'—oh, well he knew 'em all an' six more; but Bill said it wasn't learnin' the tricks that counted, it was learnin' to think for himself. Bill used to put obstacles in his way, so that the pup would have to cipher a while to figger out how to work it, an' this was what Bill called stretchin' his intellect to match his enviroment. He was some the solemnest pup I ever see, an' it was kind o' creepy to see him come to the shack, open the door, slam it after him, wipe his feet on the burlap, look into Bill's face, an' give a short bark. This was to ask if Bill had any new jobs for him.

I had it all planned out that the pup was to sleep in the wagon shed; but this didn't look good to the pup, nor to Bill, neither. When night would come, Cupid would go through his lessons, eat his supper, an' fling himself slaunchways on the wide bunk. He didn't weigh more'n sixty pounds, but they was the solidest sixty ever wrapped up in a dog hide. He wouldn't mind no one but Bill, an' it was all I could do to get room enough on the perch to hang on. Then Bill would open up his vau-dee-ville show, an' when he'd simmer down, the pup would begin to chase jackrabbits, which was the most devilish-lookin' sight I ever see. He'd lay there with his eyelids rolled up, an' his eyes turned inside out, givin' short barks an' jerkin' his legs.

"Bill," I sez one night, "I ain't no chronic coward, but doggone me if I want to be mistook for a jack-rabbit, an' have this bulldog sock his ivories into me."

"He ain't no bulldog," snaps Bill. "It looks to me as if you might learn purty soon that he's a brindle bull-terrier!"

"Oh, I know that all right, an' I'm willin' to swear to it," sez I, "but just now it's his teeth, not his ancestors, that are botherin' me. If I'm to be mistook for a jack-rabbit, I ain't nowise particular just which kind of a bulldog is goin' to do the mistakin'."

Bill, he smiled sadly an' walked over an' stuck his naked finger right into the pup's mouth. I looked to see it bit off, but the pup only opened his eyes, looked foolish, an' tramped down another acre of imaginary grass; finally goin' to sleep again an' usin' my feet for a piller.

Talk about grit! That little cuss was willin' to fight any-thing that walked. We took him out to the herd one day, an' after he'd been kicked an' tossed an' trampled, he got on to throwin' a steer by the nose, an' from that on it was his favorite pastime. He played the game so enthusiastic, that I finally sez to Bill, "Bill, you mustn't forget that Colonel Scott has other uses for these cattle besides usin' 'em for dog exercisers." From that on, Bill made the pup be a little more temperate in the use o' steers.

The muscles on that pup got to be like hard rubber, an' you couldn't pinch him hard enough to make him squeak. He allus took a serious view o' life except when the' was a chance for a little rough an' tumble; then his face would light up like an angel's. Pullin' on a rope was his idee o' draw poker, an' he could wear out the whole bunch of us at it. Bill fair idolized him—fact is, we all thought a heap of him; but I'd 'a' liked him a mite better if the' 'd been more bunks in the shack.

If he got cold, he'd scratch your face till you let him under the covers, an' then when he got too hot, he'd pull the covers off an' roll 'em into a nice soft heap, with himself on top. He never overlooked himself much, the pup didn't. First I knew, I got to missin' a right smart o' sleep that really belonged to me; 'cause, while I'm opposed to speakin' ill o' the absent, I'd just about as soon try to sleep with a colicky hoss as with Bill an' the pup. When the pup wasn't chasin' imaginary jack-rabbits or live fleas, Bill was jumpin' up an' down to write somethin' new into his book; until Kid Porter swore that if any more came, he was goin' to leave.

I like a dog the full limit, but I never hankered to sleep with 'em, not when they have fleas; an' when they don't, they allus put me in mind of a man 'at uses perfumery. I tried to devise a plan for sleepin' on the floor, but I couldn't engineer it through.

"No," sez Bill, in a hurt kind of a tone, "I wouldn't inconvenience you for the world. Me an' Cupid will sleep on the floor." Well, there I was. I'm as tender-hearted as a baby antelope, so I just turned it off as a joke, an' got to sleepin' in the saddle on the return trip.

Nothin' on earth made Bill so mad as to call the pup a bulldog, though if he wasn't one, he sure looked the part. I knowed it wouldn't do to take too many chances, so me an' the Kid used to post the boys, an' when one of 'em would drop in an' say as natural as though he was chattin' about the weather: "That's a mighty fine London, brindle, bull-terrier you-uns have got," Bill's face would light up as if he was the mother of it, an' he would turn in an' preach us a sermon on dogs. That was why you liked Bill; he was just the same all the way through an' if he was friendly when it paid, you was certain sure he'd be just as friendly when it cost.

Colonel Scott's niece came out to visit him some time in May, an' we heard of her long before we saw her. 'Bout every one we met had somethin' to tell about what a really, truly heart-buster she was. She learned to ride, an' one afternoon she an' the Colonel struck our outfit just in front of a howlin' storm.

The' wasn't no show to get back to headquarters that night, so we smoothed out the wide bunk for the lady, an' us men planned to flop in the shed. She sure had dandy manners! She pitched in an' helped us get supper, an' we had about everything to eat that a man could think of—side meat an' boiled beans an' ham an' corn-bread an' baked beans an' flapjacks an' fried potatoes an' bean soup, an' coffee so stout that you couldn't see the bottom in a teaspoonful of it. We just turned ourselves loose an' gave her a banquet.

As soon as the dishes was off our hands, we started in to be jovial. Me an' the Kid wasn't just altogether at home, but Bill was right in his element. He played, an' him an' her sang, an' they talked, an' it was the most festive function I ever see; until the pup came in an' jumped up on the wide bunk where she was settin'. "Oh, take that horrid bull-dog away!" she squealed.

I dreaded the result; but I sez to myself, "Now surely that doggone ijit won't throw a call-down into the lady." but he did. "Miss Johnston," sez he, "that ain't no bulldog. That's a high-bred London bull-terrier. How would you like to be called a Chinaman? Come here, Cupid."

It was like throwin' a bucket o' water on a bed o' coals. Bill was like an oyster from that on, an' the girl looked as if she'd been slapped. I was mad all the way through. It's all right for a man to be crazy, if he'll only keep it private, but the' ain't no sense in tryin' to get the whole balance o' creation over to his side.

The Colonel thought it a mighty prime joke to have his niece called down over a bull pup, an' he chuckled about it consid'able. Next mornin' he made Bill promise to come over an' visit him; but the girl said HER good-byes to me an' the Kid. From that on, Bill was over to headquarters half his time, but it didn't do him much good. The girl wouldn't stand for the pup, an' Bill wouldn't go back on him; so it looked purty much like a deadlock.

One Sunday about the first of August, we was all sittin' in the shade of the shack, lookin' down into the valley. The shack backed up against a massive crag on the edge of a high plateau. The road from headquarters came in from the North, wound around a steep butte, then along the top o' the cliff to where it slid down into the valley to Danders.

We heard the thud o' hoofs an' turnin' around, we saw the Colonel's niece tearin' down the road on a big hoss. It was a plain case of runaway, an' I felt something break inside my chest. They were headin' straight for the top o' the cliff, the hoss was goin' too fast to make the turn, an' we was too far off to beat him to it.

We simply stood there like a flock o' sheep, without a single thought among us. The' didn't seem to be a thing to do, but just watch 'em plunge two hundred feet into the ravine. I glanced at Bill, but I hardly knew him. His brows was drawn down like a wildcat's, his jaws was clamped so tight you could hear 'em grit, an' his eyes seemed to smoke.

I looked back to the road again, an' there was the pup, standin' down by the road watchin' the hoss runnin' toward him. I touched Bill on the shoulder, an sez, "Can the pup do anything, Bill?" Bill gave a sigh as though he had just come back from the dead, an' in a voice that wavered an' trembled, but still rang out like a trumpet, he yelled: "Throw him, Cupid, throw him!" Lord, man! I wish you could have seen it. The mane bristled up on that dog's back an' his muscles bulged out till he looked like a stone image. We heard him give a low whine, like as if he knowed it was too big a job for a little feller like him. But did he try to flunk it? Not him. Then I knew 'at he wasn't neither a bulldog nor a bull-terrier, but a little sixty-pound hero, willin' to pass out his life any time 'at Bill would draw a check for it.

We fair helt our breath as he backed away from the road an' took a little easy gallop until the hoss was near even with him. Another dog would have blown his lungs loose, tellin' what he was a-goin' to do; but Cupid never said a word. His lip curled up till you could catch the glisten of those wicked white teeth of his, an' then when the hoss was right alongside an' it looked as if he had lost his chance, he gave a couple of short jumps an' threw himself for the critter's nose.

Well, I can't rightly tell you just what did happen then. I saw him make his spring an' swing around full sweep, hangin' on to the hoss's nose; but from that on the whole earth seemed to be shook loose. The boss keeled over like he was shot, the girl seemed to turn a somerset in the air, an' light all in a heap, with one arm hangin' over the edge of the cliff. We heard a shriek, a little smothered yelp, an' then we ran down to them.

Bill looked first toward the girl an' then toward the pup, an' it was tearing his heart apart to tell which one he would go to first. Finally he ran to the girl an' carried her back from the cliff. He knelt an' put his ear to her heart, then he took her wrist an' after what seemed a mighty long time, he gave a little sigh, an' sez, "Kid, run for some water. Run! What do you stand lookin' at me for?"

The Kid, he certainly did run, while Bill stepped over to where Cupid was layin', still an' quiet, but with a piece o' the hoss's nose still in his grip. The hoss's right shoulder was broke an' he couldn't get up, but was thrashin' an' strugglin' around. "Get your gun an' put that hoss out of his misery, Happy," sez Bill, an' the' was somethin' in his tone that filled me plumb full o' the spirit of action.

When I came back, the Kid was pourin' a bucket o' water over the girl, an' Bill, with the tears rollin' down his cheeks, was feelin' over the body of the little bull-pup. I put the muzzle to within an inch o' the soft spot in the hoss's forehead, an' fired. The hoss's head sank, an' then I gulped a couple o' times like a flabby galoot, an' sez, "Bill, do you reckon the brindle bull-terrier'll pull through?"

"Get me some o' that water," sez Bill. When I got it, he showed me a place where the whole o' the pup's scalp had been kicked loose. I couldn't see what good water was goin' to do, but Bill wouldn't give up. "I can't find where the skull is broke," he sez, "an' maybe the water'll fetch him around."

He poured some water over the little feller's face, but it didn't seem to be no use. He just lay still with his head on Bill's knee, an' I knew it was all up with little Cupid; but just to please Bill, I gave him a flask, I happened to have, an' sez, "Give the little feller a drink, Bill. He never was used to hittin' it none, an' it'll have a powerful effect on him." Bill opened the pup's mouth an' poured in a tol'able stiff swig, an' by cracky, the pup opened his eyes, an' when he saw Bill bendin' down over him, he tried to wag his little tail.

Well, Bill took that pup up in his arms an' hugged him—an' if the' 's any one in this crowd that feels like laughin', it'll be healthier for 'im to step outside.

Then Bill picked up the pup, an' motioned for me an' the Kid to tote the lady up to the shack, an' we did it, though it wasn't fittin' work for a couple o' ridin men. She had fully come to when we reached the shack, an' we laid her on the wide bunk. Bill put the pup on the narrow bunk, washed out the hole in his head, an' tied it up with a clean handkerchief. Then he crossed over an' spoke to the girl. I could easy tell by his voice that the last time they had parted it had been a little stormy.

"Miss Johnston," he sez in a low tone, "are you sufferin' much?"

She owned up to a perfectly rippin' headache, an' said she was sore all over; but it was her ankle 'at pained her most. Bill started to look at it; but she reddened up an' tried to draw it under her. Bill never paid any attention to her, but sez calmly, "I've had consid'able experience, Miss Johnston. A great deal depends on promptness. Now just let the limb lay natural till I remove the shoe."

Me an' the Kid started to break for the foothills, but he set me to makin' bandages, an' sent the Kid after some more water. We was losin' our age fast, an' Bill's voice sounded like grandpa's. He said it was a corkin' bad sprain, but he tied it up an' wet down the bandages; an' then he sent me to headquarters after the spring-wagon, an' the Kid to Danders for the doctor.

We both got back before daylight, an' by that time Bill an' the girl had come to a purty harmonious agreement concernin' the proper standin' of a brindle bull-terrier. When I came in he was holdin' the lady's hand—an' I was the only one what reddened up.

CHAPTER NINETEEN
BARBIE MAKES A DISCOVERY

Jessamie, that was Miss Johnston's real name, had been ridin' one o' the Colonel's high-breds, an' again orders at that; but the Colonel was purty comfortable like at the upshot. Bill was fitted out with a pedigree an 'a bank account what made him a parlor guest purty much everywhere he went, an' on top o' that it tickled the Colonel a heap to have things ironed out by the bull pup himself.

I didn't much suppose when I see that sorrowful pup pikin' back the track that he was doomed to achieve prominence an' fame, but Fate had him entered on her book all right, an' he made so everlastin' good that it wouldn't have surprised me a mite if they'd have run him for Governor.

You just bet your life the other feller never got him again! Why they'd 'a' had to bring the whole standin' army to filch that dog away from Bill after the big doin's. Out here in Wyoming it's a test of class—owners of one of Cupid's pups are first-class, others belong to the herd.

It was two weeks after the accident that us four—countin' Kid Porter—was sittin' in exactly the same place back of the shack; only this time, Bill was pullin' the pup's ears. Bill hadn't spent overly much time with us the last fortnight, an' we were talkin' it all over, when hanged if we didn't hear the thud of hoofs again, an' I reckon we all turned blue.

Cupid himself appeared a shade disgusted at the prospect of an encore. He had only just shed his bandages, an' the flap on his lid was still too tender to scratch, so that you can't hardly blame him for takin' the narrow view of it. We jumped around the corner of the house, but the' was two riders this time, an' while they was spinnin' along at a purty merry clip, they had control of the hosses all right. Both of 'em was girls, an' one of 'em was Jessamie. When I see who the other was, I felt as though I was standin' on the outer edge of a fleecy cloud. It was Barbie. I ducked back around the corner of the house.

Bill, he ran down an' helped his lady to alight, while Barbie flopped herself off her mount an' ran up to Cupid. Oh, they know a heap, dogs do. Cupid took just one look in her eyes, an' when she squatted down on her knees, he tried to get into her lap an' they made a heap o' fuss over each other. I could tell by her eyes that Jessamie felt a shade jealous, 'cause Cupid hadn't quite forgiven her for slightin' him at the first. I was watchin' 'em through a chink in the shack and I was feelin' purty glum myself, to think that Barbie would spend all that time on a dog an' never give one little inquiry about me.

Well, they examined the spot where Cupid had made his tackle, an' the dent in the earth where the hoss an' Jessamie had lit, an' then they meandered up to the house to see just how helpless we'd been, aside from Cupid.

"Well, you all had a share in it;" Barbie was sayin' as they neared the shack. "Cupid did the actual work, you trained him for it, and Higinson had the kind of a nerve that don't melt under fire."

"Sure thing," sez Bill, "I own up that I was plumb petrified, an' Cupid wasn't carin' much one way or the other; but Hank Higinson never lost his self-possession a second,"—this was all bosh, 'cause I was purty nigh stampeded, an' that's the simple truth.

"Where is he?" sez Barbie. "I want to see him an' then I can tell just about how much he could do on his own hook."

I was feelin' a sight better. I saw exactly how it was. Bill an' all the rest o' the fellers had done exactly what I had hinted at an' hadn't divulged my identity, an' Barbie hadn't the slightest idea that I was in the state. Those people who know precisely the right time to disobey orders, are a big help to humanity; but they're mighty scarce.

Bill, he opened the door of the shack, an' sez, "Come on out. Hank, a lady wants to be introduced to you."

I stepped to the door feelin' wonderful bashful, but when Barbie saw me, she went several different colors an' shouts:

"Happy, Happy Hawkins! What on earth do you mean by bein' here?"

Her voice was trembly an' accusin' an' reproachful an' glad an' a lot of other things; an' I found it mighty hard to come back with a joke, quick enough to suit me. I felt sort o' flighty, with her big dark eyes lookin' into me, an' while I was stutterin' she opened up on me an' give me a good old-fashioned scoldin'—an' I felt dandy. Bill, he was troubled some with startin' eyes. Jessamie was breedy all right, but compared to Barbie, she looked like a six o' suit alongside the queen o' trumps.

"Why," sez Barbie, turnin' to Jessamie, "everything always goes right when Happy's present. I might have known from your description that it was Happy who saw the only way—"

"Oh, pshaw, now," sez I, breakin' in, "I didn't do a blasted thing. Cupid here was the master workman on this job, while Bill—"

"That's all true enough," sez Barbie, "you have the gift of hidin' yourself in your work; but I can see you just the same."

It was certainly comfortin' to hear the way she went on about it; but it was a little too cold-blooded for my nerves, 'cause I hadn't done a thing this time but make one small suggestion; so we finally compromised by admittin' that now an' again, I was picked out to be the nail on the finger of Fate. Sometimes I rather think that comes purty close to hittin' me.

Jessamie had graduated from the university where Barbie was goin', at the close of Barbie's first year. They had met, an' remembered each other; an' as soon as the news of the doin's had reached the Diamond Dot, of course Barbie piked over to make a call. The outcome was that when the Colonel sent out a man to take my place, I rode back to the Diamond Dot with Barbie, an' it was mighty good to be there again.

Jabez give me a good firm hand-shake, an' didn't rub it in about the silkworms; so that everything just slid along as smooth as joint-oil, an' I had a good opportunity to estimate the benefit of Barbie's schoolin'. She was a heap more changed than I had supposed at first; the' was a way she had of holdin' her head an' walkin' an' talkin', that showed me quick enough that money spent on her edication wasn't nowise wasted.

But she went back to her last year soon after this, intendin' to be the best maid at Jessamie's weddin'. This weddin' was a curious thing an' opened my eyes purty wide to the ways of women. I'd 'a' been willin' to bet my saddle that the one man she never would marry, was Bill; but she owned up herself that she had made up her mind to marry him the first night they met. She wasn't quite sure of it until him an' her had the fall-out over Cupid, and that settled it. She said a man who had the spunk to stick up for his dog the way Bill did would be a purty handy kind to have around the house, an' she was just tryin' him out to see how far he'd go. She was actually fond of dogs all the time, especially bulldogs. A girl-baby three years old could have fooled Methusaleh in his prime, an' that means after he'd had about six hundred years of experience. She's a wonderful invention, woman.

All the while before Barbie left, she was tryin' to plan out what use she was goin' to put her edication to. Sometimes she was minded to go on the stage, at others lawyerin' looked good to her, but most of the time she seemed to think that a female doctor would come nearer fittin' her than anything else.

Me an' Jabez worried about it a heap; but we was wise enough to hide it. We knew that Barbie carted around at all times what they call a spirit of combativity, which fattened on opposition, an' we preferred to let her scrap it out with herself, hopin' that what she finally decided on would be all for the best.

Jabez said good-bye at the edge of the ranch, while I drove her over to Webb Station. I kind o' fought shy of Danders 'cause it seemed to me that the' was always some kind of a job waitin' for me there, an' Barbie had left me a heap of work for that winter. "Have you learned anything yet?" she asked me, after the train had pulled into sight an' we was shakin' hands.

"Not a thing for certain," sez I. "I've stumbled onto several rumors, but they always went out. Do you still study over it much, Barbie?"

"Never a day goes by but what I study over it," sez she. "There isn't anything I wouldn't give to know about my mother—all about her."

"Are you sure, Barbie?" said I.

She thought hard a minute, an' then she threw back her head an' looked into my eyes. "Yes," she said, in a low tone, "I'd give everything—even the love and respect I feel for my father."

I gave a little shiver. "Barbie," I sez, "I don't think you'll ever have to pay that high a price. I never saw your Dad cruel in cold blood, an' he's purty just."

"Oh, I would rather die than find out that he'd ever been cruel to my mother; but I do want to know about her; and some day I will." She squeezed my hand hard and her eyes were wet with tears when she stepped on the train; but she tried to smile, she sure did.

CHAPTER TWENTY
RICHARD WHITTINGTON ARRIVES

Well, that winter rolled by without a break. Me an' Jabez had just about learned how to take each other, an' we didn't stretch our harness to the snappin' point. Bill Andrews had finally got tol'able well acquainted with me also, an' was able to savvy that while peace was my one great desire, the' was some prices that I wouldn't pay for it.

We was all het up when the graduation day finally came, an' we didn't do a lick of work on the ranch; just gathered around the ranch buildin's, polishin' up her harness an' hosses, an' talkin' about her in hushed voices. She had won honors an' medals an' one thing or another until I reckon we felt purty much as Mrs. Washington did when she was cleanin' house to welcome the father of his country after he had showed England where to reset the boundery stakes.

Barbie had wrote us that she was goin' to cut out a string of invitations as long as your arm and pike right out for home as soon as she had finished her part of the program, an' we weren't able to do a tap until she arrived. At first I was minded to drive down after her, an' then I decided that it would be better for me to stay at home an' line up the boys in some sort of style to receive her. Spider Kelley went after her and as soon as they hove in sight I had all the punchers charge down an' shoot their guns off in the air. They was wearin' their gaudiest raiment an' shoutin' their heads off, an' she owned up herself that it topped anything she ever saw in the East. She stood up in the buckboard an' took off her hat an' swung it about her head and shouted, "Boys, you're just bully—every one of you!" an' say, the' wasn't a puncher on the Diamond Dot that wouldn't have given up his hide to make her a pair o' ridin' gloves. Jabez had waited back at the ranch house an' he was tremblin' when we left him to ride down an' meet her.

Here she was, comin' back for the last time with all the learnin' of the earth packed away in her head, an' niched up with more degrees than a thermometer; but it hadn't changed her heart, not one grain; an' when she saw the home buildin's with ol' Mount Savage sittin' up on his throne an' all the little peaks bowin' before him, like pages to a king, she jes' threw out her arms as though she would take in the whole outfit in one big hug, an' her eyes filled up with tears as she sez, "Oh, Dad. I love it! I love every inch of it, every line of it, every shade of it; an' I've hungered an' thirsted for it all these years—an' for you, Dad, for you most of all."

Well, you should have seen Jabez. Beam? Why, I reckon you could have lit a cigar on his face, an' he fluttered around like a hen with one chicken an' that one a duck. He couldn't quite believe that it was all true and that he was actually awake. He had worried so long about her cuttin' into some new game as soon as her schoolin' was done that he hardly dared rejoice for fear it would wake him up; but it didn't take her long to begin enjoyin' her old freedom again. It took us some longer to adjust ourselves to her, however.

Now she hadn't changed such an awful sight, an' yet the' was somethin' about her 'at made you feel like touchin' your hat when she issued an order. Not that she was uppity nor nothin'; she rambled around playin' with the colts an' the calves, an' rompin' with the dogs, an' fairly stackin' up the whole place in little heaps. An' she rustled up her old sombrero an' leggin's just as though she had never set a hoof off the range. Still, the' was somethin' about her you couldn't quite put your finger on; but which you knew in your heart was there all the time, awaitin' till she made up her mind to call it out; like a handful o' regulars givin' dignity to a scrawny two by twice fort in the Injun country.

We took up our ridin' again, an' just as I was gettin' used to it, along comes a feller lookin' about two thirds starved. His clothes was ragged an' soiled, he had forgot his baggage, he was on foot (an' when I say on foot, I don't only mean that he was dispensin' with the luxury of a pony; he was also unemcumbered with soles to his boots), but he had indoor hands, a back as straight as an Injun's, an' a way of flingin' up his head an' drawin' down his brows when you spoke to him sudden, which proved 'at trampin' was only a sideline with him. He put in an application as cook for the home gang.

Ol' Cast Steel looked into him: examined his eyes, his hands, an' the way he carried his head. Then he spoke kind o' slow an' drawly. "Cook?" sez he. "We'll, I'd be willin' to bet 'at you've stayed up till three o'clock a heap more times'n you have ever arose at this wholesome hour. What can you cook?"

Well, the feller he laughed, an' sez, "You win. I own up 'at I ain't no cook, nor I ain't no cow puncher; but my pension has stopped an' my appetite is still runnin'. I never yet recall readin' no notice of any cook what died of starvation."

Jabez grinned. "I don't ask no man about his past," sez he. "No man knows nothin' about his future. As for the present, you can help with the cookin'. Flap Jack is due for his bender, week after next, an' if you can learn the trade by that time you'll come in handy."

'Twas the first time I ever heard of Cast Steel vary his hirin' speech; so I knew 'at he too had the feller spotted for a stray; but he rolled up his sleeves an' started to peel spuds for the evenin' slum. He said that his name was Richard Whittington, an' while he didn't talk overly extensive about himself, he wasn't nowise offish nor snarly. He did his work up to the limit too, an' even of Flap Jack didn't complain as much as he generally did whenever he was furnished with a little extra help. The peculiar thing was the way 'at Barbie treated him. She came down to the cook shack soon after he landed, with a lot of Jabez' old clothes an' a pair of boots, 'cause anything in distress got to her heart by the shortest cut. She came lopin' along with about fifteen dogs, whistlin' an' hummin' an' sort o' dancin' up in the air like a young angel; but the minute she saw him she sobered up, an' after he had thanked her, which he did in book langwidge, she simply pulled down the blinds an' locked the door. It was mighty curious an' set us all to talkin', 'cause she treated us fellers just as friendly as the rest of the stock; but Dick made a bad impression right at the start, an' we kept our eyes on him for the first crooked move.

He was a restless feller, was Dick, allus askin' questions about breeds an' fencin' an' winter feeds an' marketin'. Said he liked to have somethin' to study about when his hands was workin'. Barbie left one of her books out in the wagon-shed one day an' Dick found it. He curled right up on a cushion an' begun to read. That was the very day 'at Flappy was to start off on his periodical, an' he had made all his preparations so that everything would be in apple-pie order. When dinner went by an' no deputy showed up he ground out several canticles of profanity; but when supper time hove in sight and nairy a report from the substitute hash-herder, he fairly stood on tiptoe an' screamed his woes into what they call the wel-kin; an' you can bet that Flappy made her welk all right.

He had been training for this jag for full three months, an' the thirst he had built up was somethin' for the whole ranch to be proud of; an' all the boys was full of sympathy an' interest, an' wanted him to have every show in the world. They wanted his mind to be utterly free from care, so that he could give his full attention to tackin' up a Diamond Dot record that would arouse the envy of the entire West, an' Flappy was in fine shape to do it.

We all started out to find Dick, whether he was still hidin' around the ranch or had started to hike; but it was Barbie herself who found him. She came racin' along with a herd of dogs, friskin' an' rompin' the same as they was; but when she came onto Dick readin' her book she simmered down immejet. When he looked up an' saw her he seemed like a feller wakin' up out of a dream. It didn't break on him all at once; but when it did, he looked as guilty as a sheep-herder. He stood up an' bowed an' helt out the book an' stammered, an' all in all, it was painful to watch 'em. None of us was able to figger out why they acted this way ever time they happened to meet; but they did.

Well, after he'd apologized a couple o' chapters she told him 'at she was nearly through with the book, an' if he'd come up to the house after supper she'd be glad to let him take it. After supper up he went to the house an' sent ol' Mellisse in for it. When he got it he went back to the cook-shack an' stayed up all night readin' it. One of the boys what got in about two o'clock said 'at he was just about half through with it the second time when he came along. Books is the same as opium to some folks. After that Barbie used to send him down books purty often, an' he used to get a world of comfort out of 'em.

One afternoon when Dick was cookin' up a stew Jabez came out an' sat on a cracker-box talkin' to him. He allus seemed to have a likin' for Dick, an' used to chat with him right consid'able. This afternoon he got to spreadin' himself about how much money the place handled every year an' how much the' was invested in it, an' what a great thing the cattle industry was to the entire country. Jabez had his vanities all right, an' he used to parade 'em occasional an' got a heap o' comfort out of 'em. Dick went along seasonin' an' addin' an' stirrin' an' not seemin' to pay a mite of attention, until finally Jabez got tired of appreciatin' himself, an' sez, "Well, what do you think of this little plant anyway?"

"Do you like the scenery around here, or do you have to live here on account of your health?" sez Dick, sort of unconcerned like.

Jabez looked at him about a minute to kind of get the drift of his remark, an' then he sez, "What do you mean by that?"

"Why," sez Dick, "you ain't makin' two percent profit, an' I was just wonderin' what you stayed here for—if it wasn't for somethin' else beside the filthy looger."

Jabez, he jumps to his feet an' goes all through it again, tellin' all he has took in an' all he has paid out; while Dick kept attendin' to his pots an' pans the same as if he was stone deaf. Jabez rattled on an ended up with: "An' this here ranch has the best water an' the best range an' the best shelter of any ranch in the state. What do you think of that?"

"Why, I think it all the more reason why it should pay a business profit," drawls Dick. "Only last week I heard you complainin' somethin' fierce because you had to put up for a new freight-wagon. The great trouble with you is that you don't have no system. You need a manager, a man who takes an interest in modern progress, a man who sees that the rest o' the men pay a profit. I don't mean a foreman, you got plenty o' them. I mean a business man. You ain't no business man; you don't like it."

Well, Jabez was stupefied. He'd never had no wage-earner dump advice on him before, an' here was a tramp, as you might say, who started in by telling him that what he really needed was some one to run his business for him. He didn't fly up through. He just rose an' gave Dick a searchin' look, an' then he meandered up to the house; an' you could tell by the very droop of his shoulders that what he was doin' was thinkin'.

The upshot of it was that when Flappy was hauled out to the ranch the next week, an' as soon as he got so he could tell fire from water, Dick fitted up an office in the North wing; an' about fifteen minutes afterward we all felt the difference. From that on everything ran like a round-up. Dick didn't boss none, he just pointed out the best way, an' we did it. All those answers we had told him about calves an' winter hay an' such-like had simply gone in one ear—an' stuck to the inside of his mental gearing. He discovered that Jabez had been stuck for further orders on most of his supplies, an' had allus managed to win the bottom price whenever it came his turn to make a sale.

Well, Dick was a perpetual surprise party. You could tell by the color of his skin that he was an indoor man; but he sat a hoss like a cow puncher, an' as soon as he got things runnin' to suit him on our place he got to makin' side trips to the other ranches. He would spend two hours talkin' about the weather; but at the end o' that time, he knew more about a man's outfit than the owner himself. Then he ordered out a lot of stock papers, an' the first thing we knew, we was askin' him questions about things 'at we'd allus supposed we savvied from tail to muzzle. He seemed to like me more'n the rest, an' chose me out to be his ridin' pal an' what he called an A. D. Kong, which was simply the French for messenger boy; but Dick never unloaded a lot of talk about himself. You wouldn't notice it, but he allus managed to have the other feller do most o' the talkin'.

When winter came he took a trainload o' cattle clear to Chicago an' brought back twenty bulls—dandies! Big white-faced fellers with pool-table backs an' stocky legs, an' they sure made the other stuff look like the champion scrubs of creation. No one in our parts had ever seen such cattle, an' for the rest of the winter we helt a fair an' booked enough orders for calves to make a man nervous. Jabez had gone along, an' it must have ganted him consid'able to heave out the wampum for that bunch; but you should have seen him swell up when folks got to talkin' about 'em. He was game though, an' gave Dick the credit. He thought Dick was the whole manuver by this time.

Barbie an' Dick had got over givin' antelope starts every time they met; but they wasn't what you would call friendly by a long ways. Dick had worn a rough lookin' beard when he first arrived; but afterward he had trimmed it to a point, an' it made him look some like a doctor. His ears were set tight to his head, an' he had a proud nose; but it was his hands an' his eyes that set him apart. His hands were fair size but white, an' they stayed white. They had a nervous way of fussin' around with things whenever he got to thinkin'; but after all, the thing that was the final call was his eyes. They were bright an' set in under heavy brows; but they never seemed tryin' to bend you, like some eyes do, they just seemed so completely sure of what they saw, an' they seemed to have seen so much beforehand, that a feller was tempted to stick to the truth in front of 'em—even when it wasn't altogether convenient. Dick was the first cold-blooded man I ever liked, an' he was sure cold-blooded at this period.

CHAPTER TWENTY-ONE
HAPPY MAKES A DISCOVERY

Now dogs an' Barbie was allus exceedin' intimate. Dogs just doted on her, an she recipercated full measure; but she had one dog what was only a dog by what they call an act of courtesy. It must 'a' weighed fully two pounds, an' had bushy hair at that. It had a bark to it like one o' these intellectual dolls what can say Ma-maa, Ma-maa, but the critter was as proud o' this bark as though it shook all the buildin's on the place. The blame thing wasn't physically able to inflict much more damage than a mosquito, but it was full as bloodthirsty, an' it had took a keen disregard for Bill Andrews.

Bill Andrews was still the foreman, an' one day he was on his way to the office to make a report to Dick when this imitation dog came sailin' around the corner an' took a grab at his leg. He had a brand-new pair of pants on, an' they was outside his boots. You know how corduroy tears when the dye has been a bit too progressive. Well, the pup loosened up a piece like a section of pie. Bill Andrews lost his Christian fortitude, give that toy muff a kick that landed him fifteen feet—an' Barbie came around the corner, an' Dick came out of the office at the same time.

The poor little pup was a-layin' on his back yelpin' like a love-sick bob-cat; a white rage came over me an' I pulled out my gun; but before I could use it Dick had sailed into him without a word. Bill Andrews was too flustered to pull his own gun, so he put up his hands, but it didn't do no good. Dick caught him under the chin, an' the back of his head struck the ground several moments before his feet arrived. It was a beautiful blow; I never seen a neater. I don't reckon Barbie ever did either; 'cause as soon as she had gathered up the pup she walked up to Dick an' sez, "I want to thank you for this, an' to say that I am in your debt to the extent of any favor what's in my power." Course Dick was locoed the same as usual. His face looked like the settin' sun, an' he couldn't pump out a word to save him. Them two found it mighty hard to overcome the first prejudice they'd felt again each other.

Bill Andrews he set up after a bit, with his hands on the ground, bracin' himself while he was tryin' to recall the history of the few precedin' moments. Dick looked down at him calmly an' said, "As soon as you have apologized to Miss Judson you may come into the office and we shall transact our business." Then he lifted his hat, whirled on his heel, an 'stalked inside like as if he was a colonel.

Bill Andrews was purty tol'able low-spirited; but he handed out as affectin' an excuse as he could dream up, and as soon as Barbie had spoke her piece he slouched into the office purty consid'able cargoed up with conflictin' emotions. I'd ruther shoot a man an' not kill him, than to be the cause of makin' him look ridiculous before a woman—that is, a revengeful sneak like what Bill Andrews was.

As soon as he an' Dick got through with their talk, an' it was a purty tol'able lengthy confab at that, Bill Andrews went to the boss an' tendered in his resignation. Cast Steel accepted it mighty hearty, 'cause Barbie had just been callin' on him; an' that very mornin' Dick made Pete Hanson foreman.

Next night the office safe was opened an' fifteen hundred dollars was took. Every one thought right away of Bill Andrews, an' the ol' man sent us out in pairs to scour the country. The' wasn't much scourin' to be done, how-ever, 'cause we found Bill Andrews on the next ranch, an' they was ready to swear 'at he hadn't left it all night. The' wasn't no one else that any one felt like suspectin'. Jabez wasn't the man to weep over upsettin' a can o' condensed, an' purty soon the theft was forgot an' everything was runnin' along as smooth as forty quarts o' joint-oil.

The ol' man kept dependin' more an' more on Dick, until finally Dick got to signin' checks, orderin' all the supplies, an' takin' full charge; while Jabez spent most of his time taggin' around after Barbie. They was like a couple o' young children; but Barbie wasn't quite so high-headed with Dick after the dog affair, an' they got to ridin' together quite a bit themselves. Barbie was just as good friends with me as ever; but I could see—any one could see—that Jabez was willin' to call Dick a son-in-law just the minute that Barbie was.

By the time he had been there a year Dick was the big head chief, an' the ranch was boomin' along like a river steamboat. He allus got the best of everything in the way of supplies, an' every laddie-buck in the West knew of it; so 'at a Diamond Dot puncher didn't throw up his job just for exercise. The' was a swarm o' white-faced calves, an' about half of 'em wore other fellers' brands, which was a receipt for a lot of fancy money, so 'at Jabez was as well satisfied as the men; an' even Barbie had come to own up that Dick was the fittin'est man in those parts. I could read every thought in her head, an' it hurt me to think that at last I had dropped back to second fiddle; but I could see that Dick had had chances that I hadn't had, an' —an' I allus aim to play fair, so I took to ridin' alone an' workin' harder than I was used to.

She could strum a guitar till you'd be willin' to swear it was the heavenly harps of the Celustial Choir; an' she an' Dick used to loaf around in the moonlight makin' melody 'at was worth goin' a good long ways to hear. They sure made a tasty couple, an' all the boys used to like to see 'em together. In fact, the whole Diamond Dot was as match-makey as a quiltin' bee.

One moonlight night I'd been up to ol' Monody's grave, an' I came walkin' back about half-past nine. It was more'n twelve years since Ol' Monody had passed over, but it didn't seem that long. Just as I turned a corner; I heard a laugh that seemed to float to me from a long ways back in the past. It was Jim Jimison's laugh, an' as I came around the corner of the house there he stood with his back to me, talkin' to Barbie. "Well, for the Gee Whizz!" I cried. He turned, an' it was Dick. We looked into each other's eyes a moment, an' then I forced a laugh an' went on to the stallion stable, where I sat down to puzzle it out.

It wasn't very long before Dick came to me an' held out his hand. I took it, an' we gave an old-time grip. "I was wonderin' how long it would be before you saw through me," he sez.

I got the moon in his face an' looked at him a long time. Of course a dozen years and the beard made a lot of difference, but not near all. When I'd left him, he was only a boy, a boy all the way through, —looks, words, actions; while now he was a man an' a sizey one at that. It ain't years alone that make any such change. I knew in a minute that Jim had been through something that was mighty near too narrow to get through. "Well," sez I, "what's the story?"

"You put me on my feet, Happy," sez he, "an' after you left I just kept on goin'. I tended to my stuff, an' I improved it an' I took on new ranges, an' I made it go, I sure made it go. Then the Exporters Cattle Company got after me. My range was needed to fill a gap between two o' their ranges, an' they tried to make me sell.

"I didn't want to sell, I was makin' money an' I was layin' it up; and I wasn't ready to stop workin' at my age, so I fought back. I didn't stand any show. There's a bunch o' these big companies that are all the same, under different names, an' they fought me on the ground an' on the railroads, an' at the stock yards; they tried to turn my men again me; they had my stuff run onto their range, an' then tried to prevent my gettin' it back. I didn't mind their open warfare; but their underhanded ways drove me wild. One o' their agents used to dog me around every time I'd go to town. He'd grin an' ask me if I wasn't ready to sell out YET. I finally closed out the cattle, an' started to raise only horses. One night my three thorough-bred stallions had their throats cut, an' then next time I went to town he came in when I was eatin' my supper, grinnin' as usual, an' asked me if I thought raisin' hosses would pay.

"I knew what his game was an' tried my best to hold in, but I couldn't help tellin' him that I didn't suppose it would pay quite so well as hirin' out to murder hosses would. This was enough for him; he called me everything he could lay tongue to, and when I rose to my feet he pulled his gun. The other men in the room were beginnin' to sneer at me, but I knew the consequences, and started to leave. He grabbed me by the shoulder an' whirled me around. 'Git down on your knees,' he sez, 'an' 'pologize to me.'

"That was my limit. My cup was nearly full of coffee, an' I dashed the coffee in his face, hoping to get hold of his gun. But he jumped back an' fired. He missed me, an' I hit him in the center of the forehead with the coffee cup. It was big an' heavy, and it—killed him. This was just what the bunch wanted; but in spite of their precautions I got away, came north, and got into another business; but that didn't suit either; so here I am, with the worst gang in this country achin' to get track o' me."

"How long ago was this, Jim?" sez I.

"Call me Dick," sez he. "It was about four years ago now. I leased my land for more'n enough to pay taxes, but I suppose it will all blow up sometime, an' they'll get me in the end."

"I don't suppose the' 's any way to go back an' square it, is there?" sez I.

"Hell, no!" he sez, bitter as death. "They own Texas."

"Haven't you any friends there who would swear it was self-defense?" sez I.

"I've got plenty of friends there—that's how I got away; but they don't dare to fight that cattle crowd in the open," sez he.

"Looks purty bad," sez I.

"It's rotten bad!" sez he. "But this is business all right. Whenever I hear any one talk about the morals of business it drives me wild. The' ain't any morals in business. The best it ever is, is straight gamblin'—I say the BEST it ever is, is straight gamblin'"—Jim's voice was gritty with wrath—"while at the worst," he went on, "it stoops to murder, wholesale and retail, it ruins homes, it manufactures thieves an' perjurers an'—"

"You remind me of a feller named Fergoson," sez I. "He said that at the best, business was stealin'."

"I like him," sez Jim, or I suppose I better say Dick. "I like him. You couldn't fool him with a lot o' pleasant names for things. He dealt in the spirit of a deed. I like him."

It wasn't much peculiar that I hadn't recognized the boy. As he talked, I could see the caged tiger glarin' out through his eyes, an' I knew that something wild would happen if the bars ever broke.

"I'm mighty sorry, Dick," sez I.

"Oh, I ain't through with 'em yet. I'm not clear out of the game. You don't need to think 'at they've broke me," sez he.

"I wasn't thinkin' o' you," I said in a low tone.

He drew in his breath, an' the noise he made was half way between a sob an' a groan. "My God!" he said between set teeth. "Do you think that I haven't carried that cross also? But I've changed a lot in five years, an' they won't think of me at the Diamond Dot. Happy, I've got a scheme for organizin' the cattlemen o' the Northwest to fight that Texas crowd an' whip 'em out o' the business. I know the game from A to Z, an' if I can just work it through without comin' out in the open I can beat 'em."

"Mebbe," sez I, "but it's exposin' her to a mighty big risk."

"I'll never do that, whatever happens," sez he.

"As long as this Texas crime hangs over you, it hangs over her too," sez I, "an' as soon as your fight gets under way they'll turn your record inside out, an' you know it."

He gripped his hands together an' punched a hole in the ground with his heel, an' you could tell by his face that he was mighty sorry he couldn't have picked out the face he'd have liked to have under his heel instead of the ground. Finally he put his hand on my shoulder an' sez, "Well, Happy, you allus did have the gift of hittin' the nail on the head; an' I'll promise that no matter what comes up, I won't do anything to risk the happiness of—of Barbie. You just remember to keep on callin' me Dick, an' I reckon I'll be content to let the revenge part go, an' just settle down with my head under cover. They didn't remember me in the Chicago stock yards, an' you didn't recognize me; so I suppose it's safe enough, if I just keep quiet."

We shook hands, an' he went back to the house; but I could easy see that he was troubled. I stayed out with the stars purty late that night. It was clear an' bright an' peaceful when I looked up, but when I tried to look ahead it seemed misty an' dark an' gloomy, so I looked straight up for a long, long time; an' then when they soothed me, as they allus do, I went to bed an' slept like a log.

CHAPTER TWENTY-TWO
A FRIENDLY GAME

About three days after this, a slick lookin' feller came ridin' in about sun-down, an' of course they booked him for supper an' bed; a stranger didn't want to expose himself to a meal at that outfit, less'n he was in the mood to eat. He was a fine easy talker, an' he had indoor hands too, an' one o' these smiles what is made to order; what you might call a candidate's smile—a sort o' lightin' up in honor o' the person bein' addressed. Barbie had a bit of a headache, 'cause her cinch had broke that mornin' while she was havin' a little argument with a bad-actor; an' about eight o'clock she give us the fare-you-well an' fluttered up to bed.

So the four of us—me, Dick, the stranger, an' ol' Jabez—sat there smokin' seegars an' tellin' anecdotes. About nine Piker, which was the name the stranger had handed in, sez, "Do you gentlemen ever indulge in a little friendly game?"

Now Dick had never throwed a card in his life, to my knowin'. The ol' man used to play some, but he was mighty choicy who he played with; while I—well, o' course, I played. Dick didn't say anything at first, but he give the stranger a long an' a curious look, as though he was tryin' to place him. He looked so long that both me an' the ol' man noticed it. "I don't care to play," sez Dick, blowin' a ring o' smoke to the ceilin'.

The ol' man had been trottin' along without a break for a consid'able of a stretch, an' the proposition looked amply sufficient to him, so he sez pleasantly, "Well, now, boys, it wouldn't be a bad way to spend the evenin'. We could make the stakes small an' we could have a right sociable time together."

'Tain't altogether wise to jump hasty at another man's idee of size. I had seen the ol' man sit in a game where steers was the ante an' car-loads the limit; but at that time I thought I knew just a little wee mite more about the game than any other man what played straight, so I sez, "Well, I'll set in a while; but I don't care to lose more'n a hundred dollars"; which was just what I'd saved out for a little vacation I was ruminatin' about.

"Oh, we'll only play a quarter ante an' five dollar limit," sez Jabez. "Come on, boys, clear the table an' let's get started."

Dick didn't seem to want to play at all, but after the ol' man had coaxed him a little he drew up his chair an' we started in. The old man's deck was purty tol'able careworn an' floppy, an' the stranger sez, "I happen to have a couple o' new decks what have never been opened. We'll open one in honor o' the occasion."

"This deck is good enough," sez Dick, an' he spoke purty harsh. As me an' the ol' man looked up, our glances met an' we showed surprise. Dick wasn't a bit like himself; but the stranger didn't take no offense, he just smiled a bit careless an' put his cards on the stand, sayin, "Well, I'll just leave 'em here handy, an' if we decide to use 'em later we can open 'em up. For my part, I like a new deck."

"So do I," sez the ol' man. "I'm sorry mine are so bum. I meant to send for some new ones a long time ago, but I allus forgot it."

The stranger took out a healthy lookin' stack o' gold, Dick an' Jabez did the same, an' my little squad o' yella fellers looked purty tol'able squeezy. Dick was tremendous sober; his face was pale, his eyes were hid away beneath his brows, an' kept dartin' here an' there like the eyes of a hawk. Now for me, I allus have a curious promonition when anything is goin' to happen, an' I began to have it bad.

Still the longer we played the easier Dick got in his ways, an' purty soon he was smilin' as open-faced as a dollar watch. We played along nice an' gentle; my luck arrived early, an purty soon the yella fellers begun to percalate in my direction. About half-past ten Piker had to dig up some more funds, an' he sez, "It's gettin' kind o' late, boys, let's raise the edge a bit. Hawkins there has had all the luck so far, an' when it changes we ought to have a show to get back our riskin's."

"All right," sez Jabez, "we'll double."

"The stakes suit me all right," sez Dick. "In fact, I'd ruther split 'em."

I was feelin' purty consid'able opulent myself, so I voted to double.

"Three to one," sez Piker, "the stakes are doubled."

"The original agreement can't be changed durin' a game without the unanimous consent of all the players," sez Dick, speakin' like a judge; "but as the rest of you wish it, I'll give mine."

From that on the luck shifted. Two or three times I see a queer look steal across the ol' man's face; but everything was out in the open, as far as I could see. I played even Steven; but the wind shifted plumb away from

Jabez, an' he lost steady. Part of the time Dick corraled the pots, an' part of the time me an' Piker provided shelter for 'em: but no matter who won, the ol' man lost.

Twice he frowned purty serious, an' once I caught him givin' Dick a queer hurt look. The ol' man hadn't a drop o' welcher blood in his make-up; but cheatin' was spelled in mighty red letters to 'im. Dick was smilin' now as sweet as a girl baby, an' makin' funny, joshin' remarks, which was a new turn for him; but at the same time the' was somethin' in his face that wasn't altogether pleasant.

When midnight arrived Dick an' Piker was each about two thousand ahead, I was slidin' back to taw, an' the old man was payin' the fiddler. We had doubled the edge again at eleven, an' were usin' both the strange decks, changin' every few deals. Then the luck began to settle to Dick. Two out of three times on his own deals, an' every single time on Piker's deals, the devidends slid into Dick's coffers, while I was growin' resigned to havin' had a good run for my money. Jabez' face was drawn an' worried, which was queer, 'cause he was allus a royal loser.

At last we had built up a four-story jack-pot, an' every feller's face wore the take-off-your-hat-to-me smile. It was Dick's deal an' we all held three cards except Jabez who had furnished openers. He only wintered through a pair, but after he looked at his draw he settled back to enjoy himself. I held three kings an' a brace o trays. It looked to me as if that jack-pot belonged to Happy Hawkins. The peculiar expression had wore off Jabez' face, an' his eyes had a glad glint in 'em. I was only in for my table stakes, so I didn't make much of a noise, nohow; but the other three kept boostin' her up till it begun to look like a man's game all right.

"If you'll excuse the limit, I'd like to show my appreciation of this little hand by bettin' a hundred on it," sez Piker.

"I'm willin'," sez Jabez, "an' if it goes, why, I'll see your appreciation an' raise you five hundred."

"I don't have any more vote," sez I, "just enjoy yourselves."

"Oh, no, Happy," sez Dick, as serious as a hangman; "no matter if we raise the edge every hand, you must vote on it each time. We must be perfectly regular, you know, because this is merely a friendly little game to pass away the evening, you remember. I shall make no objections."

Jabez had slid deep into his chair, an' now he had a fierce scowl on his face. "That was MY toe you was a-pressin'," he sez, lookin' Piker between the eyes.

"I beg your pardon," sez Piker, laughin' easy; "I thought it was Silv—I mean Whittington's. I wanted him to keep still until after this hand was out. Then I'll be willin' to quit or go back to the old limit, or keep right along with the lid off."

I glanced at Dick; an' talk about jerk-lightnin'! Well, I can't see yet what kept Piker from gettin' scorched; but Jabez was in a good humor again from lookin' at his royalty, so he turns to Dick an' sez, "Now, Dick, Piker's company, you know, an' I reckon we'd better humor him. What do you say?"

"Off goes the lid," sez Dick.

They bet around awhile longer until nearly all of Dick's money was in the pot an' Jabez had a neat little pile of checks representin' him. Then Dick bet his balance an' called. We all laid down with a satisfied grin. Jabez had queens full on jacks, Piker had three bullets an' a team o' ten-spots; Dick had a royal straight flush, an' I had a nervous chill. Three aristocratic fulls an' a royal straight! Nobody spoke, an' the money stayed where it was, in the center of the table. Finally the ol' man sez, makin' an effort to speak cordial, "Well, I've had enough for one evenin', I guess I'll quit."

"Now, boys," sez Dick, in a low, husky voice, "I don't believe in gamblin'. I only went into this to be sociable, an' I want you all to take your money back."

We sat an' looked at Dick with our eyes poppin' out, 'cause that wasn't our way o' playin' the game in that neighborhood. Suddenly the ol' man whirled an' glared at Piker. "What the hell do you mean by pressin' my toe?" he growls between his set teeth. "This is the fourth time you've done it to-night."

Piker seemed confused, an' mumbled an' stammered, an' couldn't hardly speak at all. "It ain't my custom to play with strangers," sez Jabez, an' he was fast gettin' into the dangerous stage, "but you are my guest. I won't take my money back, but if Dick is willin', I'll write him a check for yours an' you can take your condemned filthy gold an' get out o' here."

"I ain't askin' my money back," sez Piker. "I'm game, I am; but I can't savvy this scheme o' dividin' up after the game." He paused a second, an' then sez clear an' distinct, "This ain't exactly the way 'at Silver Dick used to play the game when he made a business of it."

Piker leaned back an' stared at Dick in a sneerin' sort of way; while me an' the ol' man stared at him with our eyes poppin' out. Silver Dick, Silver Dick: every one in the West had heard of Silver Dick. It didn't seem possible; but as me an' Jabez sat gazin' at him, we knew 'at our Dick was Silver Dick the gambler, an' the smoothest article, accordin' to reports, 'at ever threw a card. Dick didn't say a word; just sat there with his face pale as a sheet, an' his glitterin' black eyes dartin' flame at Piker's nasty grin.

"I see you don't recognize me with a full beard," sez Piker; "but down at Laramie they called me Jo Denton. It was my cousin, Big Brown, that you shot."

"Do you happen to know what I shot him for?" Dick's face was as hard as marble, an' his voice was as cold as ice.

"I wasn't there at the time," sez Piker in an irritatin' voice, "but I know that it was because he spoke about it bein' a little peculiar that you held such wonderful good hands on your own deal."

Dick didn't make no reply, but he slipped his hand inside his shirt, an' I knew he had his gun there.

"I say that this was the EXCUSE for your shootin';" Piker went on, bent on gettin' all the trouble the' was; "but I allus believed, myself, that it started over the woman you was keepin'."

Dick's gun flashed in the air; but quick as a wink ol' Cast Steel knocked it up with his right hand, an' struck at Dick with his left. The bullet crashed through the ceiling, an' Dick grabbed Jabez' wrist at the same instant. Piker made a quick snap under the table, a gun went off, an' the bullet tore through the slack o' Dick's vest an' spinged into the wall behind him.

Then I kicked off my hobbles an' sailed in on my own hook. Dick had allus been white to me—an' back in the old days he was the squarest feller on earth—so I felt mightly relieved when I caught Piker in the center of the forehead with a full left swing. It was a blow 'at nobody didn't have no grounds to complain of. The chair flew over backwards, Piker's feet made a lovely circle, an' his head tried to insinuate itself into the mopboard. He remained quiet, an' I started in to satisfy my curiosity.

"Stay where you are," commanded Dick, an' I stuck in my tracks. "No man is allowed to doubt my deal without havin' something to remind him of it. I ain't a-goin' to kill that snake now; but I do intend to remove his trigger fingers."

Dick still held Jabez by a peculiar twist in the wrist 'at made the ol' man wince a little; he held his gun ready, an' calmly sized up Piker's hand, which was flattened out again the wall. I stood where I was, an' the room was so quiet it hurt your ears.

A grin of wolfish joy came into Dick's face as he stood there with his gun back of his head an' his thumb on the hammer—of course he was a snap-shooter—these nervous fellers allus are. It seemed as if we had all been in that same position for ages, when suddenly a voice said, "Why, Dad, what's the matter?"

It was Barbie with her hair all rumpled up an' a loose gray wrapper on. Dick dropped his hands to his side an' turned his face away; while Jabez put his arm about her an' told her that we had had a little mix-up but that it was all over now an' she must go back to bed. She reared up an' vetoed the motion without parley; but the ol' man finally convinced her, an' she agreed to go if we'd promise not to stir up any more trouble. Me an' Jabez promised quick, but Dick never said a word. She looked him in the face mighty beseechful, but he wouldn't look at her; an' when he finally promised not to START any more fuss his voice was so low you could hardly hear him.

She was pale as a ghost, an' Dick's voice made her all the more suspicious. "I'll not go one step," she said at last, sinkin' down in a chair; but Dick walked over to her an' asked her to step into the next room with him a minute. They only talked together a few moments, an' then we heard her give a stifled sob an' go back upstairs. I never see such a change as had come over Jabez. His face was drawn an' haggard like the face of a man lost in the desert without water.

The time had come at last when another man stood between his daughter—his greatest treasure on earth—an' himself. I remembered what Friar Tuck had said about the time comin' when she'd be all girl an' would stand before him with the questions of life in her eyes, an' I pitied him, God knows I pitied him.

CHAPTER TWENTY-THREE
CAST STEEL

Jabez had got the rope on himself when Dick came back, an' he spoke to him in the voice of a father sayin' farewell to the son who had gone wrong once too often. "I don't care nothin' about the money, Dick," he said. "You'd 'a' been welcome to all I had; but I can't forgive you about my little girl. You made her love you, you schemed to do it, an' you came here with that end in view. I trusted you from the ground up, but I can see a heap o' things now 'at I wouldn't see before. I had a letter written from Bill Andrews tellin' me 'at he had heard you brag 'at you intended to get holt o' my money, an' that it would pay me to search you instead o' suspectin' him—"

"Where was the letter from?" asked Dick.

"Laramie," sez the ol' man.

"Kind o' curious," sez Dick, an' his vice was as bitter as the dregs o' sin; "that's where Denton came from too."

"You deceived me all along," sez the ol' man, not payin' much heed to Dick, but speakin' mostly to himself. "You know 'at what I hate worse'n anything else is deceit—an' here you've been fast an' loose with women—" Dick tried to say somethin', but the ol' man stopped him. "That was bad enough," he went on, "but I'm no fool; I know the world, an' I could forgive you a good deal; but hang it, I never could forgive you bein' a professional gambler—a man that lives by deceit an' trickery an' false pretenses. Lookin' back now, it strikes me as bein' mighty curious how you got the best o' Piker's deals too. Was Piker or Denton, or whatever his name is, a gambler too?"

"He was," answered Dick in a low tone.

The ol' man squared himself, an' his face was as fierce as the face of an ol' she bear. "Of all the human snakes I ever heard of, you crawl the closest to the ground. You come here an' act as square as a man can until you have made us all think the world of ya; an' yet in your black heart you were all the time plottin' to get my money, usin' my little girl as a burglar would use a bar to open a safe with. Even then you couldn't wait in patience; your inborn cussedness forced you to steal an' cheat—and yet, boy, I could almost forgive you for deceivin' me, but I can't never forgive you for deceivin' my little girl. You stand there with a gun in your hand an' I stand here with none; you brag 'at no man can't doubt your dealin' without havin' cause to remember it; but I tell you to your teeth that you're a sneak an' a cheat an' a low-grade coward."

Dick stood with his head thrown back an' his left hand clenched, while his right gripped the butt of his gun so fierce that the knuckles stood out white as chalk an' the veins was black an' swollen. His bosom was heavin', his teeth showed in a threatenin' white line, an' all the savage th' was in him was cryin' kill, kill, kill!

He tottered a little when he took a step toward Jabez; but he laid the gun on the table with the butt pointin' towards Jabez, an' then he went back to the wall an' folded his arms. He stood lookin' at Jabez for a moment, an' then he sez slow an' soft an' creepy: "Every word you have said from start to finish is a lie; and you yourself are a liar."

The ol' man choked. He loosened the collar around his neck, fairly gaspin' for breath; an' then he grabbed up the gun an' held it ready to drop on Dick's heart. A curious expression came over Dick as he looked into Jabez' face; a tired, heart-achy smile as though he'd be so glad to be all through with it that he wouldn't care a great deal how it was done. Ol' Cast Steel was livin' up to his name if ever a man did. The' wasn't a sign of anger in his face by this time, nothin' but one grim purpose, an' it was horrid. It looked like a plain case o' suicide on Dick's part, an' I was just makin' up my mind whether or not it would be polite to interfere, when the door opened noiselessly an' Barbie stood in the openin'.

She seemed turned to stone for a second, an' then she gave a spring an' grabbed the ol' man's arm. "Jabez Judson, what are you doin'?" she said, an' the' wasn't much blood relation in her tone.

The ol' man lowered his gun an' sank into a chair, while Barbie stood with her hands on her hips an' looked from one to the other of us. Then it would be the time for our eyes to hit the carpet. "Now I want to know the meanin' o' this," sez she, "an' I want the full truth. This is nice doin's over a game o' cards. I wish I had thought to set up a bar, so you'd all felt a little more at home. What's it about?"

We didn't none of us seem to have a great deal to say, but just stood there lookin' foolish. Finally Dick came out of it an' sez, "I have been accused of cheatin' an' lyin' an' stealin'. The circumstantial evidence is all again me, so I shall have to go away, but you remember all I told you out in the other room—an' on our rides across the plain, an' on our walks in the moonlight; an' Barbie, girl, don't you believe a word of it.

"Good-bye, Happy—I know you an' you know me. Jabez Judson, I know it ain't no use to attempt any explanation; but I give you my word of honor—an' I set just as much store by it as any man in all the world— that I never stacked a deck o' cards in my life, an' I never held a single underhanded thought again you; while as for Barbie—well, Barbie knows. Good-bye."

Dick turned on his heel an' stalked out o' the room, Barbie dropped into a chair sobbin', an' me an' the old man continued to look like the genuine guilty parties. Then it occurred to me that mebbe it would be wise to see if Piker was worth botherin' with. First thing I did though was to see where he had helt his gun when he fired beneath the table. The' wasn't no gun on the floor, an' I couldn't nowise savvy it.

He had one gun in his holster, but he couldn't have pulled it out without bein' seen, an' he couldn't have put it back, nohow. I was plumb mystified, an' had about give it up when I came across it. I own up it was a clever dodge, but snakish to an extreme. He had fashioned a rig just above his knee, an' when he had sat down the gun had been pointin' at Dick all through the game, an' nothin' but Jabez makin' Dick move had saved him. It was a blood-thirsty scheme, an' I felt like stampin' his face into a jelly.

His head was still bent over an' he was black in the face; but when I straightened him out an' soused a lot o' water over him, he came out of it, an' I fair itched to make him eat his gun—knee-riggin' an' all! He sat up an' began to tell what a low-down, sneakin' cuss Dick had allus been. I let him sing a couple o' verses, an' then I sez: "Now, you look here, you slimy spider. Dick's too busy just now to attend to your case an' if you don't swaller them few remarks instant I'll be obliged to prepare you for the coroner myself. I've knowed Dick sometime, an' I've knowed several other men; an' I know enough to know that such a dust-eatin' lizard as you never could know enough to know what such a man as Dick was thinkin' out or plannin' to do. An' furthermore, you're a liar in your heart, an' still further more, I don't like your face; an' one other furthermore—the longer I look at you the madder I get! My advice to you, an' I give it in the name o' peace an' sobriety, an' because the' 's a lady present, is to start right now to a more salubrious climate—you an' your knee-gun an' your black lies an' your marked decks. Do you hear what I say? Are you goin' to go?"

I was surely losin' my temper; the' was a blood taste in my throat, an' when I asked him the question I kicked him gently in the chest, just to let him know 'at I was ready for his verdict.

He was a coward. He just lunched himself away from me on his back an' whined somethin' about only tryin' to show us the truth an' not wantin' any trouble, an' a lot o' such foolishness; but I soon wearied of it, an' grabbed him by the collar an' yanked him to his feet, an' sez, "Now answer me one question—who told you that Dick was here?"

"Bill Andrews," he sez; an' I opened the door an' kicked him through it: but in a minute back he comes, cringin' like a cur. "Don't send me away until after I see what direction Silver takes," he whimpered. "He never forgives; He'll kill me if he sees me; let me stay until after he starts."

I laughed. "Why, you fool you," I sez, "if he SHOULD happen to ruin you beyond repair you don't imagine any one would put on mournin' do ya? But if it's goin' to make your mind any easier I stand ready to give you a written guarantee 'at he won't use any knee-gun to do it with. Now you get; I'm strainin' myself to keep from spoilin' you on my own hook."

I was in an advanced state of bein' exasperated, an' I walked up to him intendin' to brand him a few with the butt of his own gun, when Barbie spoke low an' cold, but in a voice fairly jagged with scorn: "Let the creature alone; I don't want Dick to soil his boots." Barbie's voice had lost its college finish, an' she was in the mood to do a little shootin' herself just then.

Dick finished his packin' in short order, an' went out an' saddled his pony an' rode away toward Danders an' Laramie. We all set like corpse-watchers for half an hour longer, an' then Jabez straightened up an' sez to Piker; "Take your money out o' that pot an' never get caught in this neighborhood again. Your partner started toward Laramie; when you see him tell him I'll send the full amount o' the pot to him as soon as he sends me his address. You can also tell him that I'll kill him if he ever sets foot on this ranch again."

Barbie was standin' at the window lookin' out into the moonlight which had swallered up the best part of her world. When Jabez finished speakin' she turned around an' looked at Piker. "I can't figger out just whose dog-robber yon are," she sez; "but next time you go gunnin' for Silver Dick—you better take the whole gang with you."

It fair hurt me to see Barbie's face, so hard it was an' so different from the real Barbie: but it warmed my heart to hear the way she made that Silver Dick ring out. Oh, she was a thoroughbred every inch of her, that girl was. Piker didn't say a word; he just picked up his coin an' walked out o' the room, an' I raised up the window an' drew a deep breath. The blame pole-cat had managed to slip out an' saddle his pony about supper time, an' in a second he dashed away toward Webb Station, mighty thankful in his nasty little heart that he wasn't bound for hell, where he rightly belonged.

"Did you ever know Dick before he came here, Happy?" asked Barbie.

"I swear to heaven that I never knew that our Dick was Silver Dick until this very night," sez I; "but I'd be willing to stake my life on his word, an' I'd take it again the word of any other livin' man—bar none."

"Thank you, Happy. Good-night." She held her head high as she walked out o' the room; but I knew that livin' serpents was tearin' at her heart.

Ol' Cast Steel sat for an hour, his chin on his hands an' his elbows on the table, lookin' at the pile of money an' checks on the table before him.

"Gold, gold, gold!" he mutters at last; "it builds the churches an' the schoolhouses an' the homes; an' it fills the jails and the insane asylums an' hell itself. It drives brother to murder brother, an' neither love nor friendship is proof against its curse. It starves those who scorn it, while those who pay out their souls for it find themselves sinking, sinking, sinking in its hideous quicksand until at last it closes above their mad screams. God! if I only had my life to live over!"

That was just the way he said it, deep an' hoarse an' coning between his set teeth; an' I felt the hair raisin' on my head. He looked like a lost soul, an' the whites of his eyes showed in ghastly rings around the pupils.

"You take this rubbish, Happy," sez he, turnin' on me. "You're too much like the birds an' the beasts for it to ever injure you. Take it an' spend it—drink it, throw it away, burn it up, destroy it, an' when it is gone come back here an' live in the open again an' you'll never be far from the spirit of God."

Well, I knew it was ol' Cast Steel who was speakin', but it was mighty hard to believe it. "I don't mean no disrespect to you, Jabez," I sez, edgin' toward the door, "but I'll see you damned first." An' I slid outside an' straddled a pony an' rode till the dawn wind blew all the fever out of me an' let the sunshine in.

CHAPTER TWENTY-FOUR
FEMININE LOGIC

Well, the Diamond Dot was sure a dismal dump after that. Every one had liked Dick; but they didn't know how much until he was snuffed out like the flame of a candle. The ol' man had me make a stagger at fillin' Dick's shoes; but it wasn't what a truthful man would call a coal-ossal success. Dick had left a lot of directions, tellin' how to judge the markets an' how to make improvements without feelin' the cost, an' a dozen other things that. I had allus supposed was simply a mixture o' luck an' Providence; but it wasn't in my line to figger things out on paper. Give me the actual cattle an' I could nurse 'em along through sand-storm an' blizzard, an' round 'em up in the President's back yard; but at that time they didn't signify much to me when they was corraled up on a sheet of paper. When it cane to action I was as prepossessed as a clerk at a pie counter; but I didn't have the slightest symptom of what they call the legal mind.

The' wouldn't much 'a' come of it; but one day Barbie came out of her daze an' walked into the office where I was sweatin' over some of Dick's prognostications, stuck a pencil behind her ear, an' waded into 'em; an' from that on I took off my hat to a college edication. Dick may have been on the queer all right, but he was smooth enough to hide it. Anyhow, ol' man Judson's bank account was a heap plumper'n it was when Dick had his first whack at it, an' Dick had drawn a mighty stately salery himself. But he earned it, for the ranch was in strictly modern order an' runnin' on a passenger schedule.

It allus gave me a hurtin' in the chest to see either Barbie or the ol' man himself those days. The' was a set look in Barbie's eyes; cold an' unflinchin' an' defiant. I once saw the same expression in the eyes of a trapped mountain lion. The ol' man's face was all plowed up too. He reminded me of an Injun up to Port Bridger. A Shoshone he was from the Wind River country, an' he had the look of an eagle; but he got a holt of some alcohol an' upset a kettle o' boilin' grease on himself. He lived for eight days with part of his bones stickin' through, but never givin' a groan; an' I ain't got the look of his face out o' my system yet. Jabez reminded me of it a heap: an' he was just about as noisy over it too. I never supposed that the Diamond Dot could get to lookin' so much like a desert island to me. I got to feelin' like one who had been sent up for life, an' I would sure have made a break for freedom if it hadn't been for the little girl. I couldn't bear to leave her.

One of the saddest things I ever see in my whole life was the difference between the way she an' Jabez acted an' the way they used to. I've heard preachers beseech their victims to live in peace an' harmony together, an' not to quarrel or complain; an' right at the time it didn't sound so empty an' mockish; but when you come to boil it down the' ain't nothin' in that theory. Why, I'd seen the ol' man hunt Barbie all forenoon just to pick a quarrel with her; an' they would fuss an' stew an' revile each other an' keep it up all through dinner; an' then go off in the afternoon an' scrap from wire to wire; but they was enjoyin' themselves fine, an' addin' to their stock of what is called mutual respect. Every time one of 'em would land it would cheer him up an' put the other one on his mettle; an' they certainly did get more comfort an' brotherly love out of it than most folks does out of a prayer-meetin'; but after Dick went away the' wasn't no more quarrels. No, they was as differential as a pair of Japanese ambassadors; an' she never called him Dad again—never once! an' I could see him a-hunngerin' for it with the look in his eyes a young cow has when she is huntin' for the little wet calf the coyotes has beat her to. It was allus, "Yes, sir," or "No, sir," until I could almost hear the ol' man's heart a-breakin' in his breast.

She never complained none, Barbie didn't. She plowed through her work as though it was goin' to bring him back to her; an' when she couldn't think of anything else to do she would tramp off to the hills or ride like the wind over the roughest roads she could find. Time an' again she wouldn't be able to sleep, but would steal out o' the house, an' we could hear her guitar sobbin' an' wailin of in the night; but if Barbie herself ever shed a tear it never left a mark on her cheek nor put a glaze to her eye.

The' was one knoll not far from the house which commanded the view a long way toward Danders in one direction, an' a long way toward Webb Station in another, an' she spent about ten minutes each evenin' on this knoll. Oh, it used to hurt, it used to hurt, to see that purty little light-hearted creature makin' her fight all alone, an' never lettin' another livin' bein' come within hailin' distance. At times it was all I could do to keep from goin' gunnin' for Dick myself.

Once she sez to me, "Happy, if any mail comes to me I want to get it myself, an' I want you to see that I do get it."

"Barbie," sez I, "as far as my feeble power goes you'll get your mail; an' if it happens to involve any other male—why, from this on, I'm under your orders." She was grateful all right, an' tried to smile, but it was a purty successful failure.

Soon the winter settled down an' the snow blotted out the trails, but she never heard from him. The ol' man had wrote to the postmaster at Laramie, an' he had answered that Dick had allus played fair accordin' to the best o' his belief. He went on to say that Dick was generally counted about the best citizen they had; but that after he had shut Big Brown he had pulled out an' no one knew where he was. He said 'at Brown hadn't died, which was a cause for sorrow to the whole town. He also said that Denton would be a disgrace to coyote parents. He furthermore went on to state that Dick still owned quite a little property in Laramie. The old man showed me an' Barbie the letter; but it didn't help much.

When Thanksgivin' hove in sight the ol' man dug up a bottle o' whiskey, an' put on a few ruffles to sort o' stiffen up his back; an' one day after dinner he sez to Barbie, "Now you just stay settin'." She was in the habit of estimatin' just how little nurishment it would take to run her to the next feed, gettin' it into her in the shortest possible time, an' then makin' a streak for it.

"Now, little girl," sez Jabez, tryin' to look joyous an' free from care, "you are leadin' too sober a life. I want to see you happy again. I want to see you laughin' about the house, like you used to. Can't you sort o' liven up a little?"

"I might," sez she, with the first sneer I ever see her use on the ol' man, "I might, if you'd give me the rest o' the bottle you got your own gaiety out of."

Cast Steel's face turned as red as a brick, an' his fist doubled up. "That's a sample o' your idee of respect, is it? You're gettin' too infernal biggoty. Now you pay attention. I want to have a little gatherin' here Thanks-givin'. Will you, or will you not, see that the arrangements are attended to?"

"Yes, sir," sez Barbie, lookin' down at her plate. "How many guests will the' be?"

"Well, how can I tell?" sez Jabez. "Can you get ready for twenty?"

"Yes, sir," answers Barbie, never liftin' her eyes.

"Yes, sir; yes, sir; yes, sir!" yells the of man. "I get everlastin' tired o' your 'yes, sirs.' Am I or am I not your ol' Dad?"

"If you prefer, I can call you father," sez she, like she was talkin' to the moon through a telephone. "Dad is not correct English; it is a kalowquism."

This was allus like a pail o' water to the ol' man. Nothin' stung him any worse than to have her peel a couple o' layers off her edication an' chuck 'em at him.

"Do you know what is apt to happen if you keep on pesterin' me?" he sez, glarin' at her. "Do you think 'at you're too big to be whipped?"

She raised her eyes an' looked at him then. Poor feller, he could 'a' torn his tongue out by the roots the minute it was guilty o' that fool speech; but she didn't spare him. She let him have the full effect o' that look, an' he seemed to shrivel up. "I reckon you're big enough to whip me—once," she said; "but I'm of age, an' I'm mighty sure 'at that would be the finishin' touch 'at would break the bonds what seem to hold me to this house. I probably have bad blood o' some kind in me; but I'm not so ill-favored but what I can find a man to go along with me when I do conclude to go." She looked at me, an' the ol' man looked at me, an' I felt like a red-hot stove; but I straightened back in my chair, an' I cleared my throat. "I ain't no mind-reader," sez I, "but I'm bettin' on that same card."

The ol' man couldn't think up a come-back; so in about a minute he pushed back his chair, upsettin' it an' lettin' it lay where it fell. He went up to his room, slammin' the door after him, an' Barbie got out a pony an' galloped off to the hills.

But the ol' man hadn't give up his project. He opened it again, an' was mighty crafty in the way he handled it, until finally he engineered it through. The' was purt' nigh forty of 'em who arrived to make merry over Thanksgivin'. Some of 'em came the day before, an' some of 'em two days before, an' some didn't arrive till the day itself, 'cause they had lived such a ways. The' was four women an' three unmarried ladies, countin' Miss Wiggins, the Spike Crick schoolmarm, who was a friendly little thing, though a shade too coltish for her years. Most o' the men was still liable to matrimony.

Jabez had an idee in his head, an' it didn't take no ferret to nose it out, neither. He was extra cordial to the store-keeper from Webb Station, an' a young Englishman by the name o' Hawthorn, finally settlin' down to Hawthorn an' playin' him wide open. We had a mighty sociable time, an' whenever we wasn't eatin' we played games. Barbie did just exactly what of Cast Steel played her to do. She was too red-blooded to let an outsider see 'at she'd been bad hurt; so she brazened up an' laughed an' danced an' sang, an' showed 'em games they hadn't never dreamt of before.

Most of 'em went home by Sunday night, but Hawthorn was prevailed upon to stay a week longer. He had a little ranch up in the hills, an' seemed a well-meanin' sort of a feller, but slow. He belonged to the show-me club, an' had all his facical muscles spiked fast for fear they'd come loose an' grin before he saw the point himself.

Barbie see through the ol' man's lead, an' she took her revenge out on Hawthorn. She would lean forward an' hold his eye, an' say, in the sweetest voice you ever heard, "Oh. Mr. Hawthorn, I want to tell you somethin' that happened at school;" an' then she would start in an' tell some long-winded tale 'at didn't have no more point than a mush room, an' as she told along she would call his attention to certain details as though they was goin' to figger in at the wind-up. When she would reach the end she would break out in a peal o' spontunious laughter; while he would look as if he had been lost in the heart of a great city without his name-plate on. Still, he had a certain breedy look about him, an' before the week was up she grew ashamed of her-self an' showed him a good time.

He was one o' these sad ones—sentimental an' romantic, with a bad case o' chronic lonesomeness; an' one twilight he told her a pathetic little love story about a girl back in England what had had sense enough to cut him out of her assets when he had trooped over to this country to punch a fortune out o' beef cattle. This had been about five years previous; but his heart still ached about it—though it hadn't cut his appetite so you could notice. She treated him mighty gentle after this, an' when he started to ride away Jabez had the look of a man what had filled his hand.

In about a week he came over an' stayed for a couple o' days, an' he showed up at Christmas too; an' about once a week after that he'd drop in an' stay four or five days. Early in March he paid a visit to his own ranch to ready things up for spring, an' the day after he was gone Jabez sez to Barbie at dinner, "Now, Mr Hawthorn is a gentle man. He asked me for the honor of winnin' your hand in holy wedlock; an' I have give my consent."

Barbie went along eatin' her meal, an' purty soon Jabez sez, "Well, did you hear what I had to say?"

"Why, certainly I did," sez Barbie, calmly.

"What have you got to say about it?" sez he.

"Oh, nothin' in particular," sez she. "It was very polite in him to ask, an' very kind in you to give your consent; but I can't see as it interests me much. I can't see that he has any show of winnin' the hand. I promised that once, an' I ain't never got the promise back."

"Yes," snaps Jabez, "an' who did you promise it to? To a sneak who didn't care a pin for you but was only after my money. If he was honest why didn't he ask me, the same as Hawthorn did?"

"Of course I can't tell for sure," sez she, without raisin' her voice or changin' her expression, "but I thought at the time that it was the hand itself he wanted, an' not merely permission to set an' wish for it. In this life a man generally gets what he asks for. Dick got the hand."

"Seems to set a heap o' store by it," sez the ol' man, edgin' up his voice cruel an' tantalizin'. "Where's this Dick now; when did you last hear from this winner of hands?"

It was a fierce stab, an' Barbie went white as a sheet; but she faced him cool an' steady. "I ain't never heard from him since the day he left; but I trust him just the same. The hand will be his when he chooses to claim it; or if he never comes back at all—why the hand will still be his."

Cast Steel got on his hind legs an' struck the table till every dish on it jumped, an' I rose a bit myself; but Barbie only curled her little red lip. "Curse him," sez the ol' man, "curse him, wherever he is an' wherever he goes. He has ruined my life an' he has ruined yours; an' if he ever steps foot on this ranch again, I'll—"

"Stop!" sez Barbie, springin' to her feet. "You give me more sadness every day I live than Dick has altogether; but for pity's sake don't bind yourself by a threat. Wait till he comes back, an' be free to meet him like a man, not like a thug pledged to murder."

"What do you know about him?" sez the ol' man, sittin' down. "For all you know, he may be robbin' trains for a livin'. It would be right in his line."

"For all I know, robbin' trains was where you got your start," sez Barbie; an' the ol' man's face turned gray an' his eyes stuck out like picture nails. He wasn't used to gettin' it quite so unpolluted, an' it gave him a nasty jar.

"How do you know 'at he ain't livin' with the woman he kept over at Laramie?" sez Jabez, tryin' to get the whip hand again. "How do you know he ain't married?"

"An' how do I know 'at you ever was married—" she stopped short, bitin' her lip an' turnin' red with shame. "I know it's well nigh hopeless to plead with a natural bully," she sez in a new tone; "but I do wish 'at you'd let me alone. You're destroyin' my respect for everything. I can't stand this much longer. If I can't live here in peace I'll have to hunt a new place to live; but as long as I do stay here you will have to act like a man—even if you can't act like a father. I think that in the future I shall take my meals alone."

"I do want to act like a father, little girl. That's what I want most of all. If you would only go back to the old times, if you would only get this sneak out of your head"—Jabez had started in gentle an' repentent, but the minute he thought of Dick again he flared out white with rage—"an' you might just as well get him out of your head, 'cause he's the same as dead to you. I hate him! I hate every sneak; an' I hate every lie—spoken or lived, I hate a lie!"

The ol' man leaned forward, shaking with anger, an' Barbie got up like a queen an' walked out o' the room as though she was steppin' on the necks of the airy-stockracy. She went to the office, an' after a couple o' minutes I follered her, expectin' to cheer her up a bit; but she wasn't mournin' none; she was workin' like a steam engine, with her face cold an' white except for a little patch o' red in each cheek; an' when she raised her eyes to mine I knew 'at the ol' man had gone a link too far.

After me and Barbie had taken up Dick's work we had divided his wages, an' she had a nice little roll of her own corded away. I didn't ask no questions, but it was plain as day that she had jerked up her tie-rope; an' the next time Cast Steel used the spurs he was goin' to be dumped off an' she was goin' to flit the trail for Never-again. I didn't blame her a mite; an' though I didn't pester her with queries nor smother her with advice nor sicken her with consolation nor madden her with pity, I did give her the man-to-man look, an' she knew 'at all she had to do was to issue orders.

It was that very afternoon that she started to correctin' my talk an' stimulatin' my ambition, an' tellin' me about it never bein' too late to mend; an' while I couldn't quite decide just what she was drivin' at I saw that when she found she couldn't trust her cinches any longer we was both goin' to jump together. About five o'clock she put her hand on my shoulder an' sez: "We've been mighty good pals, Happy Hawkins; an' while you ain't parlor-broke nor city-wise, any time 'at anybody counts on you they don't have to count over."

She walked softly out o' the office, an' I sat until it was long after dark. I couldn't believe 'at she was desperate enough to marry me; I could see the gulf between us plain enough, an' the higher you are the plainer you can see the difference; but I could see that unless Jabez changed his ways, why, the oldest man the' was couldn't tell how far Barbie would go. I didn't think a bit of myself, I can say that much; all I looked at was what would make her the happiest, an' she was welcome to take my life any way she wanted. If she chose to drag it out for fifty years, or if she selected that I cash it in the next hour, my only regret would be that I hadn't but one life to give her.

CHAPTER TWENTY-FIVE
THE WAYS OF WOMANKIND

Things went along purty much the same after that; but I could see 'at the ol' man sensed a new tone in things, an' he begun to look agey. He was still gallin' on Barbie, but I couldn't help but feel mighty sorry for him. He had paid all them years 'at she was away at school, out o' the joy of his own heart, lookin' for his pay in the time when she'd come back an' be his chum again, an' here they was with a wall of ice between 'em an' nairy a lovin' glance to melt it down.

The' come a warm spell toward the last o' the month; an' one evenin' just as we was finishin' supper we heard a cry o' distress in a man's voice— an' the cry sounded like "Barbie!" I reckon all our hearts stood still, an' I reckon we all thought exactly the same thing. In about a minute the cry came again, an' the ol' man jumped to his feet an' pulled his gun. "If that's Silver Dick," sez he, "I'll kill him."

Barbie had also sprung up, an' she looked him square in the eyes. "If you harm a hair of his head I'll—I'll do some shootin' myself."

She pulled a little gun out of her bosom, an' we all stood quiet for a moment. It was easy to see 'at she wasn't bluffin': but I'm purty sure that Jabez an' I had different ideas as to what she meant. Jabez thought she meant him self; but he hadn't got the name o' Cast Steel for nothin', an' a sort of a grim smile crept onto his face. We stood still for a moment, an' then we went out together, an' before long we heard the sound again—a long, waverin', ghostly call in the gatherin' twilight.

We hurried along, an' purty soon we saw a man lyin' across the trail. The ol' man held his gun in his hand, an' so did Barbie, while I walked a step behind doin' a heap o' thinkin'. If the ol' man killed Dick, Barbie would shoot herself; if any one stopped the ol' man that one would take on weight exceedin' fast, unless he crippled the of man first. I finally made up my mind that I would try to overpower the ol' man without hurtin' him, an' ol' Cast Steel was built like a grizzly. I didn't enjoy that walk as much as some I've took. When we got close to the figger lyin' in the trail we all walked a little crouchy. It looked quite a little like Dick; but when we saw it wasn't nothin' but that fool Hawthorn with a busted leg, we three looked like the reception committee of the Foolish Society.

I hustled back an' got Hanson an' a couple o' the boys and an ol' door, an' we fetched him home an' put him to bed an' sent for the doctor—an' that was the worst luck that ever happened to ol' Dick. You know how a woman is with anything hurt or sick; they're the same the world over. A right strickly wise married man would have everything broke except his pocket-book, an' then he'd be sure o' lots of pettin'. They allus want to spoil a feller when he's on the flat of his back. When he's walkin' around on his own feet all he needs to do is to express a desire, an' they vetoe it on general principles, an' after they've talked themselves dry they send out an' get the preacher to finish the job; but when that same vile speciment of masculine humanity gets some of his runnin' gear damaged, why they bed him on rose leaves, feed him on honey, an', good or bad, they give him whatever he wants. This particular feller wanted Barbie, an' Barbie was mighty gentle with him.

Sometimes it seems to me that the only men who can understand a woman are the men who work a lot with the dumb creatures. Take an animal now, wild or tame, an' it hates to confess a weakness; it'll just go on head up an' eyes flashin' till it drops in its tracks—so will a woman. Take the fiercest female animal the' is, an' it's all mother on the inside. Why, they're everlastin'ly adoptin' somethin' 'at don't rightly belong to 'em. Sometimes they go to work an' adopt a little straggler that in a regular way is their daily food; an' it ain't no step-mother affair neither, it 's the real thing.

The wild animals are the best to study, 'cause the tame ones have been some spoiled by associatin' with man. Well, the wild animals spend all their spare time dressin' up an' cleanin' their clothes, an' when it ain't absolutely necessary they hate to get a toe wet; but when it comes to love or duty, why fire, water, nor the fear o' man ain't goin' to stop 'em; so again I sez 'at the man what can savvy the wild animals can get purty nigh within hailin' distance of woman, an' that's gettin' close; but you want to remember this, no animal never tells the truth to an outsider. The principle part o' their life is spent in throwin' folks off their trail, an' they allus make their lairs in the most secret places. If a feller ever gets to know 'em even a little he has to be mighty patient an' mighty careful, an' above all things, he mustn't never get the idee that he knows every last thing about 'em the' is to know, 'cause no man never knows that. Some men try to estimate a woman by their own earthy way o' doin' things. 'T would be just as reasonable for a man who was purty wise to the ways of a pug-dog to get inflated with the idee that he had a natural talent for hivin' grizzly bears.

But to get back to my tale: this Englishman had fallen on his feet all right, even if the connection to one of 'em was busted up a bit. I was around 'em a good bit, bein' forced to consult with Barbie about things, an' I was able to piece out the method he was usin'. He wasn't such a fool as he looked, by consid'able many rods. He talked a heap about the sacrifice he had made for the girl back in England, an' how much he had loved her an' how much Barbie had comforted him, although even yet he could not forget her. Once Barbie asked him what her name was. For a moment he didn't answer, an' then he sez in a low voice, Alice LeMoyne. I lifted my face quick an' gave him a look, but he wasn't noticin' me. I didn't say anything; but I couldn't help wonderin' if this Alice LeMoyne had anything to do with the dancer what had married into the Clarenden family, an' then died. It was an odd name, but still I didn't reckon the' was a patent on it.

Finally I could tell by their talk that Barbie had told him about Dick, an' then I knew the jig was about up. He allus spoke o' Dick in a gentle, soothin' way, makin' every excuse for him; an' this made her think him a noble-minded feller! an' the most natural outcome was for 'm to just bunch their woes an' cling together for comfort. She allus used to sit by his side in the twilight, singin' sorrowful love songs to him, an' once I caught him holdin' her hand. You see she was just naturally hungry for somethin' to pet an' care for; luck offered a spavined Englishman, an' she was tryin' to make the best of it.

Jabez savvied this to the queen's taste, an' he got gentle an' lovin' to Barbie, an' did all he could to square himself; so that poor old Dick wasn't much more'n a memory, which is one o' the complications absence is apt to cause after it gets tired o' makin' the heart grow fonder.

But hang it, I didn't like this Englishman more than the law required. The' didn't seem to be much harm to him; but he had washy eyes, an' he was too blame oily an' gentle. I never heard him swear all through it, an' it ain't natural for a real man to stand on his back for eight weeks without havin' a little molten lava slop over into his conversation. It was all I could do to keep from stickin' a pin into him.

"Barbie," I sez one day, as innocent as an Injun, "I over-heard our honored guest tell you that a girl by the name of Alice LeMoyne put a crack in his heart over the water."

"Yes," sez she, with a sigh.

"It don't seem to be a popular name," sez I. "I've met lots o' women who wasn't called Alice LeMoyne."

"It is probably French," sez she.

"It does sound like a circus, that's a fact," sez I. "Well, you break it to him gently that Alice LeMoyne is dead. Don't ask me any questions, but do be careful not to shock him, he seems purty high strung."

You might as well use sarcasm on a steer as on a woman; Barbie went up to Hawthorn with her eyes full o' pity, while I waited below an' made up pictures o' the crockadile tears he'd pump up for her. All of a sudden she gave a shriek. I hit the stairs, goin' forty miles an hour, an' there was Barbie with her hands clasped, lookin' down at the Englishman.

Well, he was enough to make a snake shriek. He was layin' there with his head jerked back, his eyes wide open an' pointin' inwards, an' lookin' altogether like the ancient corpse of a strangled cat. His hands was doubled up tight, an' the' was a little froth on his lips. I'd never seen nothing like that before, so I threw some water in his face. That's about all the rule I know for any one who is missin' cogs, an' I poured enough water on him to please a duck. He didn't respond for some several minutes, an' when he did come out of it he looked loose all over. I helped Barbie get some dry stuff under him, an' then I went down, wonderin' what kind o' dynamite for him they'd been in that name I'd sent up.

I tried to convince Barbie that his wires were all mixed up an' he wasn't healthy; but she argued that it showed a loyal nature to be so affected by mention of his old sweet-heart, an' tried to pump me for where I had picked up the name. It looked too much like a chance shot to me; as this guy had only been among us a few years, an' I gathered from Bill Hammersly that the Alice LeMoyne I was springin' had journeyed on, some several years earlier.

But the Englishman continued to repose on his bed o' down, Barbie read to him, cooked little tid-bits for him, an' he opened up his nature an' gave a new shine to his eyes; while Jabez—well, Jabez was buoyant as a balloon, an' sent here an' there for nick-hacks an' jim-cracks an' such like luxuries. He got to callin' Hawthorn "Clarence" an' "my boy," an' kindry epithets, till even a casual stranger would 'a' knowed the' was a roarin' in the ol' man's head like a chime o' weddin' bells.

Hawthorn was able to crutch around a bit by the first o' May; it was an early season, an' the' was a great harvest o' calves at the round-up. I was in work up to my eyes, an' sort o' lost track of the doin's except when Barbie would have the buckboard hooked up an' come out to the brandin' ground. The weather was glorious, an' you couldn't have blamed an Injun idol for fallin' in love, so I lost heart an' was two-thirds mad nine-tenths o' the time.

Jabez had had a hard siege of it an' it showed. His face was lined, his hair was white at the temples, an' the' was a wistful look in his eyes which was mighty touchy. Barbie was more chummy with him too, an' they was edgin' back to ol' times; but I was darn glad to see Hawthorn finally admit that he was sufficiently recovered to drive over an' see what had become of his own lay-out.

The very first meal that we et alone, however, showed that the old sore wasn't plumb healed over yet. Jabez couldn't wait any longer, so he called for a show-down as soon as our food began to catch up with our appetite. "Has Clarence popped the question yet, honey?" sez he.

"About twice a day on the average," sez Barbie, chillin' up a trifle; "but I don't think he stands much chance. I like him an' he is kind an' good; but I don't reckon I could ever marry him."

The ol' man didn't flare up, same as he would have once. He just sat still, lookin' at his plate, an' that was the hardest blow he had ever struck her. She asked me twice that afternoon if I thought he was failin'.

Next day at dinner Jabez finished his rations, an' then leaned back an' looked lovin'ly at Barbie for a minute. "Little girl," he sez, "I know 'at you don't like to hurt me intentional; but you have give me a mighty sight of heartaches in my time. I have allus aimed to do what seemed best for you, an' it has generally been a hard job. I haven't complained much; but I'm gettin' old, child, I'm gettin' old. It's not for myself, Barbie, it's all for you, for you an' for—for the mother you never knew; but who made me promise to watch over an' protect ya. I can't speak of her, Barbie; but when I meet her out yonder I want to be able to tell her that as far as I was able I've done my part.

"This Dick has been gone a year, an' never a word to ya to let you know even whether he's alive or not. This ain't love, honey; he was only after my money. Now Clarence is honest an' open; why can't you take up with him, so 'at if I'd be called sudden I could go in peace. It would mean a lot to me to see you in good hands, honey. I'm afraid 'at Dick'll wait until I'm gone, an' then come snoopin' around, like a coyote sneakin' into camp when the hunters are away. Don't answer me now, child; just think it over careful. I've generally let you have your own way, but I do wish you'd give in to me this time."

Was Jabez failin'—was he? Well, not so you could notice it! Course he wasn't quite so physically able as once; but I never saw him put up a toppier mental exhibition than he did right then. Barbie didn't have a word to say that afternoon until about five o'clock. Then she suddenly looked up from some reports we was goin' over, an' sez, "Happy, if you had gone away from me like Dick did, what would be the only thing what would have kept you from comin' back to me?"

"By God, nothin' but death!" sez I, without stoppin' to think.

The color rushed to her cheeks as if I had slapped her; an' then it oozed away, leavin' her white as chalk, while I bit my lip an' pinched myself somethin' hearty. I had wanted to compliment her I suppose, if I'd had any motive at all; but what I had done, when you come to look it square in the teeth, was to ask her to cut an ace out of a deck with nothin' left higher than a six spot. I ain't what you would call inventionative; but I could 'a' done a blame sight better'n that if I'd taken the time to think, instead o' simply blurtin' out the truth like some fool amateur.

"Well," sez she, finally, "Dick was twice the man you are, so he must be—dead."

We didn't say anything for some time. Vanity ain't like a mill-store about my neck; but at the same time, whenever any one plugs me in the face with an aged cabbage, I allus like to make a some little acknowledgment. Of course I knew that she was handin' me one for my fool break; but she did it in cold blood, an' if it hadn't been for her bein' so stewed up in trouble, I'd have made her furnish some specifications to back up that remark. Twice is a good many, but I let it go.

She sat lost in study for a while, an' then said, mostly to herself, "I reckon I might as well take him"—my heart popped up in my mouth till I liked to have gagged, but she went on—"he's honest an' kind, an' he's been true a long time to his first love. I hope he'll stay true to her after we're married; I know I'll stay true to mine"—then I knew she meant that fool Englishman. "Anyway, father has been good to me," she continued, "an' I don't set enough store by my own life to risk spoilin' his."

"I suppose that mis-shapen stray from the other side is twice the man I am, too," sez I. She put her hand on mine an' sez in a tired voice, "Ah, Happy, you've been my staff so far through the valley, don't you slip out from under me too"; so I swallered hard a couple o' times an' let it go.

She sat still a long while, lookin' out the window an' up to the of gray mountains; and as I watched her with her lips tremblin, an' her eyes misty, with courage winnin' a battle over pain, I saw the woman lines of her face steal forth an' bury the last traces o' girlhood. After a time she sez softly, "Poor ol' Dick, I wonder how it happened"; but never one tear got by her eyelids—never one single tear.

From that on it was plain sailin'. Barbie didn't put up any more fight to either of 'em. She told 'em open an' fair that she would never in the world have consented if she had thought that Dick was still alive; but if they was willin' to take what part of her heart was left why they was welcome to it.

Jabez was pleased at any kind of a compromise 'at would give him his own way, an' Clarence, poor dear, wasn't a proud lot. The flesh-pots of Egypt was about all the arguments needed to win his vote, confound him. I used to give him some sneerin' glances what would 'a' put fight into the heart of a ring-dove; but he was resigned an' submissive; so 'at I had to swaller my tongue when I saw him comin', for fear I might tell him my opinion of him an' then stamp his life out for not bein' insulted.

The first of November was selected for the weddin' day; an' Jabez told 'em 'at his present would be a trip to Europe an' a half interest in the ranch. Clarence sort o' perked up his face when Jabez told him about it; an' I thought he was goin' to suggest that they cut out the trip to Europe an' take the whole o' the ranch. I had the makin's of a good many cyclones in my system those days.

CHAPTER TWENTY-SIX
A MODERN KNIGHT-ERRANT

I was lonesome once. I don't mean simply willin' to sit in a game, or to join a friendly little booze competition, or feelin' a sort of inward desire to mingle about with some o' the old boys an' see who could remember the biggest tales—I mean LONESOME,—the real rib-strainin' article when a man sits in a limpy little heap with his tongue hangin' out, a-wishin' that a flea-bit coyote would saunter along, slap him on the back, an' call him friens.

I was out in No-man's land with just a small bunch o' mangy cows, an' the grass so scarce I purt' nigh had to get 'em shod—they had to travel so far in makin' a meal. It was hot an' it was dusty an' it was dry—the whole earth seemed to reek. My victuals got moldy an' soft an' sticky, my appetite laid down an' refused to go another peg; 'I was just simply dyin' o' thirst, an' every single drop o' water we came across had a breath like the dyin' gasp of a coal-oil stove, expirin' for a couple o' fingers o' the stuff they float universities in.

Now I'd allus supposed that the' wasn't anything left to tell me about bein' lonesome; but when it was finally settled that Barbie was to waste herself on that imported imitation of a hand-made mechanical toy, I found out that heretofore I'd been only dealin' in childish delusions. The whole Diamond Dot seemed to rest right on top o' my soul: the air didn't smell sweet, I got so I'd lie awake at night, food grew so fearless it could look me right in the face without flinchin'; but one night I saw Merry England with his arm around Barbie's waist, an' that settled it. By the time I had regained my self-control, I was twenty miles from the ranch, an' I knew that if I went back it would be to make arrangements for the last sad obsequaries of Clarence the Comforter.

I had about three hundred bucks in my belt, so I wended my way to Danders an' sneaked aboard the East-bound without attractin' the notice of ol' Mrs. Fate or any o' the rest o' the Danders bunch. I got out at Laramie, an' they all knew Dick an' was proud of him an' eager to learn what had become of him. One thing else I found out, an' that was that he had been keepin' a woman all right, an' that she was livin' there yet; but never went out without a heavy veil, an' the' wasn't any way short o' physical force to get to speak to her.

I figured out that Dick wouldn't care to go back to Texas, so the chances were that he was either in San Francisco or England. I didn't know anything about England, so I went to Frisco. I prowled around for a couple o' days exactly like a story-detective; an' by jinks, I turned up a clew. That feller, Piker, was the clew, an' when I spied him in a low gamblin' room I made some little stir until I got him alone so I could talk to him. I hadn't hurt him none; but I had been tol'able firm, an' he was minded to speak the truth. He told me that Dick was in the Texas Penitentiary for life—that he had surrendered himself up, an' that this was what had give him life instead of the rope.

I knew the gang what had put him there, an' I knew that his chances for gettin' out were about as good as if he was in his grave. I was stumped an' I knew it; so I sez to Piker: "Piker, you may think that I'm allus as gentle as I've been with you; but if this ain't the truth you've told me I'll get your life if I have to track you bare-footed through hell."

He swore by everything he could remember that it was the solemn truth, an' then I turned him loose an' I turned myself loose too. The boys down at Frisco was certainly glad to see me, an' we sure had a royal good time as long as my money lasted; but when it began to dry up they seemed to lose interest in me an' had a heap o' private business to attend to.

One mornin' I noticed that I was dead broke; so I drilled down to the dock an' sat on a post. Pretty soon along comes a little fat man, an' he looks me over from nose to toe. I don't know why it is, but as a rule a city man takes as open-hearted an' disembarrassed an interest in me as though I was a prize punkin' or the father of a new breed o' beef cattle. After he had made up his opinion he smiles into my eyes an' sez, "I like your face."

"You soothe me," sez I. "I was just thinkin' o' havin' it remodelled; but now I'll leave it just as it is."

Well, he laughs an' slaps me on the back an' sez, "I like your style. Want to take a ride?"

"What on?" sez I, for he seemed purty blocky an' fat-legged for a ridin' man.

"On that there sailboat," sez he, pointin' to a thing about the size of a flat-iron with a knittin'-needle stickin' out of it. I give a little think, an' I sez: "To tell you the gospel truth, Bud, I ain't never been on a sailboat in my life; but I'm game to play her one whirl if you'll just wait until I get my breakfast."

"How long will it take?" sez he. "Deuced if I know," sez I. "I've been waitin' hereabout two hours already an' the' ain't none showed up yet."

"Why don't you go to a restaurant?" sez he.

"I thank you kindly for the suggestion," sez I; "but the same brilliant idee occurred to me a little over two hours ago, an' all my finger-nails is wore to the quick tryin' to scratch up enough change."

He studied my face a moment, then he chuckled up a laugh, an' scooted over to an eatin'-house, comin' back with a lot o' stuff an' some coffee. Then we got into the boat an' begun to sail. Oh, it certainly was grand! By the time I had made it up with my stomach we were out on the Pacific Ocean, an' I felt like Christopher Columbus.

Enjoy myself? Well. I guess I did! I felt like a boy with copper-toed boots an' a toy balloon. Then things began to churn up wild an' furious. Fatty said that Pacific meant mild an' peaceful—the darned, sarcastic, little liar! The storm that was presently kazooin' along was fierce an' horrible, an' that dinky little soap-bubble cut up scand'lous.

We went jumpin' an' slidin' ahead, tilted away over on one side, but Fatty never turned a hair; he said it was nothin' but a capful o' wind, an' he sat in the back end o' the boat with a little stick in his hand, hummin' tunes an' havin' the time of his life; but give me a bunch of blizzard-scared long-horns for mine.

I never knowed a boat was so human. This one bucked an' kicked an' reared up an' tried to fall over on its back, the same as a mustang; while I held on with my teeth an' wondered if it was a put-up job. Then I began to feel as though I had partakin' of a balloon. I gritted my teeth an' swallered hot water constant; but it wasn't no use; purty soon that beautiful breakfast began to fight its way to liberty. Layer after layer, up it came; an' all the while mebbe I wasn't feelin' like a tender-foot, with that fat little cuss puffin' his pipe in the back seat, as happy as a toad.

After a bit he looks at me purty sympathetic like, an' sez, "You seem to have a weak stomach."

"Weak?" I yells. "Weak! why you doggone son of a pirate, it kicks like a shotgun every time it goes off. Weak!"

We stayed out on our pleasure trip the best part of the day, me layin' with what used to be my head jammed under the front seat, while my liver chased my stomach up an' down my backbone, tryin' to squeeze out a few more crumbs o' that breakfast. You can believe me or not; but when noon came that double dyed villain got out the grub an' began to eat—even goin' so far as to ask me to join him. A hog wouldn't 'a' done it. We came back; about five o'clock, an' by the time we reached the landin' place I was feelin' fine. An' hungry— Say!

When we got upon the platform an' started to walk up-town Fatty sez to me, "What are you goin' to do to kill time now?"

"Time?" sez I. "Well, now, I dunno as I feel any inborn hankerin' to slaughter time; but if the game laws ain't in force I wouldn't mind flushin' up a covey of fat young ham sandwidges."

"You're a funny cuss," sez he.

"I am," sez I; "an' I hope I won't come sudden in front of a lookin'-glass. A good hearty laugh just now would be purty apt to puncture my stomach—it's jammed up so tight again my backbone."

"You don't seem to like this community," sez he.

"I don't know," sez I. "It's been a mighty long time since I tasted it; but I have an idy that I'd enjoy some served hot with a couple o' porterhouse steaks smothered in cornbeef hash an' about three pints o' coffee."

He chuckled up another laugh, an sez, "If you had a good job here would you be apt to settle?"

"Settle?" sez I. "You needn't worry much about that; I'm no tight-wad. When it comes my turn to settle I generally fish up a handful an' say, 'Here, take it out o' that an' keep the change.'"

He looked at me a minute without speakin', an' then he said, as though he was thinkin' aloud, "You seem to be mighty well set up."

I was hurt at this. "Your ticket entitles you to one more guess," sez I. "Any time anybody got set up in my company since I struck town the bartender allus managed to sneak me the checks without gettin' caught at it. The' must 'a' been a cold snap here, an' all the easy spenders got froze up."

"No, I mean you're wonderful well built," sez he. "Kin you ride a hoss?"

"I can," sez I, "if he's kind an' gentle, an' I manage to get a good grip on the saddle horn, an' he don't start to lopin' or somethin' like that."

"Do you know what a knight is?" sez he.

"Yes," sez I, "I do when I'm home; but since I've been here I ain't wasted none of 'em in sleep, so I ain't right certain."

"No, I don't mean that kind," sez he. "I mean the soldiers of long ago who used to wear steel armor an' fight with spears an' rescue maidens an' so forth. I believe I can get you a job at it for a month or so, at three dollars a day."

"Now look here, Bud," sez I, "them three dollars look mighty enticin' to me, an' I ain't no objection to rescuin' the maidens; but I move we cut out the steel armor an' the spears. If the' 's any great amount o' maidens in need o' rescuin', I could do the job a heap quicker with my six-shooters."

"Oh, I don't mean to be a real knight," sez he. "I want you to advertise tobacco."

"Say," sez I, "perhaps you never noticed it; but after you've been livin' on air for some time you get so you can't tell whether it's yourself or the other feller what's crazy. I came down to this town because my appetite was clogged up an' wouldn't work; but I'm cured. I'm the most infernally cured individual you ever set eyes on, an' I'm goin' back where food ain't too blame proud to be seen in company with a poor man."

Well, I broke through his crust that time, an' we sidled into a feed-joint, where I pried my ribs apart while he un folded his plot. It seemed the' was a brand of chewin' tobacco what had one o' these here knights on the tag, an' I was to dress up like the picture an' advertise it. The man who was to do it had sprained his ankle, an' Fatty's brother was huntin' up a new man. Fatty said he'd get me the job.

Well, he did, an' next mornin' I started out in a tin suit with a sort of kettle turned upside down an' covered with feathers for a sky-piece. I certainly made an imposin' sight, an' all I had to do was to ride around an' fling little plugs o' tobacco out o' my saddle-bags. But the' was draw-backs. The' generally is.

Take the real native-son brand of Friscoite, an' he'll tell you 'at Frisco an' Paradise are sunonomous. I used to like to argue 'em out about it. One day I had a thirty-third degree one pointin' his finger in my eye an' beatin' his palm with his fist, an' spreadin' himself somethin' gorgeous. He never curbed his jubilization nor altered the heavy seriousness of his expression; but in the most matter-of-fact way in the world he backs over to the door-jamb an' begins to polish it up with his spinal column. If ya'll notice you'll find most o' the coats in that locality has curious little streaks up the back— but it ain't polite to ask questions about 'em.

"Look here, Bud," sez I, interruptin', "I know all about your golden gates an' sea lions an' cosmopopilic civilization; but how about your fleas?"

"Fleas!" sez he. "Hang the fleas! I'll tell you about them. The devil He tried an experiment; he wanted a place so fine to live in that man wouldn't have no inducement to try to get to heaven; so he studied all the cities an' the towns—an' then he made Frisco. The experiment worked to perfection; everybody what lived there was perfectly satisfied, an' the preachers couldn't make 'em believe 'at any place could be any better. But the good Lord, he was powerful fond o' the Friscoites, so he finally figgered out the little red flea—an' then even Frisco had a drawback; not enough to give the town anything of a black eye; just enough to leave one little talkin'-point in favor of everlastin' bliss."

Well, these here fleas was consid'able of a talkin'-point with me all right when I was takin' the part of a canned knight. They used to congregate together in the valley between my shoulder-blades, an' I'd get off an' back up again a lamp-post, but it wa'n't no use. I couldn't reach 'em, an' the' ain't no way on earth to scare 'em. Finally I hit upon a plan of wearin' a couple o' feet o' chain down the back o' my neck an' givin' it a jerk now an' again. It was only just moderately comfortable; but I had the satisfaction of knowin' that it was more of a bother to them than it was to me. A suit of armor ain't no tenement house, it's only meant for one. But when they got on my face they had me beat. I'd forget all about bein' sealed up, an' I'd take a smash at one an' bat the kettle over again my forehead until I had both eyebrows knocked out o' line.

I carried a spear with a little flag on it, an' rode a hoss built like a barrel. He had been in the brewery business all his life an' looked the part. About the only item in the whole parade that put me in mind of myself was my lariat. I smuggled that along for company, an' so I'd have somethin' to work with, provided anything turned up.

Fatty had give me a book called "Ivanhoe" the night before I started out, an' it was full o' pictures about knights knockin' each other about with spears; an' I bet a hat it was fun to be a real one an' not have no tobacco to advertise, but just nothin' to do except jab each other with spears. I reckon a corkin' good one like Ivanhoe himself or the Black Knight got more 'an three a day for it too; but the one best bet is, that the vigilance committee those days didn't take on much superfluous fat.

I enjoyed myself first rate, an' upset a couple o' delivery wagons because they wouldn't make way for me, roped a runaway steer 'at had the whole town scared, an' chased a flat-head clear into the Palace Hotel for throwin' a pear at me. Fatty's brother confided to him that I was the best advertisement they'd ever had.

Still I allus get weary o' doin' the same sort o' thing day after day. That's what gets me about livin' in town; it's so blame monotonous. Out on the range now a feller can allus be expectin' a little excitement even if he ain't enjoyin' it right at the time; but in town it's just the same thing over an' over again. It's bad enough at any time; but if you want to soak yourself plumb full o' the horrors of a great city you want to wear a tin suit with an iron kettle strapped on your head that you can't take off without help. I got so blame disgusted drinkin' steam beer through a straw that if any one would 'a' dared me I'd 'a' signed the pledge.

If it hadn't been for the children I'd probably got hysterical an' been voted into the uncurable ward; but they thought I was the finest thing out, an' I used to give 'em little plugs o' tobacco for souvynears. I used to read "Ivanhoe" at night an' tell stories to the kids the next day. Some o' them thought I was a fairy godmother; an' I generally had such a gang troopin' after me that we looked like an orphan asylum out for an airin'. I allus did like children.

Well, one day I was out at the foot o' the hill neighbor-hood on Sutter Street. A lot o' cars was blockaded, an' a herd o' kids stood lookin' on. I stopped an' talked to 'em, an' the' was one little girl, just for all the world like another little girl I used to know, away back yonder in Indiana. She had the same confidin' smile an' the same big, wide open eyes; an' I felt a sort o' lump in my throat when she looked at me. She had that same queer little look that Barbie'd had when she was a child too. Her mother was named Maggie, which also happened to be the name o' the little girl I had known clear away back when I'd been a school-boy. All of a sudden I felt lonesome again; so I give the kids the slip an' skirted the car.

I started to ride up the Hyde Street hill on the other side, an' say, it was a hill! Steep? Well, it was about all Mr. Hoss could do to climb it. While I was wonderin' if I hadn't better let that part o' town go unadvertised I heard a rumble, looked up, an' saw comin' over the square o' the next street a big wagon loaded with lumber an' runnin' towards me down the hill. The' wasn't no hosses hitched to it, an' the tongue stuck straight out in front. It was comin' like a steam-engine, an' like a flash I remembered Maggie on the other side o' the car. That wagon would 'a' weighed six tons, an' any fool could see what would happen when it struck that street car.

For a second—for just one second, which seemed to last a thousand years—I was turned to stone. I could hear the crash; I could hear the screams; I could feel the horrid scrunch as car, wagon, an' all ground over poor little Maggie; and then everything cleared up, an' I could think ninety times a minute.

I turned my rope loose an' backed ol' Mr. Barrel up on the sidewalk in the wink of a hair trigger. I looked down at the hoss, an' he would have weighed a full ton himself; but I knew that he wouldn't have sense enough to brace himself when the jerk came. It was comical the way thoughts kept flashin' through my head—everything I had done, an' everything I might have done, an' a heap more beside; but the thing that worried me most was the thought that a mighty good story was about to happen, an' the chances were that I wouldn't be the one to do the tellin' of it afterward. I can talk about it easy now, but I wasn't BREATHIN' then.

On came the wagon, an' it looked as though nothin' under heaven could stop it. A strange feelin' o' weakness swept over me for a minute, and—and—darned if I didn't pray, right then. The pressure lifted like a fog, an' I sat there as cool an' still as though I was Ivanhoe, darin' the whole blame outfit to come at me in a bunch; an' I was some pleased to notice that a little group had gathered to see the outcome. My knees dug into the hoss's ribs as I circled the rope around my head, an' then at just the right instant I gave the foreleg throw. Well, it landed—everything landed. As soon as the noose caught the tip o' the tongue I yanked back on the brewer until he must 'a' thought his lower jaw had dissolved partnership.

The' never was any neater work—never. The noose tightened well out on the tongue, an' when the strain came the wagon turned in toward the sidewalk, runnin' in a big circle on the outside wheels. The jerk had lifted ol' Uncle Brewer, who didn't have gumption enough to squat, plumb out in the middle o' the street, an' just as the wagon climbed the curb an' dove into the basement office of a Jew doctor the rope tightened up with me an' the brewer square behind. It didn't last long; the' was only one cinch to the saddle, an' the first jerk had purty well discouraged that; the brewer had grew suspicious an' all four of his feet was dug into the cobble stones; the wagon was lopin' along about ninety miles a second, an' when the tug came me an' the saddle an' the tinware an' about four thousand plugs o' tobacco made a half-circle in the air an' plunged through the first story winder onto the dinin'-table—an' the family was at dinner.

Nobody was hurt; but I wish you could have seen the eyes o' that family—an' their hands—yes, an' their tonsils too. They didn't seem fully prepared. After a time the doctor got his heart to pumpin' again, an' he roars out, "Vat are you doin'—vat are you doin'?"

"I'm advertisin' tobacco," sez I, tryin' to cut the kettle off my head with a fruit-knife.

Then he did the wind-mill act with his hands an' rolled up his eyes an' sez, "Vell, mine Cott, man, dis iss no vay to atfertice dobaggo!"

"Mebbe not, ol' sport," sez I, thinkin' o' the way that wagon had dove into his office, an' takin' a general survey o' the dinner table; "but if you're game at all you got to own up it makes a strong impression."

He was a comical little cuss, an' it amused me a heap to see how excited he was. He spluttered an' fizzed away like a leaky sody fountain, while the rest o' the tribe kept up a most infernal squawkin'.

By the time I had the tobacco an' the balance o' the trimmin's picked up an' got back to the street again I found the rest o' the population gathered together to see who was holdin' the celebration; an' from that on my stay in the city was a nightmare. The passengers in the car gave me gold watches an' champagne suppers, the Jew doctor wore himself to a bone tryin' to find out whether it was me, the lumber company, or the tobacco firm which had to pay the piper; while the newspaper reporters pumped me as dry as the desert. The tobacco company kept me on double pay, because when it came to what they call a publicity agent I had played every winnin' number open an' coppered all the ones that lost.

That car had been loaded with a group o' the real, genuine gold-sweaters, an' they entered into a fierce competition to see which could load me down with the finest watch an' load me up with the finest champagne. They got me to make 'em after-dinner speeches an' do fancy stunts with my raw-hide—ropin' wine bottles off the waiters' trays an' such—until we got as friendly as a herd of tramps. They even got me into a long-tailed coat an' a bullfrog vest; but I didn't take kindly to that, 'count o' there not bein' any handy place to tote a gun except the tail pocket, which I never could have got at in case the trouble was to slop over.

I kept lookin' for little Maggie, an' one day I found her. I bought her a couple o' pounds o' candy an' a lot o' new dresses; an' I took her out to her home in a carriage. Well, this home o' hers was a thing to wring the heart of an ossi-fied toad. It was up near the Barbery coast, where they kill folks for exercise. She an' her mother was livin' in two miserable rooms, her mother doin' washin' an' Maggie runnin' errands; but they was as near respectable as half-fed people ever was in the world, an' it made 'em hustle to even keep half fed, too, 'cause they was in competition with the Chinks, who don't have to eat at all—that is, not regular food.

An' would you believe it, her mother was the little Maggie I used to know away back yonder in the kid days when all the world was just like a big, bulgey Christmas-stocking. She had married a good man, an' had come out to the coast with him on account of his health, an' he had flickered out without leavin' her much but a stack o' doctor's bills an' little Maggie. She had struggled along ever since, an' it made my heart ache like a tooth to see the sweetness an' the beauty o' the little girl I used to know come to the eyes o' this poor tired woman an' smile—smile the same old smile like what she used to when I'd given her an apple, or when she'd written me a little note an' sneaked it across the aisle.

Well, I didn't stay long. I had a special swell function to attend that night, but next mornin', when the Turkish-bath man was willin' to risk the peace o' that locality by turnin' me loose, I gathered up a peck or so o' watches an' cashed 'em in. I reckon I got beat some; but anyhow, I drew down somethin' over sixteen hundred in yeller money; an' I took them two Maggies down to the train an' shipped 'em back where the little one would have a chance to grow up like a flower, with plenty o' green grass an' sunshine about her, an' the mother could put on a clean dress afternoons an' visit 'round a little with the friends o' long ago.

After they was gone everything seemed mighty gloomy an' damp an' lonesome, an' I entered into the social festivities most enthusiastic. The' was somethin' about both these two Maggies that kept bringin' Barbie before me, an' what I felt most like doin' was to bolster up my forgetfulness. It wasn't very long, however, before I noticed that my quiet an' simple life hadn't in nowise fitted me for refined society, an' I made my plans to bid it a fond farewell. I'm just as cordial a friend as whiskey ever had; but my con science rebels at floodin' my vital organs with seventeen different colored wines at one meal. I've been infested with pink elephants an' green dragons an' I never com plained none; but hang me if I can get any comfort out of a striped yellow spider ten feet high on horrid hairy legs.

I was sittin' in the Palace lobby one mornin' wonderin' if I'd bump my head should I happen to sneeze, when in come one o' my pals. His face lit up when he see me an' he came over holdin' out his hand. I held out my own hearty enough; but I sez in a warnin' voice, "Now, before you ask me the customary question I want to inform you that I positively don't want a drink, neither now nor this evenin', nor never again."

"Pshaw," sez he, "I'm goin' to pull out for home to day, an' I don't want to go without a farewell libation to the good times we've been havin'."

"I'm goin' to pull out, myself," sez I, "but I went on my farewell libation last night. Where might your home be?"

"Texas," sez he. I straightened up.

"Know the governor?" sez I.

"Some," sez he, his eyes twinklin'; "he was my sister's youngest brother."

"Your sister's youngest brother?" sez I, an' then I tumbled. "Say," I yelled, jumpin' to my feet, "you don't mean that you're it yourself?"

"That's the history," sez he; "but if it's just the same to you, I'd rather you didn't work up much of a story about the way I've handled this town since you saved that car."

"Do you really think 'at I saved your life?" sez I.

"Why," sez he, "if that wagon had ever hit the car the' wouldn't 'a' been anything left but my teeth to identify me by, an' I ain't never had one filled yet."

Well, I took one drink with him an' I told him the straight o' that cattle ring an' how Jim Jimison had surrendered on account o' the best little girl that walked, an' that he was the all around squarest boy the' was. I didn't cork up any natural eloquence I happened to have, an' I was some sorry 'at ol' Hammy couldn't have heard that plea. It was dramatic, an' I'll bet money on it. The outcome was, that he swore he'd have Jim out o' the pen as soon as he could get back an' do the signin'. He was a big man with steel gray eyes, an' by jing I felt good over it; but I stuck to the one drink proposition.

CHAPTER TWENTY-SEVEN
THE CREOLE BELLE

Well, now, mebbe I didn't feel fine! I'd have a real man for Barbie to marry purty soon, an' it was a good job o' work to send that washy-eyed Englishman back to his one-hoss ranch to learn hove to act grown-up. I was all squared around now. Up to that mornin' I couldn't tell where on the face I did want to head for; but now I knew. I wanted to bee-line straight for the Diamond Dot an' light the joy-lamps in Barbie's eyes again. When I had given my life to her the' wasn't no strings to the gift. I hadn't said that my happiness was to be considered at all, nor the happiness of any one else on the whole earth except just her own, an' I was wild to be back.

I was makin' up my mind to sneak away without seein' any o' the glad band—those Frisco fellers are terrors when they take a fancy to ya—I mean the thoroughbreds, the toppy lad with rolls 'at a ten-year-old boy couldn't up-end without strainin' himself. I hated to do it; but I'm only human, an' when I'm in earnest about bein' delivered from evil I allus get up early in the dawn an' get a good start while temptation is still enjoyin' its beauty sleep.

I had just got my will power properly stiffened up, when lo an' behold, I was slapped on the back an' a merry voice exclaimed, "Happy Hawkins, by the Chinese Devil!"

I glanced up into a bearded face with two twinklin' eyes an' an outdoor look about it. I recognized the eyes all right, but I knew I hadn't never seen 'em in that sort o' trimmin' before; so I sez in a dignified manner, "I'm exceeding glad to see ya, but who the 'll are ya?"

"Ches!" sez he. "Ralph Chester Stuart—Great Scott, have you lost your memory?"

Well, by the Jinks, but I was glad to see the boy, an' we hid away in a private room with two pure an' proper lemonades before us. He was a genuine minin' engineer, an' had been havin' lots of queer experiences. He wanted me to sign up with him, promisin' me that we'd have change of bill twice a week; but I finally prevailed upon him that I had aged considerable since our didoes with the goat, an' all of a sudden he ups an' sez, "By the way, old hat, I've got you news!"

"Yes?" sez I. "Where'd you get it?"

"Why, about the Creole Belle," sez he.

"Creole Belle!" sez I. "Well, tell it, tell it. Why don't you tell it?"

"Oh, fudge," sez he; "it's been long enough on the way, an' I reckon it'll keep a minute longer. The Creole Belle was a gold-mine named after a woman."

"Good or bad?" sez I.

"Good," sez he. "Paid two hundred dollars to the ton in spots."

"I meant the woman, confound ya," sez I.

"Well, it seems that she was a purty square sort of a woman," sez Ches, "but I didn't suppose 'at you'd care much about her. The mine—" I groaned. "Well, you fool me," sez Ches, seein' I was in earnest. "The' was a purty florid romance mixed up in it too; but I didn't suppose you was interested in such things, an' I didn't pay much heed to that part of it."

"That's allus the way when a boy does anything," sez I, with peevishness. "Now you set there an' think up all you can about the deal—everything."

"Well," sez Ches, slowly, "it seems that a couple o' young Easterners came out to find their fortune. They was the true Damon an' Pythias brand o' partners, an' stood back to back durin' a protracted spell o' good, stiff, copper-bottomed misfortune. They finally located a mine that looked good-natured an' generous; but it was a fooler. One day it coaxed 'em an' next it give 'em the laugh. Finally they each got down in turn with mountain-fever an' a beautiful young girl nursed 'em. She was there with her father, who was workin' a claim near by. He was an odd sort of chap to be minin'— though come to think of, that's not possible, seein' that all kinds o' men—"

"Ches," I breaks in, "will you kindly get on with that tale, or must I shake it out o' you?"

He seemed mightily surprised, but he went on: "Well, the girl was a beauty, an' she had a gigantic maid—"

"Monody!" I shouted.

"Keeno!" shouts back Ches, some exasperated.

"Now that wasn't slang nor sarcasm what I was usin'," sez I, smoothin' it over. "That gigantic maid you mentioned is part o' the tale that you don't know yet."

"Well, naturally, while they was bein' nursed they both fell in love with her—"

"With Monody?" I yells.

"No, you ijot, with the girl!" Ches was gettin' flustered. "She was a corkin' handsome girl, an' they all called her the Creole Belle. To be strictly honest though, they didn't really fall in love with her. They both loved the same girl back in Philadelphia, an' they just took to the Creole Belle as a sort of a substitute. Now the ol' man an' the big maid watched over the girl careful, an' the' wasn't no harm come of it; an' when the mine finally got to handin' out the gilt without jokin' about it, the two pals got to goin' off alone an' thinkin' o' the girl back East. They had four or five miners workin' for 'em by this time, an' they was gettin' the dust in quantities. Finally they got together about it. It seems that they had an agreement that neither one would propose to the girl without the other's consent, but they had each been makin' gentle-love in their letters to her, while she didn't seem to know which she liked best."

"Where'd you learn all this?" sez I.

"Oh, I've been askin' all the of miners I've met," sez Ches, "an' at last I found one who knew the whole of it. All of 'em knew something; things ain't done secret in a minin' camp, an' all the boys got interested. Well, they finally agreed to play five hands o' draw for the first chance to propose. If the lucky one got the girl he was to pay the loser half the profits. If he lost an' the second feller got the girl on his proposal, he was to get mine an' girl both. They was still fond o' the Creole Belle an' she was fond o' them—from all accounts they was men above the average, all right. Well, they played the five hands an' it was even bones at the fourth show. Then Jordan made a crooked move o' some kind, an' Whitman called for a new deal. It was the first suspicion that had ever raised its head between 'em, an' they looked into each other's eyes a long time; then Jordan dealt again an' Whitman won.

"He wrote to the girl, an' after a time she answered, sayin' yes. Jordan an' Whitman wasn't such good pals as before; but when the girl was due to arrive they started down in the stage to meet her, both together. Just as they was goin' by the of man's claim—Ol' Pizarro, or some such a name as that he had—the stage lost a front wheel an' Whitman got a broken leg. They took him into the ol' man's cabin, sent a man on hoss-back after the doctor, an' Whitman insisted that Jordan ride on down to meet the girl. They'd had a hard time gettin' the girl to consent to come at all; but she was an orphan with only a faithful servant for a family, an' she had finally give in, seein' as Jordan would be there as her best friend; an' now Whitman forced Jordan to go down an' meet her." I remembered the letter 'at little Barbie had made me read, an' I was able to guess the rest.

"Well, Jordan met the girl, an' the servant who had tagged along,—the name of the servant was Melisse, if you want all the details."

"I knew it," sez I; "go on."

"He brought the girl back to where the Creole Belle was tendin' to Whitman in a mighty gentle an' tender way. The girl didn't seem to care much for Whitman when she saw him, an' that very day they had it out. She didn't make no fuss, she was a game one all right; just said that it was a mistake all 'round an' left on the next stage, goin' to Frisco.

"Whitman was laid up six weeks, an' by the time he was out Jordan told him that he was ready to propose to the girl on his own hook. Whitman agreed, Jordan made his play, got a favorable answer, an' Whitman made over a full deed to the Creole Belle. Just at this time ol' Pizzaro cashed in, an' the first thing Whitman knew he was married to the Creole Belle, had sold his wife's mine an' started to leave the country. Down at the station he hears a chance word that gives him a tip, an' he leaves his wife there an' goes back to the mine. He accuses Jordan of havin' told the eastern girl that he was already married to the Creole Belle when she came out to marry him herself. Jordan denies it, but they fight, an' it's sure a bad fight. Jordan gets three bullets in his body an' only laughs about it; but he shoots Whitman twice, so that fever sets in, an' it was reported that he died. Anyhow, he's taken down to the train an' put on board, out of his head; an' was never heard of again.

"Jordan hid his wounds purty well, bein' a man o' wonderful grit; but just when he was gettin' around again one o' the boys what Whitman had done a good turn to picks a quarrel with Jordan, an' Jordan still bein' stiff from the wounds he was hidin', gets the worst of it, is hammered up with a pick-handle an' left for dead. He don't die, however, he works the Creole Belle mine till he's taken out about a million, an' then she closes up an' he gets out o' the country for keeps. That's all the' is to that tale. Now you tell me what part of it you're interested in."

"Was that all you heard about the gigantic maid?" sez I.

"You certainly have a healthy appetite for gossip," sez Chez, laughin'. "But I did hear more about the maid: she came back to that part a few months later to square things up with her lover. He didn't appear willin' to square, an' they found him in his cabin one mornin' with his throat tore out by the roots, an' they found her clothes on the bank o' Devil Crick; so that ends her story. She must 'a' been some devil herself."

"No," sez I to chez, "the worst any one can call her is a man; an' it wasn't altogether her fault that you can call her that, I'll stake my soul on it."

Ches was ravenous to learn why it was that I wanted all that old scandal dished up; but I was too busy to tell him right then, an' he was goin' to leave in an hour to overlook some new findin's out in Nevada. We promised to write to each other, an' I told him that probably I'd be willin' to take a job with him in a month or so; an' then he skinned out to make ready, an' I got busy on my letter. Letters never was one o' my chief delights; but I wrote to Jim, tellin' him enough o' the details to throw a bluff into Jabez; but not enough to put Jim wise to the tale. Just gave him the right names an' the name o' the mine an' told him to bluff that he knew it all; but not to speak too free; an' that would suit all around an' put Jabez into a nervous condition. I sent this letter to the governor, tellin' him to give it to Jim personal, an' to hustle things for a quick finish.

I posted my letter an' started up to the desk to pay my bill, when I had another turn. I stood still with a shock, pinchin' myself to see if I was in my right mind or only sufferin' from an extra foolin' hang-over. A jaunty young chap with out-standin' clothes, an' a brindle bull-terrier was registerin' their names, an' if I was in my right mind I knew them folks for true. I was feelin' exuberant to a dangerous limit, an' I sneaks up an' unsnaps the bull-terrier from the leash what the porter was holdin'. Well, it was Cupid all right, an' he was bugs to see me. He started jumpin' up on my shoulders an' makin' queer sounds, an' I pretends 'at I'm scared to death an' duck an' dodge around that office until I have all the inmates standin' on the furniture an' yellin' police.

Bill runs around after us tellin' me not to be frightened, an' givin' Cupid a tongue-handlin' that would 'a' stung a deaf alligator. When I can't hold in any longer I rolls over on a dievan—that's what they call a hotel sofy—an' get Cupid in my arms an' make a sound as if he was stranglin' me. Bill gets Cupid by the collar an' jerks him off, an' then I stands up an' sez in a hurt an' dignified voice, "It seems darned funny to me that I can't welcome an old friend without you interferin'."

He give me one look—I was festooned a little out o' the ordinary—an' then he begins. First he'd sing a chant about how tickled he was to meet up with me, an' then he'd sermonize most doleful about how untasteful it was to commit such a havoc as that in a hotel lobby, especially with a dog what had been trained to have quiet an' refined manners. I finally refused to hold my safety valve down any longer; an' I grabbed him under the arms an' waltzed him over the marble, while Cupid frolicked around us an' Bill kicked me on the shins. I had had too many things happen to me in a small space o' time to be altogether sane, an' it took a good many kicks on the shins to get me down to a practical basis again. Bill was plumb disgusted; but Jessamie, who had seen the last part of it, had to join in with the rest o' the crowd an' have a laugh.

Bill refused to eat unless we could have a private dinin' room. Not on Cupid's account neither; he'd got civilized enough to stand for Cupid bein' treated like a dog by this time; but it was me he was scared of, an' I sensed it, an' refused to feed with him at all unless it would be in the main mess hall, an' Jessamie voted with me; so Bill had to give in.

He didn't want to make the contrast too strong, so he slid into a dark suit instead of the real caper, while I wiggled into my champagne apron an' marched in like I was a foreign delegate. Well, you should have seen Bill—his mouth took on the triangle droop, an' his lamps was stretched to match. I was entirely at home, et with the right forks, joshed the waiters, an' when my friends began to drop over an' pass the season's greetings, an' I presented 'em to Bill an' Jessamie, an' Bill saw that they was nothin' at all but cream, I bet you a tip that he was the worst locoed man in topsy-turvy Frisco.

We had a hard time throwin' the gang off the trail; but I finally sent 'em over to the Pampered Pug restaurant, while I took Bill an' Jessamie to a quiet little spot to hold our own reunion. They had just come from a trip around the world—they was still on their honeymoon, in fact; an' I had to listen to a heap o' Sunday-school story adventures 'at they'd been havin'.

After a while, though, I nudged Bill hack to the Clarenden family trail, an' he said 'at they had stopped for over a month with his friends in England, an' was posted up to the minute.

"Well," sez I, as though I was inquirin' after an old pal, "how's the Earl?"

"They're plumb out o' earls in that family," sez Bill. "The old one's dead an' they've hunted high an' low for the strays an' can't even find Richard."

"They won't need him," sez I. "The younger son is still in good order, an' when the proper time comes I'll spring him on 'em; but I doubt if he takes the job after all."

"Confound you, Happy," sez Bill, "I never can tell whether you're jokin' or not on this subject. Deuced if I ever could see where your trail could have junctioned onto the Clarenden family."

"Son," sez I, "I'm a store-house o' knowledge, an' I'm about to open the flood-gates an' pour it forth. How many Alice LeMoynes did you ever happen to hear of?"

"Only but the one," sez Bill. "It was a fake name probably, an' one was all they ever struck off that die. What about her?"

"Oh, nothin' much," sez I, "only a stray Englishman happened to pull that name on us a while back, an' I wondered where he came into possession of it."

"You got somethin' up your sleeve," sez Bill, who was a mite too observin' at times; "what is it you want to know?"

"Nothin' at all," sez I; "I know all I want to now."

"What kind of lookin' feller was it?" sez Bill.

"Purty harmless," sez I; "watery blue eyes, fair size, purty good lookin', nice manners, book-talker, owns a little ranch; oh, he won't set no important rivers on fire."

Bill studied awhile. "How old was he?" sez he.

"Why, he's about my age, in years," sez I.

"It might be Richard—if Lord James is still alive, Richard is the heir apparent," sez Bill. "How long have you known o' this feller?"

"Oh, this ain't Richard," sez I. "He ain't got epolepsy nor insanity; he's just stingy an' stupid."

"How do you know he ain't got epolepsy?" sez Bill.

"'Cause he don't bark like a dog nor froth at the mouth, nor he ain't afraid o' water," sez I.

"You're thinkin' o' hydrophobia," sez Bill. "Epolepsy is sort o' fits."

"Well, by gum, he did have one fit!" sez I.

"What kind?" sez Bill.

"Why, I worked a trick on him, an' he stiffened out an' his eyes got set, an' he was the sickenest lookin' human I ever met up with," sez I.

"That's it!" sez Bill, "an' you say he knew about Alice LeMoyne?"

"That's what give him the fit," sez I.

"I bet it's Richard," sez Bill. "This will make a story for me, an' you can work things for the reward. Where is he?"

"Say, you come along with me to the Diamond Dot," sez I. "Things are goin' to happen promiscuous up there after a bit, an' you don't want to miss it. Never mind about the reward. I'm goin' to handle this affair just as if the' wasn't such a thing on earth as the Clarenden family."

"You make me tired," sez Bill; it allus was spurs to him to cut him out of a secret. "You try to pertend 'at you're nothin' short of a world power; but I bet you're just flim-flammin'."

"Nothin' 'at Happy Hawkins'd do would surprise me," sez Jessamie. "Now that I've seen him in a dress suit, hob-nobbin' with the bun-tong, I'm prepared for anything." She was a good feller all right.

Well, we chatted along a while, an' they told me that they wanted to see Frisco an' the Yosemite Valley, an' then would head for Colonel Scott's, where it'd be handy to drop over to the Diamond Dot at any time.

"Well," sez I, "I'll write you some letters of introduction to a few o' my friends here, an' mebbe after you've seen Frisco, all you'll want will be rest—just plain, simple rest; less'n your ruggeder built than me."

So sure enough I wrote 'em a parcel o' letters, pickin' out about the most persistent spenders the town could show, an' it made me laugh when I pictured Bill tryin' to lug home the list o' stuff they'd load him up with. I packed up for the early, train, an' then as it wasn't worth while to waste the handful o' minutes left o' that night, I got back into my workin' togs an' went out for one last Turkish bath. I'm mighty partial to Turkish baths, an' I wanted to let 'em know that I was perfectly sober at least one night o' my visit.

It was gray dawn when I came out o' the buildin', an' even in Frisco that's a shivery period. In spite of me holdin' all the good cards in the deck, an' knowin' just about how I was goin' to play 'em, I was lonely an' down-hearted there in the dawning. All I wanted was Barbie's happiness, an' I was goin' to give it to her full measure an' nairy a whimper: but if it could just have been my home-comin' instead of what I was goin' to do, that would light up her world for her, I reckon I could have FLOWN all the way back to the Diamond Dot.

I turned a corner an' came face to face on Piker. He was lookin' downcast an' harried, an' I bought him a drink. He had told me where Jim was, an' I didn't try to forget it. I sat down an' talked to him an tried to soften his crust an' get him to agree to make a new try-out o' life.

He finally got purty mellow an' told me some o' the steps down which he had stumbled, an' how slippery the'd been when he'd tried to climb back. I confided to him a lot o' my own mishaps, an' he got purty near up to the mourner's bench, when all of a sudden he gets bitter. "You're just like all the rest," sez he, "you make all kinds of allowance for a good lookin', proud sort, like Silver Dick; but a feller like me—you allus give the verdict again a feller like me, an' you know it."

"Dick ain't been no saint, I know," sez I; "but at least he was out in the open, while I can't quite get over that knee-gun you wore."

"Out in the open, was he?" sez Piker, with a leer. "Didn't he get to your ranch an' try to land the daughter o' the boss—an' him a married man all the time!"

I reached across the table an' got him by the collar, jerked him to me, an' flopped him face up across the table. "You lie," sez I. He shook his head, an' I felt a cold streak hit my heart.

I loosened up on him an' let him set up, an' he said 'at Silver Dick was married to the woman at Laramie, an' he knew it. I tried to bluff him out of it, but he stuck to it, finally sayin' that I had him, an' could finish him if I wanted to; but that it was the God's truth, an' he'd stick to it.

As I looked into his eyes I knew beyond a doubt that he was dealin' straight; an' as my plans toppled over an' came tumblin' about me, I felt like walkin' down to the dock an' endin' it all. Put this passed in a flash; it wasn't my turn yet to think of myself. There was little Barbie with the two serpents creepin' toward her, an' my place was at her side till the fight was fairly won.

CHAPTER TWENTY-EIGHT
THE DAY OF THE WEDDING

I had struck the Diamond Dot in a tol'able wide variety o' moods; but I never felt like I did the mornin' I came back to ditch Barbie's weddin'. I knew 'at the chances were 'at I'd break her heart; but I had only one course open, an' I didn't intend to waver. I had gone on through to Laramie, an' had found 'at Silver Dick's wife was still there, livin' her locked-in life. Then I came on back through Danders to Webb Station where I hired a feller to drive me to within a mile o' the ranch house. All he knew was that the weddin' was to come off in three weeks.

Jabez an' Barbie was both glad to see me; but I didn't make much explanation for leavin' without notice, an' I didn't tell all about my trip. Just told 'em about my experience as a knight an' on the boat an' such. Barbie was purty thin an' a little under color; but her grit was still keyed up to full tone. I had a good long talk with her that very afternoon, tellin' her that I had found out a lot o' stuff about the remnant she was thinkin' o' marryin', an' tried to get her to test him out an' find out where he'd come from an' what he was; but she seemed numb, an' told me that she would not think it friendly if I said anything evil against the man she had to marry. I couldn't understand her, she didn't seem like the same old Barbie; but the more I hinted the more froze-up she got, so I dropped it.

Then I told her that I had found out that Dick was even worse'n this one; an' she opened up on me an' we had a purty square-off talkin' match. She wouldn't listen to me, an' she wouldn't pay any heed to my suggestions; an' I was consid'able out of patience. I was afraid if I turned her again Dick she might marry this Hawthorn thing, an' if I turned her again him too soon she might run off with Dick on the rebound; so I was purty much hobbled, an' made a botch of it. Finally she turned on me. "We've been good pals, Happy," sez she, "an' we'll be good pals again some day; but you're not playin' square now—I can tell by your actions. I almost believe 'at what you're tryin' to do is to—" she stopped with her face red as fire.

"Well, say it," sez I.

"Is to marry me yourself," she blurted out.

I didn't say anything for a long time. I made every allowance for her, an' I knew 'at some one had threw it in her face, 'cause this wasn't one of her own brand o' thoughts; but I'm not all horn an' bone, an' when I saw that she intended to go her own gait I made up my mind that she'd know at the end of the course that she might have saved herself several hard bumps.

"Barbie." I sez, an' at my voice she turned her face an' looked a little frightened, "I ain't denyin' that I'd rather marry you than be sure of gettin' into Heaven; but I want you to remember one thing, an' that is that if I ever do marry you it will be because you ask me to yourself."

We rode side by side back to the ranch house, an' her head wasn't held an inch higher than mine nor her lips shut a grain tighter. I was willin' to be used for a bumper; but I couldn't stand everything even when I knew 'at she'd been hounded beyond endurance. From that on Barbie was some cool to me; but I wasn't there for a vacation, I had a duty to perform. Poor little Barbie, she didn't act much like a bride elect. Jabez wanted a weddin' that would be the talk for years; but Barbie said no, that she felt more like a widder than a maid, an' she didn't take much stock in turnin' a second weddin' into a circus. I didn't say nothin'. The ol' man didn't contrary her much them days, so he dropped the subject; but he sent all the way to Frisco for a store full o' fixin's an' a couple o' women to engineer the construction of 'em.

A full week passed without me hearin' from Dick, an' then I telegraphed to the Governor. I waited at Webb Station till I got the answer. He said 'at he had give Dick my letter an' that he had left two days before. That kept me on edge 'cause I wanted to see him when he first arrived; so I kept a couple o' the boys watchin' each road; but day after day dragged around until I got desperate. For all I knew Silver Dick had enough black blood in him to take advantage of me an' just fly his kite. He might have got news from England too, an' all in all I was agitated.

Two days before the ceremony was scheduled I gave him up an' made a run to Laramie. I wasn't sure just what I would do, but I was minded to get all the evidence I could. I tried to get speech with Dick's wife, but she wouldn't pay any heed to my knocks, an' finally the lights in the house went out. I scented trouble; so when a couple o' men pounced onto the place where I'd just stood they found me immejetly behind 'em, an' I rapped 'em on the heads before they could express a sound. I heard a noise at the keyhole an' I whispered in, "If you want to save the life o' Silver Dick, open the door."

I waited a minute an' then the door opened an inch, but a chain kept it from goin' any wider. A woman's coarse voice sez, "What do ya want?" I couldn't believe that this was the woman, so I sez, "I want to speak to the other woman, an' it's got to be done quick."

Presently a soft, gentle voice sez, "What is it?"

"Silver Dick is in the Texas penitentiary, sentenced to be hanged for a murder committed there in April four years ago. He'll be hanged a week from to-morrow night if some one don't make a plea for him. It takes a woman to do such a job as this—are you game?"

"Why, he couldn't have done it," sez she. "He was here all that spring."

"Are you willin' to swear to it?" sez I.

"Oh, I don't want to appear in public—but of course I will, if the' ain't no other way."

"You won't have to if you'll come with me to-night. The Governor of Texas is up here on a huntin' trip; he'll be at a party to-morrow night; all you'll need to do is to wait in a room where I'll hide you until he gets into a meller mood—I know him well—an' then I'll bring him to you an' you make a plea for him. You can be his wife or his mother or daughter—or anything you wish."

"I'll go," sez she, in a quiet tone, an' I breathed free; an' as soon as she opened the door I dragged the two men inside. They were Greasers, the same as the old woman what had first talked to me; an' I turned 'em over to her a' took the woman with the soft voice down to the train by a back street. She still wore a heavy veil, an' I never looked at her—not right straight—but I could see that she walked with her feet an' held her head on the top of her neck; so I was purty certain that if Dick did return an' try to finish the weddin' as the star performer she'd give us an interestin' exhibition.

Spider Kelley was at the station when I got off the train. I turned the woman over to him, tellin' him to bring her out so as to arrive the evenin' of the weddin', not to talk to her, an' not to let Dick see her should he chance to come back that way; but to smuggle her into the office as soon as preparations for the ceremony got started. I still half looked for Dick, but I thought I had things blocked out, no matter what turned up, an' I flopped on my hoss an' rode him at about his best.

Everything around the house was whirlin' with preparation; but Barbie was about the palest lookin' bride 'at ever got ready to toe the scratch, I reckon. The Hawthorn critter had stayed over at his own ranch for the last week, an' Barbie wouldn't 'a' had no search-warrant swore out if he had sent over word that it looked so good to him that he had decided to continue to remain there for a million years.

The guests had arrived plenty early, an' whenever Barbie would stumble on to a bunch of 'em she would head up an' get right rompy again. We had about a ton o' stuff cooked, 'cause we was tol'able thoroughly experienced on the neighbors. Folks out our way ain't nowise uppity about such matters. All you need to do is to hint that a little celebration is goin' to be pulled off an' you can count on their presence; an' if so be 'at you've forgot anybody's invite, why like as not they'll hear about it anyway an' be on hand in plenty o' time. The weddin' was scheduled for Wednesday evenin' at eight thirty; but by Sunday the house was full an' the grounds looked like an Injun camp-meetin'.

Jabez, intended to give Barbie the full penalty; none o' your squires for him, nothin' but Friar Tuck, who was one o' these here Episcolopian preachers what sport a full regalia an' a book o' tactics calculated to meet any complication a human bein' is apt to veer into. Some say they're just Roman Catholics, gone Republican, an' some say that they're the ones who started the first strike—I don't know much about it myself.

He hadn't arrived by seven o'clock, but we didn't worry none; he might have had to come fifty miles, an' he never had any time to waste.

We'd had a sort o' light supper at four o'clock, an' it was intended to have the weddin' feast after the performance was finished. It was just eight o'clock when Friar Tuck swung off his pony an' as many of the crowd as could gathered in the big dinin' room an' waited for the words to be said. Spidier Kelley came an' told me that he had locked the woman in the office, an' that she was behavin' herself reasonable, so I knew 'at the finish wasn't far off. The tables an' chairs had been taken out, the intention bein' to dance in the store-room after the ceremony, an' while the dancin' was goin' on to set the banquet in the dinin' room. Oh, it was all planned out like a theater show: Jabez had a full orchestra too, three fiddlers, a guitarist, an' a fifer; an' they began to play solemn music, like they allus do at a wedding. It's a toss-up which is the most touchin', a weddin' or a funeral,—a feller's takin' a mighty long shot at either one.

The whole crowd was on edge, but myself was strained to the breakin' point. Just as the old clock struck the half hour the orchestra pealed forth a march, an' they all came struttin' in, slow an' stately an' top-heavy, accordin' to the city way. Jabez was in a brand-new suit o' black store clothes, an' had a mighty proud look on his face; he was wearin' gloves too. Barbie was a-leanin' on his arm, an' she was wearin' a dress 'at would 'a' made some o' the queens crane their necks a bit, I reckon. Hawthorn had his nerve with him, an' wore a low-necked vest an' a droop-tailed coat. I had my own rig like this hid away in the stallion stable; so it didn't jar me none; but some o' the boys had a hard time chokin' back their grins. It was the first weddin' I had ever seen where the groom hadn't wore a silk handkerchief around his neck.

They all met in front o' Friar Tuck, who was standin' under a tissha paper bell with about four miles o' ribbon tied to it. I couldn't see Barbie's face on account o' the veil she was wearin'; but she held her head high, an' I knew she was ready to take all the jumps without balkin'. The Friar had one o' these voices 'at never seem to say an idle word, an' the room got as still as though it was a trial for life; which ain't so mighty far off the mark, that bein' the usual sentence, an' out our way we don't count it game to get pardoned out for a new trial.

I was on pins an' needles durin' the openin', but Friar Tuck boomed along until he arrived at the part where it sez "If any man knows just cause why this here couple should not be joined together in holy wedlock let him make his kick right now, or forever after hold his peace." The room was as still as the grave, an' I had just taken a full breath, so that I could make a clean throw, when a deep voice at the back of the room sez: "I think that I know a cause. I don't believe the girl is doin' this of her own free will."

We all whirled around, an' there stood Silver Dick. Dusty he was an' travel-stained; but as he loomed up, straight an' tall, he certainly did look like a man. His beard was gone, his face was pale with a sort of unnatural whiteness, an' he was ganted down in weight a little; but all the same he put up a great front as he stood with his hands on his hips, his head thrown back, an' a grim smile on his face. Quick as a flash the ol' man, who had half expected this, pulls a gun out of his pocket an' drops it on Dick, while the crowd politely splits apart to give 'em a fair show. Barbie had settled back, an' I caught her in my arms an' held her a moment; but all the time my eyes were on Dick as though I'd been charmed.

Never in my life have I seen such a figger of a man as him, as he stood there alone an' unfriended. His hat was tilted back a bit, an' his short wavey hair rippled across his forehead, his mustache had been shaved off and his lips somehow reminded me of the muzzle of a gun, they was that firm; while his eyes—man, he had the greatest eyes in the world. Blue steel they was, but never for a moment free from some hidden fire. When he smiled they danced; when he frowned they blazed; but to-night the' was a new darin' in 'em,—a confidence, a purpose, an' a strength that defied Death himself.

He had changed a heap since we'd seen him last. His face was as smooth as a woman's, his hands were white, an' his clothes looked like picture clothes out of a book. He didn't speak for some time, an' then he said: "Is your gun broke, Mr. Judson, or do you think it would be only the square thing to talk things over first? I think I can interest you. I am not armed; perhaps you would be more comfortable if you lowered your gun until you were ready to shoot."

The' was a sting in his slow, sarcastic tone, an' a scowl came over Jabez' face; but he lowered his gun just the same. I didn't want to soften any toward Dick so I had to keep grittin' my teeth as I watched him, 'cause bluffin' a man like Cast Steel, armed an' ready, was a stirrin' sight, an' Dick looked as if he had the backin' of an army.

"Mr. Judson," sez Dick, "when I left here your daughter was promised to marry me, an' I promised to write as often as possible; but after I started in to clean up my record I was denied the privilege of writin'. I am here now, with my record clean; the' ain't no spot on this earth where I don't feel free to go—an' now I claim her hand."

"Claim her hand, do ya?" sez Jabez, with a wicked leer. "Well, you allus was better at claimin' than at gettin'. I don't want to sadden my daughter's weddin' night, but if you ain't minded to go your way peaceable I'll have to spoil ya."

"Barbie," sez Dick, an' his voice was meller as a flute, "don't ya love me no more?"

She raised her head an' looked at him, but she couldn't speak, so she only nodded her head.

"Will ya marry me?" sez Dick, an' we all waited a long time for the answer.

Once or twice she tried it, before her voice finally got back to her, "Dick," she sez, "I waited for ya a long time, an' I never heard from you; so I thought 'at you had either forgot me or else you were—were no longer living; an'—oh, Dick, you have no idee how hard it has been for me. You can't imagine how often I refused, nor what a lonely life I was forced to live; but I've never ceased to love you, an' I allus told 'em so. Now I am half married to another man; an' I don't see what we can do."

"Well, I see what we can do!" blurts out Jabez, raisin' his gun again. "We can go right on with this ceremony. You have give your word, an' the word of a Judson is bindin'. As for you, you sneakin' card-sharp, I'll give you just ten to state your intentions."

Jabez started to count slow an' steady with his left forefinger, while he held his gun above his right shoulder ready for the drop. His face was white an' his eyes blazed like live coals. The' was no time to waste now; Dick had a card up his sleeve, an' this was his chance to take the trick, or he'd spoil my own game. The room was so still it hurt you to breathe. Somebody sneezed, an' it sounded like a boiler explosion.

"Judson," sez Dick, an' he was smilin' now; but it was the chillin' smile I had first seen durin' the card game. It wasn't a pleasant smile. "Judson, I did not cheat durin' that game, an' I never did cheat, although gamblin was my business. You have become a fanatic on the subject o' truth, an' I propose to tell you some. You are a bully; you have bullied this girl in order to make her consent; and you are a coward, a miserable coward. Any man afraid of his own past is a coward; and your past stands back of you like a ghost, doggin' your steps awake, an' hauntin' your dreams 'sleep. You preach the truth; but your entire life is one black—"

"Stop!" yells Jabez, holdin' his hand over his heart, but gettin' the drop on Dick, although his face looked like the face of a man long dead. "Say another word an' a bullet will drive it back through your teeth."

"All right," sez Dick, still smilin' his cruel, hard smile; "but you have only counted up to five, an' you gave me ten. You're surely honest enough to stick to your own agreement. Begin to count now, while I start the tale about Jack Whitman an' the Creole Belle—"

When Dick mentioned the name o' Jack Whitman both o' Jabez' arms fell to his side; an' when Dick spoke o' the Creole Belle his legs shut together like a pocket knife; an' he crumpled down on a little padded bench they had fixed up to kneel on. His face was gray, an' his eyes had a scum over 'em, while his mouth hung open like the mouth of a man dyin' of old age. Barbie gave a low, waverin' call: "Oh, what have you done, oh, Dick! Daddy, Daddy; what's the matter Dad?"

She jumped to his side, an' after tearin' off her veil she knelt at his feet; but he drew his hands feebly away, an' refused to touch her; while a look of sorrow—sorrow an' pain an' shame, swept across his old gray face, an' his lips trembled so 'at he couldn't talk.

I glanced at Silver Dick; he stood there with his lips set tight, his eyes cold an' hard, an' I knew 'at he was ready to make his kill, cost what it would.

"Oh, Daddy," pleaded Barbie, "don't look this way. Tell me what it is all about. Don't turn away from me, Dad; I don't care what it is, or whether it is true or false—I am ready to forgive you, an' to love you. Look at me. Daddy. I care more for you than for any one else in the whole world.

"Yes," she sez, standin' up an' flashin' a look into Dick's eyes as fierce as they had ever shot themselves. "Yes, an' if you think to win me by strikin' down my old Dad, why—we have both been mistaken, an' I despise you!"

Silver looked as though she had struck him in the face with a whip; the hot blood swept up to his hair, an' then left him ghastly white again; while she put her hand on the ol' man's shoulder an' looked like an eagle protectin' her brood. I looked around for Hawthorn, who had become entirely forgotten. Gee! how I envied him his chance just then; but there he stood, lookin' like a white rabbit bein' tried for murder. The girl looked at him too, gave him one long scornful look; then she looked back at Silver, standin' all alone like the statue of a king; an' then she looked up at me. "Happy," she sez, "you never failed me yet. Clear this room—clear it of every one but just ourselves."

"Clear the room," I yells. "Come, friends, this is the time to step lively. You can go into the store-room an' dance if you want to, but the weddin' has been postponed."

They filed out in good order, all except Dick, Friar Tuck, an' Hawthorn. Hawthorn stood leanin' again the wall, lookin' at Dick as though he was seein' a ghost. I tapped him on the shoulder. "Git!" I sez, "your number didn't win nothin'." He gives a start, then down on the floor he flops with his eyes turned in an' his mouth frothin' a little. Friar Tuck straightened him out an' began to rub his hands; an' I turned to Dick.

"Now, it's your turn to go," I sez. "I'd advise you to go clear to England, where you'll find good news."

He came toward me as if he didn't see me, an' when he reached me he said: "You better go along too, Happy. I want to talk to them alone."

"Jim," I said, usin' the old name, "I don't want to do you harm. This game is up; you'd better go along peaceable."

He looked at me a moment in surprise, an' then his face got haughty, an' he put out his hand to push me aside. I took him by the arm an' swung him over against the wall. At first he couldn't seem to understand that I was in ear-nest, an' then his hand shot to hip an' breast; but he had spoke the truth, he wasn't armed. I had him covered, an' he sneered into my face without speakin'. I walled over an' examined him, but he didn't have even a knife. I didn't have the heart to drive him forth like a dog, so I sez, too low for the rest to hear: "Jim, I know the double life you've been leadin'; but you can't break Barbie's heart. You're a married man, an' I know it."

"You lie," he sez, clear an' cold. It was just the word I needed.

I crossed the room an' laid my gun on a chair, an' then I turned to him. "We're equal now," sez I. "The winner gets the gun."

He wasn't as strong as I was, quite; an' he was some out o' condition; but he had had trainin' more than me, an' for a few minutes he stood me off; an' then as he struck at me I grabbed his wrist, his left wrist, with my right hand, shot it in close to his body, an' clamped it behind his back; while I got his throat with my left. Slowly I brought him to his knees, my fingers all the time workin' deeper into his throat, while his right kept jabbin' me till it made me grunt. No one tried to interfere at first; but then he got too weak to strike. Barbie said sharply, "Happy Hawkins, stop that at once!"

"I'll stop as soon as he promises to go without further trouble," sez I.

She got up an' came across the room to us like a flash, an' seized the wrist that held Jim's throat. "Let him alone, Happy," she said fiercely.

I gave him a little push that sent him to the floor, an' then I picked up my gun. Jim rose to his feet; but the starch was purty well taken out of him, an' of course this touched her heart, she bein' a woman. "Are you hurt, Dick?" she sez sympathetic. "Yes, I'm hurt," he snaps back, glarin' at me; "not at what he's done, but at his lies."

"It's no lie," sez I.

"What was it?" asked Barbie—of Jim. He didn't answer for a minute, an' when he did his voice shook; but he looked into her eyes as he answered: "He said I was married."

Barbie drew away with a sharp gasp an' looked at him in horror; then she looked at me with her face all drawn up with anguish. "I tried to prepare you for this three weeks ago, Barbie," I sez, "an' you—you know what you threw in my face."

"Oh, Happy, Happy," she whispered, "it's not true, it's not true—say it's not true!"

"It is true, Barbie," sez I, an' she gave a scream.

"It is not true," sez Dick, an' she glanced from one to the other.

"I can prove it at once," sez I; "she's here to-night."

"Who?" asked Dick with a start.

"The wife you left in Laramie," sez I.

"Good God, you haven't brought her here, have you!" shouted Dick, an' Barbie a queer, heart-broken little laugh. "It's true, it's true," she sez. "You have convicted yourself, and it's true. Happy,"—she went on speakin' to me,—"of all the men I have ever known you are the only one that has been always true to me. You said that you would never marry me unless I asked you to—prove to me that this man is already married, an' I'll marry you. I'll get down on my knees an' beg you to marry me. The world seems full of wolves an' I want a man I can trust."

She was wild, an' the look in her eyes frightened me; but she came over an' put her hand on my arm, an' said: "Prove it, prove it, an' then let us go away together!"

"She's out in the office," sez I. "Shall I bring her in here?"

"No," sez Dick. "Happy, for heaven's sake don't do anything hasty."

"Bring her in, bring her in at once!" sez Barbie. "This is my wedding-day, an' my father wanted it to be the talk of the whole state. Bring her in!"

Just as I reached the door it opened, an' the strange woman came in with old Melisse, who was makin' queer throaty noises like a dog. Her veil was raised, an' I stepped back in surprise. She was an elderly woman with gray hair, white at the temples, an' dark eyes that rested for a moment on Dick, for a longer second on Barbie, an' then stopped when they met the starin' eyes of of Cast Steel, who had staggered to his feet.

He stood there with his hands clutchin' the side of his head, an' his lips movin' rapidly, but not a sound comin' through 'em, an' then his knees gave way beneath him, an' Friar Tuck eased him back to the little padded bench. The hands of the strange woman were clasped on her breast; but even when the rest of us started for Jabez she didn't move.

CHAPTER TWENTY-NINE
THE FINAL RECKONING

It hurts me inside to see anything plumb beaten. I've hunted a lot, an' I'm as keen on the trail as a terrier dog an' durin the fight I don't have no disturbin shudders; but after I've won an' I see the light of joy an' hope an' freedom fadin' out of eyes that have been so bright an' fearless, the' 's allus somethin' 'at swells inside o' my breast an' makes me half sorry 'at all fights can't end in a draw. The' 's one kind of nature which I never yet was able to figger out, an' that's the nature that can rub it in on a fallen foe.

Poor old Jabez, I'd judged him an' I'd judges him harsh; but when I saw him go to pieces there on the padded bench I just seemed to go to pieces with him. When I saw the strength leave him like the steam from an engine as the flood reaches its fire-box; when I saw the hands that thought they was strong enough to shape the future danglin' between his crooked knees, an' the eyes that had never before asked mercy lookin' up glazed an' pitiful, why, it felt to me as if I was just tryin' to send the strength out of my own body into his. Poor ol' Jabez, he was cast steel to the finish, no spring, just simply rigid an' stiff, till at last he broke.

But runnin' the universe is no job for a human; every man would choose to look his best when he's to meet the one woman; but if Jabez had still been standin' like a rock an' lookin' out at the world through eagle-eyes the woman at the door wouldn't never have spoke to him. When she saw him tired an' broken an' heart-sick of life itself, the mother in her finally tore out all the wrongs o' the past, an' she crossed the room an' took one of his hands an' said, "George, you mustn't give up, you mustn't give up now."

Barbie was holdin' his other hand, an' the ol' man looked first from one to the other while big tears gathered in his open eyes an' rolled slowly down his cheeks. I tell you it was a touchy sight, an' I was sweatin' like a fish when ol' Friar Tuck tip-toed over an' put one hand on my shoulder an' the other on Jim's, an' said: "They'll get along better without us, boys. Let's just step outside till they call us."

Oh, I tell you that Friar Tuck was a sky-pilot for true! We sneaked stealthily to the door, passin' ol' Melisse on the way. She was huddled up on the floor prayin' in Spanish, an' Friar Tuck rested his hand on her head a second, an' then we went out into the night air—I can taste my first breath of it yet.

He went over to see how the crowd was doin' in the storeroom, sayin' that he thought he'd get some eatin'-things under way to sort of ease the strain—he knew a human all right, the Friar did. Jim an' I walked out together under the stars, an' I told him my side of it; an' he told me that he had met Jack Whitman when he was runnin' a gamblin' place close to the New Mexico line. Whitman ran it on the square an' he had saved Jim a lot o' money one night, an' then afterwards Jim had helped to stand off a hold-up gang, an' a strong feelin' had grew up between 'em. Whitman had told part of the story, but made out that Barbie's mother was his own sister. When she had left Jabez an' the child—I don't know, myself, just why she left him. It started when she found out how he had lied to Whitman an' mighty near killed him; but just all that happened, before she burned out her brand and skipped, I don't know to this day, but they was both purty high-headed an' nervy in their youth, an' I've often suspected that Jabez' conscience didn't get to workin' smooth until after he was left alone with the child on his hands. It sometimes happens that way.

Well, anyhow, when she had left him she had gone to the southern part of California, where she'd got a job teachin' school. Whitman had located her, an' when her health gave out he had sent her money without lettin' her know where it came from. Whitman had follered minin' till his wife died, an' then he got to speculatin' in stocks, finally gettin' cleaned out full an' proper, an' then he started to gamblin' in earnest. It was from him that Jim had picked up most of his idees about business an' gamblin'. When Whitman himself had died he had turned Barbie's mother over to Jim.

She was livin' on a ranch in northern Colorado at this time, on account of her health. When Jim got cleaned out by the cattle crowd, an' opened his joint in Laramie, he brought her over to keep house an' be company for him. He pertended to be the son of a wild uncle she'd had, an' he fixed up a believable tale to go with it. All the while he'd been at the Diamond Dot he had supposed that she was Whitman's sister—she went by her maiden name of Miss Garrison, an' she had never told him her full story, simply hintin' enough at times to let him know that she had gone through the mill.

He had never pieced things together until I had sent him my letter, an' then he guessed how it was, an' puttin' what I told him onto what she an' Whitman had told him, he saw it all. He didn't know what had made her leave Judson, or rather Jordan; but he said he was positive it was his fault, as she was some the finest woman he had ever met, exceptin' of course her own daughter.

We talked it all over there in the starlight, until ol' Melisse came an' called us in. I didn't want to go; I was tryin' to cut myself out of the game entirely an' forget that I even existed; for the' was a cry in my heart that wouldn't hush, an' I wanted to be alone; but when Jim insisted I braced up an' went in.

Ol' Jabez looked a heap better, but still shaky; his wife had a tender half sad smile on her face, while Barbie was radiant with the joy she had waited for so long; she had kept her father, she had found her mother, an' she was about to meet—her lover. I saw the Sioux Injuns doin' the dance once, where they tie thongs through their breast muscles an' circle around a pole. Every now an' again they'd fling back their full weight on the thongs, an' their faces would light with savage joy. That was the kind of joy I felt when I saw Barbie's face.

Her mother smiled into Jim's eyes when he came in, an' Jabez stood up an' held out his hand. "Do you want to marry her?" he said.

"That's the only wish I have," sez Jim.

"Then she's yours, an' I thank God she's got a true man," sez Jabez, puttin' Barbie's hand into Jim's. I turned my face away.

The first thing I knew I felt a hand on my shoulder an' another hand taken' hold of mine. I turned an' looked down into Barbie's face, but I couldn't bear the light in her eyes. I turned my face away again—an' my lips were tremblin', the blasted traitors.

But she turned me around until my eyes looked down into hers, an' they were swimmin' in tears. Her little soft hand clasped my big rough one, tight an' warm, an' her voice was husky as she whispered, "You—you won't care much, will you, Happy?"

"No, Barbie," I sez between my set teeth, "not much"; an' by God, I smiled.

"An', Happy," she went on, "my home will allus be your home, an' anything that is mine is yours; but my heart ain't mine, ol' pal; an' so—an' so we can't help it."

"No," I sez, an' I was back in the saddle again this time. "No, little gel, we can't help it; but we can allus make the best of it; so I vote that we don't disappoint the crowd; but go on an' have a weddin'."

She backed away from me a little, while her face took the color of a rose, an' her eyes went to the floor; an' then I turned to Jabez an' said: "Jabez, I've took a mighty sight off you in my time without ever puttin' up one little squeal; but if you send this gang away to-night without a weddin', why, I quit you for good."

The' was all so wrought up that I was about the steadiest in the room; an' in about two minutes I had 'em lined up, an' the crowd back in place an' Friar Tuck in full regimentals under the tissha paper bell.

Before we could begin, however. Jabez mounted on a chair an' said in a new, soft voice: "Friends, in all my life I never told but one black lie. I may have spoken falsely through ignorance, or to spare sorrow to my child; but I never fought through the temptation but once, an' got whipped by it. I told one black lie, an' it was the blackest one ever told, I reckon. It brought me my money an' my wife; an' my load of shame an' sin an' contempt—it lost me the best friend I ever had, an' it led to my losin' my wife for most o' my journey. All my life I've tried to live down that lie an' to fill every man I met with a reverence for the truth, an' that's what makes me so blame ashamed of the way I've treated Dick. I ought to have seen quicker'n anybody else the kind of a fight he was a-makin', an' pitched in an' helped him instead of findin' him guilty, on the first suspicion, an' tryin' to make his life as sour as mine has been. But"—here Jabez put his arm about Barbie's shoulder, an' looked down on her a moment—"it was all on account o' this little girl."

Then we all gave a cheer an' Friar Tuck tied the knot, after which every one opened the sluice-gates o' their hearts an' let the sociability gush forth in a torrent. I stuck around until the dancin' began, an' then I flopped myself on a hoss an' rode, an' rode, an' rode. The air was cool an' crisp as it swept over my face; but it was a long time before it took the fever out of my blood. Finally I circled back to of Monody's grave an' got off an' sat there till the sun came up, fresh an' strong. Ol' Monody had taken the burden 'at had been handed to him, an' had borne it along to a mighty fire finish; an' it made me ashamed of myself, so I got to my feet, gave myself a shake, an' rode back to the ranch house.

CHAPTER THIRTY
THE AFTERGLOW

I didn't look for anybody to be about that early after the night that outfit had put in; but just before I reached the corral I saw Barbie an' Jim ridin' slowly toward the stable. They was ridin' close together an' lookin' into each other's eyes, an' I'm glad to say that even that soon I felt nothin' but joy in the sight. A little farther on I spied Jabez an' his wife standin' on a knoll, lookin' at the sunshine, an' before I reached the house I saw two others swingin' up the trail on a lope. In a minute I made out Bill Hammersly an' Jessamie. For just one second I did feel a little bit out o' the world; but by the time they rode up I was able to welcome 'em with a joke.

"We lost our way," sez Bill. "Is it too late?"

"It's never too late," sez I. "But I'm right down sorry that you didn't arrive last evenin'. We had about as stirrin' a weddin' here as ever you see."

"Who was it that Barbie married?" asked Jessamie.

Just then Jim an' Barbie came around the corner o' the house, an' I sez: "Mr. an' Mrs. Bill Hammersly, allow me to make you introduced to the Earl o' Clarenden an' his bride."

They was totally devoid of remarks for some time. Jim was the first to speak, an' he seemed a trifle put out. "What do you mean by such nonsense, Happy?" sez he. Then they all looked at him on account of him usin' the tone he had. I turned to Barbie an' sez easily: "I was tellin' Bill down at Frisco about a month ago that I rather doubted if Jim here would take the job; but if so be that he wants it, it's open for him. If not, that Hawthorn thing has the next chance."

I stepped back a few paces after this an' let 'em talk it out. Jim was the most flabbergasted of any, Barbie looked a little bit frightened; but Jessamie sez: "If Happy Hawkins sez 'at you're the Earl of Clarenden, why you might as well give up. He has inside information on every given subject, an' things don't never happen until he's had his finger in it somewhere." Jessamie allus was a good feller.

An' that's the way it turned out. Jim an' Barbie went back to Clarenden on their honeymoon, an' Barbie's taken the lead over there the same as she'd do anywhere. I stayed right at the Diamond Dot 'cause Jabez didn't seem able to get along without me; an' I hit work harder than ever. Now I oversee the Diamond Dot, Jim's place down in the Pan Handle, which is full stocked an' runnin' easy with the ex-governor's backin', an' also the ol' Colonel Scott ranch which Bill and Jessamie fell heir to.

Jim an' Barbie an' the children come back every summer; Bill an' Jessamie an' their outfit hop in on me most any time, Ches an' his bunch drop in for a week or so now an' again, an' if I ever do get lonesome I just sneak my full-dress uniform out o' the hay an' go down to Frisco for a little easin' off o' the guy-ropes. Oh, I haven't had to petition to congress to have my name changed; I'm Happy. I'm happier than any human ever had a right to be, an' life never drags none—at least not in the daytimes. The' 's dozens o' boys named after me, an' only the recordin' angel knows how many dogs an' ponies. Take it as a big gatherin', an' if any one yells, "Happy, you rascal, get out o' here," Why the' 's a general stampede.

Barbie's allus extra kind to me, as if she still felt that the' was somethin' left for me to forgive her; but my goodness, the' ain't a thing. It wasn't her fault—she couldn't never have loved me—not in the only way I wanted her to. And it ain't my fault—I couldn't help but love her, an' the' was only one way that I could love her, an' that was world without end. I'm not sorry I loved her; why, the' ain't nothin' in life I'd take for this love of mine—and it is mine. The' ain't nothin' can ever take it away from me, the' ain't nothin' can ever put a limit to it; an' though it has burned in my heart like fire, I reckon the worst it has ever done was to burn up the natural-born evil I started out with. I ain't mean-hearted nor jealous—I can't even understand it.

I can easy see how a feller would kill a man for ill-treatin' the woman he loved; but I can't see how he could marry a girl who didn't love him with all her heart. An' Jim, he's been square. They're happy, an' I stand afar off watchin' 'em; an' some way when I'm out in the starlight—when it seems that I ain't lyin' on the earth at all, but floatin' slow an' easy like an eagle restin' on his wings—I seem to share in their love, an' I don't seem to grow old.

I don't reckon I ever will grow old, 'cause love is—love is—some way MY love is like the starlight itself; an' the starlight don't scorch an' weaken an' pester like the sun; it soothes an' softens an' lifts a man up where it's calm an' steady and—and pure.

The longer I live the fonder I grow o' the stars. It don't take as much sleep for me now as it used to, an' I never was dopey; so the' 's mighty few nights 'at I don't have a little visit with 'em. I know now 'at they keep whirlin' an' circlin' away up there; but they never deceive a body. You can allus keep track of 'm, an' when the seasons change an' you can't see 'em for a while, you know 'at they're tendin' to their duties just the same; an' somehow it kind o' holds a man to the trail when the trail is gettin' rougher than he thinks he can stand.

I've got a heap o' friends, men an' women of all kinds; an' when they come to me ragin' an' bitter, I just take 'em out an' show 'em the stars; tell 'em the ones who are about to go on a long journey, but who will come back again when they're due, an' not a minute late. The' 's something about the stars 'at allus seems to take the wickedness out of a human. I've had 'em come to me—men an' women both—with murder in their hearts; but after we've visited a while with the stars they either sigh or sob—but they allus go away clean an' rested.

It's a funny notion; but sometimes I feet like as if I'd like to be a star myself; away up above the worry an' selfishness of the world, an' helpin' to bring peace an content to those who look up to me. It's a funny notion— especially for a feller what's follered the trail I have.

Me an' the preachers lock horns purty often; but they're all right, most of 'em, when you treat 'em like humans an' make 'em play fair. One of 'em happened out here on a visit, to sort o' rest up, an' he called me some kind of a Persian name an' read me a little book called The Other Wise Man. I reckon I know that book, all except the big names, by heart; an' if one of my stars would ever cut out o' the herd an' go off, slow an' stately on a new trail, why I'd foller that star—God knows I'd foller; an'—I wouldn't let on to no one else except you—but, way down, deep in my heart, I'm hopin' that sometime I'll get the chance.